A TROUBLEMAKER NEVER CRIES

Genta Sebastian

ISBN: 978-1-942594-09-3

Where to find Genta Sebastian:
Facebook @ https://www.facebook.com/gentasebastian
Existing on the Edge of Effectiveness: www.gentasebastian.net

A TROUBLEMAKER NEVER CRIES

Dedication

For Minha Trafulha
My Lesbian Wife – My Life
Heroine of My Heart
Forever

Where is Terceira?

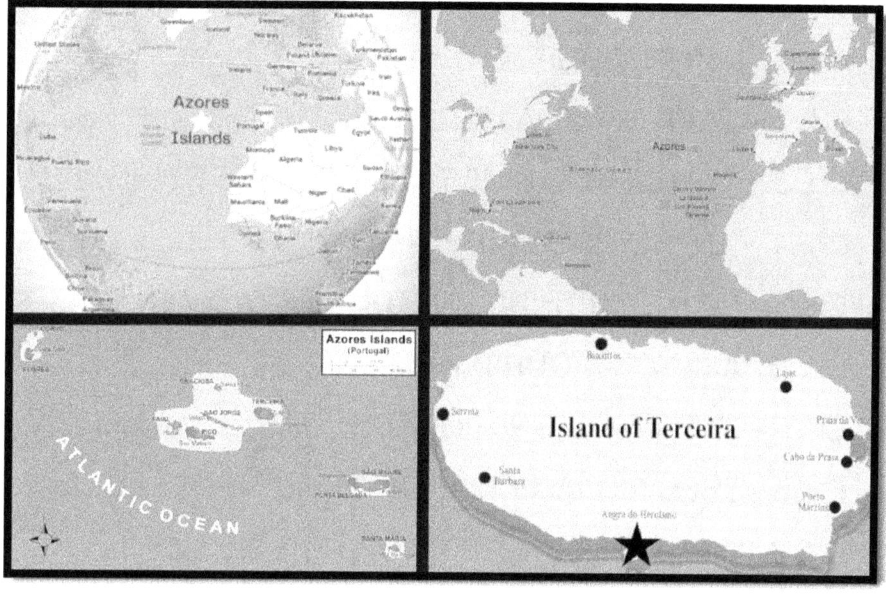

TABLE OF CONTENTS

Introduction

Any self-sufficient archipelago, isolated for centuries, eventually suffers from a limited gene pool. A concerned Mother Nature springs into action when inbreeding threatens the health of her islands' children. For five decades across three generations, the number of lesbians and gays not only doubles, it triples. Instead of the usual five to ten percent of the population, fifteen to thirty percent are born.

By limiting their mating options the Great Mother drives desperate heterosexuals abroad in search of spouses to bring home to their parents. The newcomers bring more than strange cooking, ways, and traditions. They stretch the boundaries of social acceptance. Happily, this means young people can easily find others like themselves, band together, and create supportive groups. Sadly, it also makes them easier targets for bigots and bullies.

Mother Nature knew full well a population rich in homosexuals creates a unique situation in any time and place, much less the repressive 1950s on the old-world Catholic island of Terceira where our story begins.

What was she thinking?

Ch. 1 - Her Personal Triumph

Autumn, 1959

On a dark moonless night when she was eleven, Vitória hunkered down out of sight, glad she'd worn a jacket to guard against the chill winds of October. The cool salt air whipped her dark curls briskly, stinging her eyes. She was lying in wait for her first victim. *I'm ready.*

Vitória wiped tears with the back of one hand and motioned sharply for her older brother, Johnny, to lie flat on his belly. "Don't scrape your feet," she hissed, hypersensitive to any sound or motion. "Want them to hear you?" They were hiding up on the flat space beside the chimney of the whorehouse.

Vitória knew Johnny sometimes wondered why she, three years younger, dreamed up the schemes that routinely got them into trouble. She pulled a strand of hair from her eyes, a little sorry to have dragged him into this with her. *Being a boy, and almost a man, he is taking the bigger risk.*

"This is more dangerous than swiping oranges and we'll probably get caught," he whispered back, fanning the flames of her guilt. "We're not playing war games like this afternoon." She pretended not to see him wipe cold sweat from his brow.

Silently waiting for her prey, she refused to let fear intimidate her. Instead, Vitória let her thoughts drift back to their afternoon's adventure. Her grin went unseen in the darkness until she nudged Johnny, who turned to look at her. "But it was funny." His answering grin blazed between them in the darkness as they both stifled giggles.

After school that afternoon they'd joined their friends to play war, a game created by watching American movies. It was one of those crystal blue afternoons when everything seems sharper, colors are brilliantly vivid, every smell is richer, even sounds carry clearly. The crops were in from the field, leaving the children free, and the joy of being alive flooded their souls.

Johnny was the captain of one team and as usual when it was his turn, he chose his sister to be the scout. He and Carlos, captain of the other team, tucked the target high up in one of the trees in an orange orchard. Inside its leafy darkness, it would be difficult to find, and Johnny lived to challenge Vitória. She hated to fail.

Every boy brought his own weapon, a slingshot. Small pocketknives had carefully carved each from pieces of old lumber left lying around the village of Lajes. Vitória and Johnny spent hours searching for the right sized pebbles to use as weapons during these war games, and that afternoon their pockets were heavy with them.

The cool wind fanned the grass as members of both teams hunkered down low, creeping along. The objective of the game was to first find the target and knock it to the ground while staying invisible to the other team. If spotted, every stone they had would be launched at their opponents, who, of course, did the same if they were seen first. Whichever team knocked the target to the ground won. It was always good fun and a favorite game.

Determined to lead her team to victory that afternoon, Vitória kept her eyes sharp to find the target, an old white shirt stuffed with dried cornhusks. Having set herself the task, nothing could distract her. The players on her team furtively patrolled through tall grass, watching for the other team, following her as she searched. When she shouted and pointed, the whole team dropped to their knees. As one, they took aim at the white shape hidden high in the tree and fired.

Back on the cold rooftop, she watched Johnny rub his eyes as if to wipe the memory from his mind, a move that made her giggle aloud. "I tried," he muttered. "I tried to stop you, but you let fly. You didn't listen, you never do. Then you shot again!" His hand tried to smother his own giggle, which didn't work; it burst out of him anyway.

"And again! I reloaded over and over, but we couldn't knock that stupid target out of the tree. I couldn't understand why." She shrugged her thin shoulders. "I was shooting as hard as I know how!" Vitória cocked her head to one side, making a comical face.

"You finally ran out of ammunition," Johnny said, forgetting to keep his voice down.

"Hush Johnny, keep quiet!" She and the whole team had turned to her brother for an explanation. "Your eyes were big as a cow's." Unable to follow her own order, she imitated the horrified voice of her brother that afternoon. “That’s not the target! That’s a man!”

He chuckled ruefully. “You cowards dropped like stones. So did I,” he admitted. “We all did.”

“Stop! Stop! Oh. Oh! Lord, help me!” Vitória now pitched her voice to imitate the man they’d heard shouting from the trees. Their whispered laughter floated away in the dark sky to be carried on the wind.

When they’d heard the farmer’s agonized cries, the group scattered like dandelion seeds freed by a brisk breeze, a strategy based on the concept that if chased, fewer would be caught. But whoever was up in that tree didn’t see them, thank God. He was probably busy watching the sky for another shower of stones to rain down on his luckless head.

Once safely away, such an adrenaline rush coursed through Vitória she’d felt invincible. It seemed natural to follow up with their current endeavor. She’d talked fast that afternoon and explained what she had in mind to her equally excited brother. Johnny agreed enthusiastically then, but the damp evening air cooled his impulsive side. He started having second thoughts.

“Maybe we should just go home.” He looked like a mouse searching for a hole. “We can get into a lot of trouble.”

Vitória knew just what to do with the anger she felt at his timidity. She saw him wince slightly, bracing himself against the steely glint in her eye as she twisted to face him. A hot flush of success flooded her, but she hid it. Johnny needed to follow their usual routine to find his courage.

“Go home, chicken,” she hissed. “Escape to your safe, warm bed. Your *little* sister will handle this all… by… herself.” She paused long enough for her anger to sink in its teeth.

“A man has only his word; what does that make you when you break it?” She normally stomped her foot at this point but that would give them away, so she snapped her fingers instead. “You told me you’d help me!” She snarled, glaring with as much disgust as possible. “You’re nothing but a lying coward!”

Johnny groaned, but Vitória showed no mercy. She knew her brother well, and this same challenge always goaded him. “Admit it, most of the time we don’t get caught. If we’re lucky, tonight will be one of those.”

Finally, Johnny crossed himself. She heard him utter a quick prayer asking the Lady to help them succeed. Nodding at her, he turned back to watch the road.

Darkness had fallen, dinners been eaten, animals tended to, and men would start arriving soon. Neighborhood gossip said most of the whores' customers showed up alone. Others came in rowdy groups looking for cheap sex, but a fight was free and almost as fine an entertainment. Vitória didn't know which idea excited her more, to carry out her plan or see a fistfight.

They stayed perched, motionless, on the flat area around the chimney. Practically invisible under the moonless sky, they made sure to stay that way as the first of their prey finally came into view. Two men, wearing light jackets against the autumn chill, cheerfully approached the whorehouse.

Taking a deep breath, she nudged Johnny. Each dipped an old paintbrush into a large tin can they'd hauled up to the roof. For a week Vitória used that can as her toilet, saving her pee for this evening's business. With fully loaded brushes, they took aim at the men below while making the sign of the holy cross, whispering, "In the name of the Father, the Son, and the Holy Ghost." The clinging muck spattered on the heads of their unsuspecting targets. One glanced up and the children ducked out of sight. He held his hand out, palm up as if checking for rain.

Two weeks ago the man who lived next door rented half of his house to prostitutes, shocking the neighbors and Mom. Not because of the women themselves – their mother never let society dictate her friends – but because the business was being conducted right next door. Mom, as true a Christian woman as ever lived, would never take matters into her own hands. Instead, she endured with quiet dignity her inescapable proximity to sin. *Something must be done, and I'm just the one to do it.*

"Rain, already?" asked one man as the door to the whorehouse opened. The children peeked over the ledge.

"Too early," answered the other. "Beatrice! My beauty."

"Raphael." The woman stood before them guardedly, her nose wrinkling. Dressed in a clinging red dress and matching pumps, she did not move aside to allow the men in. "Too early for what?"

"Rain, what else?" answered the first, gesturing toward the sky. The whore blinked slowly several times and raised a hand to fan the air in front of her nose. Raphael caught a whiff and raised an eyebrow at his friend.

"Don't mind him, he's drunk already. Let us in." He moved forward to enter, but once again, the woman in the doorway did not budge. "Beatrice, sweetheart, what's wrong?" Raphael asked, reaching for her.

"Enough," announced the whore, brushing away his hands. "You drink too much and wet yourselves, okay, it happens. But then you come here and think we'll let you in?" The door slammed shut, and the two men stared at each other in dismay.

"Do I smell of piss?"

His friend sniffed at Raphael twice, then a third time. "I don't know, it could be piss. Maybe it's that cheap beer you drink." He kicked the door of the whorehouse and turned away. "Screw them."

"That's what I was trying to do," snorted Raphael, and the two men wandered up the road laughing and sniffing each other.

Up on the roof, the children silently stifled their laughter, afraid someone in the house would hear them. "Good job," whispered Johnny with feeling. Even though Vitória was a girl, she always came up with great pranks. "This is one of your finest."

"Do you think it will work?" his sister whispered, but before he could answer she put a finger to her lips, listening. The two lay flat as possible where they were, willing themselves to be invisible.

Kicking at cobblestones, shoulders hunched and hands stuffed in the pockets of a light jacket, the next man approached quickly from around the corner, taking them unaware. He had already knocked on the door when they baptized him. Tall and thin, the stranger waited unconcerned, showing no sign he was aware of being wet. Johnny raised an eyebrow at his sister. She shrugged.

Beatrice once again answered the door, patting her black, high beehive hair in place. Pretty, in a calculated way, her eyes glittered like black diamonds by the light of kerosene lamps within. Her carefully painted red lips smiled, but above them, her slightly crooked nose wrinkled as it had before.

"Thomas at the docks said to say he sent me." The young man offered her an ingratiating smile, clearly no stranger to the procedure, only the house. "He says he'll expect you to adjust his rate accordingly." A folded bill appeared between his first two fingers. The man tucked it into the cleavage exposed by the whore's red dress, trailing his fingers over her skin.

Beatrice leaned back into the house. "Hey, Slim!" she bellowed. "Here's one for you." She plucked the bill from between her breasts and handed it to the slender redhead wrapped in a green kimono who appeared beside her. "Smell for yourself," she said, gesturing at the smiling man standing on their doorstep. "This one stinks like the others I told you about, doesn't he?"

Slim's long-lashed eyes rapidly checked the bill's denomination and stylish clothes of her potential customer. Smiling, she sniffed the air in the young man's general direction. "He most certainly does not," she declared, pulling him in with a sunshine smile and midnight eyes. Beatrice grunted as she closed the door.

"Guess we missed him," said Johnny.

"I don't think so," Vitória said, her voice low thunder rumbling in the distance. "She just didn't care."

Beside her, Johnny nervously kept his peace. They'd get caught for sure if his little sister let her temper loose. Most of the time she controlled her anger, but occasionally Vitória exploded, damned be the consequences. That was fine with him as long as he was nowhere around when she erupted. Although she didn't care about whippings or going without supper, he did.

On she went. "Mom says it doesn't matter, but it does. The gossips are painting our mother with the whores' sin. It's only fair we do a little painting of our own in return." Vitória's voice started to rise and Johnny made a shushing motion, afraid she'd be overheard.

The girl's voice dropped in volume if not intensity. "Oh, shush yourself," she muttered crossly.

Overhead, clouds teased the moon, their number and size increasing. The children were getting tired and fidgety when a drunken chorus of voices approached. Half a dozen men lurched into view, stumbling into each other. They grew louder, trying to sing a popular song out of tune, unable to harmonize, and slurring the wrong words. All wore canvas pants and rough wool shirts, the clothing of fishermen. Fresh-shaved, hair freshly trimmed and washed, they were just off a month of commercial fishing and eager to spend their pay.

The children, stiff from inaction and the chill wind, were a bit over-enthusiastic flinging Vitória's pee at the group of jovial men. Certainly more than one reached up to touch his hair, checking the sky for molesting birds. The smell on their fingers disgusted those who touched a wet spot, but by then it was too late to do anything about it. The door opened and golden light from within beckoned the eager men.

A woman with bleached blond hair, her voluptuous figure clearly seen under a filmy negligee, greeted them. “Ah, good to see you! I see you brought friends. Fine, just fine. I’m glad you found us in our new home. Come on in.”

She held open the door, and the first man passed by her. “What? Wait! Come back here, you,” she called after him, raising her hand by way of stopping the others from following him inside. “Come back here.”

She didn’t have long to wait. An angry Beatrice pushed him toward the door. “Okay, if it’s not piss,” she was arguing, “then your sweaty fish stink still has no place among us. Get yourself a bath and sit in it for a week before you come back.” She shoved the protesting man out the door to stand next to his puzzled companions.

“But we bathed,” complained one. “Look, we’re clean-shaved.”

“Apparently the men of Lajes can’t smell themselves anymore,” sneered the woman who opened the door. “Take our word for it, you stink.” Several men nodded in unconscious agreement. The women’s laughter rang through the night. The blond started to close the door.

“Now look,” said the first man, stepping forward and putting his hand up to block the closing door, “we have good money to spend. You’ve got good women in there.” He winked at the blonde’s see-through nightie. “Surely we can figure something out?”

“Well,” mused Beatrice with a sigh, “we are having a slow night.” She looked them over with a keen eye. “Okay, double the usual rate, and we’ll take you as you are. Regular price and we’ll throw in a wash, courtesy of the house. I’m sure the girls will be happy to help.” She clapped her hands. “Okay, which is it going to be?” Beatrice let the men pass through. Once more, the road went dark as the lamplight was shut within.

It doesn’t matter if they smell bad or not. Vitória brooded on the rooftop. *Maybe we did all this for nothing.* She rolled her eyes.

The two stayed on the roof undetected until midnight but no more adulterers or fornicators appeared. A bone-chilling fog rolled in from the sea. About to call it an evening and slip home to warm beds, the children heard muted male voices coming down the road. They dipped their brushes for a last attempt to drive sin from the neighborhood.

Two men, both wearing the broad-brimmed straw hats of farmers, fell silent as they came within view of the whorehouse. Where storm clouds now blanketed the sky distant lightning threw shadows, concealing their faces. A hand reached out and knocked on the door.

Vitória, followed quickly by Johnny, muttered, "In the name of the Father, the Son, and the Holy Ghost," and took aim, making a large sign of the cross in the air.

Their sudden movement startled a pigeon in the coop below. "Oo-oo-oor," she clucked reproachfully, which caused the men to look around just as the opening door revealed the sultry Slim. The young man sent by Thomas stepped past her and out into the night, whistling a jaunty tune.

Luckily, the red-haired beauty distracted the men who didn't look up at the roof. *It's amazing really*, thought Vitória, *how few people ever look up. Miracles happen right overhead, and they never know it.*

"You, too?" the prostitute asked. "What's wrong with the men of Lajes? Don't any of you bathe?"

One of the men smelled his armpit. The other shrugged his shoulders. "I washed before I came over here," he said, defensive.

In the dark, Johnny shot Vitória a panicked look and the hair on the back of her neck rose. Then the other man spoke.

"Wouldn't you know it'd rain piss on a whorehouse?" He laughed.

Johnny's voice squeaked; Vitória's almost disappeared. "Father," they whispered. Without another word, they lay flat and stayed absolutely still.

"You think that's funny? Do you even have the cost of a basic?" the whore complained. "Beatrice." Her voice was muffled as she called into the house. "I'm leaving. The men in Lajes are pigs." She started to close the door, but their father shoved his foot in the door.

"Now, now," he soothed in a voice his daughter had never heard before. "Pretty girl, let me come in." He leaned toward her and whispered something the children couldn't hear. Slowly they lifted their heads to see.

The prostitute finally laughed. "You goat," she teased. "Randy and ready are you?" She pulled the front of her silky green kimono open. Her black underwear was molded to light skin. She posed, dropping the robe as she slowly turned to show off her truly remarkable backside. The children stared, as did the men who were both nodding their heads. "Go to hell," she shouted at them and slammed the door.

"What the hell?" Their uncle, Father's youngest brother, was fuming. "Gaspar, what's got into these broads?" It was a term an American singer was making popular, and Sal Mendes liked to use it.

Vitória felt the wind knife through her at the fury in her father's voice, a tone she *had* heard many times before. "Stupid woman, ugly donkey's ass." He kicked the door once, then again, but it stayed stubbornly shut.

He punched it, then spun around and stalked off in the chill dark. His cowed brother followed, an invisible shadow.

"We've got to get home." Johnny draped his long legs over the side of the ledge, feeling for the pigeon coop. He misjudged and landed with a thump. Several birds startled, complaining loudly in the dark.

"Who's there?" From the other half of the building hustled the owner, Mr. Diaz, the man who rented to whores. A kerosene lamp swung in his plump hand. "Who's pestering my pigeons?"

Johnny jumped from the top of the coop to the branch of a nearby fig tree. Within seconds, the broad leaves hid him. Vitória lay flat, not moving.

The owner got to his coop and held the lamp up to check inside. Half the birds woke and feathers flew from the opening to float gently to the ground as they muttered their displeasure. "Oo-oo-oor, oo-oo-oor," The man counted his flock, then satisfied they were all there, glanced around and up toward the roof and chimney. "Ew. I'll clean out your coop tomorrow."

Each held their breath and looked at the other, hidden eyes finding the same.

The old man craned his neck to see up and down the road, checking for suspicious persons. Finding none, he headed back to his warm bed, entering the same doorway they'd been aiming at all night. Vitória hoped some of the muck down there would stick to greedy Diaz. It was understandable he'd rent half his large house after his sons married and wife died. It was inexcusable to rent to prostitutes. *This isn't that type of neighborhood.*

Johnny watched Vitória leap easily, and silently, from roof to pigeon coop and down to the road. They ran swiftly next door, arriving just as the thunderstorm broke. Without wasting time, they split up. Johnny entered the house through a window in the front room where he slept, and his younger sister did the same through one in her bedroom left propped open with a rock.

Safe in her own room, she washed her hands, face, feet, and butt with water she'd left in a basin. Her heart pounded like a trapped bird, exhilarated and afraid. *Father! The one possibility I never considered.* Her head ached.

Vitória slipped into a nightgown and slid between white sheets her mother sun-bleached regularly. She thumped the side of her head, berating herself for not thinking of everything. *Why didn't I consider him? Now I'll get my butt kicked, sure.* She steeled herself to get through it without a whimper. She would not give her father that satisfaction.

She had discussed this with friends, other tomboys like her, who joined her in the stand of trees behind her mother's house Sunday nights. When dealing with discipline from fathers, uncles, or brothers, each had developed her own way of getting through it without crying, sharing strategies with each other. Vitória, however, was the only one who claimed to simply not feel the pain, until afterward anyway.

"How can a whipping not hurt?" her friend Juana asked once.

"Oh," she answered blithely, "I have bruises afterward that hurt all right. But during it, I send my mind elsewhere. Once I even asked Father, 'Are you finished?' I was so far away it surprised me when he stopped. That just made him madder, but I honestly didn't realize. My mind ignores the pain because I go somewhere other than this stupid rock."

Mostly she imagined herself in America, that far off land where glamorous movie stars lived magical lives. She knew one day she'd live in that fabulous country, no matter how impossible it seemed. While her father beat her, her mind traveled into the future visualizing a life far away from her current reality. Vitória worked so hard at being somewhere else her focus left no room for pain. She wouldn't allow it.

She stretched luxuriously in bed, letting the threat of punishment fade away. As she mused over the day's adventures, she offered the stars outside her window a delighted grin. She hadn't had this much fun in a long time. *It's worth whatever happens.*

It wasn't a surprise her father went to prostitutes. Vitória yawned in the darkness as she clenched her hands into fists under her chin, allowing her memory to wander… *Sylvia.*

When Vitória was very little, only five or six, her father took her with him to the café where he cooked to pay his bar tab. She brought customers plates of food, and they tipped her with sweets, soda pop, or cigarettes.

Sylvia was a whore who used the café to find customers. In her late twenties and desperate to look younger, she wore tight dresses cut low on top and high on the bottom. Bright makeup heavily painted her thin face, doing nothing to hide the exhaustion in her eyes. She haunted the café from noon to the early hours of the morning, flirting men into buying her cheap drinks and picking up the odd customer. Sylvia had become a prostitute after getting pregnant in her teens. The baby was stillborn, but her family kicked her out anyway. She passed from one man to another until it became her way of life. Men had fun with her, maybe genuinely liked her, but no one would marry her.

Gaspar Mendes thought his youngest daughter too naïve to figure out his trysts with Sylvia. *He still doesn't know I know*. She yawned again and stretched, releasing the tension in her fists. It confused her how often adults misjudged her abilities. *They think I'm a silly child, but all it takes to figure out what's going on is to listen and act dumb*. She'd been doing it as long as she remembered.

Not that I caught on for a while. She writhed in remorse, remembering her stupidity. It wasn't until she was seven that all the little pieces of the puzzle fit together for her. *I was so dumb*.

Every now and then, she'd look around to find her father gone from his usual place at the stove in the kitchen. When she asked, the boss always explained he was on a break. She knew it was a lie; Father wasn't on any break. Every time her father left the small, hot kitchen, he yelled for a glass of wine to cool his throat; it never failed. That's what finally made her suspicious. He would never go without his wine if he were at the café. So where was he?

It took longer for her to notice Sylvia's absences at the same time and longer still to figure out what they were up to. After all, the whore was often away for different periods of time, so it wasn't unusual for her to be gone. But when Vitória did see the pattern, she wasted no time in checking it out.

She kept her eyes and ears open as she brought plates of food from the hot, steamy kitchen out into the main dining room, moving faster than usual. When she heard her father ask for a break and not shout for wine, she hid outside to watch where he went.

First Sylvia came out the front door, walking casually down the street until entering the little house she lived in. A few moments later, her father left through the back door of the restaurant. He stretched and scratched, then pulled a hand rolled corn-husk cigarette from his pocket, lit and puffed on it as he followed Sylvia's footsteps, throwing it aside as he entered her door. Vitória waited a short while, then crept up to peer through the windows.

In the safe darkness of her bedroom, she twisted convulsively onto her side and snuggled deep under a blanket, trying to forget what she saw over that sagging dirty windowsill four long years ago. Her father had been seated on a chair, pants and underwear down around his ankles, head thrown back and breathing hard. Sylvia kneeled on the floor between his spread legs, her head bobbing up and down in his lap. The only sounds were her father's groans and the slurp, slurp, slurp of the prostitute's tongue. Sylvia's brightly painted fingernails gleamed on the pale flesh of his thighs. The scene disgusted her, and she'd cried in the bushes where she was hiding that day. Vitória went back to the restaurant with a whole new understanding of her father.

Those who grew up on any of the nine Açores Islands in the 1950's were no strangers to the idea that sex was a sin. *No one ever talks about it except the Priests and they have nothing good to say about it.* Parents were shamefully silent on the topic, but truly vicious gossip was easily overheard at any gathering. Curious children learned to denounce, loudly and publicly, anyone who differed from the sanctified definition of normal.

However, Vitória also learned early in life that women of the island believed their men needed prostitutes to satisfy excessive, unnatural desires. Friends of her mother complained when their husbands went to prostitutes but were still thankful their men were satisfied. "Good women don't do those things," she heard more than once, "so let bad women do them."

She knew her father was strict, even cruel on occasion; she'd dodged his fists and feet too often to deny it. But until tonight she'd never thought him crass enough to frequent the whorehouse next door. *I thought he had, well, more class than that.*

In the darkness of her bedroom, she felt her face flame with anger at the insult to her mother. Now she could think of him with complete contempt rather than offer even the token respect she owed a parent. If he did find out her pee baptized him and kicked her tailbone until she couldn't stand, she'd refuse to cry and force her mind to go to America, where girls could do as they wished.

Her father often beat her because she liked wearing pants instead of skirts. It was perfectly fine with him until she started going to school. And he'd also started kicking her ass whenever he caught her smoking although he used to think it was funny when customers at the café gave her lit cigarettes to smoke.

Father says I have to give up playing with boys and dress and act like the other girls in Lajes. He hates me because I want to keep doing the things I've always done. She didn't know why her father suddenly changed, but she didn't want to and resisted him at every turn. Not feeling the pain of his beatings was her personal triumph, somehow evening the growing score between them.

As her exhausted eyes finally closed, she felt herself drifting off to sleep. Thinking of all the frustrated men who went home to their wives wearing her pee, her father and uncle among them, her lips curved upward one more time in the darkness. *Serves them right.*

Ch. 2 – Tattles Like a Little Girl

The Next Day

Vitória woke to a day that looked like a dream, high white clouds scuttling playfully across a vibrant blue sky. All day long, she felt lighter than air, almost able to fly.

She left the schoolyard that afternoon walking with her best friends Margarida and Alexandra, the three of them dressed in simple skirts, white blouses, and colorful sweaters for school instead of their preferred pants. They would meet later in the woods behind Mom's house, wearing boy clothing they'd stolen from clotheslines.

Vitória kept glancing at the new girl who walked ahead of them. Ana had two long golden braids that hung heavily down her back. Blonds are rare among the Portuguese, and she'd never seen anything quite as beautiful as that hair glinting and glittering in the bright afternoon sun. Her fingers itched to reach out and stroke it, to feel the weight and softness of it.

Dawdling to stay behind Ana as they walked up the cobblestone street toward home, Vitória watched the pretty girl in front of her. Her friends busily discussed their fourth-year teacher, Professora Alameda, the only one ever to instill a love of learning in them.

Although Vitória was smart, Alexandra brave, and Margarida quick, their first three schoolmistresses ignored the most spirited girls. They were stashed in the back of the classroom, as far away from learning as possible. There they first recognized fellow outlaws of the soul, became best friends, and supported each other. They were castaways together, much easier than slogging against the tide alone.

Their fourth year was different. Professora Alameda recognized their neglected talents, and the girls bloomed. Her students weren't hit because they were ignorant, rather taught with patient kindness. Instead of expecting their illiterate parents to value homework, she provided time during the day to help them herself. Vitória discovered how much fun it was to learn. Instead of being ridiculed and made to feel stupid, she was encouraged and applauded. She and her friends were more than a little in love with their teacher.

They were discussing something the Professora said in class when a swarm of boys ran past them, shouting and laughing. As they reached and surrounded the timid new girl trudging ahead, each one yanked cruelly on her long braids. Tears popped into Ana's eyes as she tried to break away from them.

Vitória's schoolbooks hit the ground as she ran up the street and started pounding on the boys, grabbing their much shorter hair and pulling it fiercely. "There! How do you like it? You don't? Then leave Ana alone!" She added to this advice several well-placed kicks and a few roundhouse blows.

The boys scattered good-naturedly, knowing all too well what damage Vitória could inflict. As they fled, she felt Ana's thankful smile like a gentle touch on her face and knew she wanted more. Suddenly she had a deep desire to see Ana smile like that every minute of every day.

"Thank you…" the shy girl said, blushing when she realized she didn't know the name of her rescuer.

"Vitória." Surprisingly just as shy, she shrugged. "Ana, right? Third year? I saw you at recess standing by the building." Their eyes met briefly, and each offered the other a smile. Then, just as swift as when she came, Vitória ran back to her grinning friends.

In the habit of childhood, everything was forgotten within moments. Up the street in an unused field, the boys started a quick game of soccer, calling to Vitória who ran joyfully to join in. She was the only girl who did, however. Not even Alexandra or Margarida could break this barrier. At one time, the boys tried to keep her away too, but having sampled her fists and seen for themselves her ability to play, they began counting her as one of their regular team members. She now played in all their games and punched any boy who dared suggest otherwise.

Short, scrawny, fast, and very strong for her age, Vitória soared up and over the head of the surprised goalie to slam the soccer ball down with the top of her foot, scoring. Standing victoriously among her cheering team, she saw Ana watching and basked in the warmth of her admiring gaze. Vitória grinned and waved, glad the blond was looking at her instead of one of the boys.

Not far from where they played leaned Mrs. Alvares on her veranda gate, sharing a few words with whoever passed by on the street. She was one of a legion of older women, mostly widows, who cleaned their houses in the morning and then grew their tits on the gate tops, gossiping and judging. Mrs. Alvares always had something to say to Vitória when she saw her playing with the boys, and today was no exception.

"Hey, you *maria rapaz*, you twisted tomboy!" The dirty insult flashed through the air. "Why don't you stop trying to be a boy and learn to sew like a good girl?" The old woman's eyes glinted evilly in the sunlight as she waited to judge how her barb landed.

Vitória glanced hastily from the gray-haired crone trying to rob her of her moment to the golden-haired beauty still watching. To be called a maria rapaz in front of others was a very bad thing, something she learned the hard way over the last few years. It meant she was too different, a tomboy with a debased quirk, a s/he, neither one nor the other. Just hearing it was enough to make her father's face blow up purple with rage. Vitória needed to walk the narrow tightrope of revenging herself on this woman without putting herself in line for a beating.

"I would have, but your Gabriel enrolled in my place at the sewing school," she answered in a short, vicious whisper. Mrs. Alvares blanched at the mention of her son who'd run away and never returned, tightening her lips into a straight line. She crossed herself and stared down the length of her nose, assessing Vitória as nothing but a sassy child.

"You watch what you say to your elders, girl." The old busybody heaved up the ponderous weight of her bosom and shuffled back inside her house. Vitória grinned at Ana and waved saucily to her friends before going back to play with the boys.

Sometime later, she noticed the small group of girls who watched the game had all gone home to help with dinner. As they did every early evening, the usual gathering of women around the common well across the street began assembling.

Vitória and Johnny had discussed last night's adventure as they walked to school this morning. Thinking a girl could pass unnoticed, and anxious to know if they were in trouble or not, he gestured to her to go over and listen in. She threw him a withering glance but drifted to within hearing range of the chatting women. Unwilling to be sent home to cook, she also made sure to stay out of the direct line of sight of her mother and aunt, two of the dozen or so women.

"My Jaime came home last night smelling like the hogs. He told me he got drunk and missed when peeing; can you imagine that? Men are such animals!" said one woman in disgust.

"My Manny also smelled bad," announced another in surprise. "Said he walked through a pig pen in the dark."

"You know, my husband came in late last night and his shirt was wet… I mean sopping wet!" rose a third voice. "And it was cold last night, you remember?" Vitória angled herself so she could see the woman look thoughtfully at the first two. "He's never washed a shirt in his life, my Izzy." They nodded in agreement. Men on the island didn't do laundry. "He said he fell into the lagoon, but then why were his pants dry?"

There was a general hubbub as the women broke into smaller groups for discussion. Vitória scooted behind the broad behind of a woman standing close to her mother and listened.

"Sal smelled bad last night too," she heard Tia Maria say and sensed rather than saw her mother nod in agreement.

"Well, I know where my husband was last night," a woman Vitória couldn't see until she moved a little to her left said morosely. "He was at *that* house." She tossed her head over her shoulder as they all focused on her. "He was furious because they turned him away. And he stunk."

The women turned as one to glare at the whorehouse, and she heard her mother's distinctive sigh. Vitória moved back behind the big woman to avoid her gaze.

"How do you stand it, Amalia?"

"What choice do I have?" Her mother answered calmly. "Yes, a lot of men have been in and out of there lately." She heard Mom's voice begin to rise with excitement as she mentally put all the pieces together, and Vitória wished she could see her face without being seen herself. "Do you suppose somebody managed to dirty the men who went there last night and got them sent away, stinking for their wives to find out?" She could hear the grin in her mother's voice even though she couldn't see it.

Once again a hubbub of excited discussion rose. Before long, the group decided some brave woman of Lajes, spurred by righteous indignation, managed to mark the prostitute's customers last night. Many were loud in their appreciation of the unknown woman's courage, challenging each other to admit who did it. Many suspected her mother, who denied it repeatedly. No one admitted to the great and glorious deed.

Vitória ran back to her brother, pulling him out of the game so they could whisper together. "We're safe," she told him. "They think only a grownup could do anything so brave!" They laughed together, pleased with their prank and even more satisfied to get away with it.

A month or so later, they were playing with their friends after school when they heard Mom's voice drifting through the deepening dusk calling them home to eat. A single kerosene lamp, a golden warmth filled with delicious aromas, lighted their mother's kitchen.

They washed their hands in the basin of water set out for them, then sat on the bench along one side of the long table. Vitória was careful not to glance at the two empty seats across from her. Grandfather had died six years ago, and Grandmother followed him only a short year later. She missed her grandparents terribly, although no one ever spoke of them anymore. The house became hollow without them, the center missing from the shell. Grandmother always filled their dinner table with grand tales of days gone by, entertaining them all. Vitória's favorite story was about a day a woman saved the island of Terceira.

"Five hundred years ago," Grandmother always began, "evil King Phillip II of Spain wanted to invade and use our island in his war to conquer Portugal. He sent ten Castilian ships carrying a thousand soldiers, who landed in Salgueiros Bay and caught the people there by surprise. They rounded up and imprisoned every man and set fire to the houses and fields, destroying everything before them. Can you imagine, sweetie?" Young Vitória's vivid imagination did its best.

Grandmother would pause at that point in her story, her squinty brown eyes grow round with wondrous pride. "One young woman, Brianda Diaz, became a true hero that day. She watched them burn her family's farm and chain her father, brothers, and fiancé. Determined and almost as stubborn as you, little troublemaker," her toothless grin teased her wayward granddaughter, "she summoned all her courage, strength, and bravery to save the rest of the island and rescue the men."

Vitória loved the next part best. "Tell how she did it!"

"Riding bareback, Brianda raced across Terceira calling for everyone to gather their cattle and bulls. Following her directions, they herded nearly a thousand of the huge animals to the enemy's location and with shouts and musket shots stampeded them down upon the unsuspecting invaders. Hundreds of Castilians drowned in the panic fleeing to their ships, giving us time to rescue the prisoners and get our defenses up. They say that when the battle ended only fifty Spaniards survived to tell the tale."

She and Grandmother always cheered then, both proud a woman, not another man, saved their people. That story always ended with,

"Remember child, women are every bit as strong, if not stronger, than men."

And her father, if present, always added, "Nonsense."

Vitória could still hear her grandmother's sweet voice rising and falling as she told this story, building the tension. They'd laughed so hard at the picture she painted of the Castilian soldiers' faces when they saw the bulls descending upon them and their mad scramble all the way down to the rocky shore. "Brianda scared them so much they threw themselves into the sea, preferring death to a mad Terceiran woman and her bulls!" While Grandmother lived, their dinner table rang with mirth. That is, until she became a widow.

Sitting silently at the table waiting for Father to wash his hands in the basin and join them, Vitória's mind drifted farther back to the day Grandfather left her, when she was too young even for school. She was his favorite grandchild and felt the familiar clutch of her heart as she remembered him telling her so, many times.

Don Francisco, as everyone called her mother's father, loved Vitória more than anyone else ever. After Alice, their older sister, got married and went to live in her own house with her husband, Vitória was left in his care. While her parents worked the fields, Johnny went to school, and Grandmother tended house, the two became inseparable, doing everything together.

Grandfather taught her whatever she wanted to learn. He showed her how to use tools and take proper care of them, helped her draw up plans and make things, and taught her that if she wanted something badly enough, she needed to work hard to get it.

"Only one thing stands between you and your dreams – you. Learn what you need to know, use every bit of yourself to work for it, and you can get anything and go anywhere." He himself had been born on the mainland, then traveled to Brazil before finally settling on the third island of the Açores.

"You say Brazil is very beautiful." The little girl stared into his vivid blue eyes, so unusual. "Why stay here? Why didn't you return?"

Her grandfather's rich laugh filled the house. "Because, my little love, your grandmother is even more beautiful."

Vitória loved her grandfather beyond reason. His obvious pleasure in her, delight at her quick-wittedness, and joy in her bravery and integrity established a strong sense of self-esteem in her as she grew. They spent every waking moment with each other, and every day after lunch she would sit quietly at the foot of his bed, waiting for him to wake from his frequent naps. He always had, until…

She sat on her chair patiently all that afternoon, quiet as a mouse so as not to wake him, but his eyes didn't open. Even when her mother knocked softly on the door and poked her head inside, he hadn't woken up. And then things got noisy, confusing, and crazy. People were crying, adults were running in and out and about the house, and no one thought to explain anything to her, a frightened child forgotten in their midst.

Grandmother washed and dressed her beloved husband in his finest suit, then wound him in a clean white sheet. They laid him across four pairs of chairs set facing each other in the main room. Then they waited until a long black wooden box arrived. Vitória passively held Johnny's hand as two men transferred Grandfather from the chairs to the box, but panicked when they started to close the lid.

Her five-year-old mind reeled at what she saw. *What are they doing? Don't they know that Grandfather is only sleeping, and he'll wake from his nap soon, just as he always does?* Young Vitória realized that if they put the heavy lid on the coffin he might not be strong enough to push it off without her help. She had to stop them or crawl inside with Grandfather so she'd be with him when he woke. Her breath struggled from her closed throat.

As the men finished and lifted the coffin to carry it from the house, she wrenched her hand from that of her older brother and launched herself at them. She hit and kicked blindly, hysterically, screaming at them to put him back down and open the coffin again.

Her grandmother, aunts, and mother were weeping loudly and didn't see what she was doing. Her father brusquely reached out a strong hand and grabbed her thin arm, thrusting her back toward her brother. Father hadn't said anything to her, just glared. Then he and the other men carried her grandfather away. Vitória thought then that Father had been glad to take Grandfather from her. She cried until uncountable tears finally washed the pain from the memory.

Her sweet grandmother disappeared in much the same way only a short year later. Bereft and alone, Vitória reached a terrible conclusion: she had done something so bad it drove her good grandparents away. She was always getting into mischief, couldn't seem able to stay out of trouble, and often purposely angered her parents. Her unhappy grandparents must have decided to leave. *They abandoned me.*

Day after day, and then week after lonely week, she sat on the step of the veranda. With no one to watch her after school, which she had just begun, she wouldn't go in the house. Neighbors told her parents about her daily outdoor vigils. They tried to convince her to wait indoors for them to return from the fields. She said she would but then didn't, continuing to stand watch faithfully. She convinced herself that if she sat there long enough her missing grandparents would eventually walk by and then she would throw herself on them and apologize. She would plead with them to come home until they returned to her. In sunshine, fog, and rain she sat on the veranda, watching and waiting.

Mom ladled soup in Vitória's bowl, which shook her free of her reverie. She glanced at her brother sitting next to her. Johnny had largely ignored her up until the time when sitting outside in the rain gave her fever. She grew very sick, and there were doubts she would recover. Their mother, already grieving the loss of both parents, prepared to also bury a third child having lost two sons in infancy. Father ignored her. But her scared brother had tried his best to fill the emptiness in her heart. He ran errands to earn money to buy her candy and told her stories about what they would do together when she got better.

I didn't want to get well. I wanted Grandfather and Grandmother back.

Her obvious hopelessness had gnawed at Johnny, and a belief that she would actually die of loneliness made him sit and read to her every day until she slowly regained the color in her pale cheeks. He began dragging her along behind him when she was well enough to go out, hoping to build up her strength. That was how Vitória first got a chance to play with the boys. Johnny also gave her a taste for competition, a job he still took too seriously. She nudged his ribs, flashed him a smile, and stuck her tongue out at him.

The family settled into their dinner; only Mom rose once from the table to pass out pieces of boiled fish. It was their custom to eat in silence unless Father chose to speak. So they were startled when a thunderous knock sounded on their door. Her father shared a glance with her mother, and then both turned to look at their daughter. She clasped her hands together tightly under the table and froze.

Father rose and opened the door. Standing on the veranda was Irene Rodrigues holding her son Henry by the arm and glaring angrily past Father straight at Vitória. "Gaspar, Amalia, something has got to be done about that girl!"

Oh no. No. No. No. She felt a large lump effectively close her throat, gagging her as she tried to swallow. She blushed furiously as looks between her parents flew over her head. Her mother sighed and sat up straighter while her father turned to face the irate mother, both already clearly resigned to hear something terrible.

"What has she done now?" Her father's voice blared across the room, ringing with the promise of punishment. Vitória twisted her hands in her lap, willing the woman to disappear. Unfortunately, that never worked.

"It's Henry. She hurt him so badly that I've just come from the pharmacist. You will pay me for the medicine I had to buy!" Mrs. Rodrigues' eyes blazed a hole into the top of Vitória's bent head. "That maria rapaz of yours pulled his penis until it's swollen like a donkey's!"

Her stunned father only gaped at the woman. Johnny tried to stifle a loud guffaw that managed to escape him nonetheless. Her brother's eyes danced delightedly from Henry, who was holding one hand protectively over his groin, to Vitória sitting next to him stewing in her own combination of horror and delight. He grinned a knowing grin.

Mom glared at Johnny, silencing him. "I want to know what happened." Looking at her husband, she nodded for him to bring the woman and her son inside. "No need for the neighbors to hear more than they already have."

Once the door was closed, Mom rose calmly from her chair and approached the mother and son standing in her warm kitchen. This was her domain. Here, she ruled.

"Irene how, exactly, did my daughter get her hand on your son's penis?" She spoke calmly and clearly, as if she said this sort of thing every day.

Vitória silently cheered. Mom had been unraveling the rumors that surrounded her for a long time and could tell when a story was more than it seemed. She took a chance and looked sideways at the group to see what was happening.

Mrs. Rodrigues grew suddenly still as this question had not occurred to her before. She looked at her son, whose face had just gone pale. She shook him by the shoulder and demanded, "Well, Henry? Answer Mrs. Mendes!"

"She…she just grabbed it," he said, almost under his breath.

"And you're sure it was our Vitória that did this?" she heard her father ask. She saw her mother shake her head, knowing that was the wrong question to ask. Of course, it was Vitória who did it.

"Yes, yes, I'm sure," the boy hurried on, but Mom was not quite ready to proceed and held up her hand for silence. Vitória watched her mother surreptitiously.

"Henry, did you let Vitória put her hand down your pants?" she asked.

The twelve-year-old boy squirmed under her direct eye contact. "No!" he blurted. "No, I didn't." He looked nervously at his mother, unsure if she would approve of this answer. Irene Rodrigues beamed proudly at her son, reassuring him slightly. The miserable girl at the table tensed.

"Well, if Vitória didn't go into your pants, was your penis out of your pants?" continued Mom.

The rattled boy nodded gratefully before thinking, and added, "I was showing it to the girls."

Mrs. Rodrigues gasped so sharply Vitória was convinced she'd swallowed her own tongue. The furious mother cuffed her son sharply on the ear. "What do you mean you were showing it to the girls?" she screeched as Henry howled.

At this Johnny couldn't keep quiet any longer. "He's been doing it for a while now," her brother blurted out. He spoke to the room as a whole, keeping his eyes on his sister. Vitória had sense enough to keep hers focused on the tabletop.

"Margarida told me that he's been showing his weenie to the girls every chance he gets. The girls scream and run away. That's why he does it. Vitória knew, and this afternoon he teased a new girl, asking if she wanted to see it. According to Margarida, Vitória walked right up to him past all the other girls and asked if he wanted to show it to her. When he took it out of his pants, he expected her to run away screaming like the others. But not my sister." An odd tinge of pride colored his voice. "She just grabbed it and started twisting."

Vitória glanced up just long enough to see her father wince at the image and then resigned herself to the beating she had earned. *I knew I should never have touched that boy's ugly weenie.* But Henry was a bully, always terrorizing the girls by exposing his penis and wiggling it at them. Besides, he'd stolen Ana's attention.

Occasionally, girls stayed to watch the game. Some watched the boys, but several watched her. It made Vitória feel good, and she played better because of their presence. That afternoon, when Ana quit watching her to deal with him it was the last feather off the chicken. Vitória decided to teach him a lesson.

Henry had grinned wickedly at her when asked if he wanted to show her his weenie. She didn't know what she was going to do until she saw him unbuttoning his trousers. She laughed when Henry's eyes widened in surprise as she reached for it, but when she grabbed that soft little thing and started twisting they quickly filled with tears. *Big baby. Can't even take a little pain. Tattles like a little girl.*

She was so busy with her thoughts she'd lost track of what was happening in Mom's kitchen. Vitória reluctantly drew her attention back to her parents and the intruders knowing her father would already be formally apologizing for his daughter's bad behavior. He would give money to Mrs. Rodrigues to pay for the medication she bought and after they left he'd take off his belt and begin on her. It was always the same. *Why can't I stay out of trouble?*

With a shock, she heard Mrs. Rodrigues say, "Amalia, I'm so embarrassed. I don't know what to say except I'm sorry. Gaspar I promise you, when his father hears about this Henry will be punished until he can't sit down for a week."

What happened? Her father was staring at her in stunned surprise. *What did I miss?* Mrs. Rodrigues apologized for interrupting their dinner and dragged Henry to the door by the back of his shirt collar. Vitória kicked herself for drifting off. She watched silently as the two left the house and her parents returned to their places at the table.

She searched her mother's face, finding only laugh lines playing around the corners of her tired eyes. Mom ladled another piece of fish in Vitória's bowl, an unusual event in itself. The girl looked at her father, who was staring determinedly at his own dinner, fighting to suppress a smile. Then she looked at Johnny grinning wide as a fool.

As if at a silent signal, they all picked up their spoons and returned to dinner. Unspoken praise filled the silence, which only confused Vitória even more.

It was the first thing she brought up when she met her friends in the woods behind her mother's house next Sunday evening. A small fire was already crackling, cheerfully beating back the seasonal chill. A half dozen girls, ages ranging from nine to fourteen, sat around on the well-worn ground, a secret group afraid to realize they'd formed a club.

"She called you a maria rapaz in front of your parents?" asked Margarida, aghast. "She actually said it that way?" Her friend's mind reeled at the ramifications of such a thing.

"Yes, I told you she did. I thought Father was going to explode when she said I twisted his penis!" Vitória laughed. "But what I don't understand is why they reacted that way. Especially my father. I mean, he didn't yell at me or hit, even after finding out I touched a boy."

"He's proud of you," announced Alexandra with confidence.

"What are you talking about?" Vitória scowled. "He's never been proud of me a moment of my life. When I was born sickly, wasn't he heard saying he thought I would die and the sooner the better?" Alexandra couldn't deny it. Gaspar Mendes had said it to her own mother when she'd visited the new baby. She'd heard the story told often, with gusto.

"I think she's right, though." Margarida nodded at Alexandra. "It sounds to me like they're both proud of you. And I know Johnny is. He said as much when I told him what you did." She slapped Vitória soundly on the back and roughened up her voice. "Hell, even I'm proud of you!"

The six laughed together as easily as butter melts. *I'm lucky to have such friends.*

"Well, I think you were crazy to do it," said Berta, a small wiry girl with glossy black hair worn in a single braid down her back. "I wouldn't want to touch a boy's weenie!" She shivered. To soften the sting of her words, Berta offered Vitória a bag of fried fava beans she'd stolen from her mother's pantry. That night, the group feasted on those and a loaf of corn bread snuck from Tina's home, which they dunked in tin cups filled with red wine pilfered by Margarida.

Vitória ruefully agreed. Her hand still felt dirty after that contact, even though she had scrubbed it with lye soap several times. "But it was worth it to see the little pig squeal." She laughed at her own daring, just beginning to believe she might get away with it. The other girls joined in her laughter, a shared joke they would enjoy many times. They lived for such small victories as these.

"Where's Juana?" asked Margarida to fill a slight break in the conversation. She tossed a fava into the air and caught it neatly in her mouth.

Olivia tossed another bean up in the air and over the fire for Margarida to catch, which she did. It was one of the few things their tall gangly friend did really well, and they helped her show off her talent whenever possible. "Well…" The skinny girl pulled her braid over one shoulder and leaned in conspiratorially, waving the rest of them to do the same as if afraid someone might overhear them. Seated in a loose circle a hundred meters from the outhouse behind Mom's house, they were hidden from prying eyes by a fringe of fruit trees. No one ever walked back there, or practically no one did, but they all leaned in to hear anyway. "It's terrible," Olivia whispered. "Everyone on their road is talking about it. Juana's brother-in-law punched her. They say he broke her teeth."

Each girl leaned back into the dark instinctively searching for cover, silently digesting the news. It wasn't the first time something like this happened to Juana. It wouldn't be the last time something like this happened to any one of them. No one met anyone else's eye, each sitting on her island of experience.

Juana was two years older, a full head taller than, and twice as wide as Vitória. She couldn't help swaggering when she walked. Her face had never worn the softness of a curved cheek or full lips. It was a strong, honest, masculine-looking face, and the unfortunate hint of a mustache furthered that impression. With wide shoulders and narrow hips, she bore a distinct resemblance to a bull.

Juana's mother had tried curling her hair, dressing her in the most feminine clothing, even applying makeup. Nothing made her look girly. She looked just like her father. Although her parents loathed letting her dress in trousers she looked even more ridiculous when wearing skirts. They hadn't given up, however, and were determined to force their daughter to become a proper young lady. That meant they turned a blind eye to, when not blatantly approving of, their son-in-law doling out physical correction.

To her credit, Juana had tried for years to satisfy them, trying constantly to look demure, wearing her hair in a long braid carefully wound around the crown of her head. She shortened her steps until she resembled a dog mincing along on its hind legs. She attended every Mass with her mother. She even tried flirting with boys. "But it always ends up the same," she told them one night not long ago. "The boys wander off repulsed while I watch with a little regret and a great deal of relief."

Vitória looked around the circle of shadows thrown by the firelight and knew that each of the girls was sending healing wishes to their missing friend and would offer up prayers for her tonight. It was something the tomboys did for each other. Juana would return to them sooner or later and they knew she would be changed.

Every beating changes a person, but ones that leave visible wounds are the worst. Everyone sees what's been done. People would throw judgmental looks Juana's way, approving of a family trying to bring their willful daughter into line. The scars from those battles were more than skin deep and each girl sitting around the fire had her own. It was what made their club membership private, shared pain were the dues.

As luck would have it, they had each other. It would have been a hundred times harder to get through bad times if they didn't have this group of friends and their weekly gatherings. Not far away Juana lay on her cornhusk mattress in pain but knew at this moment, around this campfire, six people wished her well and hoped to see her again soon. That might be her only comfort tonight.

They were a real family. The girls, tomboys all, were sisters of the soul. With each other they found the comfort and support they lacked in the rest of their lives. Vitória and the others knew that no matter what, they would always have a place around this fire.

For some it was all they had.

Ch. 3 – You Can Call Me Traf

Winter 1959 through Spring 1963

Just like all the islands of the Açorean archipelago, Terceira grew up through the murky waters of the Atlantic one layer of lava at a time. A glittering green gem when seen from above, the quilted fields are broken by sloping hills built up around the volcano's base by thousands of years of flows and earthquakes. The coastline is rugged; sharp volcanic rocks and steep cliffs protect most of it. Bays and manmade breakwaters shelter boats from ravaging waves during storms.

Luscious flowers grow in the wild, a riot of color, carefully carried home to be cultivated in growing villages. Bananas, figs, oranges, grapes, an entire multitude of delicious fruits dot the land. People who harvest extra *this* trade it with people who grow extra *that.*

During spring, summer, and autumn the humid island climate changes from caressingly warm to stifling hot. But in the winter, Terceira can be a cold, lonely place filled with drifting mists and bone-chilling rain.

One bitter February day the weather fit Vitória's mood perfectly. Looking at the schoolbook in her hand, she worried. *I only had one more year to go and then Professora Alameda showed up. Now, it matters that I can't read well.* She couldn't just imitate the other girls anymore. *I've squeaked by so far, but that teacher is too smart to fool for long.*

She asked her best friend, Hermione, who lived in a little house up the road, to help her. Hermione was four years older, already fifteen, but still unmarried. Being the daughter of an unwed mother left her lonely and ignored with no friends except Vitória. A kindred recognition of being different had bridged the years between them for as long as either could remember.

"Of course I'll help," her best friend assured her. They worked every day after school with Hermione reading aloud words that were difficult for Vitória to decipher. The older girl would write the homework answers, which the younger would copy in her own hand.

Handwriting had been an issue between her teachers and Vitória since the first year. They tied her left hand behind her back every day in her first three years in school. Professora Alameda released her, but she found her left-handed writing was almost as difficult to read. But she kept at it, repeating everything Hermione taught her.

Months passed this way until one Saturday, as they worked in Hermione's bedroom, her mother, Betty, came home unexpectedly and found the two girls together. She shook her head slightly when her daughter looked up. Hermione tried to look unconcerned but became obviously distracted. Whenever Miss Betty's employer had a headache she was sent home early from her job as a maid meaning there were no leftovers from her lunch.

"Vitória," her mother said kindly, drawing the younger girl's attention from her daughter's hunger, "you're having trouble letting the letters make sounds for you, aren't you?"

"Yes, Miss Betty." She shook her head. "No matter how many times I draw them, I don't remember the sound, or it doesn't sound like what I hear when others say it."

"Come with me, child," said Miss Betty. "Let me see if I can help you puzzle through it."

"You can read?" Vitória asked while following her to the kitchen table, more than a little surprised. Except for teachers and priests, most adults she knew couldn't.

"She taught me everything I know." Hermione held her head high.

Miss Betty ran one hand over her eyes ruefully. "Yes, I can read. I was at school on the mainland, and did well, too." She shook her head as if to empty it of memories, then sat down beside Vitória. They started connecting letters to sounds, starting with the vowels. Consonants followed, and as the girl began recognizing words, she also started spelling properly, which made her proud enough to improve her handwriting. It made for a long afternoon but by the end of it the student discovered the magic of reading. Hermione sat alongside them, cheering her on all the way.

"Thank you, thank you, Miss, uh, Tia Betty!" Vitória didn't wait to see if being raised to the status of an aunt suited her tutor. She gathered up her books and slate, then turned to hurry home to her mother's good cooking. She turned back and impulsively gave Hermione a big hug. "I'll see you tomorrow," she promised.

Racing home, Vitória ran to her room and dug out the saved coins she'd earned one by one by running errands for people. Taking all five, she ran to the bakery and bought two sweet pastries and a loaf of corn bread. Then she hurried to the dock and along the way purchased some potatoes. With the last two coins she haggled fresh mackerel from the fishermen. She ran all the way back to Miss Betty's house, placed her gifts on the doorstep, and banged very loudly. She darted back up the walkway and was halfway home waving her thanks before Hermione opened the door.

That evening as they cleaned up the supper dishes, Vitória asked her mother about their neighbor.

"Betty was a beautiful young girl," her mother reminisced. "Her family was the richest on the island with a home in Lisbon that the children used when they were at school. They had nannies, cooks, and maids, even a car with a chauffeur."

Vitória tried to reconcile that image with the worn, but kind woman who lived down the street, and couldn't. "What happened?"

"A smooth-talking boy who belonged to her social set talked her into…" Mom stopped. "How old are you again?"

"I'll be twelve next month, Mom."

"Already?" Her mother sighed. "Then you're old enough to know." Handing Vitória a plate to dry, she reached back in the hot water for another one. "Betty was more than pretty. She looked like one of your American movie stars at the theater. All the boys were after her, which made her think of herself as a prize to be won." She handed her daughter another plate to dry. "She put the boys through their paces, asking impossible things of them, challenging them to fight for her. One night that's exactly what happened. Two of her best boyfriends, former best friends, turned on each other. One was badly beaten. The other claimed her as his prize."

Vitória put the stack of dried plates on the shelf in the cupboard. "Claimed her as a prize? Like he owned her or something?"

"Well yes, in a way. He thought he could do what he wanted with her."

"What did he want?"

"He wanted what all men want."

"What do all men want? Money? Love?"

"Vitória, people don't always marry for love. That comes with time and hard work to the lucky. How old are you again? Surely some of those girls you talk with have spoken about what happens between men and women." Mom blushed as she built up the fire in the brick oven and started measuring flour into a large bowl for bread. "Go collect the eggs and your thoughts while you're at it, my trafulha."

She called me her little thief, a troublemaker, just like Grandmother used to. I kinda like the sound of that. Vitória whizzed through the penned area of the yard collecting eggs from nests defended by sullen hens. The girls she met with in the woods never spoke about men, except as bullies and the dispensers of discipline. But Johnny had changed since growing taller and pointed out to her roosters mounting chickens, bulls with cows, billies on top of nannies, and the silly rabbits who would go so fast and then fall over when they were done. He laughed, so she laughed. Now he talked a lot about girls and how he wanted to kiss them, and other things. The way he described it, it sounded like something she might like to do… but not with boys.

"You mean sex, right?" Vitória bustled back into the warm kitchen, depositing the ten eggs onto a waiting towel so they wouldn't roll away. She cracked them open and added them to the mixture in the bowl.

"Right." Her mother's blush had faded while she'd been outside, but now it deepened again. "Anyway, Betty got caught. When she told her mother, she was turned out of the house, a disgrace to the family. The news spread throughout Lajes like feathers in a storm. Betty's friends turned their backs on her, afraid they'd be tainted by her shame."

"How do you know all this?"

"Six months before Hermione was born, Betty bought her house. Her father gave her enough money for that, at least. With a baby on the way and no husband, she needed someone to talk to." Mom had the most sympathetic ear in the village of Lajes, largely because she could keep secrets and almost never gossiped.

"After Hermione arrived Betty started working as a maid, carting the baby along with her. She told me if she never let that boy lie with her she might have been a professora or even a nun. She loved reading, although I doubt she has much time for it now. We talked, once, about her teaching me to read." Amalia looked at her daughter blankly. "But who has time for that nonsense, right?"

She laughed, kneading the dough with strong hands, punching, folding, and slapping it in every direction. "Just remember, Vitória. You can work hard an entire lifetime to build an honorable reputation, only to lose it all at the speed of gossip. An hour of pleasure can lead to a lifetime of drudgery."

As Mom covered the rising dough with a damp towel, she looked sideways at her headstrong daughter. "What heartaches will you face, my unusual child who breaks every rule?" She shook her head. "I worry about what's in store for you but I will always be here to help any way I can." She caught her youngest child in the rarest of hugs.

With Tia Betty's tutoring, Vitória became one of the top students in school. Her grades were so good, in fact, that Professora Alameda provided an extra fifth year.

The teacher had to argue long and hard with Gaspar Mendes. First about the worthiness of his daughter as a student and second, whether a girl destined to spend her life as wife and mother should bother to attend. However, when the stubborn woman insisted she would pay for the extra year from her own meager salary, he reluctantly gave in.

Over the course of the next year, as many of her former classmates found jobs as servants, worked their parents' fields, or even married, Vitória excelled in school once more. In early summer, displaying her best student's final exams as evidence, Professora Alameda visited Mom's house to ask about continuing Vitória's education. The teacher admitted she had taken the intelligent thirteen-year-old as far as she could on the island of Terceira.

Mom also wanted to send her daughter to the mainland to study, not so much because she valued education but because it was one of the last things her father asked of her before he died. His voice still sounded clearly in her memory. "Make sure Vitória goes to school. I've always been sorry I didn't see to your education, Amalia. She's every bit as smart as you were at her age. Don't make the same mistake I did. The future is changing, Daughter, and a woman will need new knowledge to get along."

The two women argued strongly for a formal education, something Vitória could only get in mainland Portugal. She listened with her heart in her throat but knew her father would never let her go. Sure enough, this time he stood his ground, making quite clear to one and all that he would never agree to any daughter of his being unchaperoned so far away from home. "There simply isn't the money to waste on a girl's education." That ended the discussion permanently.

They were part of a changing middle-class. Vitória's Grandfather worked hard as a young man and had enough property at the end of his life to leave each of his five children their own fields. Each had enough to grow the food their family ate, and sometimes extra to sell at market. As landowners on the isolated island, the children of Don Francisco Cortes, including Mom, had as much as most.

But that was when they were only a dot on a map. Before Vitória was born, even before World War II, the British realized the Portuguese Açores islands offered a strategic vantage point along the long coastline of Europe. The British negotiated with the Salazar government, built an airbase in the village of Lajes, and leased it until shortly after the war ended. In 1948, the year Vitória was born, the lease expired and the English decided to vacate the base.

The Americans moved in, expanding everything and bringing their Army, Navy, and Air Force with them. They hired local people to work for them, laborers to build a large new landing field, bartenders, and cooks. Local women were hired as maids for their homes.

Americans also bought fish from local fishermen and fresh fruit and vegetables from farmers. Soldiers' wives bought clothing from local seamstresses who could copy the high styles of Paris, Lisbon, or Madrid for a fraction of the cost. Açorean nannies tended their children.

New money flowed into the local economy and while the Mendes family still had plenty to eat, it was sometimes difficult to come up with the cash necessary to buy the new things imported from overseas. It was astonishing how quickly things they never knew existed became indispensable. It seemed there was never enough money.

Now that Vitória's education had ended, her options dwindled. Considered a young adult at the age of thirteen, on Terceira girls her age were expected to spend the next few years being courted, preparing for marriage, having a wedding, and starting their own families. She would, just like every young adult, remain in her mother's house as long as she was unmarried. Since Vitória didn't want to get married that might be forever.

Boys were interested; some even asked permission to visit her at her mother's house. She always told them yes, but was never home when they called for her. The few times she got caught at home, she was happy to have the veranda wall between them and her mother just inside the door. Young men and women were not allowed to be together and unchaperoned until after they were married. Every year during Festival season her father ordered Vitória to keep away from the boys and dance only with girls. To his utter surprise, this was the only thing she'd ever given him no argument over. *What can I say? I prefer the company of girls.*

Vitória spent several years doing seasonal work at the tobacco shed in Lajes, shredding leaves and loading the machine that produced rolled cigarettes for packaging. It was tedious, backbreaking labor, and the owner was happy to hire whoever would work, even women. Every week she brought the money she earned home to her mother. It helped buy the little pleasures of their simple life, sugar, coffee beans, maybe some cocoa, or a little extra kerosene to read by at night. Even though it was hard boring work, she liked making her own money and was glad to have a job. When the men she worked with called her nasty names like maria rapaz, or twisted tomboy, and bitch, she dug in her stubborn heels and refused to be driven out. So six days every week during the autumn, she stood on her feet, hunched over a table, shredding tobacco with stained fingers. The rest of the year she helped in the family fields.

Now in his mid-fifties, Gaspar Mendes had retired from cooking in the restaurant, only tending his crops these days. Although Johnny, eighteen and a soldier in the Portuguese Army, was busy and away from home most of the time he still came to help when he could. But Gaspar's old, arthritic back needed regular help to plant, care for, and harvest the crops. Nowadays when he slaughtered animals or did the regular repair work any house requires over time, he needed someone's youthful strength and stamina.

As Vitória's vigor grew Gaspar's waned and he found himself in the awkward position of being thankful his fifteen-year-old daughter was so willing to help, even after the grueling hours she spent at the tobacco shed. This amused her, as if her growing disdain for him would ever stop the granddaughter of Don Francisco Cortes from helping in the fields he left her mother. She always had; she always would. Familial obligations, after all, were just that. An uneasy peace settled between Vitória and her father.

She had never minded hard labor; she enjoyed the physical workout as much as the satisfaction of completing a task. She knew she was a good extra pair of hands and another strong back in the fields to help with the crops. It made her feel significant to be someone others could count on.

Over the years, it became routine for Father to periodically look at the sky, squint his piercing black eyes, and pronounce it a good day for fishing. "Want to go with me?" he would ask his youngest daughter, knowing she loved to fish as much as he. Vitória would eagerly agree and they would harvest bamboo, find string or wire, and fetch the couple of hooks Father kept sharp and ready in an old bottle cork. Then off they'd go to the rocky cliffs to perch over the deep of the ocean.

They sat for hours side by side without saying a single word to each other. It was a comfortable silence, with all bitterness put aside, because each loved being outdoors and relished any moments they could snatch sitting in the salt breeze, pulling in fish. They spent a few afternoons in early summer every year mutely competing with each other over the size and number of fish they caught. Afterwards, they carried their catch home and gave it to Mom. No meal was ever as tasty as freshly caught fish.

When Vitória found herself with free time, which wasn't very often, she headed for the fishing port in Praia to watch commercial fishing vessels pulling in or setting out. Fascinated by the many varieties in the sea, she admired the size and number of fish they brought in every day. One of her uncles had taken her fishing in his boat once and she amazed them all, easily catching as many fish as any man on board.

It was not unheard of for women to fish but like everything else on their small island, only men did it professionally. The more she watched, the more convinced she became that she could do anything she saw them doing. It seemed a glorious way to make a living, much better than rolling cigarettes or planting corn. *And after all, wasn't Jesus a fisherman? The Priests in their black frocks always urge people to be more like Him, and in this way I can oblige.* She decided to crew on a fishing boat.

One bright morning in early summer, she met Capt. Mark Avila's boat and waited until his crew offloaded the catch. Once the fish were on their way to various restaurants, she squared her shoulders, straightened her spine, and walked up to the canny old seaman. Vitória looked him directly in the eye and said, "Hire me to fish for you. I can do as well as any man on your boat."

Captain Avila took a good hard look at her. In his eyes she saw herself judged as a young woman, only half grown at that. But he also saw her earnest eyes, strong arms, and listened to her well-rehearsed argument that she would work twice as hard as anyone else and pull her weight among the other fishermen. She knew he had never had a woman on his crew before – no one ever took that chance – but she'd also heard he took pride in not being superstitious.

"Be here two hours before sunset this evening. I'll let you try."

So pleased she almost clapped, the fifteen-year-old caught herself just in time. She thrust her hands deep into her skirt pockets.

The old man hid a smile in his beard. "What's your name, little fisherman?"

Vitória looked up into his honest brown eyes. She'd already decided she needed a stronger sounding name than Vitória if she was going to work among men. "Trafulha," she offered cheekily. "But you can call me Traf."

Capt. Mark barked a loud laugh. "Troublemaker? That's what you're called?"

She grinned right back at him. Many times, when in trouble for this or that, she'd heard Mom complain to God, "You took my two baby boys to be angels with You but left me this trafulha to put me in my grave."

"It's a strong name for a fisherwoman. See that you earn it," he said gruffly.

Ch. 4 – An Incredible Offer

Spring, 1963

The next afternoon, Vitória dressed carefully in some of her brother's old clothes. Walking to the dock, she reminded herself she was Traf, the professional fisherman.

By the time Capt. Mark and the first of his four-man crew arrived she was practicing sailing knots learned from her uncle. Her shining, well-scrubbed face glowed with excitement, but her hands were swift and steady as she practiced tying and untying the piece of discarded old rope. Hiding how impressed he was, the captain ordered the crew to show her how to prepare the chum and get the substantial boat under way. The men grumbled but did as they were told.

Traf knew Capt. Mark would keep a close eye on her and if she couldn't do the job, he'd be honest. He and his crew fished for their living, not for entertainment or sport, and they needed all hands on board to do their work to his exacting standards. *I'll show him he hasn't made a mistake. I'll out-fish them all.*

By the time they pulled back into port an hour before dawn, Capt. Mark would admit to himself, if no one else, that he was lucky she'd come to him first. He waited until they washed down the boat, secured all the lines, and packed the fish in baskets ready to carry to restaurants and market. "Traf," he announced to his men, "is the newest member of our crew."

As she expected, the men were more than a little shocked. The grumbling turned into loud complaints.

"She's a kid. She should be home with her mother."

"Women on boats are bad luck!"

"If you need another hand, my five-year-old son could do better than this twisted tomboy."

Capt. Mark stared them down sternly. "Over the last ten hours she learned what we taught her, didn't get sick, and did a bull's share of your dirty work." Traf was surprised and pleased that he'd seen the men heaping some of their work on her young shoulders. "And," he continued, "not to embarrass you, but she brought in thirty fish by herself, more than any of you." The men grudgingly admitted he had a point. Capt. Mark ran the best-known fishing boat on the island for good reason and they had no wish to find themselves left behind in port.

Vitória loved fishing. Professionally, she took to it as naturally as breathing. Morning or evening, she was always willing to man the boat, an eager hand and willing worker. The men soon came to respect her, much as the boys did when she joined in their sports – except one, a big ugly man called Little Pedro. The only thing little about him was his brain. He was huge, strong as a bull, twice as stubborn, and only half as smart. He seemed to take her being on the crew as a personal affront.

Capt. Mark Avila, a fairly religious man, didn't allow foul language on his boat so Little Peter sometimes followed Vitória home, hurling taunts and calling her names when their boss couldn't hear him. She hated him more every day but remained determined to ignore everything he said. She would take any amount of verbal harassment to keep her job on Capt. Mark's boat. Fishing was so much more rewarding than shredding tobacco, and it paid better too. Little Pedro would not drive her from it.

Two weeks after she started, however, a night of fishing on a tossing sea caught the crew off guard. They came in during the darkest hours just before dawn, thoroughly defeated. Everyone was tired and frustrated. No matter where they went, the fish weren't there. A surly crew cleaned the boat in the early morning light, knowing their pay would be short.

While they washed down the boat, Little Pedro let a few choice words slip off his lip. "Damned women bring bad luck. They're only good for one thing."

Traf kept her mouth set in a straight line, no happier than any of the men that no fish had been caught.

"This one's not even a woman, just a girl. Someone should beat her and send her home to her mama. Maybe that would teach her how to behave."

Capt. Mark was as grouchy as the rest of them. He stayed quiet, deciding to let her handle this situation on her own. If she wanted to do a man's job she'd have to work among men and deal with their occasional anger. He wouldn't mollycoddle her just because she was a woman. After their poor catch, he was a bit inclined to agree with Little Pedro, anyway.

Halfway through cleaning the boat, the stupid giant suddenly roared and punched the back of Traf's head, which sent her sprawling across the boat onto a coiled rope. Rough fibers skinned her cheek and nose raw. She shook her head to clear it.

"You bitch," he howled, frustrated and furious. "Sick maria rapaz. Unnatural she/he! You're a curse. You brought bad luck to our ship."

Traf untangled herself from the rope and stood up slowly. She turned and glared at Little Pedro. As irritated and tired as the rest, she'd had enough. Fire blazed in her eyes, the challenge clear. The crew stopped working, frozen in place, watching the pair as they squared off.

"Look at you, dressed like a man, doing a man's work." The giant spit overboard, scowling. "Evil jinx. You bring your perversion among us and God denies us the fish." He swung clumsily at her, his weight tilting the boat. Traf jumped easily out of his reach.

"Don't be an idiot, Little Pedro," shouted Capt. Mark. He shouldn't have let it get this far. "That's only stupid superstition. We've brought in more fish than ever since she joined us. Okay, tonight was bad. We've had crummy nights before." His words fell on deaf ears. The big man moved toward her, Goliath to her David.

A red haze rose in Traf's mind; her heart pounded with self-righteous indignation. Rage swept over her, but even within the passion of her fury she knew she could never beat the huge man in a purely physical challenge. She glanced left and right, checking her surroundings for anything that might give her an advantage and placed her feet to stay balanced.

With an evil grin, she glared up at the man stalking her. "They call you Little Pedro because of the size of your weenie, don't they?" she asked in a loud strong voice, then wiggled her little finger at him. The watching crew burst into laughter, guffawing loudly at her off-color remark, totally unexpected from a young woman's mouth.

The big man didn't stop to think. He charged. His weight tilted the boat again, but Traf readjusted, keeping her footing. She grabbed his outstretched arm, pulled him across the lever of her hip and up. Little Pedro found himself flying overboard, his airborne face contorted in comical confusion.

Water geysered as he hit the surface and everyone rushed to the side to watch him flounder. Traf threw him a line; the whole crew laughed uproariously until he'd clambered aboard. Once back in the boat he moved to tear her apart, but Capt. Mark immediately stepped between them, stopping the giant's frenzied rush with a raised hand.

"It's over," he said. "Traf's a member of my crew, Little Pedro, and since you don't like fishing with women, you can find yourself another job. You and your foul language are not welcome on this boat anymore."

"What?" he sputtered, wiping dank hair from his eyes. "You want a scrawny girl to fish with you instead of me?" He lumbered around his boss and lunged for her again. "I'll tear her head off. Then see who you want."

Gamely, Traf braced to take him on knowing this time his blow would land. She didn't shrink or try to dodge. He would probably break her in half, but she refused to back down.

Capt. Mark, a rather large man himself, kicked the giant's knees from behind sending him sprawling to the deck, then kicked him in the ass for good measure. "Get off my boat." The threat was clear and the rest of the crew hustled a resisting Little Pedro to the dock.

"You can pick up your pay this afternoon," the captain growled after the wounded behemoth. Then he looked at Traf, worry in his remorseful eyes. "He won't let it drop. You better watch your back, little lady." He clapped a big hand on her shoulder. "Traf," he amended with more than a little respect.

She grinned, acknowledging her boss and the other men with a nod. "I'll be careful," she promised them. "I know how to take care of myself. I'll see you tomorrow night."

Easy to say. She walked off. *Now, how to get home?*

She searched nervously for Little Pedro's threatening figure, perhaps hidden in a tree's branches, or crouching behind a stone wall. The same old path she walked every day of her life now seemed ominous. There was no running electricity anywhere on the island but on the American base. Deep shadows cloaked everything in those last minutes before dawn. It was not uncommon for a woman daring to walk alone in the dark to be attacked. And those were women who hadn't just humiliated a surly giant, and a stupid one, to boot.

Traf straightened, thrust out her stubborn chin, made up her mind, and did something she almost never did. Seeing Teresa's taxi, one of the few motor vehicles on the island, dark and waiting for the early morning traffic, she hastened across the cobblestone street. She would be extra careful for a while until the big idiot forgot about her. Rummaging in her pocket for money, she thrust it through the window at her drowsing friend. “Wake up, Teresa. You’ve got a paying customer.”

Shaking herself, the good-looking driver of the cab sat up straight and smiled back, her even white teeth gleaming in the dark. Teresa was an older tomboy who sometimes joined the dozen or so who now met in the woods. She had an easy laugh and beautiful face that belied her strong determination to support herself. Most people underestimated her, assuming a woman as attractive as she would surely give in to societal pressure and marry. That hadn’t proved to be the case, however. Traf respected and admired her.

Many men wouldn’t ride with Teresa, feeling it somehow demeaned them to be driven in a vehicle owned by a woman. This prejudice cost Teresa a significant amount of business. She had to do something to bring in more income, so she specialized in providing safe transportation for women during the night and early mornings. Those hours left her witness to the nightlife of the island and she knew better than most how dangerous a place Terceira could be in the dark.

“I’m so glad you were down by the docks this morning.”

“Really, why? Climb in the front, up here with me and tell me all about it.” So Traf told her first version of the Tale of Little Pedro, as it came to be known.

“Maybe you can pick me up after fishing if we get in during the dark hours, for the next few weeks at least?”

“Sure,” answered Teresa. It’ll cost you a little money, but I’ll give you the tomboy discount. Just buy my gasoline and I’ll make sure you get home okay.”

“Thanks! By then Little Pedro will leave me alone.”

“That’s the truth. He’s nothing but a bully, and he’ll find someone else to pick on when he can’t find you.”

The next day was a Sunday, and following afternoon Mass, Traf found herself with no immediate chores. She joined a chattering group of her friends standing in the village square near the common well. They spoke idly, casting about for a way to spend their free time.

Margarida’s father stored his donkeys in a nearby field, so the group decided to go over and ride them. They all raced home to grab gunnysacks for saddles and change from their best church clothes to well-worn skirts and blouses. Within minutes, they congregated once more at the edge of the field, nervously eyeing the donkeys, who returned their looks with an equal measure of uneasiness.

There were six young women and half a dozen donkeys. Traf was the last to get there, so the others had already mounted by the time she arrived. She looked at the unchosen donkey doubtfully and spread an old gunnysack over its back. Throwing one leg up and over, she jumped agilely upon the beast's back, urging it forward by grabbing its mane and tugging. The others guided their mounts with their knees, shambling together across the field. She heard them calling her. "C'mon, Vit…Traf." Their voices wafted in the warm late afternoon air, still struggling to remember her new nickname. "Catch us if you can."

But her donkey refused to move. It stood there placidly, tearing up grass from the pasture and chewing. First, she nudged it with her knees. Then she kicked it sharply in the ribs. The beast cocked its long ears backward to listen as she swore using words learned from fishermen. Not one muscle did the recalcitrant beast move. Her friends looked back at her and laughed. Juana called out, "Hurry up, *mosca tonta*, you dizzy fly."

Traf was in a ridiculous position. Here she was, a seasoned commercial fisherwoman fresh from a battle won with a man three times her size, yet unable to get a stupid donkey to move. Her pride was at stake. She had to do something to get this headstrong animal to move or she'd be the laughing stock of her friends.

Over my dead body.

She dug deep into the pocket of her well-patched skirt to pull out a long, wickedly sharp kilt pin she'd liberated from one of her older sister's outgrown skirts. Unsnapping the pin, she plunged its sharp point deep into the donkey's flank.

The wounded animal let out an unearthly noise and bolted straight ahead, forcing her to hang on as best she could. It ran so hard and so fast that she couldn't see where they were going. She heard her friends yelling frantically as they watched her being carried away. Her bones were pounding into powder and the brains in her head felt as loose, suddenly, as her bowels. When her fingers had almost lost their grip, the donkey abruptly braced its front legs and ducked, hurling her over its head and into a patch of blackberry bushes.

Dozens of sharp points attacked her from every side. More thorns tore at her as she tried to rise and separate herself from the brambles. They caught in her flesh, digging in and shredding as she fought to get free. Scores of scratches marked her face, bare arms, and legs. Each one stung like fire. Blood ran into her eyes, making it almost impossible to see.

Traf grit her teeth as her bleeding hands forced the thorn bushes apart. Greatly relieved, she scrambled out into the open field. Her friends shrieked at her, waving from their placid mounts.

"Look out," Berta shouted.

"Right behind you!" screamed Juana.

"Jump!" Margarida waved frantically.

Wiping the blood from her eyes, she turned.

Large red lips curled back from huge yellow donkey teeth filled her vision. The enraged animal charged her fully intending to bite. Without thinking twice, she hurled herself back into the brambles and there she stayed, unmoving, enduring numerous vicious stabs until her friends reported they had the animal under control. Only then did she struggle painfully out again.

"Are you badly hurt, Vitória…er, Traf?" Alexandra gawked at her with concern.

Staring at the skyline, she looked neither one way nor the other, mortified beyond belief and refusing to flinch even though her friend's innocent touch torched a fire in her shoulder.

Trudging out of the field and up the road to her mother's house she didn't utter a word. Every step a torment, the relieved laughter behind her only added to her pain. Fierce thorns as long as her thumb stuck out of her in all directions. Tears mixed with blood and stung her eyes, but she refused to let them fall. *When I get home, Mom will fix me up*. It was the only thing she allowed herself to think on the agonizing walk home.

When she finally entered the front door of her home, she found her mother and aunt Isobel chatting side by side while colorfully embroidering fine linens to sell, in the way they spent most Sunday afternoons.

At the sight of her daughter covered from head to foot in thorns, blood running in tiny rivulets down her body, Mom stopped in mid-sentence and peered, squinting in disbelief. "What? What happened now, my girl?"

"I don't want to talk about it." Traf glowered at the two women.

Mom started a laugh that rose from the very depths of her. She chuckled and whooped, chortled and guffawed. Clutching her stomach and gasping for breath, she finally wiped tears from dancing brown eyes. Traf seethed, glaring balefully at her mother as small trickles of blood ran down her forehead and arms.

"Daughter, daughter, daughter," she shook her head, "isn't it enough that you follow Jesus as a fisherman? Do you have to be crucified, too?"

Mom fell over in stitches at her joke and Tia Isobel laughed so hard she brayed just like the idiotic donkey. The two women continued to chortle over her 'crown of thorns' as they carefully pulled spikes from her tender flesh and swabbed cold tea over scratches and punctures.

As the pain subsided, Traf began to calm down but remained mute. Her soul was bruised. She went straight to bed as soon as they were done, all thoughts centered on how she would hear the story about the donkey repeated time and again, all ending with her mother's clever comment about being crucified. *Why do I have to have a funny mother?*

Sure enough, next Friday morning following a particularly good night of fishing which canceled out Saturday's bad luck, Mrs. Alvares, heavy breasts supported by crossed arms atop the veranda gate, waited for her. "I hear you were crucified last Sunday, maria rapaz. It's God's message, I tell you. Give up your mannish ways and come back to the church, you pervert."

Old witch. Traf walked by whistling, refusing to acknowledge her good mood evaporated at the gossip's words. It was one of those times, rare but inevitable, that she wished desperately she could be normal and fit in so the busybodies wouldn't pick on her. *Sometimes it feels like everyone in the whole world knows a secret and they're all keeping it from me. I don't fit in anywhere, no matter how much I try.*

Crossing the veranda to the front door of her mother's house she saw Tio Joe through the window. Tia Isobel's husband, he was a big happy man who always brought her a candy bar when he came visiting. Today was no different; he held it out as he greeted her. "Hello, little savior. I hear you crucified yourself last Sunday."

Even though she wanted to scowl, Traf couldn't help grinning at her uncle, glad to see him again. He'd always been her favorite. Tio Joe worked for the Americans on their base in the maintenance department. The candy bars he brought were American Milky Ways and Hershey Bars.

But more than that, he liked her. She could see by the twinkle in his eye that her antics amused him and she loved being appreciated. They often swapped stories, each trying to top the other in outrageous lies. Laughter was always near when this uncle visited. She sometimes wondered why her father wasn't more like Uncle Joe.

Today he was in a hurry, just stopping by on his way to work. "Why don't you walk with me to the bus stop, Vitória?" he asked, winking at her. She knew him well enough to know that meant he wanted to talk to her alone so she jumped up and walked with him down the dusty road. But instead of telling her some story too naughty for Mom to hear, he turned and spoke to her seriously.

"Do you remember your Grandfather?" he asked her gently. She was only six when the old man died. Now, at fifteen, Joe wouldn't have been surprised to hear her say no.

Instead, he received an unexpectedly fierce, "Very well."

His eyes widened in appreciation. "Well, your grandfather wanted certain things for his children and grandchildren. Not one to keep his opinion to himself, he made sure everyone knew his wishes before he died." Uncle Joe ran his hand through his hair and smiled into her upturned face. "He wanted you to have an education. You are smart enough and deserve one, but there just isn't the money. Now, I think I've found a way for you."

Her heart stopped. Traf loved learning. "What way is there, Uncle?

"The Americans are taking Portuguese into their armed services. If you join they will educate you, teach you English, a trade you can use to make a living, and give you a job." Uncle Joe spoke tenderly to his unusual niece. "It's an incredible offer, and I think it will satisfy your grandfather's spirit if you join."

Americans? America… Her thoughts whirled with possibilities. For as long as she could remember, she dreamed of going to America. *Working with Americans would only bring that dream closer.* Then common sense reined in her enthusiasm. "What would it cost for me to join?" she asked slowly. *After all, there's no sense in getting excited about any opportunity if it's too expensive. The fishing business isn't that prosperous.*

"Silly savior," teased her uncle. "You don't pay them; they pay you."

"They will pay me to learn English and a trade? Tio, have you been drinking?" She looked up at him in alarm, suddenly afraid this was another joke at her expense.

The crowded, noisy, odiferous bus came lumbering into view. As he swung up its steps, Tio Joe thrust a piece of paper in her hands. "Read this. Then go see the Americans." Waving once, he disappeared into the bowels of the bus. It took off, snorting and stomping on up the bumpy cobblestone road as he leaned out a window to wave at her.

Clutching the paper to her chest, she dared one quick look at it, seeing only one word: opportunity. Then she thrust it deep into a pocket of her work pants. Her brain buzzed like a hive of bees. Mom called her in to dinner, muttering about barbarian Americans who forced her brother-in-law to work Friday nights when he should be decently home with his wife and children. Traf hid the paper as she changed clothes, deciding to hoard the secret for a while and show the paper to her friends on Sunday. This felt like something big.

Ch. 5 - Not Something Portuguese Women Do

Summer, 1963

That Sunday night, when the group gathered, Traf waited until a fire was lit and stolen sausage was frying before she stood up, arms akimbo. "Opportunity," she said dramatically. She wouldn't say another word until she had their undivided attention.

"An opportunity is being offered that is rarer than black sheep and worth a hell of a lot more too." She paused for effect. "The Americans will give us lessons in reading, writing, and speaking English! And, they will teach us whatever trade we want to learn." She pulled the paper from her pocket with a flourish and read, "Modern jobs fit for the postwar world."

"Ah, what does that even mean, and besides, who has the money?" Berta shrugged her skinny shoulders.

"That's the best part," Traf crowed. She waved the paper over her head. "They will pay us!"

A babble of voice rose. "That's insane."

"What? Nonsense. The Americans aren't crazy, are they?"

"That can't be right."

"Let me see that paper?" asked Alexandra.

As the first generation who'd attended mandatory public school most of them knew how to read so it passed easily from hand to hand as they all absorbed the offer. Those few who had trouble got help from others.

"You're right! This is a great opportunity. Are you going to do it, Vit… er, Traf?" Margarida asked.

She tried hard to look like she didn't care too much, but inside she was still reeling with the possibility. "Tio Joe thinks it's a good idea. He thinks my grandfather would want me to do it, but my father will never agree." Her slender shoulders shrugged. "What about the rest of you? Anyone want to try to join up with me?"

Alexandra nodded vigorously. "I'll go with you. Beats the hell out of doing housework every day." When school ended for Alexandra her mother began ‘preparing her for marriage’, making her do the everyday chores of women. The repetitive, dreary housework and cooking were driving the young tomboy crazy.

“America,” mused Berta. Do you think they’ll send us to America?” Her eyes lit with visions of the world they’d seen only in movies.

“I don’t know,” put in Olivia. “It’s probably only for men.” A new face around the campfire, she’d only come to a few weekend gatherings. She pulled her long braid over her shoulder.

Her reminder about the privileges of men dampened the mood momentarily, but then Traf grabbed the notice from Margarida’s hand and held it so the firelight lit up the print. She squinted as she painstakingly looked over the words in the low light. “No. It says right here that the opportunity is open to the men *and* women of the Azores.” She broke off, laughing. “Look how the Americans spell Açores… with a ‘z’. That’ll take getting used to.” She looked around the group. “Yes. I’m going tomorrow.”

“To the base?” asked Olivia. “I mean, it’s one thing to talk about this, but are you really going to go to the base? Speak to Americans?”

“Why not?” Traf demanded. She flexed her muscles and pulled a face. “They can’t eat me.” Her façade dropped, but her back remained straight. “It’s a fantastic break. If I don’t grab it now, I won’t get another chance. I’d rather try and fail because of something I do, than just plain fail because I don’t even try.”

Finally, it was decided that Alexandra, Berta, and Tina would all meet her Monday morning after she cleaned up from fishing. They would go together and take the notice with them. Not one spoke any English, except a few phrases they’d learned at the movies. Somehow, Traf doubted “Made it, Ma, top of the world,” or “Here’s looking at you, kid,” would come in handy, and she was a little worried about how they would communicate.

The next Sunday night, before stolen wine or cornbread could be shared, Traf and her friends eagerly reported what happened to them at the American base earlier in the week. “They knew right away why we were there,” she explained excitedly to Margarida, who listened with lips parted and eyes shining. “It’s a big program, and a lot of people are interested.”

“Yeah,” interrupted Tina. “They even have people in uniforms who speak Portuguese, just to talk to us.”

"Did they say we could go to America?" asked Juana, longingly. Other voices repeated the question.

Tina, Berta, and Alexandra looked at Traf, sitting silently and cutting a slice of bread with her pocketknife. In clear deference to her they held their tongues too, helping themselves to the food and drink.

"What did the Americans say?" urged Olivia, her volume rising with excitement.

"Yes, what did they say, Traf?" agreed Margarida impatiently.

She took her time answering, refusing to speak until the noisy young women settled down. She stirred the fire, watching sparks fly up in the breeze. She needed to catch her breath. This was too exciting for simple words.

"They said…" She jumped up with hands raised over her head triumphantly, "we can join." A host of cheers and back-slapping broke out among the gathered friends. None of them really expected to be accepted.

She took a deep breath to calm the fluttering in her stomach before continuing. "They showed us pictures of all the branches of American service and told us to think about which one we want to join."

"I'm going in the Army," announced Alexandra, trying to execute a snappy salute.

"It's the Navy for me," cried Berta. "I've always wanted to see what's out there," and she gestured vaguely toward the sea.

"What about you, Traf?" asked Margarida. "Which one will you join?"

"I like the blue uniforms best. I'm joining the Air Force."

Margarida laughed in her face, shaking her head. "You're choosing your future based on uniforms?"

"Well, I'll be wearing them every day, so it does matter." The dark blue uniform had beckoned to her; she would look very smart wearing it. The idea embarrassed her, but she acknowledged the truth of it to herself.

"But that's not all they told us," she continued, eager to change the subject. "They talked about the kind of jobs we can train for, and what they'll teach us. We'll learn to read and write English. They'll teach us to fight, to protect ourselves. We'll even learn how to shoot guns." She shook her head in wonder. "They'll give us new clothes, and all the food we can eat. We can even become American citizens if we stay in long enough. And it all starts in two weeks."

Traf's voice faltered for the first time. "But they have to have signed permission from our parents since we're underage by American law." She pulled a bundle of papers from her back pocket and started handing them around. "I picked up enough for everyone. If you can get it signed and report two weeks from Monday, then you're in."

She held the last one out to her best friend Margarida who looked hopelessly back at her. "You know my father won't sign it." She sighed, ignoring the paper being thrust in her face.

"Mine won't either," Traf agreed emphatically, "if he knows what it is. So I'm going to make him think it's something else."

Margarida looked up, skepticism and hope waging war in her eyes. "How are you going to make him believe that?" she asked.

"I'll need the help of a couple of older people," Traf explained. "I think I'll ask my sister Alice and my brother-in-law Jack to help me."

"Do you think they'll do it?" asked Margarida.

"I think if I can convince Jack, he will convince Alice. If anyone can convince my father, it's Alice."

"Will she help convince my father?"

"I think after she's done with my father, he'll convince yours." Traf laughed.

Monday morning, she headed over to visit her married sister. There were fourteen years between them. Alice married nine years earlier and had two small daughters and another child on the way. Traf stopped by often to help her sister with household chores, the laundry, cleaning, and caring for her young nieces. "Woo-hoo, Alice," she called as she opened the door of her sister's large house.

"In here, Vitória."

She found Alice wearing a faded housedress cleaning her kitchen. A bucket sat beside her on the floor. In her hand, a scrub brush furiously removed the dirt tracked in yesterday. Her sister looked up, wearily pushing a stray wisp of dark hair from her eyes, the rest caught up in a colorful scarf.

"Traf. I want you to call me Traf, now," she reminded. She walked carefully around the wet spots and stood next to her older sister. "I need your help, Alice. And I need Jack's help, too."

"Well, happy coincidence, I need your help with the girls this afternoon, *Vitória*. Once I'm done here and clean up, I want you to babysit while I go to Angra. When Jack arrives for his dinner, it's ready on the stove. There's enough for him, the girls, and you. Ask him about your favor, and if he says yes, I'll be glad to help you." Alice went back to her vigorous scrubbing. Traf tried not to giggle as her sister's hard-working bottom wiggled back and forth, her pregnant belly swaying below.

While Alice went shopping, she spent the afternoon delighting her young nieces with games made up in the spur of the moment. When her brother-in-law came home from working his fields, she fetched the food from the stove and dished up the fish stew, potatoes, and bread Alice left warming. They ate together, listening to the little girls chatter and laughing at their babyish antics.

"Jack, I need a favor," she started hesitantly after dinner as she washed her nieces' hands and faces with a wet cloth.

Her brother-in-law grinned at her, rose to help gather the dishes, and took them to the stand holding the washtub already filled with hot water. Unlike most Açorean men, he helped around the house. Many people thought he spoiled his wife, but he thought of it as gentle indulgence. He often told people, "Alice is my queen."

"What do you need, Trafulha?" he asked.

"You remembered." She was so startled at his use of her new nickname that she forgot for a moment what she was going to ask him.

"You think I would forget a perfect nickname like that?" Jack laughed. "If anyone deserves to be called Troublemaker, it's you." He clapped a friendly hand on her shoulder, then bent down to sweep up his youngest daughter and took the hand of his eldest, leading them to his chair at the table. "Now, what's this favor you need?"

She added some soap chips to the hot water and swirled it around with a wooden spoon before submerging the bowls from dinner. Taking a deep breath, she looked over her shoulder at Jack playing quietly with his daughters. "I want to join the American Air Force. I need help getting Father to sign the permission form."

Jack paused for a long moment, staring at her. "What are you talking about?" he asked gently. Working part-time on the American base as a bartender for enlisted soldiers, he knew she was too young for them to consider adult. All American soldiers were eighteen years or older. His young sister-in-law was only fifteen. There was also the small matter of her nationality.

She pulled the well-creased piece of paper from her skirt pocket along with the permission slip. She handed them silently over to Jack. He read them carefully, twice, then handed them back.

"This is not something Portuguese women do," he mused aloud. "At least, it's not something they've done before. Portuguese women don't even join our own military." He thought for a moment. "So the Americans will take young Portuguese, enroll them in something they say is," he checked the paper in front of him, "an opportunity for cross-cultural interaction, and then train them as soldiers?"

"Yes, because we're already adults here. And if we stay in for ten years, our rank will convert to the adult American military."

"Why do you have to stay in for ten years?" Jack asked. "You'll be an adult by American standards in only three."

"President Salazar and the Portuguese government set it up that way." Traf shrugged. What did she care about ten years? *That's a lifetime from now.* All that mattered was that enlistment Monday was in two weeks.

"You're right. Your father won't sign it." Jack scratched the shadow of a beard on his chin. "He would never approve, your mother either."

Traf swallowed deeply, took a deep breath, and turned to face him. She blurted, "He'll sign it if he thinks it's about my diploma."

"From school?" questioned her brother-in-law, putting his daughters down on the floor to play. "But you graduated three years ago."

"Yes, I know," she answered eagerly. "But they don't send you a copy of your diploma unless you send a form from the school to the mainland, so if Father and Mom think they're signing this form to get a copy of my diploma, they won't hesitate to make their mark. He never wanted me to go for the fifth year, but I did. Now that it's done and over, Mom says she wants the written proof." Traf smirked impishly at him. "You could easily convince them. They would believe you."

If anyone was ever going to be accepted into heaven, it would be Jack. He was the most honest of souls and given to expect the best from people. Neither of her parents could read, so they relied on their oldest daughter and her husband when it came to written correspondence of any kind. They would believe whatever he said was on the paper.

Jack shook his head at her in admiration. "That would work, but only until you report to that shoe place they talk about. You'll be gone for months, and believe me, your father and mother will notice."

"Boot camp, not Shoe Place." She laughed and nodded. "I know. But once I'm already there, they can't take me out again." She drew herself up to her full height of five feet and two inches. "I am an adult, after all." At Jack's indulgent smile, she bristled just a little. "Well, I am. If I were getting married, there'd be no trouble at all."

Jack admitted that was true. Other girls her age were getting married and starting families of their own. And in his secret heart, he also admitted something else just as truthful; his coltish, tomboy sister-in-law was clearly not suited to the role of wife and mother.

Traf shifted from one foot to another, watching as he rubbed his day-old beard and ruefully shook his head, thinking it over. His wise brown eyes finally settled on her.

As much as he loved her, he was the first to admit that she was nothing like her older sister. He considered his Alice everything a man could ever want or deserve in life. She was compulsively clean, a devoted mother, a good cook, and an obedient wife meaning that she did what he wanted when he wanted it. His sister-in-law could never fit into that kind of a relationship with a man. She was fiercely competitive, individualistic, and far too independent. Marriage would be one physical altercation after another for her. She'd never back down and tragedy seemed inevitable.

Jack also knew that she'd always dreamed of going to America. He'd thought it an impossible ambition, but now here was her chance, just as she insisted would happen. Could he stand in the way of her dream? He looked at his unusual, but endearing, sister-in-law. It might even be God's will.

But could he lie to his wife's parents?

Holding her breath, Traf watched him struggle with this question. For Jack, the idea of deliberately misleading anyone ran counter to his morals. He finally said, "We'll talk this over with Alice and see what she thinks." He hadn't been quite as enthusiastic as Traf hoped, but she refused to be quashed.

When her sister arrived home a few minutes later, they repeated their conversation. Jack waited to see what his young wife would say. He was, after all, nearly nine years her senior, and worried he might be old-fashioned in his viewpoint. He counted on Alice to keep him updated on the modern world.

"Well, I think it's a terrific idea," answered Alice, surprising them both. "Vitória will never fit in around here, so she should go to America and make her way there." And, Traf could almost hear her sister add silently, *it'll get her out of here before she disgraces the whole family.* Alice knew Traf as well as anyone and had known for a while there was something, well, wrong with her. It was Alice's opinion that her younger sister was an embarrassment waiting to happen.

"So you'll do it?" Traf asked eagerly.

Jack looked at his wife, who nodded at him. "We'll do it, Trafulha."

"When?"

Alice stood up and stretched, arching her back against the swelling of her belly. "I'll be over Wednesday afternoon to pick up my laundry. Pull out the form then, and I'll help you get it signed."

Traf jumped up and gave her sister a hug. So filled with optimism and excitement was she that she ran and jumped all the way home, quieting only moments before entering Mom's house. She couldn't afford to make Father suspicious and a sure way to get his attention was to be happy, so she went straight to her room.

Sunday evening she pulled on a pair of Johnny's old dungarees under her skirt and rolled the legs above her knees. Grabbing a paper sack filled with fresh biscuits she bought at the bakery on the way home, she tried to saunter unnoticed back through the kitchen.

She walked by Mom, familiar head bent and dear to her heart. She paused to look at the intricate, bright embroidery her mother was doing by the combined light of the fire and one kerosene lamp. Then she walked casually past her father. He was rolling a cigarette and watched her with piercing dark eyes.

"Where are you going?"

"Over to Margarida's house to play some dominoes," she answered breezily.

"No fishing with Mark Avila tonight?"

"No, he isn't taking the boat out tonight. He said we'd go tomorrow night."

Mom started to rise, and Traf knew she would put together a plate of food for her to eat. Quickly she put out her hand, stopping her mother. "I spent the afternoon babysitting for Alice and ate with the family. She and Jack send their greetings." She knew her father wholeheartedly approved this kind of activity. "And your granddaughters send you kisses," she added. That sealed the deal. Mom nodded happily at her, then turned to her husband.

"Well, give my regards to Margarida's father," Father turned to face the fire.

"I will, sir," she answered, ever the obedient daughter, and disappeared out the door and into the darkness before another word could be said. She offered different excuses all the time to join her group. This was one of her favorites because she often did go over to Margarida's house to play dominoes with her father. Just not tonight.

Traf's mother knew about the girls' weekly gathering. In the beginning, when it was only the three school friends, she'd brought them snacks. When they were a little older and others started joining them, Traf saw Mom through the trees behind the firelight one night, a few meters away, listening to their talk. Through the darkness, their eyes had met in understanding. Traf never spoke of that night to her mother, who also never discussed it. More importantly, Mom never mentioned it to her husband, happily pretending she didn't know.

As Traf joined the group of young women already sitting around the dim, small campfire, she thought, *Mom really is wonderful. She's never said anything to make me feel bad about my... differences*. When Father ranted and railed, Mom often came to her daughter's defense. Just being her own spirited self could get Traf's father very angry, but her mother had managed to soften and turn away many blows in her lifetime. So busy was she with this train of thought she didn't notice two new faces sitting just outside the firelight. That was until one of them spoke.

"We brought some cakes to eat," a tall girl said.

"We put sugar on them," offered the shorter one.

Traf, who was busy wrestling her skirt off over her pants, nearly toppled over with surprise. She whirled around to see who had spoken.

Sitting in the dark, just behind Margarida's shoulder, were Iris and Isabella, two sisters from a family that lived across the street and down from her mother's house. Iris was one year older than Traf, and a dark-haired beauty with bright shiny eyes. Her little sister was two years younger and would be just as beautiful in another few years. Neither was the kind of girl who would ever think about wearing trousers, but both watched with interested eyes as Traf discarded her skirt and hurriedly rolled down her pant legs.

"What are you two doing here?" asked Margarida, surprised to see them. Not one of the tomboys believed either of the two girls walked here in the dark by themselves. They were too ladylike to be caught out after dark on their own without a chaperone.

"We heard Berta talking to Juana about meeting up here the other day, and well, we thought maybe we'd join in," explained Iris, glancing up from under long dark lashes. Isabella smiled shyly at the group and started to ease her way forward, into the circle of tomboys.

"Wait a minute," growled Berta. She raised a skinny arm to point at Isabella, stopping her in her tracks. "You aren't invited."

In silent answer, the younger girl whisked an embroidered cloth from a plate filled with slices of sugar-covered cake. It was an effective bribe in their group of growing young teens. Alexandra reached for a piece of cake as Iris nodded encouragingly at her.

Traf looked at her own sack of biscuits which on any other night would be a treat and shrugged. Then, putting down the unopened sack, she reached for a piece of cake, too. *Bread or cake? Cake wins every time, especially sugar cake.*

Making room for the sisters, the tomboys accepted their cake and their presence – at least for that night. It was the first time anyone who wasn't as different as they were wanted to join and an uncomfortable silence descended as they swallowed the cake. After all, what did two pretty girls have in common with the rest of them? The town gossips never called Iris and Isabella nasty names or belittled them. They were perfect little ladies, just like the parents of the tomboys wanted them to be. What did these 'nice' girls want?

Traf decided to break the awkward silence. She cleared her throat importantly, then looked pointedly and victoriously at Margarida.

"You did it?" asked her friend, incredulously.

"Yes, Alice got them to sign it last Wednesday." She raised clasped fists above her head, shaking them like winning boxers in the movies.

This caused a round of cheers, and some excited voices sprang up from various girls in the group.

"I convinced my mother after a whole night of arguing," sighed Alexandra. "Then it took another few hours for her to convince my father. But in the end, they both put their marks on it."

"My father signed it right away," announced Berta. "He said it sounded like a great opportunity, and if he was young enough he'd join up himself." The other tomboys looked up, amazed and impressed. Berta had the most supportive father of any of them. He even seemed proud of her, something none of the others ever experienced.

"My parents signed." Juana's quiet voice broke through the chatter. "They like the way American women officers dress and think they'll teach me to be a lady."

"You know they're going to teach us to fight?"

Juana smiled and a smoldering fire blazed to life in her eyes. “Yes, and I’m going to be their best student.”

“What are you all talking about?” chirped Isabella. “Signed what?”

Teresa took the time to explain to the sisters about the opportunity the Americans offered while the rest of the tomboys compared stories with each other.

“You mean, go in the American Army like a man?” asked young Isabella, confused.

“Yes, just like a man,” Traf exclaimed.

“Well, no,” countered Margarida. “If they get in, then they’ll still be treated like women, but like American women, not Portuguese women.”

“What’s the difference?” asked Iris, idly licking sugar off the plate with one finger.

“I don’t know, but I am going to find out,” Traf answered, laughing as she watched the pretty girl’s tongue lick off the sugar. *How…interesting.* “What about you, Iris?” she asked to see her mouth move again. “Don’t you ever want to be anything except a good little Portuguese woman?”

“What’s wrong with being a good woman?” asked Iris, blooming under the sudden attention of the tomboys. Her dark eyes grew luminous by the firelight, and she shook her head so her long hair flowed over her shoulders. Traf wasn’t the only one watching.

“Nice women don’t wear pants,” answered Juana promptly, while stretching out her legs toward the fire and admiring her trousers.

“Nice women can’t have a good job.” Teresa spoke with authority. “Or even drive,” she amended.

“Yeah, and good women have to get married and have babies,” jeered Berta.

“Nice women don’t join the Army,” added Margarida.

“Or the Navy,” agreed Alexandra.

“Or, the Air Force,” said Olivia with a snappy salute.

“Let’s face it,” Traf finished, grinning at pretty Iris. “We’re not nice women.” With that, the tomboys started laughing loudly and pounded each other on the back.

Young Isabella looked shocked but Iris met Traf’s gaze evenly. “I don’t know. I think you’re pretty nice.” She smiled appreciatively, her eyes sweeping the group of boyish young women. More than one tomboy blushed.

“Then you’re the only one who does.” Margarida snorted derisively.

"I'd like to come back another Sunday. Would that be okay?" The beauty's dark eyes flashed around the fire to take in all the tomboys but stopped on Traf's.

"Only if you bring more good things to eat," announced Berta, making the other girls laugh. "And speaking of that, Traf, didn't you bring something to share in that bag?" Even though Berta was the smallest of them she was famous for her huge appetite.

Traf tossed the sack of biscuits over the fire. The rest of the group crowded around Berta and cheered when they saw what she was holding. Watching them, Traf couldn't help but notice the difference between her friends and the two ladylike sisters, who sat courteously and waited to be served.

Waiting to be served? She snorted. *It will be a month of Sundays before that happens.* But even as she thought it, Teresa reached out and handed both girls fresh buns.

Why are they here? The question bounced against the confining walls of her mind. She shook her head despairingly. *They aren't like us. They're normal. So why are they here?* She just didn't get it. But, she had to admit she didn't really mind.

Ch. 6 - Are You a Quitter?

Still Summer, 1963

A light breeze cooled Master Sergeant Deborah Diaz's face as she stood on the sun-drenched tarmac, watching the bus full of new recruits drive up. Staff Sergeant Linda Baines joined her, both standing at ease as the doors opened and a pile of little kids tumbled out. The drill instructors looked at each other in horror, then turned to stare at the interpreter.

"You gotta be kiddin' me." Thirty-five year old Baines was a lifer. "Are these kids considered adults on this island? How did they manage to enlist?"

The expatriate Brit who served as an interpreter filled them in. "Well, President Salazar made an agreement with your government for the base, but last year the American lease ended. You don't want the Lajes base falling into the hands of the Russians or Chinese, now do you? Terceira is between the US and Portugal." The interpreter shrugged eloquently. "You know? Access to the European coast? Seems pretty important to you Americans."

MSgt. Diaz interrupted. "And the Brits before us, yeah, I know. But what has that got to do with these girls?"

"Yeah, well, to sweeten the pot, you lot agreed to let Portuguese men and women enlist. Hey, you've done it at other bases around the world." The interpreter started laughing. "Here, these girls are old enough to get married. Some of their friends are already having their second or third babies."

Diaz only grunted.

"I guess it makes sense," mused Sgt. Baines. "We come into their country bringing strange foods, clothing, and new ways of doing things. It's not a bad idea to bridge the culture gap. It's harder to hate the US military when your own people join." She looked out to the ocean, clearly visible from where they stood. "You know, the whole of this island is no bigger than Aurora, Colorado, my hometown."

MSgt. Diaz's mouth turned down as she stared at the group of girls wearing skirts and blouses (some of which had seen better days) milling around in front of the bus. They had no clue what to do, all big-eyed and gangly-legged, but eagerness and excitement radiated from them. Her eyes hardened, considering.

Traf, who stood near enough but couldn't follow the conversation, had no trouble interpreting the body language of the woman in front her. *We look like excitable kids playing a game.* She nudged Alexandra and stood still. Soon the others had caught on and stood still, looking at the two women in uniform expectantly.

Inhaling deeply, MSgt. Diaz took her time looking them over, taking special note of their leader, the one who quieted them down. Command had not warned her. Compared to her usual batch of Americans, these girls were so much smaller it made them look all the younger in comparison. She expected none of them to make it. They would all end up running home, crying to their mamas before boot camp was over. Well, not if she could help it. Squaring her shoulders, she resolved to do her best to turn this ragtag group of kids into soldiers.

The interpreter shrugged his shoulders and grinned at the two women sergeants, handing over a checklist. "They're all yours."

"Treat them as reserve officers in training," read Sgt. Baines. "What? Like R.O.T.C.?" They turned their backs to the new recruits and looked at each other, stunned again.

MSgt. Diaz shook her head. "What is this, high school? Orders are orders, but what a waste of time." However, standing on this glittering island gem set in the Atlantic Ocean she figured things could be worse. She might have ended up in Vietnam instead of Terceira. Things were heating up over there.

With a grim look, she turned to face the excited girls judged adult by their own society. She had a job to do, and she'd get it done.

By this time, several single-stripers had hustled the girls into four rows of ten, all facing toward her. She nodded at the interpreter and began speaking in English. He waited until she stopped, then repeated her words in Portuguese.

"Good day. Welcome to Lajes Field in the Açores. You are here because you've enlisted in the Reserve Officer Training Corp of the United States of America. You are here to become soldiers."

As the interpreter translated her words, MSgt. Diaz watched, judging their reactions. She had already spotted two or three that she was pretty sure would turn tail and run before the day was over. It was time to turn on the charm.

Traf watched as the American walked up and down the rows of enthusiastic girls, looking into each pair of eyes while she spoke. She had never seen such a powerful woman.

"I am MSgt. Diaz. You will call me Master Sergeant, or Ma'am. I am here to make you into US soldiers, a task it is painfully obvious will be impossible. I've never seen such a worthless group of recruits." She waited through the interpretation to see the impact of her final words, repressing a grin at several gasps of shock.

She threw the assembled girls her patented look of utter contempt. "You are the most disgraceful group it has ever been my misfortune to have been assigned. Just look at you, ragged, undisciplined and unable to stand in simple straight lines, much less stand at attention. You'll never make officers. Worthless bums, every one of you. It will be a miracle if I can make you into soldiers." Confusion rose in their eyes as her words were translated. She saw the inevitable resentment and smiled. "I'll be sending at least five of you home before the day is through."

Traf made up her mind she wouldn't be one of them. "What a witch," she muttered to Margarida standing next to her. "With a mouth like that she must be a fishmonger's wife."

They were giggling when they heard, "You think so, soldier?" spoken in perfect Portuguese. The master sergeant came to a standstill directly in front of them, blocking the sun.

Traf nearly broke her neck swiveling to look at the interpreter. He stood there sneering but hadn't said a word. It was the huge, fierce, American woman standing before her.

"You speak Portuguese?" Traf's mouth fell open and hers wasn't the only one.

"Better than you, a ridiculous child with tobacco still growing in your belly button." It was an old taunt used to tell someone they were young and inexperienced. Every child on the island heard it a dozen times growing up. MSgt. Diaz leaned in close until their noses nearly touched, smiling wickedly. "What's your name, soldier?"

"Vitória Mendes," she answered promptly. "But my friends call me Traf." She grinned up at the master sergeant, trying to be friendly. *Maybe I got off to a bad start.*

"Vitória Mendes, what?" snapped MSgt. Diaz.

"Just Vitória Mendes."

"That's Just Vitória Mendes, Ma'am," said MSgt. Diaz. Her eyes glittered like cold rain splashing the surf.

Sgt. Baines stepped up beside her and said in English, "Say, Ma'am, yes Ma'am, soldier." This the interpreter translated.

"Ma'am, yes Ma'am!" repeated Traf, understanding at once what she was expected to do.

MSgt. Diaz raised the volume of her voice, louder and heavy with even more sarcasm. "Just Vitória Mendes, do you think you've got the making of a good soldier?" Standing an easy six inches taller than any recruit, the master sergeant loomed over her, throwing an intimidating shadow. Traf blinked at her silhouette against the bright morning sun.

"Huh?" she asked, confused about what the angry American wanted for an answer. She looked at Sgt. Baines for help, but none was offered.

MSgt. Diaz doubled her volume. "Huh? Now there's a smart answer. You think you're a smart girl, don't you Just Vitória Mendes?"

"My name's not Just, it's just Vitória Mendes," she tried to explain.

"You think I'm as stupid as you are, soldier?" Her glare grew even more alarming. Traf had trouble dodging spatters of saliva flying in her face. "I asked you a simple question; do you think you've got what it takes to be a good soldier?"

"A soldier?" Traf thought the question over. "Umm, sure I do."

"That's 'Sure I do, Ma'am', Mendes," Sgt. Baines snapped at the side of her face. "The very first thing a soldier learns is to call her superiors by the appropriate rank, or address. If you speak to Sgt. Diaz during boot camp, soldier, everything you say will end in 'Ma'am' or 'Master Sergeant'. Is that clear?"

Traf looked from one American to the other and nodded. "Ma'am, yes Ma'am."

Sgt. Diaz leaned down and in, letting the sun hit the nervous recruit full in the face. "So you will address Sgt. Baines as 'Ma'am' or 'Sergeant'. We are your superior officers until you graduate and receive a Second Lieutenant rank, understand?" Traf bobbed her head in emphatic agreement. "Can you get that through your thick skull, you mosca tonta, or are you too stupid?"

"I'm not a dizzy fly." Traf flared without thinking, her fists balled for a fight. She had always resented being called an idiot. Too late, she realized her error and stood blinking foolishly.

That was the payoff, and the master sergeant pounced. "You are talking back to your superior, soldier." Her voice dropped dangerously until it was nearly inaudible, but each of the forty girl recruits heard every word. "You'll learn better before you leave my boot camp, Just Vitória Mendes, starting tonight. Report to me after dinner." Master Sergeant Deborah Diaz stalked off.

Sgt. Baines and the interpreter swiftly took them in hand, which was good because the other girls were every bit as confused as Traf. They herded them first to get supplies, and then to the barracks to store it all.

The barracks were miracles of construction with twenty bunk beds, ten on either side of a wide aisle leading from the door to the showers in back. Two lockers stood at the foot of each bunk, and a shelf hung on the wall between the sets of beds. Amazed by the cotton-stuffed mattresses so unlike their own corn husk ones at home, the girls learned how to make beds the US military way. Sgt. Baines showed them how to store their brand new uniforms, underwear, boots, and sundries. The girls' eyes gleamed with pleasure, most having never seen such plenty.

When they entered the mess hall, the group as a whole stumbled into each other in stunned silence. Not one of them had ever seen anything like it. The hall dwarfed the barracks, with enough tables and benches to accommodate up to five hundred at a time. A long line of steaming pans held unusually spiced food with exotic scents. They got in line behind uniformed soldiers, both men and women, holding strange rectangular plates divided into sections.

And what food it was. Uniform wearing men, covered by white aprons like waiters, dished up a huge variety of American edibles. Although they didn't have names for much of the food that was available, each one seemed more delectable and alluring than anything they had ever eaten before. When Sgt. Baines warned them to take only what they could eat, they looked at her in amusement. Not one of them had so much at home that there was ever any waste. It was not the Portuguese way.

After a dinner that went far too fast, Sgt. Baines made them practice lining up and saluting. MSgt. Diaz found them, eager as puppies and just as clumsy, and stood watching from the gathering shadows behind their barracks for a while.

As always, the wheat separated from the chaff. Some of the girls had trouble getting the salute down, but not the tomboys. They took to saluting like birds to flying. Perfect mimics, they imitated Sgt. Baines' every move. Traf was working on getting her shoulders square when the master sergeant walked up more decisively than any man and shouted one word only, "Mendes."

Sgt. Baines snapped to attention, throwing her master sergeant a sharp salute. The recruits imitated her as best they could. Waving Traf forward, the drill sergeant strategically stepped to the rear, creating a stage for her superior officer in front of the lined up girls.

Traf took a few steps forward and faced Master Sergeant Diaz, throwing her a snappy salute.

"Ma'am, yes Ma'am," she said, her eyes sparkling with triumph. She had questioned Sgt. Baines carefully over dinner about what she'd done wrong and tried to figure a way out of this troubling misunderstanding.

Sgt. Diaz stood still as a statue, and twice as tall. "Soldier," she began, "you have the mistaken idea that you can talk back to your superiors. You did so repeatedly today." Her cold eyes blinked once. "I am assigning you KP for the next three evenings."

Traf had no idea what KP meant, but she gathered by the expression on Sgt. Diaz's face that it wasn't going to be fun. "Ma'am, yes Ma'am," she offered hopefully. Maybe it wouldn't be as bad as it seemed.

"You will report to Sgt. Kelly in the kitchens. He will assign you whatever chores need to be done. I will check with him to see how you are performing." Master Sgt. Diaz glared down the row of girls, checking them over as if to select someone else to share the duty. Each one stood as still as could be. They didn't know what KP was either, but they were more than willing to let Traf find out and report back to them.

Sgt. Baines got her to the right place, and Sgt. Kelly made good use of the interpreter to make sure Traf knew what she was supposed to do. Peel potatoes. Lots of potatoes. Mountains of potatoes. So she peeled from 1900 hours until 2330, when she was finally allowed to creep back to the silent barracks. No one else was awake by the time she got there, so she lay staring at the ceiling for a good long while, wondering what she had gotten herself into.

The next two days were very busy. Three times a day they ate fascinating food. While every island girl had eaten fried eggs with bread, a quick filling meal, not one had ever considered combining them in this delicious new concoction; French toast served with sweet liquid syrup. To a one, they refused to eat hot dogs until Sgt. Kelly explained it was pork, not a real dog. Colorful fruits, like apricots and strawberries, and peculiar vegetables such as Brussel sprouts and celery, surprised their tongues. And potatoes! Grated, scalloped, fried, and mashed, potatoes at every meal.

The new recruits learned the basics - the correct way to brush teeth and shower, what proper marching was supposed to look like, and not just how to salute, but to whom and when. Their brains whirled busily, absorbing information and when they thought they could take no more, they practiced marching for hours, guaranteeing total exhaustion. Every night Traf reported to the kitchens and Sgt. Kelly just as the other girls got time to relax, chat, play games, and have a little fun.

Private First Class Ben Glaser yelled at Traf for not taking enough peel off and then Sgt. Kelly criticized her for cutting too deep. First she peeled too slowly, and then too fast. Nothing she did seemed to please and she grew tired of trying. Her back ached, and her fingers bled as she mastered the art of skinning potatoes the military way. Traf sat in the kitchen each night, cursing the mother who gave birth to MSgt. Diaz and counting off the time until at last, the fourth day arrived. Finally she was free after dinner.

Small groups chattered among themselves, but the tomboys, Margarida, Berta, Juana, and Alexandra, were eager to see their friend again. Boot camp allowed no time for chat except at chow and during those few treasured minutes before lights out. Her group led her to Alexandra's bunk, the only lower one between them, where they gathered every night to talk.

"What does KP mean?" asked Alexandra. Traf had filled them in, between bites at meals, about the mountains of potatoes.

"I asked Sgt. Kelly last night, and you know what the grumpy bastard said?" She made a face. "He said KP stands for Keep Peeling, but PFC Glaser told me we were on Kitchen Patrol. It doesn't matter anyhow, because now I know Diaz speaks Portuguese I'll mind my tongue. I'm going to be careful what I say. From now on I'm not going to get into any trouble."

Alexandra and Juana laughed at her outright while Berta tried hard to keep a straight face. Margarida just slapped her on the back and grinned. "Oh no, Trafulha," she drawled. "You'll get in no trouble at all."

If wishes were fishes, no one would drown. She really wanted to succeed and during the next three months she worked hard learning the rules and other things they taught her, but somehow her mouth kept tripping her up. Sgt. Diaz kept a close eye on her and always managed to be nearby just when she let loose with some complaint or earthy phrase. She spent more time peeling potatoes and learning how to scrub a bathroom floor with a tiny toothbrush than any two other recruits combined.

The potatoes made sense; people had to eat after all, and she had helped her mother in the kitchen for as long as she could remember. But cleaning a floor with a tiny little toothbrush made absolutely no sense to her when a larger brush would do the job faster and better. *Diaz thinks she'll wear me down, make me quit. Well, that's not going to happen.*

Sgt. Diaz found her on hands and knees in the bathroom one night in the middle of the third month, wearing out her fifth toothbrush. The girl was whistling a song as she worked. The drill sergeant intentionally walked through mud before entering the room and took quiet delight in watching Traf's face fall as she crossed the clean tile to stand before her. The young recruit stood up, saluted at attention, and waited to hear what was coming. She offered no complaints about the muddy tracks she'd be scrubbing in just a moment. Her face showed only the resigned look of expectation that a disciplined soldier of Sgt. Diaz's was allowed.

Traf thought she saw a glimmer of approval that vanished before she could verify it. "Mendes, when you finish here I want you to go straight to bed. Don't wake any of the others. You'll need every ounce of strength you can muster tomorrow."

"Yes, Ma'am," she answered with another smart salute, hiding vindictive thoughts behind her soldier face.

Sgt. Diaz turned away, deliberately walking her muddy boots all around the floor before leaving. She stood just outside the door listening. The cheerful whistling started up again. Yes, indeed. Young Mendes was shaping up to be quite the soldier.

In the middle of the night, at 0300 hours, Sergeants Diaz and Baines brought metal garbage can lids into the sleeping barracks. They banged the lids and shouted the recruits from their dreams.

"Wake up you slug-a-beds. Rise and shine. You have thirty minutes to get showered, dressed, and chow, then report with your packs out front.

Get moving. Get moving…" The sergeants shook the bunks of those slow to respond. Traf fell to the floor.

Groaning, she stumbled to her feet and hurried to make it outside in time. She didn't want to carry an extra pack, which was what always happened to the last one to report. So she scrambled around the others, pushing and shoving to get out the door before them. For the first time in her life, she skipped breakfast.

They spent the hours before dawn, all morning, and into the late afternoon marching a twenty-three-kilometer route across country, up and down hills, through the old fort and to the highest point. It began to rain in the early afternoon and never let up, making the strenuous march agonizing. Camping equipment in heavy packs weighed them down and their young muscles strained to keep up. Finally, their drill sergeants ordered the hungry, tired, wet, and miserable recruits to make camp.

It did not escape Sgt. Diaz's hawk eye that Traf was one of the first to get her pup tent set up, as far from the sergeants' tent as possible, and was also the first to get her soggy cold meal. She nudged Sgt. Baines, who nodded, once.

For her part, Traf could feel her drill sergeant's cold, calculating eyes measure her and find her wanting. Painfully exhausted, she and the others crawled into tents the steady rain ran through. There was nothing to sleep on but sodden, cold sleeping bags swimming in mud.

Drenched and miserable, Traf grumbled trying to get comfortable. *What a fool I was. I thought I'd walk in, they'd give me a pretty uniform, and then I'd be free to come and go from the base. Yeah, the pay is great, we make more than most of the island men, much more than I can make fishing. But no one told us it was going to be this hard.* She huddled into herself, trying to warm the chill from her bones.

It's crazy to lie here with cold water streaming all around. Her mind filled with the image of her warm dry bed at Mom's house. The idea of home had never seemed so sweet.

Thoughts of peeling potatoes, scrubbing floors with a toothbrush, and how much she hated both flashed through her mind. *Sgt. Diaz is always riding my back. It's as if she's daring me to make a mistake. Sgt. Kelly is so picky and hard to please. They're both trying to make things harder. And I'm tired of being called bad names. If I'd wanted that I could have stayed home.* By this time, she'd learned enough English to know what 'lazy bum', 'idiot', and 'good for nothing' meant. She'd gotten used to being called a twisted tomboy, impudent, and a troublemaker. But no one had ever called her lazy before. To Traf's mind, that was the worst insult of all.

I'm not a bum. I can do anything. Hadn't she worked like a man on Capt. Mark's boat? She felt her face grow hot, and she soon stopped shivering.

I don't need to do this. I'm not doing it to prove anything to anyone. If they want me to fail so badly, maybe I will. Right now, all she wanted was a warm dry bed. Dark, reckless thoughts filled her head.

Splashing in the dark she sat up, a miserable young woman who wanted her mother. *Kind, gentle Mom who always has hot food to eat, and a dry clean bed to sleep in.* Time to give up the US military with its hard work and no appreciation, and go home.

Peeking out of the tent, she looked carefully first one way, and then the other. She saw no lights glowing in the sergeants' large, dry tent, expertly set up on high ground. Scuttling like a cockroach, she snuck into the dark night.

The rain had stopped but began again as soon as she started moving. She darted around her tent and down, away from the camp. Pushing herself to an all-out run, she started down the mountain. Her heart leaped into her throat. *Free.* She ran even faster, knowing she would be home in only a few hours.

Lightning bolted from clouds to the ground; cracking thunder shook the air around her. Warm rain streamed down her face, and her muscles ached from all the marching earlier. She began to stumble, almost falling a few times until she slowed down. It was a horrible night. She couldn't wait to get home and dry.

She reached the bottom of the mountain where she'd pick up the road to go home, glad to be on level ground again. A flashlight glared out of the dark blinding her.

"Turn around, Mendes," said Sgt. Diaz quietly from her parked jeep. "You've got a long walk back up the mountain."

Traf stared at her drill sergeant with huge eyes, completely stunned. "How did you know?" she managed.

"Move it, soldier," answered the master sergeant, brooking no excuses. "I don't train quitters. Start walking."

Traf thought about refusing. She could run right past Sgt. Diaz's jeep and keep on running. She almost sank down in the mud, defeated. Instead, she turned around and walked back up to her waterlogged tent while Sgt. Diaz followed in a jeep.

During the long walk, something inside her clicked. Memories of working with Grandfather on different projects flashed through her mind. When she'd gotten discouraged, he ask her pointedly, "Are you a quitter? Because if you're the kind of person who'll quit a project before seeing it through, I don't have time to waste on you." That had made an impact and she'd never quit anything before, resolutely facing every challenge. *And I won't quit now.*

Two hours later, she finally stumbled into her tent to grab a few hours of sleep. As they started the long march back to camp, she learned she wasn't the only one to try and make a run for it. Several others tried too, but most got lost and Sgt. Baines easily rounded them up. No one had made it as far as Traf, which gave her a kind of sour satisfaction.

To her surprise, she received no discipline for having run away. For the next seven days, she was a model soldier, never answering back or getting into trouble. She made up her mind to stay so she did it right. Even Sgt. Diaz could find no fault with her.

At the end of that long week, she and the remaining recruits received their commissions as officers. There was a graduation ceremony where each of them would receive a new rank as Second Lieutenant. They had been instructed to invite someone special to pin the sparkling bars on their shoulders. Traf asked Mom and Father to attend but they refused, still furious at her deceit. So her brother-in-law, Alice's Jack, stood in for her, grinning like a proud peacock as he pinned a gold colored bar to her epaulet. Sgt. Diaz threw each of them a perfect salute at graduation, an experience Traf found particularly satisfying.

The girls were given a three-day pass after that, and Traf went home. Neither of her parents said anything about where she'd been, and neither did she. Winter was coming, and they were harvesting the fields. She put in a hard three days helping bring in the corn.

The next Monday, Traf was back on base, reporting in for the next phase of her training, proudly wearing her new Air Force uniform and bars. She looked as good in it as she thought she would. Whenever she saw a superior officer she snapped off a crisp and perfect salute which, to her secret thrill, they invariably returned.

She and Juana chose to be Air Force VIP drivers, escorting officers on their appointed rounds. Alexandra opted for a Navy career in the secretarial division. Margarida was also joining a secretarial division but in the Army, where Berta was headed for communications. Michaela, a new friend made during KP, joined the Air Force auto mechanics and was learning to work on engines. Michaela loved mischief as much as Traf did and the two hit it off right away.

A few weeks later, on her way to English and deportment lessons, Traf crossed the compound where the second batch of Açorean women recruits were being processed. She grinned, listening as MSgt. Diaz demanded of some poor wretch, "You think I'm as stupid as you are, soldier? I asked you a simple question; do you think you've got what it takes to be a good soldier?"

Noticing the newly commissioned officer, MSgt. Diaz suppressed a proud grin as she saluted her sharply and turned back to the still eager group of forty. "See that Second Lieutenant over there?" the drill sergeant asked the new collection of young local women. "I knew the moment I laid eyes on Mendes that she would be a first class officer, not like you worthless bums."

Traf, unable to believe her ears, ran smack into the flagpole in the center of the quad, making it and her head ring. Diaz fought back another grin as the brand new officer squatted in embarrassment, picking up the books and papers she'd spilled.

Recovering as best she could, she kept walking toward the set of buildings that would be her classrooms for the next year, blushing like a new bride. *Wow. Wow.*

She squared her shoulders and marched forward, head held high just as Master Sergeant taught her.

Ch. 7 - Pretty Pigeons Poised

Autumn, 1964

The next year flew by in a flurry of intoxicated learning. She spent weekdays in class, learning to read and write in English. It was a complex language, which didn't always make a lot of sense. But she kept at it, knowing that if she was ever going to live her dream of going to America, she needed to know the language. The years with Professora Alameda proved worthwhile and she picked English up quickly, practicing on anyone whenever she could. Friday nights she went to the theater with her friends and watched American movies, startled and thrilled when she finally began to follow the dialogue.

She spent weekends helping her parents in the fields until all the crops were collected and stored in gunnysacks or recycled tin cans in a dry room of her mother's house. They harvested potatoes, wheat, beans, corn, melons, tomatoes, and grapes, enough to last through the winter and growing season next year. It was hard work but her muscles were finely toned from boot camp so she was even more help than before.

Traf helped with the animals too. Her father bred and trained guard dogs which he sold to farmers and nervous soldiers. There was almost always a litter of puppies to care for, as well as chickens, rabbits, sheep, and the occasional pig her mother raised. Their animals were kept for breeding or slaughtered to be eaten. They bartered eggs with a local grocer to get what they didn't provide for themselves. During the winter months her mother carded wool from their sheep, weaving good warm blankets for the family. The extras they sold, and that funded the repairs to what they already owned.

Her parents had not accepted her choice of career, and her father, in particular, hated the fatigues she wore to work. He thought she looked quite respectable when dressed in her formal blues, but when Gaspar saw her wearing her daily uniform he was humiliated.

"Wear modest clothing going to and from the base. Carry that clown outfit to the base before putting it on. I don't want the people of Lajes to see you running around in pants like a man. It disrespects your mother and me." He finished his lecture with, "I'll kick your butt if I have to."

Once a month she received a paycheck from the Air Force. Perhaps not much by American standards, the seventy-two dollars a month was very impressive when translated into escudos, the local currency. It certainly helped out at home. Which meant she didn't need to worry about what her father wanted anymore – at all. In clear defiance of his orders, she wore her fatigues to and from work every day.

That infuriated her father who, usually in front of others, felt obliged to carry out his promised punishment. It happened one day at the bus stop as she waited with others heading for the base. She wore her fatigues and her mind was already focused on the work waiting for her. She never heard him coming. Her father's shoe connected with her tailbone, and she staggered forward into a man waiting in front of her.

"You're a disgrace!" he ranted. "You shame your family wearing pants like a man." And with that he stalked off, leaving her in humiliated pain.

One day, old man, you'll pay and dearly. For myself, and my mother's honor. She sat at the rear of the bus, plotting revenge. Traf studiously met no one's glance, in case it be either gloating or sympathetic.

Festival time grew near. People looked forward to spending time in entertainments, conversations, and eating good food. Over the months of June through October, each village, one by one, hosted their own festival, which could run several days to a week. Friends and family would come to stay until the next one started somewhere else.

Their village of Lajes hosted the final festival every year starting just as the harvests finished. It began with fireworks on Saturday night, followed by the Parade of Saints on Sunday. The statues, one by one, were gently removed from the big church on proudly decorated litters. Everyone dressed in their finest clothes and lined the streets to watch the saints pass on their way to the small church, where visiting priests celebrated a special Mass. Some penitents walked barefoot and prayed the rosary the whole way, paying promises made during the year.

Each day of a festival brought good things to eat, much visiting back and forth, new motion pictures, parades, and rides on a carousel or bumper car. Young men ran daringly through town streets taunting fierce bulls whose only restraint was a very long rope held by five pasteros, or bull herders. The nights filled with music, singing, and dancing. A time for courting, young men searched for ladies to woo. Romance filled the air, and feelings ran high.

For a week before the Lajes festival, Mom and Alice baked and cooked. Girl cousins, aunts, and friends packed the house for several days and nights. Traf, who hadn't shared her room with anyone since she was six years old and Alice got married, escaped as often as possible. She always made herself available for any necessary test tasting, however.

Their group still gathered in the woods Sunday evenings and more of the ladylike girls joined them all the time. Just as confused as when they first started coming around, the boyish tomboys came to accept their presence. Especially since they couldn't drive them away.

We try, all right, but for some reason, those 'normal' girls seem even more determined to stick around, Traf grumbled to herself, stepping gingerly around sleeping cousins, who covered nearly every inch of her bedroom floor. *Not even sneaking up on them in the dark and shouting scares them away. But they do bring delicious food; I have to give them that.* She dropped from her window, wondering what appetizing treats lay in store for her tonight and headed for the woods.

When she arrived, Margarida, Berta, and Michaela, who'd joined their group, tended a small fire. Isabella and Iris sat cozily around it with two new girls, conventionally pretty ones like themselves. Traf, disinclined even to look at them, concentrated instead on her old friends. They were soon joined by Tina, Juana, Teresa, and Lydia. Most of the tomboys sported brand new blue jeans and white T-shirts, courtesy of those who could now buy at the PX on base. The other, more ladylike girls wore colorful skirts and blouses with hand knitted sweaters to keep them warm in the autumn breeze. That night, Margarida brought hand-made candies wrapped in bright bits of paper to enjoy, courtesy of her hard-working, unsuspecting aunt. They devoured the candy and savored the tea before the conversation drifted toward the coming festival.

"My cousin says she has a boyfriend for me, can you believe that?" blurted Berta, scraping a piece of the chewy candy from its wrapper with her teeth. "I told her I don't want a boyfriend, but she just laughs at me and says, 'you will.' I don't think so." She looked around the fire shyly, a little afraid of what she'd just said.

Traf nodded at her. "I know what you mean. Mom and Tia Isobel tease me too, telling me I'm getting to 'that age'." She laughed. "Maybe so, maybe not. All I know is that I don't want one of those boys dancing with me. They smell funny." She held her nose.

"Traf!" exploded Iris, by now a familiar voice around the fire. "How can you say that? They don't smell any funnier than you do. Unless they don't bathe of course," she amended, blushing prettily.

But Teresa nodded vigorously at her from across the fire. "Yes, yes," she exclaimed excitedly. "I thought I was the only one who smelled it. I didn't even want to mention it before, but men do have a stink. When they ride in my taxi, which is rare," she added ruefully, "they fill it with their odor. Even when they're fresh from the bath, I smell it on my father and brothers. It's on their clothes, too." She looked in wonder at Traf and then around the fire at the others. "Haven't any of the rest of you ever smelled it?"

Confused heads shook but the oldest tomboy, Teresa, and Traf banged shoulders in agreement, both relieved someone else smelled the same thing.

"Well," Isabella pulled her sky-blue sweater around her shoulders, "I think you're both crazy." She waved her hand dismissively. "Men don't stink."

Teresa grinned at everyone and no one, then rose. Kneeling beside the younger girl she leaned in, drawing her nose along Isabella's hair, neck, and shoulders, inhaling her scent deeply. "Oh, yes, sweetheart," she cooed to the now bright red Isabella. "Your scent is quite unlike a man's. Women smell fresh as flowers and tasty as sweet bread." The tall tomboy rose, laughing heartily. "Men stink!" She crowed, folding long limbs into a squat at the fire, winking wickedly at the embarrassed girl.

Traf laughed at Isabella while changing the topic. "My father forbids me to dance with boys at the festival. I told him I'd obey, but under protest." She laughed easily. "I'm glad he doesn't know how happy I am to avoid them or he'd make me dance with boys." She slapped Teresa's back. "And they stink." Both laughed and the other tomboys joined in.

The two new girls looked askance at each other, then the older one abruptly snickered. All the tomboys stared.

Iris giggled. "These are my friends Gabriella and Ana."

Traf suddenly recognized golden-haired Ana from their school days together. She'd defended that little girl, fought with the boys pulling her long braids ruthlessly. Once pretty, now beautiful, those bright eyes knew

Traf the instant their glances met. Ana blushed, blinked rapidly, and looked down in confusion.

To her surprise, so did Traf.

Ana sat beside the still snickering other new girl, Gabriella. A few years older and former teacher's pet, she challenged the tomboys outright. "Well, if you won't dance with boys, who will you dance with?"

Traf stared pensively at the fire. Long habit sealed her lips. She said nothing, but from beside her Michaela finally spoke up. "We could dance with girls." Spoken soft but surely, her eyes begged the pretty young ladies seated across the fire to understand.

"Sure," self-confident Gabriela drawled, "but that's just for children. Grown women only dance with men."

An uncomfortable stillness descended upon the group. Glances flew between the tomboys who had discussed this fact for years. The crackling fire sounded loud in the sudden quiet. No one dared break the silence.

Michaela rose and circled round the fire to stand tall before Gabriela. She nodded and offered her hand to the seated girl. "Will you dance with me?" she asked in her best adult voice. Her outstretched hand held steady as every eye focused upon it.

Gabriela stared up into Michaela's eyes. The air filled with nervous excitement, a moment fraught with hidden meanings none of them understood. No one spoke or even breathed.

A look passed from one to the other that Traf never saw before between two women. It made her heart beat a little faster. She felt afraid, almost timid, suddenly concerned about right and wrong. But more than that, she wondered what it would feel like to dance with a beautiful young woman in her arms. She noticed Ana breathlessly watched the drama unfold.

Finally, Gabriela broke the tension with a great big grin, grabbed Michaela's hand, and jumped up. "But what shall we do for music?" she asked.

Teresa started clapping her hands and singing a popular song from radio. Her clear young voice led, and they all joined in. Margarida played along on her harmonica. No one sang too loudly, they were still a group hiding in the night after all, but within their circle they enveloped the standing couple with a stream of music.

The two young women captured every eye when they moved together. Michaela's arm slid easily around Gabriela's waist as she danced her around the fire. Twice they circled before the group in the flickering light, creating a surreal scene in the dark woods. When the song ended they stopped and smiled shyly at each other before laughing and sitting back down. Everyone clapped and grinned. A great relief (over what, no one was completely sure) washed over the group. But the dance shattered the fear, bringing a new awakening on a cool autumn night.

"I'm impressed," Traf told her friend. "I didn't know you could be so brave, or for that matter, were such a good dancer."

She began to wonder what it would be like to hold a woman in her arms and dance, the way a man did. Ana for instance. She jumped to her feet before her courage could fade and offered her hand to the small blond seated on the fallen log.

Her hand stayed there several long moments until she dropped it. Ana's eyes wouldn't meet hers, and after realizing how ridiculous she looked, Traf plopped back down by the fire. Iris nudged her shoulder as if to indicate she would have taken the chance.

The image of Gabriela and Michaela dancing around the fire haunted her for the rest of the week. As she studied her English lessons, she remembered their arms entwined. When learning basic self-defense, the sound of the tomboys singing in the dark filled her ears. And as she helped the women crowding her house to cook and prepare for the coming festivities, she wondered if she could be as brave.

That weekend, the Lajes festival opened with traditional fireworks, the Procession of the Saints, and a special Mass. Monday, the fun began, and Traf hurried home after class because today savage bulls would be let loose one at a time to run through the streets of her town. *Best day of the year!*

Four bulls had been herded from their fields in the hills yesterday, down to special corrals built just for the huge beasts. Each animal, branded by its owner with a number, was a prized possession. Traf was excited to see 212 among them, the fiercest bull on the island. The others would go first and 212 would be the last one to run, the grand finale. He never disappointed.

A sense of excitement built by mid-afternoon. People boarded up businesses and homes to protect them from the rampaging bulls. Balconies bloomed like gardens, draped with colorful quilts, and bleachers on hills above the street filled with young women and girls wearing their most beautiful dresses, always accompanied by a chaperone. Brightly colored scarves protected their hair from the fierce sun. The tomboys, in plain skirts and bare heads, agreed to meet in a vacant lot just above the curve in the main street running through Lajes.

Many men found their courage in beer, working themselves up to accept the challenge. Bachelors and teens sauntered up and down the street, embarrassed and thrilled to have so many beautiful women watching them. Some bought treats from vendors on the street, tossing small twists of paper holding fried fava beans or candies up to those they favored. Old men strolled behind and excited young boys between, each wishing they were strong enough, bold enough, and quick enough to run rather than hide behind stout wooden boards. Married men shepherded their families indulgently, secretly glad their wives and children meant they must behave responsibly.

A firecracker exploded overhead, signaling the release of a bull on the street, warning bars to close their doors, roadways be blocked to traffic, and anyone not running to take shelter. As the bull lunged into the road dragging a long rope from around his neck, young men from the village and a few soldiers from the base ran in front, taunting and skillfully dodging the aggravated beast's long horns. Tipped by rounded brass balls that protected from casual cuts, those horns could still gore a man when a one-ton animal put its full force behind them. Riled enough to charge, men jumped out of the way or simply ran past the line painted across the cobblestone road where the bull would be stopped. The bravest of the brave darted in to tap the rampaging creature on the forehead while others flashed umbrellas open and closed to attract the bull's attention. Each score incited the animal's outrage.

Five pastores, bull-herders, wearing traditional black slacks, white front laced shirts, and narrow-brimmed black felt hats, trotted behind holding the end of the rope. A good twenty meters long, it gave the animal plenty of room to maneuver, but it could be reined in when necessary.

After ten minutes of snorting, charging, the crowd cheering, and young men showing off, another firecracker signaled the end of the first run. The bull herders reined in and safely secured the beast, allowing bars to open their doors for thirsty spectators, traffic to flow, and giving people time to move through the boarded up street before the next run. It was always exciting to watch because sometimes people really got hurt. Over the years, more than a few men died horrible deaths making the skill and dexterity of the runners all the more impressive.

During the interludes between bulls, men dressed to impress strutted up and down the road, preening for the women sitting above. In a time-honored ritual that led to many marriages, each displayed his athleticism, daring, and bravery. Impressed women leaned down to throw them flowers or tokens to be tucked into pockets for luck.

That afternoon, Traf and the tomboys assembled in plenty of time to get seats above the last stretch of road, the place most likely to see mayhem. The first three bulls ran through, and in a few exciting instances, men escaped tipped horns by mere millimeters. During the third run, one incredibly lucky fellow, too slow from beer to jump completely free, felt the bull's horn rip his pants' leg as Teresa, Michaela, Traf, and others from the crowd grabbed his arms and pulled him out of reach.

When the final bull, 212, was announced everyone tensed with expectation. Even the vendors stopped selling and watched from safe places. During long winter nights, at dinner tables all over the island, the last run of the season would be thoroughly discussed. Everyone waited, hungry for each detail.

They heard shouting and whistling from around the bend as the first young man pulled into sight, arms and legs pumping. Directly behind him came a confusing crush of men and bull, all trying their best to negotiate through streets made unusually narrow with temporary fences protecting thrilled and noisy people. A few men crashed into each other; an American soldier fell. The crowd gasped seeing his danger, experienced runners shouted at him to play dead.

He lay completely still as instructed, hoping 212 would ignore him but wasn't that lucky. The huge beast slowed its pace, lowered its horns, and took aim at the downed man. Traf, the tomboys, and everyone in the crowd held their collective breath.

Angelo Delgado, police chief of Praia and an island favorite, darted in front of the lethal animal. An old woman from above threw down a red umbrella and began a keening chant, slapping the heavy wood railing f her balcony. The crowd followed her example as the police chief flashed the umbrella open and closed until they diverted the bull's attention. Delgado turned and ran to the other side of the street, 212 in hot pursuit. A nearby bar opened its boarded-up door long enough for the fallen soldier to be dragged to safety and closed just as rapidly.

The bull's frustrated snorting rose over the screams of the spectators as it chased Delgado's flashing red umbrella. Sharp hooves clattered on hard cobblestones. The police chief threw the umbrella at the charging animal and jumped, scraping one foot on the fence and both hands on top but 212 closed on him and struck. Victorious, the bull tossed his massive head, connected and sent the man flying up, over, and crashing down among the spectators on the other side. The five pastores reined him in, planting their feet on the cobblestones and leaning back in unison to turn the beast. 212 yanked against the restraining rope, pulling the first three men off their feet until it focused on another runner and charged down the street after him. But every voice hushed and all eyes remained on the rough wood enclosure where people scrambled until Chief Delgado was hoisted on their shoulders to wave at the crowd.

Shouts and cheers erupted on all sides. Relief spilled onto the street and sharpened eyes watched the uneventful final leg of the infamous bull's run. A final firecracker exploded as the five exhausted pastores hauled on the line and reined 212 into his waiting pen. An experienced veteran, the animal didn't resist knowing it would feast that night and be carted back to its life in the hills in the morning.

At sunset the evening came alive. The brisk autumn night thrummed, vibrating with a vitality peculiar to the festival, and no one wanted to miss it. The tomboys hurried to be near the big church named for Saint Michael the Archangel. They arrived just in time to see Lajes' seasonal electric streetlights flicker and illuminate the festival with false daylight. Powered by generators, bright strings of bare bulbs hung suspended between softer glowing gas lamps.

Musicians played in every bar. Violins, guitars, and mandolins accompanied fado singers performing songs of fate and wringing tears from many an eye. The movie theaters, brightened by their own generators, did a brisk business. The road flowed with milling joyous villagers until well after midnight. Couples young, old, and every age in between danced in the streets to lively music. People gathered around vendors selling drinks, food, and other delicacies. Games of chance benefitting church charities left the road littered with bits of paper.

The friends wandered through the evening together. Everywhere, like flowers blooming in the dark, beautiful women wore fabulous dresses. Young men dressed in their Sunday best approached girls occasionally, offering a candy bar or piece of gum as a way to begin a conversation. When this happened to one of their own, the other tomboys swarmed the cornered girl and whisked her away in a fit of giggles. The still young and untried boys stood no chance against their protective cyclone.

On the island of Terceira, a man could properly court a woman in only one way. Once she let him know his attentions were welcome, he made scheduled visits to her parents' home. If encouraged, he brought little gifts each time, flowers, chocolate bars, or wine. The entire visit consisted of him standing on the outside of the veranda wall while the woman stood on the inside. A chaperone was always within view, or at least within hearing. The entire process could take several years, but it often started at a festival.

Traf found herself the center of one young man's attention sometime before midnight. "Hey," he introduced himself, offering her a bag of popcorn. His voice had changed but squeaked awkwardly anyway, making him clear his throat. "I'm Hugo." He held out his hand to shake hers. "You look so pretty in your colorful skirt and sweater."

She didn't believe him. *How could anything so uncomfortable make me look good?* That is, she disbelieved him until she saw Hugo looking her over and smiling with honest admiration.

"I can't stop staring at you. Just looking at you makes me happy."

She felt awkward. Hugo's assertive manner told her he would ask where she lived so he could court her. It was exactly what her mother warned her would happen, and she hoped wouldn't. Michaela, sensing her discomfort, motioned for the tomboys to rescue her, but Traf waved her friends away, denying the protection of their female storm. "It's okay," she hissed at Michaela. "Maybe it won't be so bad. Let's see how this goes." She felt Mom watching and wanted to please her.

Once the tomboys left them alone Hugo leaned in. "I live across the island, in Serreta. My cousin invited me to visit during the festival. She swears only pretty girls live in Lajes." He blinked owlishly at her, almost charming in his awkwardness. "I looked around all afternoon but of all the beautiful women in Lajes only one caught my attention." He took her hand.

Traf's skin crawled, and only sheer willpower kept her from snatching it back from him.

Hugo tugged her to a vendor's stall where he bought her a sweet drink without asking which flavor she'd prefer. "I've made up *my* mind, I'm courting *you*," he told her as if his decision were law. "Only the beauty with curly dark hair, an easy laugh, and flashing eyes will do."

Maybe he sensed her disapproval when she placed the untasted drink on the stall counter and stayed silent. Comically changing his stance and attitude, he switched tone. Shrugging expressively, he dropped to one knee and assumed the stance of a sainted warrior about to do battle with dragons.

Hugo's voice grew melodramatic. "Forgive me, my lady. I knew that to win your favor I would have to brave the fearsome circle of protective females surrounding you." He made it sound like an act worthy of a great champion. Traf almost smiled, but then he grabbed her hand again.

"Assembling my courage, I cautiously approached your group of laughing girls." Acknowledging his own comedy, he winked. "You and your friends watched me like a flock of," he popped his 'p's, "pretty pigeons poised to part from my presence." He threw the back of one hand up to his forehead, feigning distress. "It occurred to me I was outnumbered." Traf struggled not to laugh aloud at the picture he painted. Hugo was growing on her some.

Aware that she was warming, he grew even more dramatic. "'Hey,' I announced into your suddenly forbidding silence, 'I'm Hugo.'" By now, she was giggling outright as he recreated their meeting only minutes ago. The young man looked quite satisfied with himself and rose to move closer to her. "But, you know the rest."

He stood there, staring at her awkwardly before suddenly pulling a chocolate candy bar from his pocket. A little too warm and slightly melted, he looked at it bleakly before offering it to her, suddenly at a loss for words. His face glowed bright red as he obviously hoped she would help him out by breaking the clumsy silence that settled between them.

Instead, Traf looked over his shoulder to see her friends holding back ferocious guffaws with the backs of their hands. Already embarrassed, Hugo's smell rose sharply to her nose, tempting her to be rude and push him out of her way. At the last moment, she remembered her promise to Mom. Winking once at Berta, she graciously accepted the candy bar.

"Thank you." She spoke demurely, watching her friends squirm with mirth.

"What's your name?" blurted Hugo, young and unsure in the ways of courtship now that he wasn't brave with humor.

"Brianda," she purred, fluttering her eyelashes at the smitten boy. Trying not to gag on his smell, she forced a shy smile.

"That's a beautiful name," Hugo murmured. "May I visit you at your home?"

"With my father's permission, you may," she cooed.

"Where do you live, Brianda?" asked the boy, clearly enchanted with her.

"The town of Praia." She tried not to let her lie turn her bright red. Michaela lived in crowded Praia by the beach. Traf lived right here in Lajes.

A silence settled between the two again as Hugo thought furiously about what else he might say to her, the proper young lady standing demurely before him. He usually made conversation easily, but she looked so pretty it drove the words from his mouth. He shifted his weight from one foot to the other.

Traf steepled her hands together and brought her fingertips to her mouth, barely touching her lips. *Hugo thinks I'm beautiful, and it's making him shy to speak. That never happened before.* The shock of it almost drove the stink of him from her nose.

The music must have finally penetrated the sound of his heart pounding in his ears, and he stammered, "W…will you dance with me?"

"Oh, I can't," she said as if she were sorry, licking her lips and watching him watch her. This was easier than she ever imagined, and twice as much fun. "I promised my father I wouldn't dance with any boys."

Hugo beamed at Brianda, the prim and innocent girl clearly devoted to obeying her father. What a good bride she would make for him. He struggled to think of something else he could say to impress her, but his mind went blank. He stood there, staring into her eyes, which disconcertingly stared right back into his own.

The silence stretched between them. Traf did nothing to alleviate the young man's discomfort. Hugo shifted his weight once more. He cleared his throat, twice. Finally, Margarida took pity on the poor boy, or simply grew bored, and reached past him to grab her friend's arm.

"Come on, *Brianda*," Margarida said loudly and decisively. "We have to go now." She pulled Traf along with her, and the whole group of tomboys broke into excited giggles as they left the stunned boy standing alone on the road.

"You're terrible!" scolded Iris, looking much more beautiful to Traf than she imagined she ever could. Brilliant in a bright red skirt and sweater, the feminine girl said, "That poor boy will be scouring Praia looking for Brianda."

“Well, let him look. At least, I can tell my sister I have a boyfriend,” Traf announced, thoroughly pleased with herself. “Maybe Alice will leave me alone about that now.”

“Yeah, right,” teased Teresa, laughing. “She won’t be satisfied until you’re well married and pregnant.”

“Well, that’s never going to happen with Hugo or any other man,” she answered with a wicked grin. “Men stink!” They both laughed and bumped shoulders as they wandered away in the dark.

The group of friends meandered over to some people dancing in a decoratively lit street corner. As they stood and watched, men and women in colorful clothes swirled by. Traf saw her father sitting with some of his friends drinking wine, smoking cigarettes, and laughing. He looked stiff and constricted in his Sunday best.

Looking around to locate her mother, Traf stopped dead in her tracks suddenly appalled. Mom, wearing her finest dress, danced with a small boy of four or five in the middle of a dozen whirling couples. Laughing and gay, her head thrown back and her feet nimbly keeping time to the sprightly music, she made quite a sight.

“Oh, Mom,” her daughter groaned, totally embarrassed. *Why, oh why, do I have to have a mother who dances as if no one is watching?*

Michaela, watching Traf’s mother, laughed and grinned mischievously at her friend. Traf’s answering glare became a challenge. Michaela reached for Gabriela’s hand at the same moment Traf reached for Iris. For one frozen moment, they all stood still. The other tomboys watched them, amazed, nervous, excited, each with bated breath.

Traf wanted to step into the dancers but hesitated. Then Gabriela smiled at Michaela and nodded. Iris watched them move off into a dance and finally twitched her head at the dancers. Traf swung the pretty girl out, in, and among the moving couples. Soon other tomboys divided into couples too, dancing with the ‘normal’ girls who had befriended them. They claimed the center of the street for themselves and grinned at each other as the adults dancing around them smiled indulgently over their heads. To the wide world of grownups, they were pretty young girls pretending to be adult. In reality they were the exact opposite: adults, pretending to be little girls.

It was a good thing Traf’s parents couldn’t read the true feelings in her heart as she held soft Iris in her arms, swaying to the music. They danced until the musicians went home for the night, and the string of electric lights sputtered out.

Ch. 8 - Their Socially Mandated Surprise

Spring, 1965

Traf jumped eagerly out of bed. *It's finally here! This is it! The day I drive solo!* She dressed hurriedly and hustled out to the main room. Her mother was already making breakfast for her, fried eggs and potatoes this morning. Traf knew Mom would tease her, she was so hungry. Sometimes it seemed as though she just inhaled all the food given to her and kept looking for more.

She seated herself eagerly at the table, but even her enthusiasm for the day's activities didn't blind her to the fact her mother's usually sunny disposition was under the weather. She looked around and saw her father was gone. Well, that wasn't strange. In the old days, he often took off for the fields before sunup. But he hasn't done that for at least two years now. *Odd.* She looked at her mother more closely.

Mom was fifty-nine years old. She had been forty-two when Traf was born. It embarrassed both her parents, she knew, to have another child so late in life. She was a whoops. But her mother always seemed so young, even now still running foot races and beating her. Mom tended the fields, animals, and her family, and did all the little things that kept a household running; the baking, cooking, cleaning, washing, and hundreds of other chores that made them comfortable day in and day out. And through it all, she always kept a cheerful demeanor.

Although, her mother did occasionally get angry with Traf's Tia Isobel, Mom's younger sister. Memories of the few times she had seen Mom lose her temper brought a grin to her face. It was quite something to see and hear, full of colorful turns of phrases and gestures broad enough to sweep a theater. So, after taking a careful look at her mother's sorrowful face, she sat up even straighter.

"What's wrong?"

Her mother threw her a confused look, then consciously settled her face into complete composure. "Nothing is wrong, Miss Busybody," Mom answered curtly, plocking a plate down in front of her.

Traf knew she'd been dismissed and should let the matter drop, but she wasn't built that way. "Mom," she said earnestly, "what is it? Can I help?"

Her mother sat down at the table across from her and tried to smile, a miserable failure. "No one can help, my little troublemaker," she said.

The use of her baby nickname gave the room an air of melancholy. A single tear trailed down her mother's weathered cheek, shocking Traf. It vanished as soon as it appeared, and in its place, her mother's face settled into stern lines of resignation.

"You might as well know the truth about men, Vitória." Her mother spoke to the air, unwilling to look her in the eye. "They want things, and because they are men and have money, they go out and buy them."

Traf tried to decipher the meaning of her mother's words. Was she talking about a new dog, or tool, or something her father bought without talking it over with her? "Where is Father?" she demanded, realizing after she spoke that her words sound sharp and confrontational.

It nearly broke her in two when she saw her mother wince at her words. "He didn't come home last night. I don't think he'll be home tonight, either."

"Why?" Traf demanded, unable to keep her voice neutral.

"I don't know for sure," answered Mom. "Mrs. Alvares tells me someone saw him around the café." Her voice dropped almost to a whisper, then she continued more strongly, "Vitória, don't ever spread gossip. It's like a feather pillow; once it's opened and the wind catches the feathers, you'll never get them all back again. That's the way it is with rumors. Even if what Mrs. Alvares says is untrue, she's telling everyone the story. Soon it won't matter if it's the truth or not."

Traf was still confused, but it was becoming clearer every moment what happened. *Father has gone off with a mistress.*

"Mother!" she exploded. "Who is with Father?"

Her mother's face darkened with shame, and in a voice so quietly beaten it stunned Traf, Mom said, "He's with a woman named Sylvia."

The name didn't surprise her although she tried hard to look shocked for her mother's sake. Adrenaline saturated her muscles, bunching them up for action. It was one thing when he'd been more or less discreet, but now he paraded his depravities around in public, disgracing her mother's good name. Hate roiled in her belly.

Mom's next words did surprise her, however. "Of course, when he comes home we won't mention it to him." She fixed her headstrong daughter with a firm stare. "Will we?"

Traf's fury exploded. "What do you mean? You'll let him come back?"

"Of course. This is his home."

She jumped up from the table, leaving her meal cooling and uneaten. "I don't understand you, Mom!"

"I know you don't, sweetheart," answered her mother soothingly. "But one day, God willing, you will."

Traf stormed out of the house and marched down the street, trying to release some pent-up frustration. She threw a wicked glare at Mrs. Alvares and her huge bosom resting atop the gate.

"You walk like a man, twisted tomboy," crowed the old gossip. "Take after your father a little too much, don't you?" She cackled.

Ignoring the old biddy as she passed by, Traf's mind seethed. *Should I go to Sylvia's house, confront her and demand she leave Father alone? Or should I keep my head high and eyes blind, remaining above the fray, like Mom?* Either way, she felt tied up in a tizzy of contradictions as she boarded the bus to the base.

Thoughts of revenge plagued her as she crossed the base to her classroom, but they faded away when her name was called to take her first solo drive in an automobile. "Mendes, front and center," ordered her instructor, Sergeant Vincent.

Shivering with excitement, Traf slid behind the steering wheel of a car. It was an automatic and since Açorean women were shorter than average American soldiers, blocks of wood were taped to the pedals.

"Remember your lessons, Mendes," advised Sgt. Vincent. "You've done this with an instructor sitting beside you and you'll be fine by yourself if you remember what you've been taught. Don't panic." Her sergeant sounded like the nervous one.

Mentally reviewing everything she learned, she adjusted the rear view mirror and checked her side ones as well. Then, being sure to signal first, she pulled carefully away from the curb and off on her own across the airfield.

I've never moved so fast in my life. Normal objects looked different as she whipped past them at thirty miles per hour. Although she had ridden in buses and taxis, this was completely different. This machine was under her control and moved at her command. She proved it to herself by moving the steering wheel subtly, adjusting the vehicle accordingly. She flexed her foot and the vehicle surged forward then slowed again under her direction. What an incredible feeling of freedom…and power.

Too soon her turn was over and reluctantly she returned to the starting place, aware she'd have to wait until tomorrow to drive again. She knew the minute she stepped out of the car she'd chosen the right career field. *Nothing can ever be as exhilarating as driving!*

The next few months flew by. Although the miracle of vehicles and how to operate them filled her days, her time at home was often tense and silent. Her father came home three weeks after he left and not a word was spoken about his absence. In fact, Traf pretty much quit speaking to her father altogether. Even though she technically abided by her mother's wishes, her disgust was palpable in the house.

Her father, who still growled whenever he saw her dressed in men's clothing, returned it in equal measure. Their self-righteous piques threw up walls of defense in both of them. They finally battered them down one afternoon when Traf arrived home early and found her father drinking wine in the middle of the afternoon.

"Where's Mother?" she asked as she entered the kitchen where Father sat with legs crossed, leaning back in a chair. "Out taking in laundry to support your lazy ass, I guess?"

Her father sat up straight, planting both feet on the floor. "How dare you speak to me that way?" he demanded. "What gives you the right?"

Suddenly it all boiled over and she stared him down while quietly ticking off items on her fingers. "One, I bring home more money than you do. Two, you sit at home while she cleans other people's houses and washes their clothing to buy your wine and cigarettes. And three," she shook her fist in his face, "she's too good for you!"

Father jumped from his chair, quivering with indignation. "You! Who are *you* to talk?" He pointed at her fatigues. "You shame your mother and me and disgrace the memories of your grandparents. You are a vile disfigurement of a woman, you piece of pig dung!"

He started toward her with his arm raised, ready to strike. She felt her training kick in and watched in surprise as her hand reached up and grabbed her father's wrist, brought it down sharply and twisted until they heard an ugly snap. Her father gasped, his face suddenly drained of all color. He sat back down on his chair hard, cradling his injured wrist as he stared at her in horror.

"Don't ever touch me again, old man," she thundered at her father. "I can sign a paper tomorrow and be on a plane to the United States that night. Juana did, and now she lives in America and goes to school there. She's free of her parents and this rock, and will never be beaten again."

Her eyes pierced him like daggers. "Believe me, Father." As she walked out the door, she snapped over her shoulder, "Raise your hand to me once more, and you'll never see me again. And stop making my mother cry."

She returned to base and requested a room in the Bachelor Officer Quarters. She stayed for a week, thankfully the same week her group received training on driving in hazardous conditions. She threw herself into the exacting work, trying desperately to forget the injury she'd inflicted on her father.

So great was her guilt she couldn't confess it, expecting nothing short of excommunication from the Priest. No one ever raised a hand to their parent. *Well, maybe a boy might when he became a man.* It was theoretically possible, although she didn't know anyone who ever had. But a woman? Never. It wasn't the Portuguese way. She knew better than that.

Seven days later she went to the doctor's office and paid her father's bill in full. She moved back in her room before he returned home that day and when she came out for dinner neither mentioned the bandage wrapping his sprained wrist. She wouldn't apologize and knew he wouldn't either, but family is family and life moves on.

Traf focused on driving through oil slicks that simulated icy road conditions, something they didn't have on Terceira. She practiced braking at different speeds safely. She learned how to gauge the weather and adjust her plans accordingly. But her hardest lesson came in holding back her urge for speed in favor of caution and safety.

It occurred to her that this was like her trouble at home; if she had only curbed her tongue, the situation wouldn't have escalated to the point of injuring her own father. He was her oil slick, and she needed to treat him like a patch of dangerous ice.

Sometimes Sgt. Vincent offered to let some of the new Lieutenants practice driving after hours. She patiently opened the training area and checked out a vehicle in her own name. One or two of them would join her for an extra hour behind the wheel. Traf never let the opportunity pass.

One Friday evening after driving for almost two hours, Sgt. Vincent invited Traf to the non-com officer's club for a drink. She readily agreed, thrilled that Sgt. Vincent, a ruggedly handsome woman whose expertise in driving seemed unparalleled in Traf's somewhat limited experience, would single her out for attention.

"Hey, Louis," the tall woman called out to the bartender, waving as they walked into the dimly lit room. The Portuguese man standing there waved back, then grinned at Traf, who recognized him immediately. He had been courting her neighbor, Hermione, for the last year or so. They were getting married in a month.

"Louis! When did you start working here?" Traf greeted him cheerfully in Portuguese.

"I got the job last week." He poured their drinks, scotch neat for the sergeant and a coffee with brandy for Traf. She and Louis had raised more than one cup together and he knew what she liked. He waved as they took their drinks to a small table in the corner.

"How do you know Louis?" asked Sgt. Vincent while taking a hearty swallow of her drink.

"He's going to marry one of my best friends next week," she answered. "He's been a familiar figure in our neighborhood for over a year now," Traf glanced curiously at her instructor. "Don't American men court American women?" she asked.

"Well, if you call a burger and a movie courting, then sure," answered Sgt. Vincent. "But I don't date men much anyway." She glanced significantly at Traf.

Instantly, the young soldier was on the alert, although she kept her face calm and friendly. Last month, Margarida had been summarily dismissed from her classes with the Navy across the base because she innocently told a sergeant how much more she enjoyed dancing with women than men. The tomboys had danced several times in the woods during the last six months when they gathered. *Who knew the Americans would take such an extreme view?* Traf had thought them somehow more advanced than that. Regardless, the tomboys took the incident as a warning. Traf started guarding what she said.

"Oh?" she answered casually as she sipped her brandy and coffee. "What do you do for entertainment, Sergeant?" She glanced up to see Vincent staring at her, but when caught she looked away.

"I was going to ask you the same thing," she said in a low voice. "What do women like us do for entertainment on this island?"

The phrase 'women like us' sent another alarm off in Traf's head, but she smiled innocently at the sergeant and pretended not to know what she meant. "Well, my mother and I go to the movies together sometimes," she offered. "But most of my evenings are spent helping in our fields."

"What about boyfriends?" Her driving instructor wriggled an eyebrow. "A pretty girl like you must have lots of boyfriends."

"My father won't even let me dance with boys yet." Traf giggled. "He says he'll tell me when I'm old enough for men to court me. It's the same for all my unmarried friends our age."

Sgt. Vincent grinned in relief and sat back, satisfied. Traf wondered if she'd been sent out on a scouting mission, and now felt relieved she'd found nothing to report. She kept smiling but reminded herself to let the other tomboys know about the incident. It wouldn't hurt for all of them to be extra careful. *Who knew the Americans could be so devious?* They finished their drinks, then went their separate ways.

In the woods two nights later the girls talked late into the evening. "Why do so many people have trouble accepting us?" Traf poked the fire with a long stick. "After all, don't we do our work as well or better than other women?"

"Yeah, what's the difference if we like women more than men?" added Berta. "What so odd about that anyway?"

"We're supposed to get married and raise children." Lydia shrugged. "But what if no man wants you? Does God, then, have no purpose for my life?"

"We go to church and pray to a god who turns His back on our prayers." Michaela spit sunflower shells in the fire. "It's true, don't deny it," she said, looking over the group. "Each and every one of us has prayed for God to change us."

No one denied it.

"Don't they think we want to fit in?"

"The problem is," Traf interrupted as the girls babbled, "we're too visible. We need a place of our own, some place to meet, and a reason to be there every night. Then no one can suggest we're doing anything wrong."

"Those Americans are very suspicious," said Margarida stridently. "I didn't know that sergeant was going to report me. She made it sound like she understood, so I told her I like holding women to dance. Then, poof! A black letter!"

A black letter meant that not only was Margarida dismissed from the US Navy but she was also permanently banned from even civilian jobs on the base. Basically, it guaranteed that Margarida would never make as much money as the girls who still worked on the base. Now she would have to carve out a place for herself among the island people like Teresa had with her taxi, or marry a man and let him take care of her.

Traf looked at her friend sympathetically. Her mind was whirring, taking a strange concept and turning it into the germ of an idea. She slowly shook her head at Margarida and winked. "Remember last winter when I loaned my Uncle Carl some money to tide him over? He gave me part ownership in that old building he owns down by the beach in Praia as payment." Her voice rose as the other girls listened.

"The place is a rat trap and it'll take a lot of work to make it livable again. It's been empty for almost ten years now and it's falling apart. But it is part mine. I'm going to talk to my uncle and see if we can buy the rest of it and turn it into a club."

"A club?" asked Alexandra, confused. "What would we do with a club?"

"Oh!" squealed quiet little Ana, usually so reticent. "I get it! We make our own club, one that's just for tomboys!" She grinned widely and gestured to the pretty, normal girls sitting there, "...and I mean all of us troublemakers. We make it a club only for women, and the men can't come in. We make it a club only for Portuguese, and then the Americans can't come in!" She looked at Traf with admiration. "What a great idea!"

"Do you think we can do it?" asked Berta, reflecting the rising hope among the girls around the campfire. "I can help with it, and I can help with the money too." Each of the four still working on the base nodded enthusiastically. This would be a good way to spend their paychecks. The "troublemakers" began planning.

But even such an exciting prospect as their own clubhouse was no match for the growing hubbub on Traf's street. The day of the big wedding was less than a week away and everyone was in the mood to celebrate.

Now grown into a shapely beauty, Hermione enjoyed nothing more than sitting in a group of young women gossiping while they crocheted or embroidered. Marrying a man she loved would be the crowning achievement of her life after growing up being ostracized as a bastard. With everyone judging her, she could have turned up her nose at Traf's boyish behaviors and snubbed her in turn, following the social pecking order. Instead, they'd become best friends for life.

Even before her daughter's first birthday Tia Betty began embroidering bedsheets, tablecloths, and towels, storing linens for just this occasion. By tradition, the bride outfitted the kitchen and the bedroom, while the groom prepared the new living room and any spare rooms. Hermione and her mother had spent weeks preparing for the ceremony and reception, cleaning, painting, and rearranging the house for after the wedding when the newlyweds would take the big bedroom and Betty move into the small one.

Knowing she had no one else in the world and how close they were, Louis had insisted his new mother-in-law stay with them. He offered to move them all to Lisbon but they decided to stay together in Betty's house in Lajes.

Traf couldn't have been more pleased. Hermione, now a grown woman of twenty-one, was as excited as it's possible for someone to be and not burst from sheer pleasure. She'd loved Louis for what seemed like forever and planned this wedding for the better part of a year. Finally her time had come. "The best possible outcome for my life!

"Oh Vitória, can you believe it? He's giving me the wedding I always knew I could never have. He's paid the seamstress for our gowns, gave Mother enough money for a real feast, even arranged for flowers to be delivered at both the church and the reception." Traf hugged her best friend as she bubbled over with happiness. "It's perfect, he's perfect, and our honeymoon in Lisbon will be perfect. My life from now on is going to be perfect!"

Traf eagerly participated in the preparations for the wedding. About fifty guests were invited to the ceremony and fifty more would join the celebration at the reception. Family and friends from Louis' side were traveling all the way from the mainland and would stay at Betty's house until catching the boat a week later on its way back to Lisbon. Wedding celebrations often lasted late into the night and into the next morning. A lot of people would need food and drink.

They butchered a pig bought in early spring and raised just for this party. A two-day process, Traf's whole family helped. The best pieces of pork were brought into the house and set to soak in wine.

The day before the church service, Tia Betty made the wedding soup in a huge iron cauldron. Louis lugged the heavy thing into her house and hung it on the hook over her hearth fire. For hours she hovered in steam, adding first one ingredient, and then another. Rich in meat, potatoes, onions, greens, garlic, and seasoned with sea salt and allspice, it would serve all of the guests. Mom baked dozens of loaves of bread in her brick oven, made of fine white flour rather than the coarser cornmeal used for every day. Alice made the wedding cake, decorating it beautifully with sweet white icing.

Johnny and Jack gave the old house a new coat of paint. Even her father pitched in, helping Louis tame the garden and prepare the yard for the reception.

While everyone bustled around them, Hermione and Traf spent an hour reminiscing while molding sugar doves as decorations. "Do you remember," Traf giggled, "the time you and I made a mud castle right in the middle of my grandmother's flower garden?"

Hermione's eyes flashed with merriment. "Oh, I thought she'd be so mad! But she didn't say a cross word to either of us, just picked a rose and put it in our tower for a flag!" The young women laughed easily together.

We've got a lot of shared memories. I'll miss Hermione once she goes into the world of married women. "You know," Traf said hesitantly, "I owe you a debt so great I'll never be able to repay it."

Hermione looked up from sprinkling sugar over a dove. "For what?"

"You taught me to read, you and your mother." Thanks and apologies were never easy for Traf, causing her to speak in a rush. "If it hadn't been for you, I might never have learned how to read or write. You changed my life." Traf hoped her real gratitude showed in her eyes.

"Your first three teachers were idiots." Hermione growled, still heated in her defense. "I can't believe they wasted your time in the back of those rooms. Harrumph!"

"I'm going to miss you." Grinning, Traf reached over and daubed Hermione's nose with powdered sugar.

"Where am I going?" Hermione swiped away the sweetness on her nose and laughed at Traf. "You make it sound like I'm sailing away from the island forever!"

"It feels like it. You're going to be a married woman now."

"That doesn't mean I won't have time for you," Hermione stopped what she was doing and turned to face Traf. "You're my best friend. That won't ever change. Even though I'll be busy making a home for Louis and me, and maybe even having a baby or three," a charming pink rose on her cheeks, "I will always make time for you." She reached across the table and patted her hand.

"I think you should get married too, Traf," she continued, surprising her friend speechless. "You're old enough now, and you need a place of your own. Think about it, your own home, your own things around you, your own man to take care of. Doesn't that sound nicer than the way you live now?"

The first two, maybe. Traf smiled wistfully, knowing Hermione had only her best interests at heart. *I wish I could tell you the truth. I like girls instead of boys.* But she didn't dare. There were some things even friendships as old and solid as this one couldn't bear. "I'll think about it," she lied, patting Hermione's hand reassuringly.

Next day, Traf woke early, nearly as excited as the bride. She had arranged with the base to have the whole day off from her studies and felt free and unfettered. Dressing in a hurry, she rushed over to see what help she could offer and spent the morning setting a long table with Tia Betty's finest linen, best cutlery, and china. Beautiful bouquets arrived from the florist filling the house with their scent, so she arranged fresh flowers from her mother's garden outside, filling the yard with joyful color. Betty's house looked brighter and more beautiful than it ever had.

The hours passed rapidly, and then it was upon them. Traf sat next to Iris and Isabella in the church, entranced by the extraordinary beauty of a bride on her wedding day. Flickering light from a hundred candles lit the golden altar and the three people standing there. The priest's voice delighted the ear as he recited magic words making two separate people one whole. Tears flowed and hugs abounded, then they all returned to Hermione's house for the reception.

Louis had set up a barrel of wine and with the guests soon in their cups happy toasts for the new couple's health, fertility, and longevity abounded. Everyone told funny stories about the bride and groom, happy to share in the joy of young newlyweds.

It took hours to serve the wedding soup. Because there weren't half enough places for everyone to sit it had become tradition for the men to eat first. Once they rose and left the table to go smoke, Traf and Alice quickly gathered and washed the dishes while their mother reset the table and served the children. After they'd been fed and sent off to play, Traf, Alice, and Mom reset the formal table and joined the women as they ate.

All evening and into the night people sang the young couple's praises, impressed and enjoying themselves thoroughly. The whole neighborhood turned out for the occasion, a true indication of the place Betty had painstakingly carved for herself and her daughter in their small, rigid community. Even Mrs. Alvares attended the festivities.

"Probably gathering gossip to spread next week." A giggle tickled Traf's ear. Although a very pretty girl in her skirts and sweaters, Iris still heard an earful from the old biddy every time she was seen in Traf's company. She felt no affection for the geriatric gossip, but plenty of respect born of anxiety rather than esteem.

"That and a free meal." Traf laughed in return. She had no fear of the old woman, merely contempt. And tonight, no one could bother her. Happy for her friends, the whole world seemed a softer, gentler place. She nodded and the two of them walked away from the lights and the festivities, out into the dark of night under the trees.

Traf liked the feeling of Iris's hand in hers. The wine they drank made her feel bold and without considering the consequences she suddenly stopped and kissed Iris on the lips. They both started away from each other, a little shocked. Eyes, wide open with amazement, met across the short distance between them. Deep within the depths of their socially mandated surprise simmered a forbidden desire. They moved together again slowly, feeling as if each were pulling the other.

They kissed again and this time no one jumped away. Traf wrapped her arms around Iris and kept on kissing. Their lips explored each other, at first tentative and soft, but soon with more determination. She led Iris deeper into the trees where they wouldn't be seen and spent the next few hours curiously learning about each other and themselves.

By the time they managed to make it back to the wedding, Isabella greeted them with reproach, obviously angry they'd spent the evening without her. Neither made excuses for their absence.

Two months earlier, Teresa brought a new girl with her to the group. The girl, Beatrice, was clearly smitten with the older taxi driver and to no one's surprise, it was returned in kind. Teresa often held Beatrice's hand while sitting with the group around the campfire, and Traf had seen them kiss more than once.

From the night of Hermione's reception on, Traf made excuses to find Iris and spend time with her.

"Why are you so close with that girl?" Alice eyed her with suspicion.

"Maybe she's missing Hermione. And you can never have too many friends, right?"

"Right, Mom." Traf ignored her sister. She'd found something wonderful with Iris and wasn't about to give it up.

From her childhood days of pilfering fruit with Johnny from neighboring fields, she knew a few secluded spots where they would not be interrupted. Whenever they could get away they explored each other's body centimeter by centimeter. Traf took the lead, thrilled to see Iris' bare breasts exposed. Tender touches led to ever-greater levels of pleasure. They barely spoke during these encounters, saving their breath for kisses.

Iris tried to return touch for touch, but somehow the girl's slender fingers on Traf's skin didn't feel quite right, and neither did exposing her budding breasts with their tender nipples. It seemed easier for her to do all the special touching and she enjoyed the feeling of being in control. Iris soon gave up trying, easily succumbing to her own desire.

Sunday nights they sat together at the fire, holding hands and sometimes exchanging little kisses. Others paired up too, Berta with Rita, Lydia and Mary Jo, and Margarida with Linda. No one talked about it, and those that didn't pair up accepted it without comment. After a while, some of the pairs broke up. New ones formed. Still no one discussed it.

There were so many thing they didn't talk about. No one said a word, for instance, when Berta quietly left the American Army in favor of returning to her mother's house and father's fields. She didn't offer a reason for leaving, and no one pried.

Instead, they focused on plans for the clubhouse. To find, and file papers with, the proper bureaucrats took time, but finally the topic of a club exclusive to Açorean women rose. There had never been another club like it on Terceira. The powers that be were a little nonplussed but agreed to check the legalities of such an enterprise.

The tomboys and their girls itched to get started on the building but had to wait for the government's okay. They shared the same dream in long night talks, imagining the place, how it would be decorated, what they would put into it, and how their time would be spent there.

On a warm sultry evening in June, Iris was babysitting her baby brother and sisters, so only Isabella came to the fire. Traf missed the feeling of Iris's hand in hers and was sorry they wouldn't slip away for a few stolen minutes of pleasure among the trees. She sat morosely by herself as the conversation flowed around her. Before she knew it the fire was being put out and everyone started to leave, some in pairs, others in groups.

"Hey Traf, you want to see Isabella gets home safely?" Teresa's voice broke through her funk. "She lives just down the road from you." They took care to see each other home in the evenings. No one wanted to be caught out alone in the dark.

Isabella stood before Traf, looking at her expectantly. Everyone else had drifted off, and it was obvious she needed to escort Iris' little sister home. Traf's eyes lit up as it dawned on her that she might still have a little time alone with Iris before their parents' return. "Okay." She shrugged. "Let's go."

She started hurrying through the woods, irritated as Isabella dragged her feet behind her. The fifteen-year-old fell farther and farther behind. Traf broke out into the street and turned to look behind for Isabella, but she'd disappeared from sight. Frightened, Traf rushed back into the trees, calling out Isabella's name softly. She retraced her steps rapidly.

"Isabella," she hissed into the darkness. "Where are you?"

"I'm up here," called the younger girl, her voice faint on the still air.

She looked up and saw Isabella on top of the covered chicken coop at the edge of Mrs. Alvares' yard. "Well, come on down here," Traf whispered in hoarse exasperation.

"No. You come up!" called the impish young woman, pulling her face back from the edge of the cement structure so she couldn't be seen.

"Stop messing around. Come down here at once!" Absolute silence met her words, so gritting her teeth in suppressed anger, Traf climbed up the side of the coop and hauled herself over the edge until she was on the flat roof. She turned to see Isabella sitting in the far corner, smiling. Her sweater was off and she sat on it, arms braced behind her. In the chilly breeze up there, Traf noticed that the younger girl was not wearing a bra.

"Come on, Isabella," she commanded. "I have to get you home, now."

"No, you don't," answered her girlfriend's sister. "My parents aren't home and Iris doesn't know the meeting's over. We have all the time in the world."

Looking at the younger girl with confusion, Traf was surprised when Isabella grabbed her hand and pulled her down to sit next to her. She was stunned when the girl put her inexperienced lips over Traf's and waited.

She pushed Isabella back and took a long look at her. She was a beautiful girl but two years younger than Traf, who also happened to be seeing her sister. This was out of the realm of her experience, and she was unsure what to do.

"I've seen you kiss Iris," whispered Isabella. "I want you to kiss me, too," and with that, she launched herself at Traf again.

It is an intoxicating feeling to be wanted. People succumb more to the pleasure of being desired rather than their own yearnings. Traf felt seductive and crushed the young girl's lips to her own. She kissed her hard, excited by the feel of the responsive girl in her arms. She heard Isabella sigh and kept on kissing her. The younger girl learned swiftly, soon kissing back with fervor.

After about an hour of petting, Traf pulled herself away from Isabella and looked at the moon setting in the west. "We better get you home," she said with some regret. "Your parents will be back by now, and you'll have to sneak in through your bedroom window."

They helped each other down from the top of the chicken coop, and that began a furious two weeks of juggling sisters for Traf. She'd spend time with Iris, then find a reason to leave and join Isabella on the roof of the coop. At night around the campfire, she made sure never to glance at the younger sister, lest the older figure out what was going on. She would pleasure first Iris, then Isabella, until her head whirled with the headiness of all that passion.

One night it happened. She was sneaking back into the window of her bedroom after a passionate session with Isabella. Easing up the windowsill, she jumped, balancing herself on her stomach. Just as she was about to heave herself the rest of the way up, a resounding pain in her butt startled her. Letting go, she turned to see what was happening, who was attacking her. The heavy wood of the window sash slipped down onto her back, pinning her in place, her legs struggling for purchase.

Through the window, she saw standing a clearly incensed Iris, face red, eyes glaring, legs braced and both arms raised overhead, holding a two-by-four. Taking aim again and again, she wordlessly, furiously, beat Traf's ass.

Unable to call out for fear of waking her father, Traf couldn't climb into the room because the window had her trapped, and she couldn't get away from the relentless pounding that Iris was inflicting. So she kicked.

Her foot finally hit Iris in the middle of her belly, and her attacker went down with a loud, "Oomph!" Pushing the window up with one hand, she climbed painfully into her room. Standing inside now, quivering with outraged indignation, she leaned out to talk to Iris.

"We're through," she whispered fiercely as she rubbed one hand up and down her aching backside. "No woman treats me like that!" But she was speaking to the air.

Leaning farther out the window, she saw Iris stalking off. "The same goes for me," the furious young woman called over her shoulder and stormed off into the night.

Humiliated and in pain, watching the first girl she kissed walk away, Traf had to admit Iris was a force to be reckoned with. She thought briefly of trying to warn Isabella.

Ah, hell. She started this affair to begin with and she's used to her sister's behavior. She's on her own. Running a hand over her still-throbbing ass, Traf didn't know whether she felt more forlorn or relieved.

Ch. 9 - A Whisper Dropped into the Silence

Summer, 1965

Her uncle, Tio Carl, was happy to sell his half of the old house in Praia. He'd tried to sell it for years, but no one had been interested. Then he rented it, but when the renters moved without paying for the last three months, he'd let it go. He didn't waste time making any repairs and stopped paying taxes on the property. It had been abandoned for the better part of eight years.

"What do you want the old place for?" he asked when Traf approached him. "The roof leaks, the windows are broken; it will take a lot of repairs."

"Some friends and I want to turn it into a club, Uncle Carl. How much do you want for your half?"

Traf's uncle was a drunk. Not a loud or obnoxious one; he was rarely truly soused, but never completely sober either. Her mother's brother had a slow and steady thirst. It took money to keep him steadily stewing, whether in homemade wine or cheap beer. "Five hundred American dollars," he announced.

"That's too much! You, yourself, said it needed a lot of repairs. Be reasonable, Uncle."

"What? Do you want it for free?" he demanded.

"Carl," called his wife, Tia Bianca, coming in with clothes fresh from the line, "don't be a fool. You'll never get another offer. Sell it to the girls for what they can afford."

Traf's aunt ruled that household. Whatever she said, went. Uncle Carl closed his eyes, sighed, and said, "Fine. Three hundred American dollars."

As Traf said, "Still too much," Bianca said warningly, "Husband…"

"As my wise wife says," he finally grumbled, "what can you afford?"

Traf and her friends had already collected what money they had between them. They'd asked other tomboys they knew from around the island, explaining their dream for a clubhouse, until each of twenty women had donated. Some put in a little more, some a little less, but in the end, they could offer him, "One hundred and twenty-five." She showed him the cash.

Uncle Carl nodded, accepting the deal, and held out his hand. "Okay. Give me the money. I'm busy today, but in a day or two, I'll go into Angra and have the deed put in your name."

Things were changing on the island. In the old days, a person's word was their bond. No one promised anything they didn't deliver, and always had a damned good reason when they could not. Having a witness to an agreement was legally binding, but after the war a different attitude spread among a certain segment of the population. Traf considered the fact that Uncle Carl was family, but also a drunk. She looked over his shoulder to see Tia Bianca shake her head in warning.

"No, Uncle. This is how we'll do it. When you're free to go, send me word. I'll hire a taxi to drive us to Angra and we'll go to the bank together to file the deed. Then I'll give you the money."

"No," announced Tia Bianca, smoothing her husband's good Sunday shirt on the table as her iron warmed on the stove. "Bring the money here after you get the deed and give it to him in front of me."

Uncle Carl grumbled but, in the end, that's what they did.

As the island warmed with hot ocean breezes, the tomboys began planning their clubhouse. They wanted to model it after the soccer clubs already operating on the island. Several of the men's teams built themselves comfortable clubhouses where they relaxed together after practices and games. Very exclusive, only invited friends and family could enter the premises. They served food and alcohol, played music, and danced. Of course, their little clubhouse for women would not be nearly as grand, but it would be all theirs.

Iris had refused to speak to Traf ever since the night of the two-by-four. She still came to the campfire every weekend, however, and made a big show of holding Tina's hand for a while. Traf missed her and soon lost her appetite for the too-young Isabella. She did not lose her hunger for female companionship, however. Traf found that she liked chasing women.

It didn't take long for her to develop a reputation as a rake. As a VIP driver, she traveled across their small island regularly. While the VIPs conducted their business, she managed to make mischief. She kept girlfriends in almost every town, sometimes two or three of them. Most of them allowed her only to kiss and maybe touch a breast now and then. A few very generous ones would let her explore their knees and slightly higher, enough to keep her always searching for more. Traf sat alone at the campfire most nights now because she chose to, although at times, she would invite a femme to come and sit beside her.

The tomboys began calling the normal looking girls, those that dressed and wore their hair like any other woman of the island, femmes. They called themselves, those who dressed and worked like men, butches. Traf was a butch. Michaela learned the terms from a doctor her parents forced her to see.

Dr. Duarte, a woman in her mid-thirties, was very sympathetic and helpful. She listened to Michaela respectfully. They talked about her feelings about women as if it was just another topic of discussion, not something intrinsically evil and demeaning. The doctor told Michaela things about herself that helped answer a lot of puzzling questions.

Then the doctor sealed the trust in her relationship with Michaela by refusing to tell her parents what had been said. It was the first time anyone who wasn't a tomboy had ever taken her side. Of course, Michaela wasn't allowed to go back to the doctor after that first visit but she brought the woman's words to the fire, repeating them for the other tomboys because they'd seared into her brain.

"Women who love women instead of men are called *lésbica*, lesbians," Michaela explained, "and there are smaller groups of us as well. You girls," she gestured to Rose, Gabriela, Ana, Beatrice, Iris, and Isabella, "you are 'femmes'. A femme is a lesbian who wears women's clothes, enjoys doing the things that most women enjoy, and is content to live her life by society's rules except that when she loves, it's another woman."

The girls nodded, recognizing themselves in the definition. That made sense. They were learning something about themselves.

"Go on," urged Teresa for the whole group. She held her body oddly tense, as if expecting a blow.

"Well, those of us who dress, walk, talk, and act like men, we're called 'butches'," continued Michaela. "Butches are broken into two groups, too. There are hard butches, also called dykes, and there are soft butches."

"What's the difference?" asked Berta. Traf leaned in, paying close attention. All the tomboys were listening just as closely. None of them had any idea there were definitions that fit them.

"The way the doctor explained it," Michaela said slowly, scrunching her eyes together as she worked to remember the words exactly, "a hard butch always dresses like a man, never wearing women's clothing." She looked at each of them as she stressed the word never. "A hard butch is a woman who tries to pass in society as a man, or if that's impossible she tries to force the world to accept her as one despite evidence to the contrary."

That description didn't fit any of the tomboys in their group. "What's a soft butch?" asked Berta, looking through the flames into the fire.

"A soft butch," Michaela explained, "dresses like a man when she's among her own kind, like us," she gestured around at the girls wearing trousers and shirts, "or find jobs where it makes sense to dress as a man. Some wear men's clothing in ways that don't show, like underwear." They all laughed at Tina, who once made the mistake of telling Berta she had taken to wearing men's underwear, rather than panties.

"They're more comfortable," the angular young woman insisted as she blushed.

"A soft butch enjoys behaving like a man, but also enjoys being a woman," continued Michaela.

"What does that mean?" asked Isabella.

Berta grinned mischievously at her from across the fire. Using both hands, she grabbed her own breasts, massaging them and moaning. "This," she said in a husky voice. The butches all burst out in bawdy laughter, while the femmes watched somewhat askance and more than a little shocked.

But Michaela was serious about definitions. "I think a hard butch might beat her woman. A soft butch never would, because she'd recognize herself as a woman too."

This sobered Traf. She glared intently at Iris, who sat with a particularly self-satisfied grin. Slowly and deliberately, Traf said, "I'll never beat a woman, no matter what she does to provoke it. That's something men do. They want to control women. The only way they can, with some of us, is with force."

"I don't want to control a woman," mused Michaela, smiling at Gabriela warmly. They had been getting along well for quite a while now. "I am a woman and I don't want to be controlled. It would steal something from me if I ever dominated someone else."

"Exactly." Traf ignored Iris, whose smirk shrank noticeably. "Men demean women to control them. For a woman to degrade another woman is to do it to herself. It's just not possible, at least for me."

"But what if your woman does something stupid?" asked Berta. She flushed a deep red as the group turned to gape at her. They all knew she was interested in Rose, a shy, dark-eyed girl who simply looked at her now. "I mean, well, isn't it our duty to correct them?"

Michaela looked at Berta, then at Rose sitting so still. "Who made you God?" she asked quietly. "What gives you the right to judge? Men think they have the right and the power to be above us, to 'correct' us into a thing of their own making. You want to be like them?" She gestured out to the big wide world of controlling men that lurked in the dark shadows, always present and a very real threat. "Would you like it if a man decided he was not only your lover but your boss and disciplinarian as well?

"But butches are superior to femmes," sputtered Berta, looking confused. "Smarter, anyway."

Michaela, Teresa, Margarida, and Traf all fell into each other laughing. They slapped Berta on the back and goaded her, chortling. Their intent was to catch a net full of trouble.

"That's right, buddy. Butches are smarter than femmes." Teresa chortled.

"We're stronger and braver, too," added Michaela, winking at Margarida.

"And no butch ever cries," put in Traf. "Not like you emotional, girly femmes." She put one hand on her hip and flounced around the fire. "Boo hoo hoo…"

"We femmes let you butches think you're smarter, that's all," Iris put in, rising to the bait. "If we don't, there's no living with you!"

In answer, Teresa swaggered around the campfire, pulling out a wad of bills. "Oh yeah?" she asked. "Who's got the money?" She spread the bills and fanned herself with them, taunting the femmes.

Shy little Rose spoke up suddenly. "Sure, you make your own money. Money gives you power." She shrugged her shoulders expressively. "But it certainly doesn't guarantee intelligence. That's a gift from God. Either you have it, or you don't." Both butches and femmes were struck dumb with surprise but nodded in agreement. Berta stared as if at a stranger.

"God is a man, that's why He favors them over women," eagerly offered Gabriela. "Mary was the exception," she added piously.

Traf looked up at the stars twinkling in the dark sky above them. "God made me the way I am. He gave me the talents to compete with men, and the need to do so. If He wanted me to be something else, He would make me need something else. How can I think that He made me wrongly? God is perfect. He doesn't make mistakes." She wasn't surprised when some of the other girls gasped. What she said was just this side of blasphemy.

"Maybe," added Michaela thoughtfully, "that's why He never answers our prayers to fix us. What if they're all wrong," she gestured out past their fire, "and there's nothing to fix because He made us exactly the way He wanted."

The rest of the evening until the fire died out, they talked about their place in the universe, just as they had many times before. It was good to have friends who sometimes felt as weird and 'other' as Traf did. It had been lonely and scary wondering if she were a freak of nature, feeling all alone until their first group of three started meeting Sunday nights. But many others sharing her little island felt the same. Over the years girls and women joined them from all over Terceira, seeking and finding comfort and acceptance. *What about the greater world, like Europe or America? Could it be that there are 'women like us', as Sgt. Vincent said, everywhere?*

Traf knew what she wanted from life. She wanted to live like a man, like her brother Johnny was doing. She wanted her own house and land. *I want a woman to come home to after working hard at a man's job. I want to give her everything she needs and as much of what she desires as possible. I want to make sweet love to that woman in the privacy of my own home, safe and secure.*

I want to be accepted on my own terms.

She also knew other things. *I don't want to wear uncomfortable clothes that hamper my movements, like skirts and high heels. I don't want to have children. I don't want to marry a man and live under his rules.* She would never be dependent on anyone for money. She'd search until she found a place with the freedom to make all the choices in her life, spend her money based on her decisions, and be no man's wife, slave, or concubine.

Sharing their outlaw thoughts around Sunday fires over the years brought her solidly to these conclusions. While not everyone was of the same mind, it became second nature for them to support each other even when they disagreed. Having felt like an official club for years, they were eager to be legally recognized, giving them a sliver of respectability.

They filed the final paperwork for the Terceira Women's Club of Praia with the proper government officials the second week of April but some objected. “The name’s so prim and proper. People will think we’re a group of church ladies.”

“That may be our legal name but we can’t call it that.” Gabriella laughed. “Our club name has to represent us.”

“Tomboys.” Berta looked offended when they laughed. “Why? That’s what we are.”

“Not all of us.” Ana fingered one of her long curls. “Some of us aren’t tomboys at all, but we still belong, right?”

“Of course we do.” Gabriella snapped her fingers. “Troublemakers. That should be our name.”

“Troublemakers?” Traf let the word tickle her brain. *Isn’t that like naming the club after me?*

“It’s brilliant.” Michaela winked at Gabriella. “That’s exactly what we are.”

Traf got the key from her Uncle Carl, and the group gathered early in the morning on Saturday the twelfth to open their new clubhouse for the first time. Excited, everyone chatted about their plans for the place, but as their hopeful group pushed open the door on its corroded hinges and peered into the dusty darkness, they choked.

No one expected to find it in such serious disrepair. Abandoned far too long, everything was covered in dust and cobwebs. Discarded trash, littered bits, and pieces of broken furniture lay strewn all over. Broken windows, like neglected teeth, grayed under layers of grime. Trails of damaging rain had leaked through the roof and down the walls over the years, ruining wood and encouraging mildew. But that wasn’t the worst of it.

Years ago, privacy-seeking lovers started using the abandoned house as a place of dark discretion. Since the outhouse fell over sometime in the past, whenever bodily needs arose, the lovers used a corner of the empty living room for their toilet. By the time the tomboys entered the place after years of misuse, the floor in that corner was rotted through by human waste and stunk to high heaven. The only good thing about the house was its location, directly across the street from a beautiful stretch of sandy white beach. Otherwise, the house they built their dreams on was a disaster.

They’d spent over a year planning this club and weren’t about to quit before they even started. They rolled up their collective sleeves and got to work.

The butches put in a tough day shoveling out and hauling away the accumulated filth, wearing scarves over their noses and mouths to keep from gagging on the odor. Everyone spent Sunday afternoon and evening scrubbing the walls and ceiling, washing everything in sight. Some of the butches spent evenings during the week, after their jobs, doing repairs. Femmes polished new glass windows to a high shine. Teresa rehung the doors and outfitted them with sturdy locks. Repairing the staircase leading to the second floor fell to Alexandra, as Tina patched holes in the roof. Ana and Gabriela treated the pervasive mold and mildew with lye and boiling water, and everyone helped apply a fresh coat of whitewash inside and out. Flush with pay from their jobs in the military Michaela bought discarded tables and chairs, Traf found an almost new refrigerator, and Margarida pitched in by buying the old gas stove and grill used in the cafeteria when a new one arrived on the American base.

They took turns scrubbing that section of the floor that had been used as a toilet, but nothing would take out the smell. Michaela even brought disinfectant from the base, but the stench was too deeply entrenched. Still, every day the femmes kept scrubbing, determined that sheer elbow grease alone would dispel the odor. Day by day, week by week, the place came together.

Their enthusiasm spilled over to some of their families. Gabriela and Ana brought in curtains and tablecloths their mothers helped them sew. Margarida's older brother helped them run wires from the new electric station to the place, one of the first civilian buildings in Praia to have it. Johnny helped them move the heavy furniture, although he laughed at the idea of a club only for women. Tina's mother suggested lemon juice and salt for the still malodorous corner of the room and even sent along the necessary ingredients. Unfortunately, even those didn't help.

Berta's father, Mr. Borba, who was very fond of his daughter, finally took pity on them. He helped the butches tear up the entire section of fouled floor and lay a new one. He also helped tear through two interior walls, opening the first floor into one long room. As they worked together, he talked to the butches, the young women who were his daughter's oldest friends. He seemed genuinely interested in them, listening when they spoke. He was the greatest man they had ever met.

Mr. Borba, who belonged to a famous soccer club in his youth, looked around their clubhouse and recognized what was missing. He used his skills as a carpenter to create an intricate pattern of different colored woods he then lay as a beautiful, raised dance floor. He knew what his daughter was. He had agonized over her as she grew up, wishing everything could be easier for her. "Well, this is one thing I can do for my Berta," he told them, and he did it with all the strength of his devotion for his only child. He wanted his beloved daughter to have a safe place in which to have fun.

Everything cost money, and their group unanimously decided that Margarida, the best of them at math, should keep a careful accounting of what they spent and who paid what. The lumber would have been completely unaffordable except that Traf found out about a building on the base that was being torn down. She approached the base commander and asked if she could have the old boards that were about to be tossed into the sea. After learning what they would be used for, he agreed. For all the wood needed to repair and build, they paid only a case of beer to the fellow who hauled it over in his cart.

When he learned from a friend about a bar for sale across the island, Mr. Borba talked to the butches. A beautiful old sturdy one made entirely of blond oak, it came to the island over fifty years ago from the mainland. They gathered enough money between them to purchase it sight unseen, based purely on his recommendation. Berta went with her father to pay the retiring barkeep his money and reported back to them that Sunday around the fire.

"It's beautiful!" she enthused. "Better than the one in the café here in Lajes. It'll cover one whole end of the room, and there's a little hatchway you can flip open and closed to get in and out." Happily satisfied, Berta smiled at her friends. She had always known her father's loving support, and now her friends felt it, too.

It seemed to Traf their little Berta stood as tall as a chestnut tree and twice as proud. "When will they deliver it?" she asked. They hoped to open the clubhouse sometime just after the first of July.

Berta lit up like a candle. "Tomorrow! It arrives tomorrow and guess what? They threw in a beautiful old mirror to hang over it." She clearly enjoyed the rest of the girls clapping her on the back, repeatedly telling her to thank her father. She told Traf later, when they were alone for a moment, "It feels wonderful to make something good happen."

As work on the clubhouse continued, the gathering around the fire on Sundays took on an odd feeling of loss. By organizing the Women's Club, they were staking a place in the community, clearly visible to the population at large and regulated by the government. It would never be the same as their hidden meetings in the woods. They would be adult lesbians, visible in a way they had never been before, and, therefore, more vulnerable. They instinctually knew they were in the last days of their innocence.

That knowledge acted as a catalyst for adult behavior. Ana left her parents and moved to Praia, where she worked cleaning houses. Lydia cleverly created a job for herself baiting trawl lines, and began building a house of her own. Michaela bought a VW bug, bright blue, which she drove to and from the base every day from her rented apartment in Praia. Alexandra decided she wasn't cut out to be a secretary in the Army and worked shoulder-to-shoulder with her father, tending their land. He deeded her ten fields, five of them prime vineyards, more than enough to be self-sufficient. Rose took a job at the local beauty parlor; Gabriela did sewing from her mother's home. All of a sudden they grew up.

That summer, nights on Terceira were sultry. When sunset made it too dark to work on the clubhouse, the group walked across the street and down to the beach. Every evening they built a campfire, keeping the tradition alive. People brought food and drink, and they sat or lay on the sand, telling stories and swapping lies. As always, they made sure they were a significant number, enough to intimidate any rowdy rascals.

Instead, those frustrated bullies turned their special brand of attention to a smaller group, one that often gravitated to the outskirts of the young women's fire. The Troublemakers weren't the only homosexuals on the island. Gay men, many of them oddly feminine in their dress and manner, took an interest in the developing clubhouse, some even suggesting it should be opened to them as well. Traf laughed when she heard; she'd never allow men in her clubhouse, much less queers.

She and the other butches looked down on these girly men. Sometimes the mere sight of them would make the women swell inside their clothes, flex their muscles, and utter insults in their direction. The butches were terribly rude when the men first started building their own campfire just a bit down the beach, throwing sand at them to make them move. The girly-men kept creeping back, however, and the women grudgingly accepted their persistence.

One night the Troublemakers heard a ruckus from the men's fire. Looking over, they watched drunk town bullies attack the men, cursing, destroying their fire, dragging, kicking sand, and beating them. The young women turned back to their fire. It was the business of men and the idea of getting involved was beyond their ken. The queers were men, and men handled their own affairs. Island women never interfered in the business of men.

The bullies were ruthless, repeatedly attacking the stubborn battered men sitting peacefully at their campfire. Night after night shouted curses pierced the evening quiet, carried on sea breezes across the sand to the women. Finally, the sounds of ferocious beatings, cries of pain, and fearful whimpering broke through the Troublemakers' collective consciousness.

Five nights after it began, the bullies arrived and started attacking the queers. *Enough.* Without a word spoken between them, Michaela, Tina, Teresa, Berta, Margarida, and Traf rose as one. Hidden by darkness, carrying firewood as weapons, they encircled the girly-men and their tormentors. A heavy plank harvested from the construction site felt effective in Traf's hands as they inched closer. She gave a sharp whistle, and the butches struck.

Bullies never expect anyone to protect their victims, especially other victims. Shrieking and howling, whacking and kicking, the Troublemakers earned their name once more. They knew these guys and owed them for many old insults and injuries. Vengeful, enraged, and empowered butches chased the tormentors down to the water's edge as the stunned and bleeding girly-men stared after them.

Bare heels kicked up frothing wavelets as the Troublemakers pounded the men mercilessly, driving them seaward. Using each other as shields, blindly seeking escape, the bruised and bleeding bullies broke away, howling like little children and limping off into the darkness.

As the last one wriggled past her, Traf raised her arm high over her head and brought down the plank of wood as hard as she could. A thud shuddered up her entire arm. She tried to pull back to swing again, but she couldn't. Her weapon was stuck.

The man she hit shrieked and grabbed at his head, bizarrely reaching for the plank. Traf pulled on it again, thinking he was trying to wrest it from her grip. He screamed, "She's killing me, she's killing me," and only then did she realize there must be a nail in the end of the plank, now securely embedded in his skull. She tugged upward and felt it come free. Her victim stumbled off into the night, crying out for friends who already fled leaving him behind.

The victorious Troublemakers scampered back to their fire, rejoining the femmes and other butches. They slapped each other on the back, regaling the group with tales of their heroic deeds. Traf showed everyone the nail in the plank, covered in blood and hair.

"I hit him so hard he saw stars."

"They won't be back anytime soon, that's for sure."

"That'll teach 'em."

They quieted, though, when the gay men approached. The girly-men, freshly patched up a bit, stood just outside the light of their fire. One of them stepped forward with a basket he thrust roughly into Traf's hands.

"Thanks," he said, his voice thick with disbelieving awe. It was a single word, a whisper dropped into the silence that could easily be forgotten, blown briskly away over the sands of time. Instead, it rang like a bell in her mind, making her wonder. *Are we the first to ever side with them?* She watched them help each other back to their fire.

The basket overflowed with fresh fruit and a bottle of wine, obviously brought to share among themselves and probably all they had to offer in thanks. Traf passed it around and the Troublemakers tasted sweet victory. The conversation drifted to the strange men, looking over to make sure they weren't within hearing range.

"Why don't they fight back, stand up for themselves?" Berta peeled a banana. "Wimps, needing women to fight their battles. Probably still suck on their mamas' titties!"

No one laughed.

"Where are their 'butches'?" Teresa spit a peach pit into the fire.

Margarida took a long pull from the wine bottle before passing it on. "Yeah, where are their big, strong, protectors?" Pulling the ever-present harmonica from her breast pocket she began playing softly.

"Probably passing as normal men." Michaela shrugged. "Their butches look like regular guys so they can't join their group on the beach without being recognized for what they are. Like you girls." She looked at the femmes. "No one knows who you are unless you're with us."

"So, we're braver than their butches are?" Ana looked at Gabriela in astonishment.

"They disgust me," admitted Teresa under the cover of Margarida's music. "Sometimes they use my taxi. I need the business so I don't refuse, but a couple of them wear women's perfume. They stink worse than normal men."

"Maybe that's their problem; they don't know if they're men or women," mused Alex, who recently shortened her name from Alexandra.

She pointed. "Georgie, the one wearing the blue shirt, you see him? Well, he was in the pharmacy buying makeup and oils." She nodded knowingly at them all, then emphasized, "Oils. You know what they need that for." She winked.

"Sure," said the always perfectly put together Linda. "We use baby oil to remove our makeup." The femmes all nodded.

Alex shook her head. "No…" she said suggestively, wriggling her eyebrows. "*Think* about it."

No way in hell would Traf admit in front of her friends that she didn't know what Alex meant so she simply nodded along with the other butches, making herself a mental note to find out what queers did with oil.

Needing to hide her ignorance and still high on adrenaline, she stated boldly, "They're the exact opposite of us lesbians!" Her next words stunned even her. "Perversions of human flesh!"

All heads snapped toward Traf then quickly away. How often had each Troublemaker heard that phrase, or one like it, used against her?

Silence dropped heavily over them; even Margarida stopped playing her harmonica. Traf's words, with all their implications, hung in the air, demanding examination.

Time expanded in a heavy introspection impossible to break. The rising full moon offered wisdom imparted by the crackle of beach fires, a soft male laugh dancing on a breeze from the men's camp to theirs, and the rhythmic waves of Mother Earth's heartbeat.

Head and shoulders bent, Traf listened and learned.

What a stupid thing to say. I didn't mean it. Those girly-men might be my exact opposite but they're more like me than the straight people who hate us both.

The ugliness of her words frightened her. *I wish I never said them, let alone ever thought them. I can't be…I won't be a bully!*

The next night the same men built their fire a little closer to the Troublemakers who didn't protest. Someone referred to them as 'our brothers' which swiftly became the accepted name; no one called them queers or girly-men anymore. Somehow, just using the nicer phrase made their attitude more pleasant, even accepting.

Gifts of food were sometimes exchanged or shared. Teresa's taxi business grew prosperous. Lydia found new customers seeking out her trawling line skills. And while the groups didn't join together, the Troublemakers began watching out for and extending protection to their new brothers. *After all, family is family.*

The Troublemakers set Sunday, the fourth of July, as the date for the grand opening of their club. Traf suggested that night because their veranda would be perfect for watching fireworks set off on the base for the American holiday, providing glorious entertainment for their special night, totally free.

The twenty butches and femmes who'd planned, bent their backs to every task, and given money to help make the clubhouse a reality, each became a charter member of the Terceira Women's Club of Praia. They received a parchment document signed by Margarida, whom they easily elected head of the membership committee. The women assured each other their clubhouse was better than either of the other two in Praia. Pride in themselves and what they'd achieved made them cocky as peacocks with feathers unfurled. They reveled in their new club, Troublemakers.

Each member spent serious time planning what she would wear to the grand opening. The butches conferred over the proper attire, discussing everything from shoes to jackets, and shirts to ties. After hotly disputed debates, they dressed interchangeably alike in dark trousers falling to a nice break over men's black loafers and white shirts pressed stiff with extra starch. Skinny bowties were in favor that year, as were jaunty black berets slouched on the side of the head.

On the other hand the femmes flittered busily, as varied as butterflies and twice as busy. Discussions and assistance raged over fabrics, lace, buttons, and bows. They met in pairs or small groups, working at a furious pace during the last few days to ensure everyone's gowns were ready in time.

Traf arranged to meet Ana at her new apartment and escort her to the opening. Dressing meticulously, her fingers fumbled while knotting her tie. It was her first date with the blond schoolgirl who'd caught her eye years earlier. Anticipation warred with caution, but the thrill of a new romance quenched both.

Traf sucked in her breath when she saw lovely Ana in her pale pink gown, hair piled up in soft curls that fell gracefully around her oval face. Already jaded at age seventeen, the butch's stomach dropped to her knees. She swallowed her tongue, tasting honey. After a long moment, she managed, "You look…stunning."

"You look beautiful, too."

Traf snorted.

Ana grinned and grabbed her hand. “I mean handsome.” She started walking. “Let’s get going. We don’t want to be late.” The glee in her voice set both their feet in motion.

Walking arm in arm, a common practice for women friends, they strolled down the streets of Praia through the gathering dusk. Traf struggled for something to say, wracked by a sudden shyness that left her unable to draw upon her past friendship with Ana, as though they were strangers meeting for the first time. The air crackled around them, heavy, warm, and sultry. Rain clouds chased across the twilight sky, alternatively revealing the first pale stars with distant flashes of lightning. The pair traveled the distance without speaking until they heard excited sounds coming from their brightly lit clubhouse. “Come on!” Traf shouted, grabbing Ana by the hand and hurrying down the cobblestone street, around the bend, and up the beach road to their new clubhouse.

The Terceira Women’s Club of Praia, forever after known by its nickname, glittered like a gem. The open door and bright windows illuminated their friends going inside. Butches, handsome in their outfits, struck poses. The femmes openly admired them, themselves a rich rainbow of swirling crinoline and lace. Excited chatter and laughter filled the air. Emotions overwhelmed Traf and a lump rose in her throat. *My friends. The family I choose in the home we built together.*

Teresa donated a phonograph, and the Troublemakers collected a variety of records to spin. The music, songs of Portuguese fado and American big band favorites, floated over cloth covered tables with candles and strewn flower petals, through new lacy curtains, and out into the breathtaking night. Hand thrown red clay bowls on each tabletop held roasted corn, fried fava beans, fresh fruit, and candies.

Shoeless to protect the beautiful woodwork, a few couples already danced on the new floor. Alex stood behind the bar at one end serving wine, beer, and soda pop. Displayed at the other, promising later delights, lay an abundance of cakes and puddings. The walls gleamed with fresh paint, and the entire place smelled of fresh ocean air and blooming roses.

“It’s everything I thought it would be.” Ana stood beaming beside her.

Traf admired the pretty girl. “Me too. It’s wonderful and just the way we planned.”

Laughing, waving, and nodding, they crossed to a table in the corner where Michaela and Gabriela already sat. They greeted their friends, just as dressed up as everyone else, and the four spent a few minutes admiring each other’s clothing. Gabriela and Ana each sewed their own gowns so their discussion swiftly evolved into the technical, leaving the butches to chat with each other.

"It's great, isn't it?" Michaela looked around proudly.

"We've done well, my friend," Traf slapped her on the back.

"We could never have done this without you. You know that, don't you?"

"I couldn't have done it alone either, Michaela. We all made this place happen; it belongs to all of us. It's proof of what we can achieve when we stick together." Traf leaned back in her chair with hands clasped behind her head and crossed one leg over the other, just like a man. Michaela imitated her and both ended up laughing. It was wonderful to feel so good, to be so free. They felt, well, normal.

Traf untied and removed her shoes under the table, then stood up and approached her date. Holding out one hand and bowing slightly from the waist, she asked, "May I have this dance?"

Nodding, her face charmingly rosy, Ana kicked free of her high heels and joined her on the dance floor. Their bodies fit together easily, and each of them wondered why she had never danced with the other before.

With Ana no longer in high heels, they were the same height and gazed into each other's eyes as they danced. Traf leaned in and inhaled her perfume.

"You smell so sweet."

"I rubbed gardenias into my skin earlier in the evening." Ana offered her neck, her smell intoxicating. They danced a second, and then a third time before resting. Breathless, Traf escorted Ana out onto the veranda overlooking the crashing waves for a breath of fresh, if somewhat humid, air. They cooled themselves as best they could in the slight breeze.

The night had darkened, the sky now a blanket of velvet above them, a million stars twinkling like the pleased eyes of a host of angels. Alone on the veranda for a brief moment, the sound of waves crashed on the beach across the street. Traf lifted a damp curl from Ana's face, leaned in, and kissed her. Brushing bare lips lightly across lipsticked ones, she lingered for a moment, then eased the contact slowly. The feather-light brush of lip on lip ignited desire. Traf wanted more, but instead of kissing those soft lips again, she drew back, savoring the sweet anticipation. Ana seemed a little flustered as they re-entered the club.

She led her date back to the dance floor where they spent the rest of the evening in each other's arms, pausing only for the firework display on the beach. Everyone crowded out onto the veranda to watch the sky over the rhythmic waves erupt into bursts of brilliant color.

"Oohs," and "Ahhs," rose all around them. Traf tried to take Ana's hand, but in front of others, the demure girl resisted. Pulling her hand away, she smiled in reassurance. The bud of Traf's interest burst gloriously into full-blown lust. Entrancing Ana captivated her.

No one drifted away as the evening wore on; rather, the entire group of twenty stayed right up until midnight, the hour mutually agreed the party should end. They shared in closing up the club; the femmes washed plates and glasses while the butches put up chairs and swept the floor. When all was done and they were ready to go, Traf handed around twenty brand new keys, one for each of the charter members. Before leaving, they watched her ceremoniously lock the door. It was a momentous gesture done in profound silence.

They broke into smaller chattering groups; as always no one walked alone. Michaela volunteered to drive anyone home who lived in another village, so six laughing young women clambered into the tiny VW bug. Gabriela waved gaily to Ana from the front passenger seat as the jovial group drove off. Later that night, she moved into Michaela's apartment.

Traf walked Ana back through the narrow cobblestone streets of Praia to her tiny apartment, their only light the occasional glow of kerosene lamps from behind shuttered windows. This time, they chatted easily about the evening, already telling stories they would share for many years. Standing in the darkness outside the apartment building, Traf kissed Ana again. This one was longer, more direct, and it ignited a fire in their bellies. When they broke apart a little breathlessly, Traf said, "I'd like to see you again."

"You will." Ana flashed a coquettish smile. "We'll both be at the clubhouse next Friday night."

Traf kissed her again, a little more forcefully. Releasing Ana, she remembered Hugo, the funny flirt. She doffed her beret and bowed low, sweeping the hand holding the hat before her. "Then, may I, a known Troublemaker, escort you to the club Troublemakers on the evening of Friday next, my lady?" She maintained her chivalrous, albeit slightly cavalier attitude.

Arching her brows, Ana answered her with a coy, "As you will, my lord. As you will." Then she disappeared inside, leaving Traf alone in the dark.

What an evening, she thought as she walked the dark streets back to Lajes. *I couldn't imagine a more perfect one if I were to think about nothing else for a week.* While asleep, she dreamed she and Ana lived happily married, accepted by friends and strangers alike.

Next Friday night, before she could knock on Ana's door, it opened. Out walked one of Traf's former girlfriends, Natalia. When they saw each other, both froze, a look of shocked recognition passing between them in that instant. Traf looked to check the number of the apartment. It was number Three-B, the same one where she'd picked Ana up the weekend before.

"You?" Traf demand. "What are you doing here?"

"Me? What are you doing here? I told you I didn't want anything to do with you anymore!" Natalia said, as imperious as ever. "I'm a married woman now, so go away!" She waited for just a breath of time, then said in a satisfied fashion, "I don't live here, anyway."

"Good. I am not here for you," Traf answered brusquely.

"Do you two know each other?" asked a voice from the darkness beyond the doorway. Ana stepped out from the shadows, her face puzzled and more than a little suspicious. She turned to face her sister, her body stance insisting upon an answer. "Natalia, do you know Traf?"

An uneasy silence settled between the three of them as they stood in the corridor of the apartment building. Ana turned to Traf. "How do you know my sister?" Natalia stayed silent, a knowing smile on her face. Digging in her heels, the younger sister glared, growing angrier by the moment.

Finally, Traf said, "Let's go, Ana. I'll explain as we walk." She turned her back on Natalia and stomped off. Ana scurried to catch up and keep the quick pace Traf set as they hurried down the two flights of stairs to the street.

"Well?" asked Ana, passing in front of Traf as she held open the door of the apartment building. "It seems you know Natalia."

"I didn't know she was your sister," Traf stated categorically. Her head throbbed violently. She did not want to have this conversation.

"Well, she is." Ana's voice held a note of irritation. "Just tell me how you know her." Shaking her head in exasperation, she turned and started striding away. Now Traf had to scurry to keep up with the incensed femme.

She reached out and grasped Ana's arm, forcing her to slow down. They took a couple of slower steps, and then Traf took a deep breath and released it with a sigh. "I dated Natalia for a while, a few months back," she said shortly, staring at Ana's nose to avoid her eyes. "It ended badly. Let's leave it at that."

Ana stopped dead in her tracks. "But..." Her mouth worked slowly, but no sound escaped. "But I've known you for years." She searched Traf's face for some explanation of her words. "Natalie is three years older and never went to school. How can you two know each other?"

The butch looked away, avoiding the younger woman's discerning gaze.

For six weeks last year, she and Ana's sister had gotten together every Tuesday night because it was Natalia's one evening off as a live-in nanny for an American Air Force Captain. The evening would start with dinner and end in teasing. To her chagrin, Traf's exploring hands had been kept above the waist. On their last Tuesday night together, Natalia hinted they would finally take things farther. She wore a close-fitted black dress that suggested a lack of underwear. She'd been especially flirtatious and playful during the evening, rubbing Traf's leg in the darkened restaurant. Afterward, anticipation rising, they walked to a deserted strand of beach, both with only one thing on their minds.

They had just found the perfect spot and started snuggling when Natalia happily announced, "I got married last week."

Shock, and a total lack of self-control on Traf's part, caused an ugly scene filled with accusations and denials. Pain seared across Traf's forehead now, a migraine of remembered pain as Natalia's angry voice filled her ears again. "So what? I used you. I was horny, and it was weeks before my wedding night. I wanted to have fun, and with you I could stay a virgin for my husband. You were my innocent guilty pleasure, but I'm a married woman now. We can go all the way; he'll never know the difference."

Traf cringed, remembering. "You never said you were getting married. You love me, you told me so yourself."

Natalia had fixed her with a condescending stare. "I do love you... as my friend."

"Only that?"

"Only that," Natalia answered firmly. "You were obediently convenient until I got married. With you, no always meant no. You stopped when I told you to stop."

Outraged over being called obedient as if she were a dog, but recognizing her own complacency, created quantum leaps of understanding. A thousand thoughts settled into place in an instant. "You don't think I'm good enough for you, not if you could marry a man!"

Now, walking beside Ana, she winced remembering her voice indignantly quivering. Traf's eyelids blinked fiercely, controlling tears she hadn't shed then, and refused to now. Her feet slowed to a stop, remembering.

"That's not how it was," Natalia had answered as if speaking to a child. "Of course, I must take the best husband I can get and give him children. To do that, I had to remain a virgin. Your hesitant touches and sweet kisses fed the hunger of my desire without destroying the dreams of my future. And now I have a rich man's name and status as his wife." She'd pulled Traf to her, attempting a kiss. Traf had wiped the back of her hand across her mouth.

"I can't believe you used me." She'd jumped to her feet, pacing back and forth in the sand. "I'm only some convenient plaything to you." Traf had whirled on Natalia. "You married someone last week, and now you want to cheat on your husband with me?" Appalled and nauseated, trying to injure as much as she'd been injured, she'd said, "That poor idiot. What's next? Will you start charging me money, whore?" Traf had lost all control then and slapped Natalia hard across the face.

Both of them froze. Traf was immediately sorry, but still too angry to admit it. Natalia straightened her tight black dress, and then glanced witheringly at Traf. "I shouldn't have expected a jealous little girl to understand." She picked up her high heels, turned sharply, and strode away, hurling over her shoulder as she left, "You'll realize the opportunity you threw away once you grow up. But don't come back to me. I won't have you."

Ana stood watching the replay of emotions run ragged across Traf's face. Her eyebrows drew together and rose in a grimace of recognition. She'd shared a bed with Natalia for the first dozen years of her life and knew the sharp sting of her sister's casual cruelty. She started walking again and Traf hurried to catch up.

"I am not my sister."

Traf looked at Ana, who seemed determined to stay a half step ahead of her. She took in the furious young woman's long legs, slender waist, and beautifully developed bosom, moving gracefully down the street toward the beach. For a brief moment, Traf compared Ana's tall, curvaceous form to Natalia's tiny, delicately petite one, then deliberately cleared her mind of the thought. Thank God they were very different, one from the other.

As she trotted alongside Ana's lengthening stride, Traf scrambled for something to say. She settled on the truth. "I didn't know you were Natalia's sister when I asked you to go with me to the opening," she said. "If I had, I might not have asked you, that's true." As they reached the bend in the road and turned to see the clubhouse a block down, she reached out and took Ana's hand, slowing her down. "In all those times sitting around the fire, you never mentioned having a sister. You certainly don't look anything alike. How would I have known?"

Swinging around to face her, Traf looked deeply into her date's wounded eyes and whispered, "But now I know. Look, Ana, we had a good time last week, didn't we? Let's have another good time tonight, and we can talk about all this as I walk you home later. What do you say?" Tugging her by the hand, she urged Ana the last few steps through the darkness to the clubhouse.

Ana had also been in a relationship the year before. The woman she lived with during that time was a hard butch who taught the impressionable girl to behave without questioning. Hard fists drove her lessons home. "Sure," she answered Traf diffidently as they swung through the clubhouse door into the lights and laughter, "later." She arranged her face in a bright smile and kept it there all night.

To Traf's pleased amazement, Ana was as good as her word. Michaela and Gabriela arrived shortly after, and once again the two couples shared a table. They enjoyed another wonderful evening full of dancing, chatting, and laughter. The butches were generous, buying drinks and treats for them all to share. Traf and Michaela also took a turn restocking food and beverages while Ana and Gabriela tended the bar, gladly serving their fellow club members.

They got along so well the four decided to meet up next Friday when the clubhouse opened again. Michaela and Traf would be busy during the week with their jobs on the base. Gabriela arranged to help Ana clean houses in Praia. They agreed to meet at the clubhouse; the two femmes would come together, and Michaela would bring Traf with her from the base.

As the entire group closed up their club that night, promises to meet next weekend filled the air. Everyone set off on their separate journeys home, careful no one walked alone. Ana and Traf waved good-bye as their two friends drove off in Michaela's blue VW.

Traf tucked her date's hand in the crook of her elbow, walking together under a beautiful night sky. Rather than heading straight for Ana's apartment, they strolled along the beach toward the port. The tide flowed out, pulling tired waves that scrabbled for purchase on the white sand before succumbing to the pull of the moon.

Traf took off her jacket and spread it on the sand for them to sit. "What is it you want me to know about your sister?" She leaned back on her elbows, legs stretched out to the sand.

"Natalie's a bully." Ana leaned back like Traf, staring straight ahead. "But maybe you've figured that out for yourself." She looked sideways at Traf, then up to the stars. "She's older than me three years, and after our parents married we shared a bed. Eventually our two little sisters were born. They kept my mother busy, so Nat and I were assigned the chores."

Ana tossed her head, a curl rising on the breeze. "She's lazy and left most of the work for me but would lie to her father that she'd done it all. Then he'd get mad and tell me to help out more. She'd always laugh about it during the night and pull my hair when I'd fall asleep, or pinch me if I didn't. I was so glad when she got the job with the Americans and moved out. Nothing changed for me as far as the work went, but at least I got credit for it."

The anger trailed away as she spoke, and now she snickered. "The Americans weren't so blind, though. The woman was a stricter chaperone than any of our aunts. Nat almost lost her job a couple of times for sneaking in late on her days off. And thanks to the American's own rules, her boyfriend didn't get any private time with her until their wedding night." Ana shrugged. "Anyway, she's a bitch and her husband's going to have to deal with her for the rest of their lives."

Thankfully, she didn't see the dark cloud swiftly cross Traf's face and disappear at the mention of Natalia's new husband. "At least I don't have to sleep with her."

She stared out to sea. "My parents aren't thrilled my only relationships have been with women but they've gradually grown accustomed to the idea. They figure I'll eventually straighten up and marry a man, the way God intends I should." Ana rose and brushed sand from her skirt. "Mom expects me to follow in Nat's footsteps." She held out a hand to help Traf up.

"Will you?" Traf tried to keep the intensity from her voice. "What'll they do if you don't?"

"Now that I've moved out, they'll probably never notice. My parents have eleven children; they are really too busy to worry, and too tired to care."

Several times as they strolled along, chatting about her past and their present, Traf pulled pretty Ana into dark shadows to swiftly steal a kiss. Each time, intense attraction surged between them. Hearts raced, pulses pounded, and lust surged.

Traf knew of only one place close by where she was sure they wouldn't be disturbed and persuaded Ana to climb before her up a ladder to the flat roof of a lobster pot storage shed. A stiff breeze blew in from the sea, whipping the femme's skirt around her legs as she climbed. Quick peeks of white panty flashed into and out of view.

The warm night air tugged at strands of Ana's hair, pulling them free from the neat bun at the nape of her neck as she sat, legs folded demurely under her on the cement rooftop. Traf reached over and tucked a loose strand behind her sculpted ear, then gently traced a line from earlobe to long velvety neck.

"Do I smell gardenias?"

Ana shivered delightfully and leaned in, tantalizingly eager, wide eyes twinkling in the moonlight. "Rose petals."

The throat under Traf's thumb contracted as her date swallowed. That sensation alone caused her loins to catch fire. The lovely girl's vulnerability and obvious desire fanned the flame throughout her body. She scooted closer as her eyes caught Ana's and held them.

Lowering them both until they lay flat, Traf leaned over and kissed her softly. "Do you want to?" she whispered into that delicately shaped ear. Her fingers picked up where she left off, trailing tender touches until they reached Ana's breast. She plucked the stiffening nipple through soft fabric, waiting for an answer.

"Yes, but," were the only words she heard. A sudden roaring in Traf's ears blocked whatever else Ana might have said. She pulled her hand away as if burned.

But? Her mind jumped from one conclusion to another. *She thinks I'm not good enough for her, just like her sister. This bitch is another lying, scheming, tease!*

Sitting up, she glared down at Ana. The younger woman cowered as if expecting a blow to land.

"If you don't want to, you don't have to. I won't force you." Traf ran the same hand of soft touches roughly through her hair, smoothing it back from her forehead. Standing up, she swung her leg over the edge of the roof and snapped, "It's not like I don't have other opportunities, you know. Save it for the worms, Ana. I'm not interested anymore."

Traf climbed down from the shed, pulled the ladder after her, and left it lying next to the building. She stalked away in the dark night, leaving a stunned Ana to her own devices.

Ch. 10 – They Are Us

On into Autumn, 1965

By the next morning, she'd calmed down a little and regretted leaving Ana up on the roof by herself. Her innate gallantry hated that she'd left a young woman to brave the night alone and unprotected. On the other hand her wounded pride crowed, vindictively glad she'd done it. She wondered what Ana would say to her on Friday when they met up at the club.

All week long, she discussed it with Michaela during their free time at the base. Since Traf's VIP driver courses were in a building close to the garage where her friend trained to be an auto mechanic, they met every day for lunch.

"Well," Michaela told her around a mouthful of Spam sandwich, a new American food they devoured with gusto, "I think you better forget all about Ana. She'll never speak to you, much less kiss you again, after you abandoned her up there." She finished her first sandwich and started on the second.

Traf chewed thoughtfully for a moment. "I bet she will. Femmes are different from us that way."

"Well," answered her best friend, "she's going all right, with my Gabriela. But from what I know about your Ana, she'll be expecting a big apology."

Michaela wasn't wrong. When they walked through the open door of Troublemakers, they found Ana and Gabriela, sitting together at the table they now thought of as their own. Ana's long beautiful hair was a full four inches taller than her friend's, teased up into a beehive that was the height of fashion. As the two butches strutted across the floor, Gabriela waved them over.

Traf uttered a polite and somewhat frosty hello to Ana. Making sure she was obvious about it, she looked over the other women in the room. Smiling and waving at a few of them, she took secret delight at the despair on Ana's face.

As Michaela swept Gabriela into the dancing, she nudged her friend as she went by, indicating the two quarrelers should speak privately. Traf walked over to the bar, bought two glasses of wine, and slid one across the table in Ana's general direction. Unwilling to be the one to break the silence between them, she lit a cigarette, crossed her arms over her chest, and leaned back in her chair.

Ana finally cleared her throat, and primly said, "I want to say, I forgive you."

Traf's face reddened as she turned to stare at Ana. "You forgive me?" she demanded. "Me? You forgive me?" She looked at the young woman's flushed face and shook her head. The best defense, she'd learned, was a good offense, so she pressed this one home. "I was the one who was teased. I was the one who was led to believe something would happen." She pitched her voice in a sardonic, mincing imitation of Ana, "Yes, I want you, but…!"

She shook her head once more and said again, "But! You're a tease, and you'll take that ice cold pussy of yours to the grave with you!" A little shocked by her own language, she nevertheless noted the triumphant delight in Ana's eyes. If she wanted to play that way, Traf could be accommodating.

Later in the evening, Ana mentioned a need to use the outhouse and asked if Traf would like to go with her. By that time, they had drunk several glasses of wine, and since she needed to go as well, Traf agreed.

As she opened the door of the two-seater, Ana grabbed Traf by the arm and pulled her in, the darkness lightened only by a low-burning lamp. Surprised, she struggled with Ana playfully, careful not to hurt her. Their lips met in a hard kiss, which neither moved to stop. Desire sparked between them.

Ana took Traf's hand and placed it on her breast. "I won't say no this time," she whispered into her ear. "Try me." Her hand pressed Traf's more deeply into her flesh, encouraging her.

"I'll think about it," the cocky butch answered coolly, disengaging herself. After doing what they'd come for, she escorted Ana back to their table. Then Traf crossed the floor to a young femme and asked her to dance. She felt the heat of Ana's eyes as she chatted with pretty Lucy in her arms. An exhilarating sense of power pulsed through her.

That evening almost no one waited until midnight to leave. Michaela and Gabriela, Ana and Traf volunteered to do the cleaning up and closing. Soon left alone in the emptied clubhouse, the two femmes washed up the few dirty glasses still left and wiped down tables while the butches disposed of trash and swept the floor. A much easier job now that the linens had been put away for special occasions and people drank beer from bottles, they finished swiftly. Turning off the lights and locking up, Ana and Traf once again stood waving to their friends as they drove off in the familiar VW.

Ana started to walk up the street but stopped when she found Traf wasn't following her. Instead, the contrary butch was unlocking the door of the clubhouse again. Opening it, she playfully waved Ana back inside, one finger over her lips.

Leaving the lights off and relocking the door, Traf pulled Ana into her arms and kissed her, hard. Using both hands, she framed the girl's beautiful face, holding it close to her own, and said clearly, "What do you want?" Traf searched soulful dark eyes for any sign of trepidation.

In answer, Ana lowered her eyelids and raised her lips, expecting a kiss. When nothing happened, she re-opened her eyes. It was evident Traf was not going to do anything until Ana spoke, so she finally said, her voice throaty with desire, "I want you. Don't make me beg."

Traf kissed her then, letting her tongue travel sensually inside her mouth. Taking Ana by the hand, she led her to the raised dance floor and they sat beside each other on its edge. Kissing, again and again, they nestled into each other. Traf scooted them back from the edge and slowly undid the tiny white buttons running along the back of Ana's dress. She lowered Ana onto her back, then leaned over to cover her in kisses again.

With one hand, she pulled the dress free of Ana's shoulders until only a cotton bra separated her from skin. She fastened her teeth over the soft material and bit gently.

Ana shuddered, then moaned as she grabbed Traf's head and pulled her face close. While kissing, she rolled to one side long enough to undo her bra, then lifted her arms as it was pulled from her. Lying on the dance floor half-naked, she watched Traf lower her head. She sighed as tidal waves of pleasure washed over her.

Raking her fingers through Traf's curls, she tightened them convulsively. At the first touch to her knee, she gasped slightly, then moaned as Traf's hand rose along her smooth thigh.

Taking her time, enjoying the delectable flavor of the younger woman's skin, Traf nibbled and teased her breasts, pausing at intervals to kiss Ana's parted lips. She tasted of wine and fresh fruit.

Trailing her hand up and down Ana's thighs, she enjoyed the tiny sounds of pleasure escaping from the woman lying beneath her. Traf let her fingers play wickedly across the white cotton of Ana's panties, over and around her hips, back and forth from navel to crotch. She slipped her fingers under the elastic waistband and pulled them down to Ana's knees in one fluid motion, enjoying the girl's gasp.

Traf was thrilled when Ana arched her back and parted her legs, inviting her in. She smiled into her neck as she rubbed the sensitive mound with her hand, finding the sweet spot she'd so far only heard about, and concentrated there. As Ana rocked under her hand, she slowly inserted the tip of her finger. Any more, and she might break her hymen, something all unmarried women avoided with horror.

It was enough. Ana moaned under her hand and began undulating her hips back and forth in pleasure. The sight of Ana below her delighted Traf's eyes, the girl's moans filled her ears, and the scent of womanly arousal tantalized her senses. Her palm ground gently, rhythmically into Ana's velvety mound. The gentle friction finally dissolved the young woman into a convulsive climax, not just once, but twice.

With each of Ana's orgasms, Traf felt the pressure of promises build inside her, right down the center of her belly. It was intense, more driving than she'd ever felt before. Waves of tension built and lessened, growing stronger moment by moment. She felt constrained, enslaved to the pleasure, yet unable to find release.

She wouldn't let it matter, however. Traf wouldn't allow Ana to return the favor even if she offered, which she didn't. It was an unspoken part of the Troublemakers culture they were creating for themselves that butches controlled the lovemaking. They took pride in never submitting to the touch of a femme. They told each other they received pleasure from the orgasms of their partners, and the satisfied femmes seemed more than happy to accept that explanation. It evolved wordlessly among them that the greater the sexual tension the butches attained, the better lovers they were.

After cuddling a bit, she helped Ana sit up and gather her clothing back around her. As she fastened the buttons she had undone earlier, she felt an unusual tenderness overwhelm her. Traf leaned down and kissed Ana's shoulder.

They spent a languid eternity just lying in each other's arms, kissing and talking in the small hours of the morning in the warm darkness of their clubhouse. Finally they left, making sure to lock up tight. Traf walked Ana home possessively, kissed her goodnight at her door, and arranged to meet the next night at the clubhouse, the first Saturday Troublemakers would be open. Then, because the busses stopped running at midnight, she spent the next hour walking back to Lajes. She thought about her beautiful Ana the whole way home, every step as light as her heart.

When Michaela's blue bug pulled up to the clubhouse the next night, however, that mood was broken, shattered to pieces. Brutes had broken every window, and the door was kicked in, now hanging loosely from broken hinges. Teresa, Tina, Margarida, and Alex were already there, and the shocked foursome gingerly picked their way through the glass shards littering the ground to meet the newcomers.

"Inside?" asked Michaela, without any real hope.

"Some of the girls are in there now. They got that too. Everything's busted all to hell. There's nothing much left," answered Teresa hopelessly. The tall butch kicked the ground. "They pissed and shit everywhere, and used it to write on the walls." No one asked what had been written.

"They stole the wine and beer too," remarked Tina sourly. "Not a bottle left anywhere, broken or otherwise. And they bashed every lightbulb in the place."

Traf stared at Ana in horror as she realized the timing. The thought of what would have happened to them if they'd stayed longer made her stomach clench. Her hands followed suit.

They all traipsed inside, righted the few chairs that weren't broken and assessed the damage. Nothing escaped the rage unleashed on the place. Smashed tables tilted on broken legs and torn curtains drooped in broken windows. The savage bastards even attacked the beautiful bar; insulting words gouged into its battered surface marred the wood. The mirror once hung with such pride now lay shattered, pieces glittering among the shards of china and glassware. Electrical wiring hung from the ceiling, yanked from its power. The dance floor, so studiously protected from their shoes, had yielded easily to ax and hoe.

As the rest of the group assembled, they met inside around the light of a kerosene lamp Berta brought to light her way home. Seeing so many long faces kept the silence ominous. A few femmes wept outright, but Traf noticed most of the butches faced the tragedy differently. During the planning stage of the clubhouse, they had discussed something like this happening. It did, and that was that. Most faced it with stoicism, most that is, but not all.

Berta couldn't control herself. She growled at the splintered dance floor so lovingly laid by her father. Then swollen red with rage, she turned on the once beautiful bar she'd been so proud to help provide. She kicked it, not once or twice, but repeatedly, compulsively.

Her foot put into motion their trauma, the shame and degradation they all shared. They watched her roar and kick for several long minutes until one by one they turned away from her impotent anger. No one could face the raw nakedness of her emotion lest it strip them of their own control.

Only Rita, her round pretty face drawn, stayed. She slipped a comforting arm around the small butch's waist, loaning her strength until Berta regained her composure and reminding her through the humanizing power of touch that she was not a freak, not something to be casually destroyed and left in pieces like the bar lying in front of them.

Long before Troublemakers became a reality, Traf noticed the femmes usually soothed the pain inflicted by the world on butches, physical and otherwise. When the butches came to the fire at night with their raw wounds of body or spirit, the femmes nurtured them, helped them heal. The softer women appreciated the butches and in a world that universally disparaged them, that, in itself, became a gift most rare and precious. They soothed raging spirits with gentle acceptance, complimenting butches on their too often underrated abilities. The femmes make it possible to keep going day after day. Their company provided a safe harbor for the butches who unrelentingly fought their way upstream.

The Troublemakers gave themselves one night to rant and rave, stomping around in the ruins, shouting and demanding retribution. They shook their fists at the darkness outside the broken windows. They wondered aloud if God were punishing them for their behavior. They whined about being different and unable to do anything about it. Finally, Michaela drove to a bar in town and brought back several bottles of wine and a case of beer. They drank together and complained until midnight.

Sunday morning, they put all that aside and showed up en masse to help with the cleanup. They swept up broken glass, removed broken furniture to see if it could be repaired or needed to be replaced. Rubber gloves were donned and disinfectant scrubbed into the fouled walls. Teresa and Michaela tinkered with the stove and refrigerator, managing to get them running again. Ana and Gabriela repaired the curtains.

On Monday, Traf left home early to make a report with the Praia police. Wearing her US fatigues, she looked out of place in the two-hundred-year-old building. Men in their police uniforms stared openly at her, leering brazenly and making crude gestures to one another. "I want to report a crime," she said with all the dignity she could muster. The men turned away, ignoring her.

She approached a man seated behind a desk. Police Chief Angelo Delgado, in early middle-age, had thinning hair that lay flat and lifeless in the heat. A single bead of sweat dripped into cold eyes that glared with recognition and disgust. "Our clubhouse was vandalized," Traf said. "I want to file a complaint."

"Against who?" he asked. A blank form lay on the desk, but he made no move to pick up a pen.

"I don't know who did it. I want you to find out who it was and make them pay for the damages."

"That new women's club, right?" Police Chief Delgado used the sleeve of his uniform to wipe his forehead. "It was bound to happen sooner or later. Inevitable, really."

Laughter rose all around her. After it stopped, she bit her lip. "A crime has been committed. You're the police. Do something about it."

Delgado rose from his desk and walked past her as if she weren't there, tossing over his shoulder, "You got what was coming to you." This time the laughter drove her from the police station.

She returned to the base in Lajes, relieved to be back among the Americans. She admired their rules and regulations, the structure of command and responsibility. *They'll see that justice is done.* Then she remembered Sgt. Vincente's prying and knew she couldn't tell anyone on base. While her commanders knew about the clubhouse, they didn't know it was a lesbian club. Asking for help would lead to an investigation, and possibly a black letter. That would destroy any chance of her escaping this lonely rock in the vast, uncaring ocean.

She told her friends there was no help coming; they were on their own, as always. It took another three weeks before the Troublemakers managed to replace everything that was broken. They started up a collection, borrowed money from relatives, and took odd jobs to replace the windows and doors, tables, chairs, and glassware. Margarida even bought a book in Angra and, following its directions, rewired the electricity. Lydia and her girl, Mary Jo, bought a smaller and less impressive mirror but hung it with justifiable pride once more over the bar.

When Mr. Borba heard from his daughter about the ruination of the clubhouse, he spent every extra hour he could steal from his carpentry job, repairing first the dance floor and then the bar, diligently sanding away the damage and polishing them to a high shine. "You're the best," Berta told her father when he finished. "The bar looks better now than it did when we first bought it!"

She hugged him right there in front of all of them, a rarity since she'd become an adult. Volumes of unspoken love passed between them in that instant. Traf knew as she watched, it was a moment both would cherish ever afterward.

Each Friday afternoon to Sunday night, they met to work. After the sun went down they plugged in the phonograph, which had been miraculously repaired, and played new records purchased to replace the broken ones. Spirits were high as they patched and refurbished. They had anticipated this and it happened. Now they could move on and forget it.

One afternoon during the renovation process, they repainted the walls of the large room. Traf felt good wearing a pair of jeans she'd purchased at the PX and an oversized old shirt she'd gotten from Johnny. She rolled the sleeves up to her biceps and tucked a pack of Pall Mall menthols, for the femmes, in one and the L&Ms she smoked herself in the other. She was thinking Ana looked cute painting the ceiling in her crisp white blouse covered with tiny embroidered strawberries, when Linda, who was goofing around with Margarida, tripped and knocked into the ladder. The paint can sitting on top flew into the air, spun around in an arc, and rained paint all over Ana as she fell. She wasn't hurt, but it didn't take much to see she was upset that her new shirt was ruined. Linda and Margarida kept apologizing and offering to pay for it. Ana accepted their apology but refused their efforts to give her money. Still, her lip quivered a little as she mopped up the wet paint with a rag.

It happened Traf had been lucky the night before. She still helped out on Capt. Mark's boat when he needed an extra hand and had caught a large eel, which brought a pretty price from restaurants that served it as a delicacy. The extra money was still in her pocket and almost as an afterthought she gave her new girlfriend the money. "Here, take this and replace your blouse."

"Oh, thank you, Traf." Ana held in her hand more than a week's pay. To her mind, this meant their relationship was becoming serious. "I'll make the most of it. Your money won't be wasted."

"I'll look forward to seeing what you do with it," Traf answered, winking saucily. They settled back into painting and with everyone pitching in they finished in record time. No more goofing around.

Every weekend night, after working on the clubhouse, they made love in Ana's apartment. In the dark, noiselessly so as not to alert the neighbors, Traf used her talented fingers to pleasure her lover over and over again. They allowed themselves only stifled moans to express their loving. Lying in the dark afterward, they cuddled until drifting off to sleep. Traf always woke while it was still dark so she could walk from Praia to Lajes and slip back into her bedroom before her parents rose at dawn. They never cared how late she stayed out at night, as long as she rose ready to work without having to be called the next morning.

Saturday, the fourteenth of August, was Troublemakers' Reopening Night and Traf arranged to pick Ana up at eight o'clock. She arrived right on time but in a foul mood. It had not been a good day for her. Since passing her exams and being certified she drove a lot, going back and forth between locations, hauling officers around the island on their Very Important Personal business. Most of the officers who visited Terceira were nice, polite, and professional, but the ones she drove around that day were curt, rude, and presumptuous. One of them, a colonel from stateside, ordered her to deviate from her designated course. When she politely refused until she could check in with her C.O., the colonel complained about her attitude. Written up for following orders, she fumed all the way home.

To top it off, when she got there her father was drunk, ranting and raving that an American car crushed one of his puppies, newly weaned from its mother. When she came through the door in her uniform he flew into a rage. It always served to remind him how he'd been tricked into signing permission for her to join the US Air Force. He cuffed her ear as she passed going to her room. It rang for several minutes before she heard clearly again.

Exasperated, in a mood to take offense, when Ana opened the door wearing a new dress Traf's mind flashed to Natalia standing in front of her in a similar garment, laughing at her. Just like her sister's gown, Ana's sexy black dress fit like a glove and accentuated all her curves. Suddenly transported to the night of her final confrontation with Natalia, Traf began suffocating with the degradation and shame of it.

She snapped, leaping to the conclusion that Ana received the obviously expensive dress from another lover, probably a male lover. Unchecked fury raged through her and without understanding what she was doing she reached out, grabbed Ana's dress at the neckline, and yanked hard, ripping it straight down the front.

Ana stared at her in horror, clutching at the tattered remnants of the outfit she'd been so proud of only moments before. She gasped, then slammed and locked her door as Traf stormed off to the clubhouse alone.

She drank heavily until well and truly drunk. When a tearful Ana showed up half an hour later on her own, a group of protective femmes quickly surrounded her. Every time one of them threw a nasty glance her way, Traf tossed down another glass of wine. Unhappy to begin with, by the time the club closed for the evening, she was maudlin. "Women," she'd tell anyone who'd listen, "you can't trust 'em." Michaela, as a best friend should, poured Traf into the backseat of her car and drove her home.

On the way, Gabriela took the opportunity to scold her. She'd heard the whole story by now, several different versions actually, and she was vehement in her friend's defense. "You gave her the money for that dress two weeks ago, you idiot. Don't you remember?"

"What're you talking about?" Traf mumbled, much the worse for wear.

"You gave her money to replace a blouse, remember?" Gabriela insisted until Traf's whirling head finally fixated on her words. "You told her you caught an eel and had extra cash. She said you insisted she take it, so she did. She spent that money on material."

Twisting around so she could face the back seat, Gabriela continued relentlessly. "She worked so hard on that dress! I should know; I helped her make it. And now it's ruined. Absolutely ruined." She flounced back around to face the dark road before her. "Damned butch."

Slowly the truth began to permeate Traf's sodden brain cells. She'd made a mistake, a really big one. Through the pounding in her head she tried to assess the damage, but that was impossible. It wasn't until the next day, sitting in her regular pew, ignoring the Mass and feeling distinctly unwell, that she finally put all the pieces together.

Still wearing her finest skirt and blouse, she went straight from church to Ana's apartment. After knocking several times Ana finally opened the door, her eyes bruised from a night of crying.

"What do you want?" she demanded, tears springing up. "Do you want to ruin this one too?" She grabbed the neck of the dress she wore to church on Sundays and tugged on it.

Traf reached out and stopped her hand, bringing it slowly to her lips. She kissed Ana's fist and gently uncurled the clenched fingers. "I want to apologize, Ana. May I come in, please?"

Ana crossed her arms over her chest and stood back, allowing her to pass. "Go ahead," she said, coolly. She stalked away from Traf still standing just inside the door, and plopped down on her couch. Hands clasped together in her lap, she waited with legs crossed, the top one jiggling.

"I am so sorry for destroying your beautiful dress." Traf cleared her throat nervously. "I don't know what happened, but when you opened the door looking so beautiful, all sexy and desirable, well, it looked a lot like the dress your sister was wearing the night she told me she was married."

Traf flinched under Ana's furious glare, shifting from one foot to the other. "You ripped my dress because it 'looked like' one Natalia wore once?" Her voice became harsh, ready to fight. "What is wrong with you?"

"I am trying to tell you," Traf said earnestly. She sat gingerly on the edge of the couch, facing Ana. "Natalia wore that dress to taunt me because he bought it for her. She wanted me to know that she was leaving my world behind and embracing his world." She rubbed her eyes with one hand. "It was a symbol of how she used me. That dress was the flag she flew announcing her new citizenship in the world of men. More than anything else, it told me, 'You're not good enough. She needs a man.' I hated that dress as much as I hated her right then."

Ana was listening. Traf hurried on, forging a bridge over awkward silence. "When I saw you in that wonderful, sexy, black dress last night, I didn't remember the stupid eel or giving you any money. All of a sudden I knew you had a male lover. I knew it, Ana," she insisted. "Don't ask me how I knew; I just knew it beyond any doubt."

"I sewed that dress with material I bought myself. I used the money you gave me when my blouse was ruined."

"I know that now." Traf nodded. "Gabriela told me on the ride home last night." She wiped her hand over her eyes again, trying to erase the memory. "Please forgive me. I know you're not Natalia."

"No," answered Ana firmly, enjoying the miserable butch's chagrin. She paused a long moment before continuing, "No, I am not my sister. I told you that once before."

"Yes, yes, you did." Traf nodded again, head bowed. "I'd like to give you twice the amount I gave you before. It's the least I can do, considering." She reached into her skirt pocket and pulled out some crumpled bills. Thrusting them into Ana's hand she continued, "Use this to buy new material or anything else you might want. Please forgive me for treating you so disrespectfully."

She waited to hear what Ana would say. The pretty young woman eyed the money in her hand, noticing it was well over twice what Traf had given her before. "This is too much," she protested, scowling, thrusting the bundle back at her. "And you'll probably just forget that you gave it to me anyway. Why should I invite more trouble?" Ana wasn't quite ready to let bygones be bygones.

Traf gently pushed her hand back. "It's nowhere near enough. There are no words to explain how sorry I am that I hurt you. I have to make do with money." She smiled sheepishly at Ana. "I won't forget this time, I promise."

"This is the last time I will forgive you for assuming I am anything like my sister," Ana stated unequivocally. She finally relented as she pocketed the money. "If you ever make this mistake again, it's over between us. I have too much respect for myself to let you compare me to Natalia." She set her mouth in so firm a line it made Traf wonder what words would pass between the two sisters the next time they met.

She sighed with relief. Looking into Ana's eyes, Traf took her hand once more and raised it to her lips. She kissed it tenderly, her bright eyes blazing as she whispered hoarsely, "Thank you, my love. I won't let you regret it."

A silence fell comfortably around the word 'love'. It was the first time they used the word between them and neither wished to disturb its gentle birth. They kissed contentedly, then made lazy love as the evening darkened around them. As Traf left to catch the last bus back to Lajes, they arranged to meet the following weekend at the clubhouse. She went home with a much lighter heart, envisioning a bright future.

On Wednesday she received a visit. Of course, her whole family knew she worked at the American base and wore the uniform of an American soldier, a topic of many heated discussions. They also knew she made American wages, much more than they made.

Tio Salvador knocked on their door shortly after dinner. Father greeted him, while her mother poured each brother a glass of wine and left the bottle on the table. Traf sat in her bedroom, reading one of the half-dozen books she checked out from the bookmobile that came to Lajes once a month. She often read late into the night, paying for her own kerosene to keep her father from complaining about the cost of the light.

She was surprised when her mother knocked on her door, asking that she join them in the kitchen. Her uncle Sal, her father's youngest brother, was in his mid-forties and the father of five children. Traf nodded in greeting as she entered the warm room, grabbing an apple to feed her ever-hungry stomach as she sat at the table. She looked from her uncle to her father, then back again.

Sal cleared his throat. "I want to borrow money, niece. Your cousin Tristan needs an operation. It's an expensive one, but if he has it, he will walk again." A few years back a horse kicked her young cousin, shattering his lower leg. They'd been told he would never walk again, a tragic fate for anyone much less a ten-year-old boy.

"That's wonderful news, Tio. I'm so happy for you, and Tristan."

Sal ignored her words and carried on. "I've already tried the bank, but they refused me. No one else has the amount I need for the surgeon, except you. I've already asked your father and he gives his permission for you to lend it to me. Will you, Vitória?" His voice held a note of desperation. Obviously she was his last hope and even though it burned him to come crawling to a woman, much less his wayward niece, he loved his son that much and wanted him to have a future that didn't involve begging. He would do what begging needed doing.

Traf's eyebrows rose in surprise. "Of course Uncle," she answered instantly. Mom tried to hide a smile of pride. Father scowled at his glass of wine, resentful his daughter could supply what he could not. Heedless of both, Traf asked, "How much do you need?"

They sat at the kitchen table talking about the operation for several hours. Traf joined the men in drinking wine at the table and made sure to pour a glass for her mother as well. In the end she loaned her uncle over five hundred American dollars, a huge sum of money. With few expenses while living at home her paychecks accumulated in her bank account. She was glad to give it to him, even knowing he had no way of paying her back.

The next day she met Tio Salvador at the bank and withdrew the money for him. He, in turn, presented her with a proposition and the deed to an old run down house he'd been slowly renovating over the last ten years, only a few blocks from the base.

"If you're willing, Vitória," her uncle offered, "I'll be glad to repay you by repairing that house, fixing it up so you can sell it for a profit. That's what I was going to do with it if this chance for Tristan hadn't come along."

Traf turned over in her mind his gracious offer. He worked for a contractor whose business was building and repairing houses. He probably did not have the money to buy the supplies necessary to finish repairing the house, or he would have done it by now. At the same time, he'd spent a decade painstakingly fixing it. With all that time to consider exactly what needed to be done, he knew the costs down to the last cent. This might very well work to her advantage.

"How soon could you have it fixed and ready to live in?" she asked, pretending to consider.

"If I buy the materials, about a year. If you buy the materials, I can have it ready in two months."

She looked her uncle in the eye, knowing that both estimates pushed him to his human limits. "I'll buy what you need. Give me a list in priority order and I'll get it for you as I can." They shook hands solemnly, a binding contract just like the old days.

Tristan flew to the mainland a few days later with his father. At a big hospital in Lisbon, the little boy's surgeon worked miracles. By the end of

August, he hobbled around in a plaster cast that covered him from thigh to toe. By the end of September, he took his first steps in two years without help, his face beaming with pride as his arms wind-milled to keep him balanced. Tristan's future took a dramatic turn upward. He could go to school again. He would have a job and be able to work in the fields to feed a family. He would grow up to be a free man, instead of a crippled dependent.

It made Traf's heart sing to hear of her young cousin's steady improvement, relishing her ability to solve people's problems. She felt strong and powerful in a way only the young, or young at heart, ever experience.

The crisp autumn days proceeded from yellows and golds to oranges and reds, and finally the browns, all the colors of the harvest. The rainy season would start soon, limiting outdoor work. Tio Sal took time off from his regular job and poured himself into his work on her house, determined to give back as much as humanly possible. He worked every minute of every day he could. When not harvesting the crops in the fields he leased to feed his family through the winter, he worked on the house. His three oldest sons pitched in, and the work proceeded apace.

Sal Mendes, an astute man, knew times were changing in the town of Lajes. Some American soldiers began looking for houses to buy or rent for their families while stationed on the island of Terceira. But they only looked at modern houses; Americans needed their conveniences. Just down the street from the base, this house would be a hot property once it was brought up to date.

He and his sons added on a bathroom with a flushing toilet, running hot and cold water in a sink, and luxury of luxuries both a tub and a shower. In the kitchen they installed a deeper sink plus a gas range and oven. He ran electricity to the house and installed light fixtures in every room. A refrigerator stood proudly humming against one wall of the kitchen. Her uncle Sal replaced the windows, enlarging them to let in more sunlight. He paved and set tiles on the veranda, creating a pleasant place to sit and visit with neighbors.

His boys spent the last half of September and the first part of the next month painting the house inside and out, then buffing and polishing the wood floor to a high shine. Artie combed the island to find attractive pieces of furniture and negotiated to buy them at bargain prices. He bought three iron-frame spring-and-mattress beds from the base, putting one in each of the bedrooms. A new hand-woven rug covered much of the floor in the main room. Finally, it was finished.

The twenty-first of October, two months from the day he'd borrowed the money, he sent young Tristan, walking on his own two feet, to the base. The boy waited for Traf outside the gate and asked her to walk with him to the house. The first time she'd seen her young cousin since his operation, his smile of joy matched hers as he took her hand and led her down the street.

In that way of mid-autumn, the crisp air held the hint of winter nipping gently underneath. Uncle Sal watched her filling her lungs with the clean, clear scent of it, his unorthodox niece still dressed in her man's uniform. He saw her swing hands with his youngest son, listening as the boy told her all about his operation.

It would be Traf's first sight of the house since she and her uncle shook hands back in August. As they walked, slowly to accommodate Tristan's still halting steps, Sal could almost see her wondering whether she'd make more profit renting the house or selling it outright. But he'd been anticipating her look of surprise, and she didn't disappoint him. His niece stopped dead in her tracks when they finally came to the house, blinking her eyes in astonished disbelief.

Where before was a small, sad, obviously neglected shack, there now stood a gleaming home, picture perfect and absolutely modern. The autumn sunset threw a rosy hue on the whitewashed walls, and the new windows winked like old friends sharing a joke. Sal stood beaming on the veranda, surrounded by his three oldest sons. As they approached, he threw his arm around Tristan's shoulders and indicated the house. "It's finished. You can sell it, or rent it, or even move into it yourself whenever you're ready."

His words rang in her ears like church bells on a Sunday morning. "Move into it myself," she whispered, looking at the masterpiece her uncle and cousins had created. "It's," she paused, at a loss for words that could adequately express her admiration. "It's …elegant," she finished, still unsure she'd conveyed her meaning.

Ten-year-old Tristan eagerly grabbed her hand and tugged her inside. Then his three brothers and father all bustled after them, proudly showing her their work. Room after room impressed her more, and she lavished them with praise. "Truly Tio," she enthused, "you should leave your boss. You and the boys should own your own business. God has given you a talent that shouldn't be wasted." They stayed with her for a short while longer, then Sal gave her the keys to the front door and herded his family home for dinner. It would be the first time in two months that he would stay around his own hearth in the evening. He'd missed his wife, but now they could relax debt-free and enjoy the sight of their youngest boy walking.

Standing alone in the living room, she took stock of her property. When she gave the money to her uncle, it never occurred to her that she would end up with such a wonderful gift. A home of her own. She could sell it and pocket the money or rent it and establish a second income as a landlord. Or… dared she think it? *I could move into a home of my own with no husband to take care of and answer to. My own home.*

She stayed until long after dark, enjoying the electric lights that turned off and on with a switch. She imagined sweet Ana cooking in the modern kitchen, and the two of them sitting on an evening out on the veranda. Dreams of making sweet, slow love in a bedroom of their own filled her mind's eye. She would be within walking distance of the base; it would save her time and money getting to work. Everything fell into place, making perfect sense.

The next night, she showed up at Ana's apartment, as agreed. They planned to go to a cinema in Lajes and see an American film, something they enjoyed occasionally. They both had their favorite stars. Ana adored Katherine Hepburn while Traf preferred Elizabeth Taylor. Tonight they were going to see The Philadelphia Story. By now, her command of English helped her translate much of the dialogue for Ana, and anyone else lucky enough to sit nearby.

They rode from Praia to Lajes where she grabbed Ana's arm and hustled her off the packed bus several stops before the cinema. "What are you doing?" the young woman asked as Traf bustled her through the closing door. "Why are we here?" Ana looked up to see the base. "Did you forget something?"

"No," Traf answered, heading up the street. "I just felt like walking the last few blocks. Do you mind?"

Ana looked at her curiously but easily kept pace with the shorter butch's stride. The crowded bus moved slowly from stop to stop, they were young and healthy, and it was a beautiful brisk evening. "No," she answered honestly. "It's a great idea."

They walked companionably for a few blocks until Traf saw her house coming up. Grabbing Ana's hand, she pulled her through the veranda gate.

"Whose house is this?" asked Ana, surprised to find herself there.

"Let's go inside," Traf insisted, opening the unlocked door and walking in, pulling Ana behind her.

"Wait! We can't!" She tried to back out, but Traf held her hand and tugged her into the main room.

"What do you think of this house?" she asked, mischievously.

"It's a beautiful house," answered Ana, glancing apprehensively around. "What if someone is home?" she asked.

"Then we'll say hello," Traf answered easily, flipping the switch that turned on the electric light fixture and pulling her into the kitchen.

"Oh!" was all that escaped Ana as she saw the refrigerator, stove, and sink with running water. She stood there in admiring silence, forgetting for a moment that they were trespassing. "What a beautiful kitchen," she cooed, her fingers trailing along the water faucet longingly.

"Come back here," Traf urged, tugging her down a hallway. "I want you to see the bathroom."

"What's a bathroom?" asked Ana, quick on Traf's heels, finally letting her curiosity carry her farther into the house.

"This is a bathroom." Traf flung open a door. Gleaming electric light reflected from a spotless window into a room of lustrous white porcelain. Ana oohed and ahhed, asking what everything did. She laughed with delight when the shower was explained to her. She even tried flushing the toilet, watching in fascination as the water swirled around the bowl.

Ana looked up to see Traf leaving the small bathroom. Hurrying to keep up, and abruptly afraid they would be found, she started for the front door. But Traf walked past the main room and into another.

"Hey," Ana hissed. "Let's get out of here before they get home!"

"Come here and look at this!" Traf called to her from inside the room, and the electric gleam of a lightbulb winked on. Ana glanced anxiously over her shoulder toward the door once more but obligingly joined her in the large bedroom.

"Look at this," Traf crowed. She had pushed two beds together earlier. She sat down and patted the huge bed covered with an American blanket. "Come here and feel this mattress!"

Ana gingerly sat down next to her, growing a little scandalized as Traf leaned over and kissed her, once, twice, and with the third one pushed her down to lie on the bed. She began to struggle as she felt Traf's hands roaming over her clothing. "Stop that!" she snapped. "We'll get caught!"

"No, we won't," Traf murmured as she nuzzled Ana's shoulder, unbuttoning the top button of her blouse. She grinned down at her lover when Ana grabbed her hand, keeping her from continuing with the next button.

"How do you know that?" demanded Ana, becoming exasperated with her girlfriend's casual attitude. "How do you know they won't come home?"

"Because 'they' are us. This house is yours, if you want it," Traf answered with a shrug. "We *are* home."

Ana sat up and blinked at Traf as her words sank in. "Wh… wait… what?"

"Do you want this house?" she pressed. "Would you like to live here with me?"

Ana jumped up from the bed. She looked around the room, finally noticing one of Traf's uniforms hanging in the otherwise empty closet. "You mean you *own* this house?" she asked incredulously.

Traf nodded her head, proudly. "Yes, it's mine. Ours, if you'll live here with me." She took both of Ana's hands in hers and gazed lovingly into her eyes. "Will you, Ana?"

A shower of kisses rained down upon her face, neck, hands, and finally her lips for an answer. Their love ignited into youthful lust in moments, all thoughts of Katherine Hepburn completely burned from their fevered bodies. They made love in their own bed in their own house and there was nowhere else in the entire world either would rather be. They spent the night planning a home of their own.

In the morning, Traf showed Ana how to work the rest of the plumbing, the gas stove, and the electrical fixtures. They spent the afternoon moving in their few possessions. With Major Brandon's permission, Traf borrowed a van from the base and used it to drive back and forth with clothing, books, and supplies.

Ana's tiny apartment emptied easily, requiring only one run. When they returned home, she made up the double bed with some of the sheets, softly scented with floral sachets she had been embroidering her whole life in preparation for a wedding night that would never come. Then she put some food staples away in the cupboards. Her clothing and sewing kit made up the totality of her possessions.

Traf's parents watched in silence as the two girls traipsed through their house. She hugged them both, briefly, and wished them well. If Traf didn't know her better, she might think she saw a tear in her mother's eye. Her father maintained a stern, disapproving silence.

The girls made first one, and then a second run, carrying out armloads of uniforms and books. As they secured the last of Traf's possessions in the van, preparing to take the final load to their new home, her mother walked up. She handed Ana a gunnysack filled with white flour, a bottle of homemade red wine, and a small bag of freshly roasted peanuts, gifts for their new home.

"My trafulha," she murmured, leaning up on tiptoe to kiss her daughter on the forehead. "God bless you." Traf hugged her mother briefly, eager to begin her life as an independent adult, but respecting her mother's nostalgic reluctance.

"I'll be right by the base," Traf whispered. "We'll see each other all the time."

"Be productive, be happy…" Mom blessed them under her breath, watching and waving as the two young women climbed into the big automobile and drove away. Only she heard her husband, who stood in the doorway.

"Be safe."

Ana and Traf spent all Sunday, after early Mass of course, in bed, shutters closed against the windows and no lights on anywhere. They made love again and again, luxuriating in the safety of their locked doors and windows. Soft skins whispered against each other, delighting the senses and intensifying their relationship.

That afternoon as they lay together, they discussed plans for the future. Traf would be coming up for promotion to First Lieutenant soon, and that would mean the beginning of overseas duty for her. She would be gone for extended periods of time in various countries, often with little or no prior notice. They discussed how to keep the house running during her absences.

She had no worry about Ana's ability to care for things while she was gone. Even though her lover was a year younger, she had proved herself good at money management when they put the clubhouse together. Ana impressed her more than once with her financial acumen. It was convincing her she could do it that turned out to be difficult.

Sixteen years old now, Ana was fifteen when she had her first relationship with a woman. Antonia, Tony she called herself, was a hard butch, one who went by a man's name and dressed like a man all the time. She sometimes beat Ana, often berating her for being stupid and ignorant. The colors from the bruises had faded with time, but they stained her soul. Nestled in Traf's protective arms, Ana confessed her fear of failure, of being unable to live up to expectations. She was convinced she could achieve nothing.

Close to midnight, Ana told Traf a secret dream she'd cherished for years. She knew she had some talent at sewing, and what she wanted more than anything was to go to a school for domestic arts taught by professionals. A school like that existed in the city of Angra do Heroismo, a short bus ride away, but she couldn't manage the tuition on what she made cleaning houses. "And besides," she admitted miserably, "I'd just fail anyway."

"I'll pay for your schooling," Traf stated, hugging her closely. When Ana only shook her head, she lectured her, "You need to have a career of your own, and I have the money for your education. A woman today," she went on, "needs an education to get along in this world."

Ana looked at her in amazement. Having brought the subject up as nothing more than a lost dream, within moments, it became attainable. She blinked, unable to quite comprehend what happened. She stared up at her lover with those bottomless eyes Traf loved so well and asked, "Am I really lying in my own bed, in my own house, being offered the chance I'd only dreamed of? Is there anything you can't do?"

Traf smoothed her hair. "Plenty, I'm afraid. Still, it'll keep you busy and out of trouble while I'm gone," she teased. "There won't be any butches teaching those classes in sewing and cooking, I guarantee you!" They both dissolved into laughter and snuggled into each other's arms.

Ana fell asleep with her head safely pillowed on Traf's shoulder, listening to her lover's heartbeat sing her to sleep.

That week, Traf took Ana to the bank and added her to the bank account. She was free to take what she needed for tuition and to run the household. The bank teller showed Ana how to fill out a check, and how to record her expenditures. She listened earnestly, learned well, and became so diligent and good at keeping the books that before long Traf began turning over her paycheck every month, leaving the bill paying and shopping to her.

Pride in her newfound accomplishments made Ana bloom, but several of Traf's butch buddies called her henpecked because she let her woman handle the money. "Better that than I lose it," she retorted. Ruefully, that happened more than once.

They settled into an easy routine. Traf left in the morning to report on base by eight. Ana caught a bus shortly after, which delivered her in Angra. She walked four blocks to her school and studied with her teachers until three in the afternoon. On her way home, she did any necessary shopping, and by the time Traf arrived shortly after six, their little house was clean and sparkling with dinner on the table. Most evenings they sat on the veranda and talked long after dark. Weekends were spent at the clubhouse with the other Troublemakers, many of whom were paired by now. Sometimes they did something special with Michaela and her girl.

As fond as ever, Ana and Gabriela grew even closer now that both were mistresses of their own homes. Everything Ana learned at school she taught her best friend. Traf often found their heads together over a saucepan in the kitchen, or in the extra bedroom they turned into a sewing room. Soon the two femmes spent every afternoon together, waiting for their butches to come home from work. Michaela began picking Gabriela up at Traf's house after work, sometimes driving all of them out to a restaurant or show.

Mom visited the new house soon after they moved in, marveled at all the modern conveniences and used a flush toilet for the first time in her fifty-nine years.

They sat on overstuffed furniture, drinking lemongrass tea prepared in the new kitchen. "What a marvelous house you have, my girl, so full of modern wonders. Your grandfather would be so pleased."

"Thanks, Mom." Traf felt proud enough to burst.

"I'm pleased to see you so settled, Vitória. I can't say it doesn't hurt to know my youngest child will never give me grandchildren." She sighed. "But seeing you and Ana living happily together makes up for it. What more could a mother want for her daughter?"

Rising to leave, she nodded at Traf rather than hugged her. "Come see your old mother once in a while. I'll visit again when I can."

Her father, however, did not visit the couple in their home and would not. Gaspar made it clear he considered their relationship unnatural and against the laws of God. He hadn't spoken a word to his daughter for weeks when one morning he looked up from the kitchen table, where he sat drinking a cup of coffee, to see Ana standing at the door. She smiled at him and asked politely if she might enter.

He wanted to refuse her, to ignore her completely, but Amalia swept past him, embracing the young woman who stood in their doorway.

"Ana! How nice to see you." She indicated the girl should take a seat at the table across from her husband.

While Amalia poured her a cup of coffee, Gaspar refused to meet Ana's eyes, instead turning his body to face away from her. His wife rolled her eyes and shrugged at the ceiling, then offered her visitor some sugar.

"Why yes, thank you," said Ana politely, helping herself. "I just wanted to stop over today and bring you these." She held out a bag of fried fava beans to Amalia, who took them enthusiastically, tasting one.

"These are delicious, Ana. Did you make them yourself?"

"Yes," she answered, grinning from ear to ear with pride. "We learned to make them yesterday at school. They showed us how to add different spices, too. I always practice what I learn at home so I won't forget. Last night I fried so many fava beans I knew we couldn't eat them all and I thought you might like some."

Ana watched Gaspar out of the corner of her eye, and what she saw was almost a mirror image of her Traf. A proud and stubborn man, he held his chin high just like his daughter. *If he's half as stubborn as she is, he won't bend easily.*

"Well, I must be on my way." She surreptitiously placed a pack of American cigarettes on the tabletop as she stood. "These are for you, Father," she whispered as she stepped past him. He still wouldn't look at her, but he nodded when he saw the small gift.

Amalia smiled appreciatively at the intelligent young woman. Her eyes twinkled as she accepted a kiss on the cheek and returned it perfunctorily. "Tell my trafulha that I miss her. Will you ask her to come by and visit soon?"

"Well," Ana paused standing at the door, "there is one other thing I wanted to mention. Vitória will be promoted to First Lieutenant in December. It would be wonderful if you could be there." Before they could say no, Ana hurried out, waving gaily over her shoulder and calling back something about her bus leaving. She disappeared into the early autumn morning.

Amalia watched her husband open the pack of cigarettes, take one out, and tap it on the back of his wrist. He stuck it behind his ear and rose slowly from the table, pocketing the rest.

"Don't even start, Amalia," he growled walking past. "I don't approve of her being an American soldier, and I won't celebrate any part of it with her. If Vitória came to ask me herself, my answer would be the same. It's not proper for women to drive, much less fight and carry guns, wearing pants like a man. It's not proper! A daughter of mine, making me a laughing stock in my own village! I ought to kick her ass..." He continued muttering under his breath as he left the house. His wife sighed, then took a handful of fava beans and popped them into her mouth.

Traf would receive the silver bar that indicated her new rank on the evening of December ninth, giving her just under three weeks to find someone to do the honors for her. First Lieutenant Mendes - the words rolled around in her head as she wondered who she could ask to pin the bar on her shoulder during the ceremony. She searched the drawers in their bedroom as she thought, pushing clothing from one side to the other.

Wandering into the kitchen she started looking through the cupboards and on top of the refrigerator. Her brother-in-law Jack, had pinned her Second Lieutenant bars on her shoulder more than two years ago. *But he told me he was so terrified the whole time he shook like a leaf and almost dropped the bars while attaching them. If he hadn't been so proud of me, he would've refused. I can't ask him again.* She opened the oven and peered inside.

Ironic isn't it? Alice is in her element when everyone's looking at her. She'd love the attention if it were seemly for a woman. Which, of course, it is not.

Moving into their spotless main room, she checked under the sofa then rummaged through the cushions. Ana found her that way her as she walked into the house. "What are you doing?" She laughed at the sight of her butch's trouser clad bottom sticking up in the air.

"I lost a pack of cigarettes." Joining in the laughter, Traf rose, took the shopping bags from her arms, and carried them to the kitchen counter.

"I gave it to your father," Ana said diffidently and pulled a fresh pack of L&Ms from a bag, handing it to her. "Your mother says you're to come by and visit."

Traf whirled on her. "You went to see my parents?" she asked incredulously. "You took Father my cigarettes?" Stunned, she stood still, clutching the pack as Ana walked around her putting away the groceries.

"I asked them to come to your promotion ceremony, too," Ana went on.

Traf's mouth shut with a snap. A pregnant pause hung in the air for a long moment as curiosity warred with her resentment. "What did they say?"

"Nothing; I didn't give them the chance." Ana pushed her lover gently to one side and began peeling potatoes. She sliced and diced, then set them frying in a small amount of pork fat seasoned with sea salt. Chopping some onion she added it to the pan, flipping its contents several times. Traf leaned against the humming refrigerator, still stunned.

Ana beat a handful of eggs, then shredded some fresh parsley into the mix. Next, she chopped leftover fried fish from last night.

Traf watched in amazement as she worked efficiently. *Just a few short weeks ago, she thought she couldn't do anything. Now she's matter-of-factly doing things others wouldn't dare.* Even while furious she admired Ana's sheer guts.

Pouring the egg mixture and chopped fish into the fried potatoes and onions, Ana stirred up a scrambled dish. She served it with fresh wheat bread baked the night before. Seated at the table with dinner served, she broached the subject again.

"You need to make up with your father."

Mouth full of good food, Traf eyed Ana as she chewed slowly. After swallowing thoughtfully, she said, "No."

Frustrated, Ana glared balefully at her. She might have learned how to get things done in the last few months, but no one could change Traf's mind once she set it.

"And don't give Father any more of my cigarettes either," Gaspar's daughter snapped. "Let him get off his lazy ass and work for his money, same as I do."

Ana stared at her, shocked. "I can't believe you speak that way about your father. Don't you owe him any respect? He is your father!"

Traf tore a hunk of bread free from the loaf. "The church says I do, but then again, the church says I shouldn't love you, and I do. I have my reasons," she continued, raising one hand as her way of saying the discussion was closed.

Ch. 11 – The Night Avengers

Winter, 1965

December ninth started out with gray skies but by mid-afternoon the clouds parted and a pale sun broke through. Busy before dawn, Ana prepared for the party they were throwing after the pinning ceremony. Taken aback to learn Traf's parents would boycott the ceremony, she realized she'd underestimated Gaspar's stubborn streak. In the face of her lover's unspoken discouragement, she regretted ever asking.

Traf's wounded heart came as a surprise. *How come Father's rejection still hurts, even though I don't try to please or impress him anymore? No matter what I do, he'll never approve of me. Why should I care if he comes or not?* Unwilling to give him the satisfaction of being unhappy, she shook it off, vengefully pleased she disappointed him as much as he did her.

Three second lieutenants received promotions that day, and the ceremony proceeded with the clockwork precision Traf had come to expect from the Americans. Louis, Hermione's husband, pinned the new silver colored bar to her shoulder. He grinned with the pride of an older brother as she received her new rank. Although standing rigidly at attention as expected, she heard Ana, Gabriela, Michaela, Hermione, Johnny, Alice, and Jack cheering for her in the gathered crowd. Over their heads, the American flag hung proudly.

Later, Ana served their guests lavish amounts of fine food she'd spent days preparing. As they ate, Traf turned to Hermione. Nodding toward Louis seated on the other side of his wife, she whispered, "Did he get nervous when he was pinning on my bar?" She was thinking of bashful Jack seated at the other end of the table, trying his best to be invisible beside sociable Alice.

Hermione chuckled and indicated her husband making a silly face at Ana as she refilled his bowl. "This clown?" She slapped Louis on the back. He turned to his wife. "How did you feel up on that stage with everyone looking at you?" she asked her husband loudly, grinning from him to Traf and back.

Ordinarily, he would have passed off some comment about how handsome he was, that it would only be normal for people to look at him and cheer, but instead he grinned at Traf on the other side of his wife. "They weren't looking at me." Obvious pride rang in his voice, forcing heat to her cheeks. "They were cheering for First Lieutenant Vitória Mendes." He raised his glass and toasted, "To the best officer in the US Air Force, trafulha though she may be! To Vitória!" He downed his glass of wine.

"To Vitória!" Everyone followed suit, and the party lingered on until well after ten that night.

As an end to a lovely evening, even though Ana urged her to sit down, she helped clean up. Having all of Friday off, a three-day weekend stretched endlessly before them. Ana had arranged to meet Michaela and Gabriela at the clubhouse Friday night. They would have a small, private celebration party among themselves.

Up early, just before sunrise, Traf put on her oldest clothes and walked several kilometers down to the beach to collect limpets, shellfish that clung to rocks along the shoreline. Before Ana finished dressing for her day at school, she had them simmering on the gas stove. They smelled fantastic, and it surprised her when Ana refused to eat any insisting she was late for the bus. *Ah well, all that much more for me.* One of her favorite treats from the sea, she settled down to eat the entire pot by herself, relishing every bite.

Gone by the time Ana got home that evening, she left a handwritten note on the gleaming tabletop explaining she'd spent her free day cleaning the house from top to bottom and was now visiting her mother. Ana's eyes filled with frustrated tears she wouldn't let Traf see. A muscle kinked in her shoulder, sending shooting pains up her neck to her head.

Since she had the time, Ana ran a bath for herself and took special care to dress beautifully. She used makeup but sparingly, like a lady. She dressed in her best and knew she looked good. She could see for herself in the small mirror in the bathroom.

When Traf got home a few minutes later, she brought the last flowers from her mother's garden. Ana took them from her as soon as she saw them and disappeared into the kitchen. She emerged a few minutes later with them prettily displayed in a glass vase, then put them on a table in the main room.

"I could have done that," said Traf, grinning broadly. She looked around the house with satisfaction. "Everything looks good, doesn't it?"

"It looks fine," answered Ana shortly. "You'll have to hurry, or we'll be late meeting Gabriela and Michaela."

Her lover's tone caught Traf's attention. She dressed in a nice pair of slacks Ana made as a school project. She put on a crisp white shirt, starched perfectly, and adjusted a black beret on her unruly cap of dark brown curls several different ways before she was ready to go. Whenever something in her life seemed a little out of kilter, she took extra care with her already natty attire.

Michaela drove up with Gabriela, and they gaily set sail for the clubhouse, chattering away. As they pulled up, however, shock struck them dumb.

Once again, hoodlums had trashed Troublemakers, yanking the door completely off this time. Broken windows stared blankly, as if unable to comprehend a second attack. As the four women jumped from the car and hurried inside to join the other Troublemakers already gathered, they smelled the human excrement spread on the walls before they saw it. Broken tables and chairs littered the room, and the bar had been savaged, predictably foul words carved deeply into its beautiful wood. The mirror that hung so brightly behind the bar was broken into hundreds of pieces. Jagged light bulb shards jutted angrily from their sockets.

This time, there were no chairs left to sit upon so they milled around in the litter and debris. People kicked glass shards around morosely, and more than a few turned away, fighting tears. Michaela disappeared in her car and came back followed by a local policeman. They gave a report to the officer, but it was clear he thought the whole thing very funny.

Traf stepped up to him angrily. "What are you going to do about this?" she demanded, gesturing at the debris.

"Do about what?" answered the officer, pocketing his report. "A little vandalism?" He looked around at them with contempt. "I have important business to take care of." He didn't say it but his look added, "And you are of no importance at all."

As he drove off, Traf looked at Michaela and then at all the young women standing around in shock. "Those bastards will never stop." Bleak looks greeted her from all sides. Not one voice rose against her harsh words. No one disagreed with her.

"C'mon," said Michaela. She took Gabriela by the hand and started back to her car. Ana and Traf trailed after them. They drove away in silence as the others morosely began to disperse. No one had anything else to say.

The next morning Traf got up and thought about heading to the clubhouse to see what repairs she could make. *Why bother?* For the first time in her life, she felt completely defeated and willing to give up. They'd poured everything they had into the clubhouse twice, and both times their work, money, and all their dreams were wasted, destroyed.

Traf headed for the beach instead, hoping to catch Capt. Mark before he left the dock. She spent the whole day out fishing. It was just what she needed to revive her spirits. She hooked a gorgeous halibut, and headed home eager to give Ana the large piece the captain gave her.

To her surprise, her lover wasn't home. She left a brief note, however, in her plain clear script: Gone to the clubhouse.

Traf left the fish sitting in the humming refrigerator and walked down the street to catch a ride to Praia.

I'll just have to convince Ana that her efforts are wasted, she reasoned to herself as the bus rattled over the old roads. They would go home and enjoy a dinner of fresh halibut rather than waste any more energy on a dream they'd never be allowed to keep. *Like the lyrics to the song says, "Don't ask more of life than life is prepared to give you."*

As she rounded the corner on foot from the bus stop, she saw an army of young women moving in and out of the battered clubhouse, easily two dozen, many of whom Traf didn't know well. They, these new members who'd joined Troublemakers as the word spread, had already removed all the broken furniture, piling it up in the front yard. Beatrice had brought the phonograph from the home she shared with Teresa and the exquisite voice of Amalia Rodrigues singing her most famous fado, "A Strange Form of Life", rose hauntingly over the hard working women, complementing their actions.

"What are you all doing?" Traf asked, dumbfounded.

"What does it look like?" answered Ana saucily, wiping her hand across her forehead and leaving a streak of dirt.

Out of the clubhouse came the tall femme Berta was seeing, Rita, carrying a broken table across her shoulders. She grinned down at Traf, then hurled the junk onto a pile growing outside the door. "We can use more strong backs. Glad you're here," she called as she turned and headed back inside the clubhouse.

Traf took a closer look at the working women. "Where are the butches?" she asked Ana.

Her lover shrugged. "I guess they'll come along later. But I'm glad you're here." Ana handed her a broom and cocked her head toward the open doorway. "You like to clean things, don't you?" she asked with a little bite to her tone. "Shall we?" she asked, leading the way back into the defiled building.

Several hours passed before any other butches showed up, looking for their women. Just as surprised as Traf at the femmes' tenacity, and although many of them considered the cause hopeless, they nevertheless pitched in and helped. Being butch, they took pride in doing the heavy work, leaving their girlfriends the less physically demanding tasks. Chaotic cleaning ensued around wielded tools, repairing what could be saved.

Around eight that night, a few people arrived who hadn't been there the night before. The devastation surprised them just as much as the bustling renovation. They stood watching, debating their ability to keep the clubhouse open. Michaela left and returned with several cases of beer. People found seats on the floor between bouts of work. An easy camaraderie settled over the group.

"It'll just keep on happening," repeated Odete, a large-boned butch who always arrived on horseback from across the island. She lived in Serreta, where she worked in her father's expansive banana fields. "It's like a game to them." She gestured around at the destruction. "We can fix it all up again, just like we did last time, and they'll still come back and tear it down!" Embarrassed by her own outburst, the self-conscious woman faded to the back of the group.

"Have you filed a report with the police?" asked Fern, the Governor's daughter. She wore a fashionable red dress and gold earrings, her dark hair swept up in an elegant twist. She'd begun coming to the Terceira Women's Club of Praia, as she knew it, only a few weeks earlier.

Troublemakers' membership had grown steadily as news of their club went around the island. To their surprise, not only lesbians were joining. Straight women found it a refreshing change from the company of men. For some, it was a relief to have a place to go where they could relax, safe from men's advances. Fern was one of these. She'd decided to see for herself and had been back every weekend since. "Well, have you gone to the police?" she insisted.

Traf turned to face the wealthy Governor's daughter and suddenly found herself speechless. She opened her mouth to explain, but not a sound came out. After struggling to find words, she dissolved into helpless laughter. Michaela soon joined her, and it was contagious.

Every one of the original Troublemakers began laughing, releasing pent-up hostility through their shared mirth. It rolled easily from them, swelling and lowering, then swelling again. Finally, it died away and in the ensuing silence, Traf once more turned to Fern. "We've made a police report. They won't be doing anything to help us. Look." She pointed toward the corner down the block. There stood two police officers and another couple of men, pointing and laughing at the "perverted lesbians" standing outside their ruined clubhouse.

Fern's lips firmed as she stared down at the corner. Before anyone could stop her, she marched down the street and demanded to know the officers' names. Surprised to see the daughter of Terceira's governor in the company of known lesbians, they both recognized her and promptly complied. Then back she marched to the clubhouse and without a further word to anyone, rolled up her sleeves, donned a pair of rubber gloves she plucked from a femme's apron pocket, and began washing down the fouled walls.

They worked hard again, everyone pitching in. With the femmes urging on the butches, they completed the repairs in record time.

"How sad there's a record to break." That irony wasn't lost on anyone.

But with a membership now grown past fifty all paying monthly dues, the increase in capital made it possible. They worked twice as hard as before, with double the workforce. To Traf's complete surprise, their straight members worked every bit as hard as any Troublemaker.

Everyone's spirits rose to the challenge, thanks to the femmes, and people wanted a huge party to celebrate. It would be their version of howling at the moon. It would also be just in time for Christmas. They broke precedent and planned their celebration for a weeknight, Thursday, December twenty-third. No one worked Christmas Eve on the solidly Catholic island.

The day started out cold and only got worse. A brisk wind blew in from the ocean and a line of dark clouds scuttled steadily over the island. Even with the threatening weather, the total membership of fifty-five planned to attend. The clubhouse glittered with candlelight, new tables and chairs looked opulent draped with holiday greenery, a third and by far the grandest, brand new mirror hung proudly behind the now twice repaired bar.

Mr. Borba had once more worked his magic on its poor tortured wood, replacing much of it. This time he had the capable assistance of another new member, Julia. It soon became obvious to everyone that Julia was a gifted carpenter after she created a fanciful pattern of interlocking darker woods for the bar front. Her dedication to the task created a breathtaking work of art, which completely covered the scarred original wood. No man could do better. By the end of their week working together, Mr. Borba hired her to work with him in his newly opened carpentry shop.

The freshly painted walls stood silent witness, clean and renewed, as the roomful of young women danced all night. They exchanged partners often, exuberant in their triumph over devastation. When Traf saw Fern glide by first on the arm of Alex, later with Tina, and still later with Lydia, she finally turned to Ana and asked bluntly, "Why does she want to be here? I mean, she's straight, isn't she? Why did she join the club?"

"She's here because she wants to be here." Ana shushed her, indicating by bowing her head they should whisper. "She came first with Teresa. Fern goes to so many social events where her father parades her around like a mare to be bred that she was thrilled to hear about a club just for women. Teresa told her about us one night when she escaped a dinner and flagged down her taxi."

Ana glanced at her seriously, then whispered, "Don't say anything against her, do you hear? She's just looking for a place where men won't paw her. We're a women's club, so let's be a place where any woman can come and be safe." She smiled at Traf and put her hand on her arm, pacifying her. "She's already been a good friend to us. I'd like us to be her friends as well."

Traf nodded. "She sure worked wonders with the police." Since taking the laughing officers' names, the two had become a grudgingly polite and respectful presence in the neighborhood. After speaking with her father, who in turn spoke to the Praia chief of police, word went out that the Women's Club should be treated like any other respectable business or club on the island. Well, Traf would believe that when she saw the clubhouse still standing after a year. But for the time being, she willingly accepted Fern and the other straight women who joined them. She still resented their presence but assumed they would eventually tire of their passing fancy. *Soon enough they'll turn their backs on the lesbians again and move on to a new fad.*

The evening passed peacefully. A triumphal spirit filled the building that suited the holiday perfectly. Ana and Traf enjoyed themselves until eleven o'clock, or so. Then the romance bug bit and they decided to go home for some privacy. As they strolled from Praia to Lajes and their comfortable little house, it occurred to Traf how many of her dreams had come true. She smiled in the dark as she took Ana's hand. They were as much a married couple as anyone else, but without the blessing of either church or state. They made a good home together and each of them supported the other in pursuing her dreams. *Many straight married people couldn't say as much.* Lost in her thoughts, she suddenly felt Ana grow still. She stopped and looked quickly around to see what spooked her.

"Didn't you turn off all the lights when we left?" Ana asked.

"Yes."

"Well, there's one on now. Someone is in our house."

"Maybe Father Christmas, or the Americans' Santa Claus?" The two looked at each other nervously.

Not many in the Açores worried about locking up their homes when away. With crime virtually unknown on the island, why bother? But as lesbians, common decency often didn't apply and anything might be happening. Traf pushed Ana behind her as she strode angrily up to her own front door and through it.

She couldn't see anyone, but the sound of running water came from the bathroom. She charged through the open door with Ana close on her heels.

Lucy, a sweet femme they first met at the fire in the woods, knelt in the bathtub, her skirt tucked up into her waistband. Ugly bruises bloomed on her battered face, one eye swollen shut. She scrubbed at her crotch with a piece of hard soap; a bright rivulet of blood dribbled down her thighs. She looked up distractedly as they barged into the room, but didn't focus on them and continued her frantic scouring, tears coursing down her face.

Ana moaned, wrapping her arms around herself as she watched Lucy, completely crushed. Traf gulped hard, then nodded at her lover. "Stay here with her," she ordered brusquely. "I'll go look around outside and make sure there's no one there." She stopped long enough to grab a loaded gun she kept locked in a cupboard in their bedroom, then she went out.

Ana kneeled next to the bathtub, gently putting a hand on the young woman's shoulder and rubbing slowly until focus came back to her eyes. Lucy gave a cry of utter despair and then suddenly slumped, falling limply into the tub. She fainted.

Traf came back into the bathroom and found Ana struggling to rinse the unconscious femme and raise her out of the tub. "No one is out there now." She took Lucy's limp form from Ana. "I'll carry her to the guest room. You go ahead of me and pull down the covers."

Together they got Lucy tucked in. A few minutes later, she came to and lay there staring at the ceiling, mewling like a wounded kitten. Turning her face to the wall, heart-wrenching sobs wracked her small frame. Within another few minutes, she fell fitfully asleep, tossing and turning, desperate to avoid the truth. Ana changed out of her party clothes and brought a chair over next to the bed. She would sit with Lucy until she woke up.

Traf burst out into the night, pausing only long enough to lock the door after her, feet pounding down the same streets and roads that seemed so idyllic just minutes before. She wanted to hit someone; she needed to break things. She ran the nearly four kilometers because it gave her angry energy something to do. When she arrived at the clubhouse she paused a moment to calm down and catch her breath, not wanting to make a scene.

She entered the room, looking to see who was behind the bar. It was Odete's night to finish serving drinks and snacks and later to close up the club with Tina, both single butches with nothing better to do. The big woman wiped down the bar and polished it until it gleamed, cleaning up. She looked over and grinned at Traf, then went on with her work. Most of the couples had already left and fewer than half the members remained to see the evening out. A few danced, some were finishing their drinks with only minutes left until the club closed for the night.

Traf crossed to the bar and gestured for Odete to lean close. They whispered together for a moment before she walked over to Tina, still sitting with several couples drinking wine. Voice low and urgent, she told the others what happened. As hard as she tried to maintain a certain level of calm, her own need to do something exploded within those present. Within moments, a company of femmes marshaled themselves, and a squadron of protective butches escorted them through the streets to Traf's house. Several peeled away to get those who had already gone home.

Odete stayed behind only long enough to turn off the lights and lock up. Then she hurriedly followed them down the dark streets. Two blocks from Traf's house, a piercing pain suddenly erupted in her shoulder. She whirled, bringing her arm up to block, knocking her assailant's arm to the side and the knife he held free. Her fist smashed up into his nose, blood splattering over them both as it broke.

"You freak!" Grabbing his face with one hand, he gestured with the other. Two men each grabbed one of her arms and pulled her wide. The one who stabbed her let go of his nose to send several hard fists into her stomach and then punched her face over and over. When her body finally sagged, they released her and fled into the night.

Odete lay on the ground for a few minutes relearning how to breathe, then rose and forced her feet the rest of the way to safety. She staggered through the open door. Stunned faces turned and shock ran through the room as everyone saw crimson streaming down the big woman's arm. Her torn mouth bled as she opened it to speak. A front tooth was missing.

"Three men," she managed, "stabbed and beat me."

Women surrounded her, supporting her as they led her to a chair. Several femmes started searching Ana's neat and orderly kitchen for clean rags and soap to wash her wounds. A hubbub of voices rose as steadily as the beat of their collectively terrified hearts.

Ana came running from the guest room at the noise. "What's happened?" After hearing Odete's story, she grabbed Traf's arm and nodded furiously. "Lucy said there were three of them." She looked around, frightened. "It was her cousin Mike. He took turns on her with two of his friends." Ana's nauseated face held eyes newly awakened to evil.

"Let's go." A quietly powerful voice commanded. To Traf's surprise, it was her own.

They swiftly decided that Alex, who had a gun her father insisted she carry, would stay behind to guard the group of femmes who now had two patients to tend. The rest of them would deal out a measure of rough justice.

A stream of impassioned women flowed with vindictive intent out into the night like dangerous lava. Twelve butches desperately needed to vent their horror, frustration, and rage. Traf led the way as they retraced Odete's steps. They found Mike's bloody knife under a bush. Traf tucked it into her belt, and they kept moving.

The butches hunted as a pack, silent, effective, and fast. Above their heads, winter stars twinkled in mocking serenity. It took only an hour to find Mike and his buddies, all three drinking hard in an unlit corner of a dark bar. Several men laughed uproariously at the story they told.

Margarida and Berta found them and reported back to the main group. They formulated a plan; they would deal only with Mike as Lucy had identified him but not the other two.

The women waited in the shadows along a dark road they knew led from the bar to Mike's house. No one thought about going home. The butches would wait as long as it took. Only Traf broke away long enough to fetch what they needed and brought back other butches who had gathered at her house. An hour passed, and then another.

Rather than allow doubts to weaken their resolve, they fanned the coals of their righteousness to flame with gossip.

"Mike's a notorious drunk."

"It's common knowledge his wife, Maria, is always covered in bruises."

"Yeah, I know her. It's true."

They knew he'd eventually come stumbling down this road; it was a shortcut to his home. The lazy bastard would take the easiest route.

"Yes, and someone said now he's started beating his kids."

"Over the years he's gotten more and more vicious."

"Imagine, raping your own cousin!"

"And on Christmas Eve!"

They watched the path with lethal patience, willing to wait as long as it took.

"Will he confess it, I wonder? Beg Christ's forgiveness?"

"Probably. People like him wrap themselves in the sanctity of doing God's work."

They glared at each other, targets of the piously self-righteous. Their anger grew.

Someone growled, "Mike's a mad dog."

"Someone should put him down."

"No one would miss him, least of all his wife."

Lucy's cousin finally came lurching along sometime in the darkest hours of early morning. Traf felt her stomach roil. *Why, God, why do you put such people on the Earth? Are you torturing us, or teaching us to be strong?*

They jumped the drunk bully and easily brought him down. Rope bound his hands behind his back. Berta knotted a blindfold securely over his eyes. They wrestled him off the road and back into the dark behind some trees, where Lydia forced some filthy burlap into his mouth, taping it securely in place.

He tried kicking at them in his alcoholic stupor but missed and rolled on his face in the dirt. Traf jumped on his shoulders and sat down hard, pinning him in place. Two others sat on his legs. Tina slit his pants and undershorts away with a short, sharp knife until he lay there half-naked.

Only then did it dawn on Mike that he might be in any kind of serious trouble. It never occurred to him that his victims had friends who might gang up on him. A stupid ruffian to whom no woman ever raised a voice, much less a hand, he found himself totally unprepared for the butches.

Tina held out an empty hand to Traf, who filled it with a dried, stiff, bristly corncob. Leaning over Mike's ear, still pinning his shoulders to the ground with her knees, Traf growled, "This is for Lucy." Tina rammed the prickly dry corncob up his rectum. He screamed, but the burlap in his mouth blocked most of the sound. Each of the butches took a turn thrusting the torturous instrument in and out his ass. Traf, the last one, thrust it farther than anyone had yet dared and left it there. She grinned like a wolf in blood lust.

"And this," she whispered in his other ear, "is for Odete!" Whirling, she grabbed the same knife he used on her friend and plunged it deep into his shoulder. Then they yanked the gag from his mouth and left him tied up, bleeding, and groaning. It wouldn't be long before somebody heard him, and to ensure his total humiliation they left the corncob stuffed up his wounded bare ass.

The vigilantes ran back through the early dawn to Traf's house. There they found an efficient group of bustling femmes. Lucy, now bathed and dressed, sat at the table in the kitchen, sipping tea. The emptiness had left her eyes, replaced by a haunted fear it tore the heart to see. Odete sat next to her, a borrowed shirt of Traf's on her good shoulder and pulled over the other, bandaged one. Her face, now clean of blood, disappeared under swelling bruises of purple, red, and green. A pot of hot, hearty pork and white bean soup simmered on the stove, as several loaves of coarse cornbread cooled on the counter.

"Sit down," said Ana invitingly, "and we'll eat." She indicated empty seats around the table. The waning moon glittered through clean windows.

The returned warriors took turns washing up at the sink. The sight of red water flowing down the drain disgusted Traf as she rinsed away Mike's blood.

The tired young women took turns eating the delicious food. As soon as one finished another would take her bowl to wash and use over again. Leaning against the walls, seated on the floor, and perched on countertops, everyone listened as the butches told their story. When they were finished, a thick silence filled the room like fog. Some of them didn't want to look at each other now that the heat of battle had cooled and they were once more in the civilized company of femmes.

"Are we as bad as him?" Traf asked into the stillness. Doubts suddenly assailed her. "We injured another human being… on Christmas Eve." The irreverence of it hit them all at once.

"What choice did we have?" demanded feisty little Berta. She stood up from the table, waving a femme to sit in her place, and started pacing the floor. "As long as they know we'll fight back, they'll keep their distance," she insisted. "Once you beat them, bullies always back down."

A few snickers among the butches were promptly quelled.

"We can't tell anyone what's happened," insisted Odete, looking at the devastated Lucy sitting next to her. "Not fathers, mothers, brothers, or sisters. No friends can know, and especially no men can know what we've done tonight. We must take it to our graves." Awkwardly, she put her good arm around the smaller Lucy, giving her a shoulder to lean on. Odete felt strangely protective of the young femme, trying to shelter her even now, knowing it was far too late.

A grateful Lucy shifted uncomfortably on the long wooden bench, then settled with a grateful sigh into Odete's shoulder, hiding her face. It would be Lucy's downfall if word of this leaked out. Gossiping old biddies would condemn her immediately. It was standing community opinion that any woman who was raped had somehow asked for it. Lucy would be branded a loose woman, her future limited to prostitution or begging.

"Will he tell, do you think?" asked Linda, looking worriedly at Margarida.

"No," reassured her butch. "What's he going to say, that a bunch of women rammed a corncob up his butt? First of all, he's too embarrassed, second, he knows the story of what he did to Lucy and Odete would come out, and third, he'd face the ridicule of his drinking buddies. But maybe,"

Margarida said, looking a little guilty, "we should send someone to make sure he's been found. What if he dies out there? He is bleeding, you know."

Lucy spoke for the first time, muttering fiercely, "Then the world would be better off." She shook her head. "He didn't care how badly he hurt me, and he wouldn't care if he killed Odete, or whichever of you he managed to catch."

"He's an animal," agreed the wounded butch she leaned against.

"My grandfather," Traf started hesitantly, giving them time to settle down and listen, "once told me about a group of men. In his time there was no real police force, no one the people could trust to right whatever went wrong. So he and some other men formed a group they called the Night Avengers. If a man beat his wife or children and no one stopped him, they would call a gathering. The Avengers would meet in the dark of night and find the man, then beat him soundly." She looked around at the other women filling her little house.

"I think we're the spiritual daughters of those men," she said earnestly. "There is no law to protect us from attacks. The church, and perhaps God, has abandoned us to our fates. If we don't protect our own, who will?"

"Night Avengers," mused Ana, refilling cups with coffee or tea. "It's got a certain ring to it." The gathered women murmured agreement. Ana raised her hand to still them, then announced impressively, "May the spirits of the Night Avengers protect us, one and all."

"May the spirits of the Night Avengers protect us, one and all," repeated the entire group of young women, just as solemnly as they intoned the responses at Church.

"And may we never betray one another, whether by word, deed, or intent," Odete added hurriedly. She looked around and found them all nodding in assent. They repeated that too. Soon after, the women started to go their separate ways. They wished each other, "Feliz Natal," being careful to leave in groups. The Night Avengers would meet again, of that all were bitterly sure.

Odete's parents gave her a small house on the other side of their fields when she grew to be a woman, so she would go to her own home in Serreta to heal. But Lucy was in no shape to return to the scrutiny of her parents. She needed a place to go and a reasonable story for her absence.

"Come to my house, Lucy," urged Odete, lisping with the fresh loss of her tooth. "I'll take care of you." She grinned ruefully at her bandaged shoulder, "And you can take care of me. Please?"

Lucy looked gratefully at the big woman sitting, imperturbable, beside her. No one else had ever made her feel safe. "Yes," she answered. "I'd love to come stay with you, but what will I tell my parents?" Her gentle face dissolved into watery tears. "I can't deal with them right now."

Teresa stepped forward quickly. "You don't have to, Lucy. You're a grown woman now, and if you want to visit a friend at Christmas, you can. I'll take your parents a message later this morning after Mass, telling them you'll be home in a few weeks. That'll give you some time to yourself." No one thought it would really be that easy, but they all pretended it would for Lucy's sake. They nodded in total agreement.

"Okay." Gratefully, the brutalized girl acquiesced, exhausted physically, mentally, and spiritually. Nothing sounded as good to her in this moment as the offer of a clean bed in Odete's house on the other side of the island. She let Teresa and the big butch escort her to the waiting taxi, and Ana and Traf raised their hands in silent salute as they drove back to the club to pick up Odete's horse.

"Some night." Traf sighed as they closed the door on the last of their departing friends. She kissed Ana's forehead.

"Some night," agreed her lover. Turning, she snuggled into Traf's arms, which held her firmly. "Why does it have to come to this? Is our love really so sinful that God must punish us like this?"

Traf had no answer for that. Truth be told, it often seemed exactly that way. Maybe God was against them. But right now, the adrenaline still pumped through her veins from the violence she had perpetrated that night. She wanted Ana in a way she never had before, needing to finish releasing pent-up energy in some life-affirming way. Traf swept her darling up into her arms and carried her to their bed, where they made love passionately before collapsing in exhaustion at dawn.

As the sun rose high in the east, their shutters stayed closed against the light. It signaled to visiting family, friends, and neighbors that they weren't home this Christmas Eve morning, but they needed the rest. More than that, they needed to escape the good wishes and merriment of the day, so at odds with their wounded spirits.

Hours later, long after nightfall, Traf woke, stiff and restless from her battle the night before. She rose and walked into the kitchen, putting the coffee pot on the stove. A glance at her watch told her they slept through the Christmas Eve Mass, so she didn't wake Ana. Let the poor girl sleep.

She tore a hunk of bread from one of the round loaves left over from last night, then munched it thoughtfully as she drank her coffee. She remembered Ana's poignant question.

Could it be true that God lets men like Mike rape and stab lesbians to punish the women for their sinful hearts? She'd heard a lot about God's wrath over the years, and yes, it did seem to fit that pattern.

It didn't make sense, though, when she tried to picture her love for Ana as sinful. *I never feel closer to God than when I look into Ana's eyes. In her arms, miracles seem possible. We share a love as pure as any straight couple I know. Surely, God wouldn't condemn that.*

Perhaps the sex was sinful? Maybe if she gave up sex she'd be a good woman again in God's eyes. She tried picturing a life with Ana abstaining from sex, but knew it was hopeless. While Ana might willingly forego sex in favor of pleasing God, Traf realized she could never live life without it. Her healthy and fierce sex drive burned with a never-satiated hunger, and she knew without a doubt that she would always make love to Ana.

A noise from the bedroom indicated that her lover was finally awake. She grabbed a second cup of coffee and tore off another hunk of corn bread, then hurried to catch Ana before she flung the blankets back to cool them off. Traf scooched under the blanket and cuddled up to her still sleepy lover, sweeping her into her arms and holding her close. With slow touches and tender kisses, she welcomed Ana back to wakefulness. Throughout the long night, sustained by cold coffee, hardening bread, and short naps, the two ignored the world before finally rising at dawn to shower and dress for the holiday.

Christmas morning dawned bright and crisply cold. Traf enjoyed watching her lover unwrap the perfume and jewelry she gave her.

Ana squealed and put everything on. Then she presented Traf with a new suit painstakingly sewn, a sharp looking Spanish black bolero jacket with matching skintight pants. A set of shirts in pale peach, brilliant white, and light baby blue accompanied it.

"You're wonderful," Traf exclaimed, examining herself in their only mirror. She put it down and twirled around. "A professional seamstress couldn't do better." She ran a hand over the fabric clinging to her muscular ass. "You should start a business. No, really," she insisted as Ana began shaking her head. "People would pay good money for stylish clothes this well made."

As much as she wanted to, she didn't wear her new suit as they spent the morning dropping in on family and friends, delivering gaily-wrapped gifts. Instead, she wore a conservative skirt and sweater so as not to shock the community's sensitivities as they visited and enjoyed holiday treats. Arms laden with presents, they returned home in the evening. Having eaten a glorious holiday meal at Alice's they weren't hungry, so they nibbled on sweet bread and drank coffee in the kitchen. They had an hour before the midnight Mass.

"Thank goodness the Americans love Christmas as much as we do," Traf said. She produced a box of American chocolates she'd bought on the base, offering them to Ana. "Oh, you know what would be good with these? That bottle of wine Teresa gave us." She opened the bottle.

Handing Traf two wine glasses, Ana reached for a chocolate. "I wonder how Odete and Lucy are doing." She nibbled on the candy daintily.

"Hopefully, they're healing together." Traf handed Ana a full glass of the deep red wine. She tossed a whole chocolate in her mouth and chewed. "Wouldn't it be wonderful if the two of them made a home together, maybe even a family?" She reached across the table to take Ana's hand.

"Yes," Ana agreed. "If ever lost souls needed one another, it would be those two. God bless and keep them."

Perhaps reminded by the familiar blessing, Traf told Ana her late night musings about God. They discussed their thoughts about being Catholic lesbians at length.

"You know," Ana mused after a while, "I've never confessed about us; have you?" She finished the last of her wine.

Traf looked at her as if she'd suddenly grown a second head. "Of course not. To a priest on this little island? Are you crazy?"

"What are we afraid of?" asked Ana. "Why don't we just confess and get it over with?"

"Well, in the first place," Traf answered her, "I'm still not convinced that what we're doing is a sin." She sat back in her chair and sipped her drink.

Now Ana looked at her with serious doubt about her sanity. "Of course it's a sin. The Bible says it's a sin. Everyone says it's a sin. If it wasn't sinful, why do they call us such vicious names?" She rose and brought the half-full wine bottle in from the kitchen, refilled her glass, and set the bottle on the coffee table.

"They're just people, as full of faults as you and me," Traf thought aloud. "And the Bible was written by men. Men who lived in a time and place that isn't here or now. And I've never heard a priest tell a single story of Jesus condemning us. He spoke only of forgiving and accepting." She paused for a long moment before finishing the thought. "Maybe the men who wrote the Old Testament wrote down how they felt, not God."

Ana laughed. "Now you're reaching for excuses," she teased.

"Maybe so. My second reason for not confessing is plain old-fashioned fear." Traf refilled her wine glass with the last of the bottle. "What if I tell a priest I'm a lesbian and he denounces me regardless of the sanctity of the Confessional? He could suggest demons corrupted me and insist I be locked up in a room for life. It's been done before," she insisted as Ana looked skeptical. "You know Ada, the older butch that comes into the clubhouse some weekends?"

"I think so," Ana answered. "She's what, thirty years old or so, with an eye that droops?"

"That's Ada," Traf agreed. "Well, anyway, she told me that her parents locked her in her bedroom and kept her there for five years because a priest told them to. She'd be there still except she escaped and hid on a ferry. That's why she came to Terceira. She was raised on São Miguel."

"I didn't know that," Ana said, holding one hand in front of her mouth. "That's a horrible story! What in the world possessed her parents?"

"A priest, I told you," Traf said, convinced. "Ada said he denounced her during a Mass one morning and then tried to perform an exorcism on her. He wanted to cast the demons out of her. Seems to me sometimes that demons fill the priests. Demons who love to torment people like us."

"Traf! You love to shock me, don't you?" Ana laughed, finished her wine, pulled on her white church gloves and inspected her shoes. "Priests are here to help guide us to heaven, not hurt us." She reached out and patted her lover's wild curls into place.

"Tell that to Ada," she grumbled but backed down. Traf only knew the few priests that had come and gone in her village of Lajes. *None of them seemed that vicious, but you never can tell*, she reminded herself. *You never can tell.* "Still," she added with obvious bravado, "one of these days I'll shock the whole island and tell everyone I'm a lesbian."

"Let's get going," said Ana with a dismissive, and most unladylike, snort. "We're going to be late." Traf tossed off the rest of her drink, then the two carefully locked their door and set off for church. The night was cold but the wine made them warm. They told silly jokes and sang Christmas carols with others walking their way.

Father Benedict always gave the special Christmas night Mass. Beautifully told in the old man's quavering voice, Traf enjoyed the story of her Savior's birth as much as she always did. A truly fabulous miracle, she believed it with her whole heart and soul. Her being swelled with overwhelming love for her God and his only Son. *What a gift to send the world.*

She lingered in the pew after the service, and before long almost everyone had gone. Ana still sat beside her, a little bewildered. A few older women, widows mostly, sat in a line outside the confessional, already saying their rosaries, fingering the beads in the same pattern they'd repeated a million times. Most people didn't choose to confess on Christmas, so only one priest heard confessions that night. Traf looked at the women waiting, and then at Ana.

"You go on home if you want to," she said, straightening her shoulders. "I'm going to do it. I'm going to stay and confess."

"I'll wait for you," answered Ana. "If you choose to confess, I'll go in right after you and confess too."

They sat there tensely, waiting until Traf's turn. She approached the tiny wooden cubicle and entered before she could change her mind. Crossing herself, she spoke by rote. "Forgive me, Father, for I have sinned. It's been two weeks since my last confession." The tiny wooden panel that separated the unseen priest from her slid back with a familiar squeak.

"Yes, Vitória?" came a voice she knew too well. "What sins do you have to confess?"

Oh no. Father Timothy. She'd made many confessions to the self-righteous priest over the years and he assigned penances with a heavy hand. He never approved of her, even before she and Johnny raided the churchyard orange tree and got caught. Traf said the rosary a hundred times for that.

The glowing faith in her God that radiated through her only moments ago converted instantly to leaden dread. Suddenly, she wanted nothing more than to get out of the tight little box into the free air where she could breathe. Pulling at the collar of her sweater, she fidgeted through her usual litany of petty crimes against the Church. She received her penance, exited the cubicle with great relief, and kneeled back in the pew beside

Ana. Traf started saying the rosary under her breath, eyes fixed on the giant image of Christ hanging over the altar.

"What did you tell him?" whispered Ana.

"Nothing unusual," Traf whispered back.

"Well, I'm not afraid. I'll do it." Ana swept into the confessional as Traf watched in horror.

Her fear grew to outrage. Their lives would change, that was certain. After Ana's confession, they would both be public pariahs, and now in an organized way rather than the lackadaisical one they enjoyed in relative privacy. Once they were denounced from the pulpit, no one would have anything to do with them. Someone would tell the Americans and she'd lose her job. Would even Capt. Mark, liberal though he might be, allow a perverted lesbian to be part of his crew?

They wouldn't be allowed to live together any longer. Her house might actually be seized or even burned to the ground. Ana would have to fend for herself, and what work could Traf find among men who knew she was a lesbian and most likely had their own ideas of how to 'cure' her? How many beatings would she receive because right now, within that small cubicle, Ana confessed their covert behavior to judge and executioner?

Traf worked to calm her breathing, marshal her terrified thoughts, and tried to finish her penance while her lover was in the confessional. Finally the cubicle door opened and Ana stepped out. From around the row of confessionals, Father Timothy's footsteps headed for the rectory.

Sliding into the pew beside her, the younger woman bent her head and began praying, fingering her rosary beads. Shooting lightning bolts sideways from her eyes, Traf silently demanded to know what had happened. Piously ignoring her, Ana kneeled and had her penance finished long before Traf was done. *But then, Father Timothy liked Ana.* He always had, and apparently still did.

Traf grinned triumphantly to herself as she realized Ana had protected their secret.

Ch. 12 – What's Wrong With You?

Spring, 1966

Traf and Ana walked home from Easter Sunday services. It was late March and wildflowers bloomed everywhere. A plane flew low over their heads, coming in for a landing. "God damn it, there's going to be a lot of new babies on the island in the morning," said Traf, carefully steering them around a mud puddle from an earlier rain.

"What? Why?"

"Because of SATA airlines. That's the second airplane I've seen land at the airport today."

Ana stopped short. Traf continued for another step before realizing she was alone. She turned. "What?"

Ana's face was a comical mixture of disbelief and suspicion. "You've got to be kidding."

"No, I'm not kidding. I saw one landing before we left home this morning, and you saw the other one right now. That's a double delivery of babies."

"Vitória Mendes, you stop that right now." Ana laughed. "You're such a clown." She took Traf's arm and started walking again. "You know how babies are made."

Aware that she'd been made a fool, Traf's anger overcame her embarrassment. "Alice told me babies were delivered by SATA," she stormed, her brown eyes turning black.

"Oh, she was just kidding," laughed Ana. "How old were you then?"

"I don't know, when her second daughter was born, I think maybe seven or eight."

"Well, there, you see? She thought you were too young to know, so she gave you the story about planes." Ana stopped short again, pulling Traf to a stop. "Wait. So you're saying you don't know where babies come from?"

"I thought they came from SATA," her butch said, angrily.

Ana wanted to laugh. Her throat tightened so her mouth wouldn't as she forced herself to stay calm. "Women have the babies," she said. "Didn't you ever notice someone get really fat, then a baby comes and they're smaller again?"

"Yeah, I know women get fat sometimes."

"That's the baby, growing inside of her."

Traf, shocked into silence, simply stared at her. She swallowed, blinked, swallowed again, and cleared her throat. "Like dogs?" she asked, thinking of Father's litters of puppies.

"And cows, goats, pigs, cats, and rabbits." Ana's eyes crinkled up as a laugh finally escaped her.

"Oh." Thoughts collided in Traf's head, banging off each other like the balls in a pachinko game. Images of livestock mating sprang up but bounced away as she thought of Father in Sylvia's house with his trousers around his ankles. Crude remarks made by fishermen, or her brother and his friends, suddenly made sense. She'd heard men refer to 'sticking it' to women many times but never associated it with the squishy pale weenie of Henry. However, she'd seen bulls mount cows, and nine months later calves came. "So a man sticks his weenie in a woman, she gets fat, and a baby comes?"

"Yes," laughed Ana. "I can't believe you didn't know this." She quieted down, then considered Traf before walking again. "Well, maybe I do believe it. Your mother never had to have 'the talk' with you, because you still don't have your period." This time, Ana steered a distracted Traf around a mud puddle. "A girl doesn't really become a woman until her first visit."

"Oh, so I'm not a real woman?" Indignant, Traf pulled up short, stopping Ana. "Could a child provide you a home, pay for your schooling, work a full-time job, and…" she lowered her voice to a whisper, looking around to be sure no one was near enough to overhear, "…make love to you the way I do?"

"No, no, of course not," Ana backpedaled swiftly. "I know you're a woman, Traf. I'm just saying that most women get their periods before they're your age."

"Oh yeah? How old were you when yours started?"

"I was twelve." One of Ana's eyebrows rose as if to say, 'See, I told you.'

"What's the big deal about getting your period?" asked Traf, again in uncertain territory. She'd heard women talk about cramps and being inconvenienced, but until she'd started living with Ana almost a year ago, she'd never really had to deal with it. Certainly, the butches never talked about it among themselves. "From what I hear, it's no fun. I won't mind if it never starts."

"Still," said Ana, a note of concern in her voice, "I talked it over with Alice, and she agrees with me that maybe you should see a doctor." Seeing the look on Traf's face, she hurried on. "Not that there's anything wrong, but most women start before now, and it wouldn't hurt to make sure everything's okay."

"You talked it over with Alice?" Traf's anger was palpable.

"She asked if you'd had your first visitor. What could I say?"

"It's none of your business," said Traf. "That's what you should have said."

Still, she began to wonder if what she'd looked on as a blessing might indeed be a curse. A week went by, and then a second, before she made an appointment with an American doctor.

"According to your chart, you're eighteen years old, is that right?" asked Captain Scott.

"Yes, sir," she answered.

"And your height is average for the local population, even if you are underweight. That may be part of what's delaying your menses. I want you to try and gain weight if you can. Eat more and exercise less."

"Exercise?"

"You're on the women's softball team, right?"

"Yes, sir. And soccer, and bowling."

"And you work forty hours a week."

"Yes, sir, but so do most of the women I know."

The doctor picked up her hands and turned them over, palms up. Calluses born of long years working in the fields and hard nights fishing looked pale under hospital lights. "You work hard, you play harder, and you're not taking in enough food to fuel everything." He grabbed a pad of paper and scribbled on it. "Give this to Sgt. Kelly in the mess hall."

"What is it?" She wasn't eager to become reacquainted with the dictator who'd forced her to peel mountains of potatoes in her first weeks on base.

"I'm doubling your calorie intake. You'll also have a milkshake at every meal," he said. "I want to see you in two months and weigh you again."

"Yes, sir," Traf answered with a grin. She'd only had one milkshake before, and she couldn't see how drinking more of them would make her period start. *Silly Americans with their crazy ideas*.

Traf's investment in Ana's education at the school of domestic arts was paying off. The young woman taught Gabriela everything she learned, thereby reinforcing her own lessons. Their two butches had never eaten so well.

But their sewing skills truly distinguished the two femmes. During the Christmas season, several of their friends had worn their designs, then word of mouth spread like wildfire, and they began to receive orders for dresses.

Women who can afford a new gown every year always search for something new. Ana and Gabriela bought fashion magazines from the mainland to see the latest trends in Lisbon, London, New York, and Paris. Skillful, quick, talented, and soon in demand, the extra bedroom in Traf's house became their seamstress shop. Women arrived at Ana's door all day long, ordering finery for the festivals and being fitted. The inexperienced femmes, flattered by the attention, accepted too many orders. "We're swamped," each explained to their butch after working long hours.

Friday afternoon of Memorial Day weekend found Traf and Michaela without companionship. Gabriela and Ana were rushed with orders to finish in time. While pleased for their girls, the two butches found themselves left to their own devices. They headed over to Troublemakers to drink beer and chat with their butch buddies.

As usual, they talked about everything and nothing until the subject came around to sex, always a favorite topic of conversation. Within their developing butch culture, a myth arose that every butch should be a sexual virtuoso. However, in reality each thought everyone else knew exactly what to do with the embarrassing exception of herself.

They knew about heterosexual sex; half of them grew up in houses so small they'd heard their parents in the night. But for young lesbians, no adult role models existed except those they'd been warned against. Of course, now parents cautioned their children about them, so each one feigned knowing everything there was to know.

Pretending to be experts, everyone surreptitiously took notes from each other. Not one felt secure about what she ought to be doing or feeling during sex. Most of them muddled through as best they could, absorbing what they could from each other. When in a group, to keep their relative ignorance unrecognized, the butches would wait for someone to take a stance on something, then either build the idea up or tear it down based on the reactions of their friends.

"I go for hours," bragged Berta. "I once spent six hours making love to one woman." Her friends pulled at their beers. Sitting in the late afternoon on the clubhouse veranda, having hauled chairs outdoors to take advantage of the summer sun, they watched the little gray lizards on the low stone wall move languidly.

"Well," laughed Teresa at last, "what's wrong with you? Why did it take so long to get her to come? I wouldn't be bragging about taking all night to get your girl to the jumping place." She stubbed out her cigarette, finished off her beer, and stuffed the butt in the bottle, balancing it on the veranda wall.

Margarida nodded, sagely. "If anything, it should be the other way around. Any butch can get a woman…" she nodded diffidently, "…*there*, but it takes one with skill to get her there in only minutes."

"I disagree," put in Tina. "I think romance should take its own time, you don't want to go too fast, or too slow." When Teresa looked skeptical she added, "But you take just enough time so your lover knows she's appreciated." Teresa nodded and Tina relaxed.

"I dunno about all that, but I agree with Berta," mused Traf, putting her feet up on the low wall, crossing them at the ankles so she could enjoy looking at her brand new Keds sneakers, fresh from the base. "I like to take my time, make sure I'm giving my lover all my attention for as long as it takes." She wiggled her feet back and forth.

"There are probably as many opinions on the matter as there are butches on the island," said Margarida, tossing a roasted peanut into the air and catching it in her mouth. "That's a lot, right there."

"No kidding." Tina leaned forward. "I think there are a lot of us lesbians on Terceira." She glanced around their group, shy about putting forth her idea, but plunged on. "I mean, a lot more than maybe there should be. And the men, our brothers, there are a whole lot of them on our island, too." She gestured out toward the beach before them, where a half-dozen small fires were kindling against the approaching evening. "They're in their own groups, kind of like ours, all over the island. An American butch told me that people like us are rare in their country. She said she didn't know any other lesbians when she was growing up and had to move to a big city to find other women like herself."

As shy as Tina was, this idea of hers came as a surprise. The other women stared at her, which made her face burn. She rose and went to the cooler bringing another round of beers, wading through thick silence as she handed them out.

"I can't imagine what it must be like to grow up not knowing anyone else like you." Traf took a deep swig from the refreshingly cool bottle in her hands. "Almost as long as I can remember, I've had you guys." She nodded at Margarida, Tina, and Berta, whom she'd known from school. "And met so many others since then." She looked now at Teresa and Michaela.

"Someone else said something to me like that." Teresa nodded at Tina. Being a few years older and a taxi driver, she'd had the opportunity to meet other, more mature, lesbians. "Do you know Agatha? She's got a big house in Angra and is from a wealthy family who sent her to the mainland for an education."

"Oh sure," said Berta, handing around a bag of fried pork rinds. "She's a poet, isn't she? I go with my father to the theater once in a while to hear her read." She stopped in mid-toss, letting the pork rind she'd just thrown in the air fall to the ground. "Wait… you mean she's a lesbian?"

Teresa grinned. "Yes. I met her through a mutual friend who was also Agatha's lover at the time. Well, we were sitting around talking one day and she said something I've never forgotten. She's twenty-five years older than me and pointed out that there are twice as many lesbians now than there were twenty years ago."

"Maybe they just weren't as aware of each other as we are," suggested Margarida.

"Or," put in Berta, "there are more of us than ever being tempted into a life of sin." A look of horror crossed her face. "What if Terceira is like Sodom and Gomorrah?"

"Or maybe," said Tina in her quiet voice, "maybe there are more and more of us being born every generation." Once again, her words blanketed the group in silence.

"I like that idea better," agreed Traf. "God is making more of us all the time, so He must have a special purpose in mind for us. But why," she asked after thinking it over for a moment, "would He want to fill our island with lesbians and gays?"

"It would certainly slow down the birth rate," suggested Berta with a wink. Everyone laughed long and hard at the idea of a whole island of women and men who did not want romance from each other.

"And speaking of slowing down," said Margarida with a laugh in her voice, "tell us again how you spent six hours with your lover before bringing her to," she cleared her throat delicately, "satisfaction." Margarida raised one eyebrow.

"Oh, sure," agreed Berta, eager to show off her prowess. "I'll speed up, or slow down, or change the location of my kisses, whatever it takes to keep her pleasure rising,"

"And your own," teased Margarida.

Berta laughed. "Well, of course. But only as long as she keeps her hands to herself."

And there it was, the great taboo, raising its wicked head again. Traf had heard the argument a dozen times, but it still made no sense to her. This time, she decided to speak up. "Wait a minute. Are you telling me butches are supposed to touch femmes until they reach wonderful orgasms, but we, ourselves, are supposed to get our pleasure only when the femme doesn't touch us?" She looked around the group, truly perplexed. "How? Why?"

Teresa barked out a laugh. "Of course. When women touch me, the sex urge dries right up, but when she's moaning, thrashing under my touch, well, it takes me up and over the top." She looked at Traf, re-assessing and perhaps judging.

"The giving of pleasure is what makes a butch happy," explained Michaela, as if that argument sealed the deal. "The more pleasure we give, the happier we are."

"But how are we supposed to get the same pleasure if our lover doesn't touch us?" Traf's frustration finally spilled over. "When I make love to Ana," she blushed but continued, "she gets very wet, starts to move in rhythm with my fingers, and ends up cresting in a wave of pleasure. Sometimes her waves are very tall, other times they are low and lazy, but I can always tell when she's satisfied. She gets sleepy, kisses me, and cuddles up in my arms, then drifts off to sleep." She ran her fingers through her hair. "But me, I'm still all worked up. I get wet, but don't have the waves like she does, and I don't get satisfaction simply by watching and touching her." Traf looked around at the others. "Don't any of you ever feel that way?"

The other five butches either sat very still in their chairs or shifted uncomfortably. None of them looked her in the eye, choosing to drink their beer instead.

Finally, Berta lit up a cigarette, tossed the pack of matches in her shirt pocket and said, “I know how to give pleasure, so I do it. Sometimes I want more, sure.” Her chin rose sharply and she looked a bit defiant. “I move around until I trap one of Rose’s legs with both of mine and then I ride her thigh until I get mine.”

“Oh, sure,” agreed Teresa hurriedly. “Yeah, we all do that.” She lectured Traf like a teacher. “Just climb on one of her legs, like Berta says, and move up and down a couple of times. You'll feel much better.”

“Why don’t you want them to touch you?” asked Traf, truly curious. Ana was so convinced that Traf wouldn’t want to be touched she never even offered to return her caresses. All her femme friends seemed to hold the same opinion.

“For me,” said Berta, “I don’t want a woman to touch me because it distracts me, makes me lose my concentration on her pleasure.”

“Yeah, right,” laughed Tina. “I don’t want to be touched because it feels wrong. I feel wrong.” She struggled to make them understand. “I’m not happy.”

“The girl is the girl, and I am…” Teresa stopped. “I’m the guy, I guess.” She looked up quickly, but no one laughed. “When someone touches my breasts, or worse, down below, I remember I’m a woman and that is so upsetting I lose all interest in sex. So when they try to touch me I grab their wrists a few times, and they get the idea.”

“My body feels wrong.” Tina blinked once, then lit her own cigarette that glowed brightly in the gathering dusk. “That’s not what I mean. My body feels wrong because it’s getting pleasure.”

“You’re not supposed to get pleasure?” asked Traf.

“No, I know what you mean,” agreed Michaela. “The more pleasure I give my woman, the better I feel. If she has a really great orgasm, I feel fantastic. If she only has a small one or doesn’t make it at all, I feel like a failure. I want her to concentrate on her own pleasure, not mine.” She and Tina nodded at each other.

“That’s what I said,” complained Berta, and they all laughed.

“So when I’m really turned on, ride her leg and make sure she has a big orgasm,” Traf summed up. She wanted to believe that her friends were right and if she did what they suggested her own desires would be fulfilled and she wouldn’t spend so many nights dazed and horny. *It seems to work for the other butches, so what’s wrong with me?* Unwilling to find out, she added, “Just don’t let her touch me.”

Teresa laughed and patted Traf on the back as she started gathering up beer bottles stuffed with cigarette butts. “Now you get it,” she agreed, offering a hand to help pull her up.

The others rose and they carried their chairs indoors. It was Friday night and they needed to go home and spruce up before returning to the clubhouse with their girls. Each left with a reinforced notion of what it meant for a butch to make love. They were secure in their knowledge of the truth because they all agreed… even the ones with doubts.

Drinking a milkshake with every meal wasn’t nearly as much fun as she’d hoped it would be. At first, it was a novelty, but with only two flavors of ice cream, vanilla and chocolate, it quickly became boring. Sgt. Kelly supervised the loading of her tray personally, giving her large portions of rich food. She wasn’t allowed to leave the mess until she’d finished it all, so she got used to bellyaches and frequent trips to the toilet.

Sometimes she felt so lethargic from overeating that she fell asleep when waiting between driving shifts. Major Brandon noticed and asked her what was going on. When Traf explained she’d been put on a weight-gaining regimen, he wasn’t surprised. She’d been seriously underweight when she was first promoted. He’d been afraid of losing one of the best Portuguese soldiers under his command, so he’d helped her hide fishing weights in her boots. She’d come in just over the official weight cut-off, but obviously someone else noticed.

“I’m supposed to get weighed by the doctor in a week,” Traf explained. “But even though I eat everything Sgt. Kelly puts on my tray I’m not gaining. The food is so rich I throw up. I can’t even look at cheese or milk anymore, and I absolutely hate milkshakes. I’d be happy to never drink one again.”

“It sounds to me like you’re lactose intolerant,” the major said. “My wife is, too. Stay away from the milk, Mendes, and cheese unless it’s been aged for several years or more. Don’t worry; I’ll speak to Sgt. Kelly for you.”

For the next week, Traf was free from the milkshakes, and although her portions were still very large they were no longer covered in creamy sauces and melted cheese. Instead, he loaded her up with bread, eggs, and beef, the foods she’d grown up on. She started to feel much better.

Standing on the scale, the doctor recorded her total weight loss with real regret. He admitted he agreed with Major Brandon. It appeared she did not tolerate milk products well, something she could have told him if he'd only asked. She'd never liked milk as a child. Her mother had always given her water, tea, or coffee to drink instead.

"Oh, and that other matter?" Traf said. "You don't have to worry about it anymore. It's okay; I got my first period last night." She faked a grimace and rubbed her lower belly as she'd seen Ana do numerous times.

"Well, good," said Captain Scott. "I'm relieved we've at least helped that situation." He mentioned casually, "You can find American products to help with your menstrual flow in the PX. We've made a few improvements over your local traditions." She felt the sting of his smug paternalism. "I'll have the nurse find you a few pamphlets to help answer any questions you might have."

"Yes, sir," agreed Traf as she left his office to visit the PX and pick up supplies for Ana. *Good, pamphlets. Reading, I'm good at. Now maybe I'll find out how babies grow in women's stomachs and, more importantly, how they get out before my own periods begin.* She figured the American Air Force didn't need to know all her business.

But the pamphlets raised more questions than they answered. Military personnel were expected to know the basics, and she didn't. Even the pictures were no help.

Traf decided to ask a pro. As one of her duties as a VIP driver, she sometimes took visiting officers to unofficially sanctioned 'clean' houses of prostitution. Doctors routinely monitored the girls for diseases, making it worth the house's time and effort to meet the base's strict requirements. Understanding she could make or break their businesses with her recommendations, the madams all made nice with Traf. While she refused their tips and/or bribes, they knew she would gratefully accept an espresso as she waited to drive the officers back to the base when they'd finished.

The next time she got that duty she drove her VIPs to the House of Bella. While not good friends, she and the house madam recognized kindred spirits in each other. Although she dressed in silk and satin gowns, wore her hair up in curls, and spoke with a lipsticked mouth, Bella was butch. The women who worked for her knew, but her clients never suspected. She knew what her customers expected from a woman who owned a whorehouse and she played the role well.

Bella appreciated the business and took a rare break, joining Traf at the bar to buy her an espresso. At first embarrassed but eventually loosening up, the VIP driver explained her situation. She finally asked, "So am I weird, or what? Is there something wrong with me that I don't get my periods?"

Bella shook her head. “No, not at all. Some women never get them. Others start later. Some start early, like your girl. We’re each of us different, Traf. You’re healthy, attractive, and smart, everything you should be at your age. Don’t borrow trouble, your own will come soon enough. You’re fine.” She pulled Traf to her feet and turned her around, looking her over from head to foot. “As a matter of fact, if playing army with the Americans doesn’t work out for you, consider working for me.”

“What? Are you crazy?” Traf laughed. “Me, lie down with men and have sex with them? For money? Hell, no. I’ll go back to rolling cigarettes, first.” Traf stopped, realizing how insulting that sounded. “Not that there’s anything wrong with it…” She stammered to a stop because she did think something was wrong with it. She tried again. “Why do you do it, Bella? You’re a butch like me. You could do a man’s job.”

“I am doing a man’s job. It’s a business,” the madam answered simply. “Maybe I made choices different than you would have made, but then maybe my options weren’t quite the same, either.” She grinned at Traf. “All right, I did it for a girl, okay? She needed protection, which came easy to me, and we could double the income if I worked, too.” She winked. “The bitch got married to my best customer, but I found others to replace her. Now I provide for seven girls and myself. That’s not so bad, is it?” Traf had to agree Bella ran a nice, safe house. If any of the men got out of line she always managed to handle the situation before anyone got hurt too bad. “Anyway, my young friend, don’t waste time worrying about your lack of a period. It will start when it starts, and not a minute sooner. And then you’ll find yourself wishing it never had.”

It turned out the expert was right. Two months later, she got her very first ‘visitor’. Ana was thrilled for her lover. Traf, not so much.

Ch. 13 – Jingle Jangled

Summer, 1966

Following her promotion, occasionally Traf was assigned somewhere out of the country. She traveled to a lot to exotic places that were only names on a map before, such as Turkey, Greece, Germany, and Spain, sometimes for only a matter of days, sometimes for several weeks or even months at a time.

Not solitary by nature, when on assignment abroad, she made friends with other WAFs, Women in the Air Force, stationed in the same place. Unfortunately, she often never saw them again. But since everyone knew their friendships might last only as long as their postings, that made it easy to strike up a casual acquaintance. If her new friends had been stationed in the area for a while, they sometimes offered to show her the sights. Near the end of a three-month tour in Spain, a WAF who had been there before took Traf to her first sex shop.

While the WAF bought a magazine with pictures of naked men and women having sex, she looked around the dimly lit place seeing all manner of things she never imagined existed. Taken aback by the displays around her, Traf uttered not one word while inside the store but her eyes took rapid inventory of everything she saw. When they left the shop to go on their next errand, she memorized the street names so she could find her way back again. Something she saw captured her imagination.

Once she returned to her room, she did what she had done as a child. She sat and thought about the thing that caught her attention in the store. She wondered if she could make one herself, but doubted she had the necessary materials. Traf needed to go back and look at it again to be sure of the design and function. However, this time she would go alone.

Four hours before catching the flight back to Lajes, Traf gathered up her courage. Dressed in civilian clothes, she took a taxi, giving the driver a written note with the street names she memorized. He leered at her but obligingly took off in that direction. By the time they arrived her palms were clammy. Traf didn't often get nervous, but in this instance she found herself almost unable to speak.

"Gracias," she squeaked out as she left the cab. The driver tipped his hat, winking knowingly.

Traf strolled casually past the sex shop pausing to look in another store window. Surreptitiously, she checked the street for any uniforms. Then she swept her gaze over the people in the street more closely, looking for any faces that might recognize her own. Since someone in the service brought her here in the first place she knew others probably knew of its existence. No sense in being casual about things. She already knew she wanted to be a lifer in the Air Force, and so far the Americans seemed befuddled on the issue of sexuality. *Better to be discreet.*

A tiny bell over the door jingle-jangled as she walked in. A curtain to the back opened and an enormous, burly man emerged who, after taking one look at Traf's frozen face, swiftly disappeared again. Prosperous shop owners, this married couple knew how to work their business because just as quickly a much shorter woman, most likely his wife, replaced him. Reading her customer's body language, she inclined her head with a warm smile and eased her ample body between Traf and the door.

My panic can't be unusual. Clearly, I'm not the only potential customer wanting to flee.

The shopkeeper, a middle-aged woman with a plain face but a large expressive mouth, spoke only Spanish. Traf had picked up some during her posting, and interpreted many words that sounded similar to Portuguese. With smiles and kind glances, the woman rapidly put Traf at her ease.

It doesn't always take language to get ideas and intentions across and the eager shopkeeper wanted to help. Traf understood her to say, "I order our inventory and am prepared to sell anything in here." So she gestured toward the thing that caught her attention during her first visit.

The woman opened a glass cabinet and handed it to her. Long and slender but with a wide flat base, it would stand straight up if set down on a flat surface. It was smooth, cylindrical with a rounded tip, and made from hard plastic, a substance with which Traf had only recently become familiar when dealing with American products.

She gazed at the storeowner, wondering if she could use it in the manner she had in mind. The matronly woman read her mind, looked amused, and pointed down between her own plump legs. Traf blinked, then broke out in a great big guffaw. The woman smiled at her. They laughed together easily, and what little tension still remained in Traf's shoulders melted away. *Obviously, my idea isn't as revolutionary as I thought.*

The shopkeeper saw Traf's relief and brought forth a leather harness from a drawer behind the counter. She showed how one fit to the other, then demonstrated over her skirt how to wear it. The plump gray-haired woman still had it on when suddenly the doorbell jingle-jangled and someone entered.

Traf hurriedly turned her face away from the door and into shadow. The shopkeeper hastily whipped the contraption from around her hips and hid it behind the counter, then surged forward to intercept her latest customer. Traf busied herself in the corner while a man purchased and pocketed a magazine.

As his back faded from the closed glass door, she turned around, her heart once again pounding against her rib cage. Her temperature rose abruptly and her face radiated heat. *I want out of here, out into the clean air, away from things that will probably get me into trouble I can't even imagine.* Panic reached for her throat, ready to kick her into flight.

The shopkeeper, sensing a good sale in danger, quickly indicated in American money the total amount due for the harness and contraption. Traf paid hastily, relieved when the woman handed her a well-wrapped bundle in plain white paper exactly as if she bought something from any other store. Although eager to bolt from the shop, she stopped and turned. "Mucho gracias."

A wide open smile transformed the unremarkable, almost dowdy woman. In a moment, she grew flirtatious, throwing her a wink and playfully swatting Traf's butt as she passed out the door into the bright sunlight. After stopping in several other stores she signaled a taxi for a ride. All the way back to the base she wondered about people she knew and their sex lives.

Oh... Oh? Oh! The mental images made her to squirm. She noticed the taxi driver looking curiously at her in the rear view mirror and decided not to think about it.

Traf stuffed the white paper package deep into her traveling bag, finished packing, and caught the transport plane home to Lajes Field. *I can't wait to show Ana!*

After reporting to Major Brandon when she returned to Terceira, she headed straight home with the day off. Walking through the front door she heard Ana talking with a customer in the sewing room. Pausing just long enough to poke her head through the door to let Ana know she was home, she unpacked and put the white paper parcel under her side of the bed. Then she took a long, luxurious shower.

By the time she emerged from the bathroom, still toweling her hair dry, Ana had finished her business and closed up early for the day. She latched the shutters on her sewing shop window, indicating she was closed for business. Then she modestly shuttered the rest of their small house. Even though it was embarrassing to have the neighbors think she took a nap in the middle of the day, it beat having someone walk in on them. The gossip would spread faster than lightning strikes if anyone saw them loving each other, especially in the middle of the day. Mere roommates to the world at large, they tried never to appear as lovers.

Safe within the darkness of their home, Traf brought forth her bundle and presented it to Ana. "Open it."

Ana smiled at Traf, already accustomed to receiving gifts from the places where her lover found herself stationed. "What is it?" she asked perfunctorily as she opened the package. But she repeated herself in confusion. "What is it?" She held it up, the pinkish plastic inflexible in her hand. "It's funny looking. What's it for?" She waggled it by its base. Ana was even more surprised when Traf erupted into laughter.

"Well," she answered with a playful leer, "why don't I just show you?" She grabbed Ana by the hand and hurried her into their bedroom. Traf experimented for several minutes, taking care to get the thing around her hips in just the right place, the pink contraption sticking out from her body at a rigid right angle. The base nestled over her briefs and it was only as she turned sideways that Ana, catching sight of her profile, began to realize her intent.

"You think you're going to get that thing inside me?" squeaked Ana.

"We'll just have to give it a try and find out," Traf answered, advancing on her lover with obvious intent. The bobbling head of the contraption made them both break out in giggles, and they fell onto their bed, into each other's arms. Under the butch's expert touch, Ana's clothes loosened and dropped away. Traf took the thing in her hand and guided it toward Ana's opening.

"Ouch, wait!" said Ana. "That's hurting me." Sharp tears of pain popped into her eyes.

Traf stopped immediately, disappointed and sorry to hurt Ana in any way. She gathered her lover in her arms and pet her, smoothing a hand over her hair. *Well, so much for that.*

Ignoring the phallus still dangling between her legs, she stretched out beside Ana and held her until the pain eased away into fading memory. Soft kisses began, then swelled into heated, desperate ones. Stationed in Spain for three months, Traf wanted this intimacy. So did Ana.

Her fingers did their sexy dance on Ana's tender flesh, tickling, stroking, and teasing. She took her time, enjoying the pleasure of watching a beautiful woman moan while being caressed, her body arching up to make eager contact. In due time, Ana's natural juices began to flow freely, palpable proof of her excitement. Her skin flushed, infused with the heated blood pulsing through her veins.

"Now try it," she urged.

Traf had forgotten that she still had the thing on, but she scrambled between Ana's legs and presented its head once more at her opening. This time, with the young woman's natural lubrication and eagerness, it slid home. Traf wrapped both arms around Ana's slender body and kissed her. Her hips began thrusting in the age-old way of procreation, a completely new experience for them both.

A memorable one in fact. So much so that neither of them could resist telling their friends about their new toy. Traf searched her mind for something to call it, and latched on to the name chuckie. She had overheard one of the American soldiers refer to his own member that way, and it sounded as good as anything else.

"Can you get me one of those chuckies?" asked Michaela when she heard about it. "I bet Gabriela would love it."

Traf grinned wickedly at her friend. "Oh yeah, she'll love it. And so will you, buddy, so will you." She slapped Michaela on the back.

Word of the chuckie spread quickly through the butches at the clubhouse. Everyone wanted to see it, so she wore it under her clothes one night. Traf took the butches outside to show them, however. It just didn't seem like something she wanted to whip out in front of all the femmes.

That little bit of paternalism didn't stop the femmes from discussing the chuckie themselves, however. Ana sang its praises and before long some of the femmes asked their butches to find out more. With a hot, humid summer in full swing, everyone wanted to explore for themselves this marvelous new toy.

One night at the clubhouse, Odete nervously approached Traf. Her big, round face red with embarrassed determination, she clearly wanted to say something and would carry it out or die trying. She stood just behind Traf's shoulder where a group of butches sat talking. Nervously shifting from one foot to the other, she waited to be noticed.

"Uh, T-traf," she stammered, although stuttering was one bane God had not inflicted upon her. "Could I speak to you a moment?"

"Sure," she said. She didn't see Odete very often, anymore. Since the attacks, she and Lucy had lived unobtrusively together in her house in Serreta. They still came to the club but less often, maybe once every couple of months.

Their physical wounds had mended by this time but both had always been shy and seemed happy just existing in each other's company. Rumors around the island said Odete's father was still actively searching for the men who stabbed his daughter and raped her friend. More than once, he'd announced he would kill whoever it was when he found them. He was a good man who loved his daughter fiercely, yet Odete and Lucy refused to tell him about Mike. Both knew he would keep his word and then spend the rest of his life in jail. Neither wanted to trade his precious life for that of Lucy's worthless cousin.

Traf hauled a chair over with the toe of her shoe, but instead of sitting the big woman looked around at the group of butches sitting at the table. The others watched her curiously, clearly wanting to know what was up. A silence settled on the group intended to make Odete capitulate, sit down, and share her words with all of them. Instead she stood still as a rock, her face flushed and perspiring.

Traf took pity on the shy butch and rose from the table to walk her outside, away from prying ears. "What can I do for you, Odete?" she asked, shaking a cigarette free from her pack and offering it to the nervous butch.

Odete took the cigarette with shaking hands, inhaling deeply as Traf lit it for her. Then she cleared her throat nervously and began.

"My Lucy," she said, making Traf grin at the term, "she talked to your Ana." Here she stopped, apparently choked by her tongue. She coughed for a moment, hoping Traf would read her mind. But Traf stood and waited, having an idea where this was going and enjoying the big butch's discomfort.

"Well, Lucy said that Ana told her about something you brought home from Spain." Again she stopped, hoping that the other butch would pick up the conversation from there. But Traf, having too much fun to help her out, continued watching her, wordless and looking blank.

"She said you call it a chuckie," Odete finally blurted out, sweat beading on her forehead and upper lip. Taking a deep breath and squaring her shoulders, she looked the smaller woman in the eye. "Could you get me one? Please?"

Traf grinned. "Sure, Odete," she answered smoothly as if this kind of thing were discussed all the time. "I'm picking some up for others, too, when I go back to Spain in a few weeks. I'll get it for you then, ok? Do you want the whole pack?" When the big butch looked confused, she explained the need for a strap, and the bottle of lubricating oil that Ana and she finally found in the package.

Odete smiled hugely, for a moment losing the chronic timidity she held around her like a cloak. "Yes! I want the whole pack, please." She cleared her throat and looked around as if to find spying eyes. "Also, could you buy me some American underclothes?" Her blush spread once again across her cheeks. "Some silky panties for Lucy and some white t-shirts for me?"

"No trouble at all." Traf had already purchased such things for other butches. "Your Lucy will love them just as much as my Ana does."

Their eyes met and Traf winked. Odete realized she'd just discussed her own sexual behavior with someone… and survived. Relief bubbled from her in a contagious giggle that grew until they both howled like dogs under the full moon.

"How much money will it take?" asked Odete, quieting down and glancing around.

Traf calculated in her head. "For everything, around ten dollars," she announced.

Odete reached readily into her pocket but had only five with her. Her face fell.

"Don't worry, my friend," Traf said easily. "You can pay me when I bring it to you."

On her next visit to Spain, she ended up buying three chuckies, one for Michaela, one for Teresa, and one for Odete. The shopkeeper remembered Traf and silently congratulated herself for having made that first sale. If she read her customer correctly, the rewards were just starting to roll in.

As soon as she returned home to Lajes a week or so later, she borrowed a van from the base and drove out to the village of Serreta. Two neat bundles, one filled with fine white American underwear, and the other with the chuckie pack, sat on the seat beside her.

Why do I do it? Traf scolded herself. *I've been gone for weeks, I've just gotten home, I've got plans for later today, what makes me keep telling people I'll do this for them, or get that?* It was irritating but she'd said she'd do it and she had only one word. *Just get it done, and then the pesky errand will be out of the way.* Pasting a smile on her face just like she did at work when driving an officer she didn't like very much, she drove on.

Lucy, surprised to see the American van stop in front of their door, saw Traf, waved to her, and ran to the fields calling Odete in. While waiting for the big butch to make it to the house, Lucy whipped up a quick breakfast, set the table, and entertained Traf.

After washing up, Odete joined them at the table. They ate fried eggs and potatoes with buttered cornbread, spending a leisurely hour chitchatting. Sitting with the young women, enjoying their hospitality, all Traf's pique at the errand disappeared. She might not know the two well, but Lucy and Odete were good, kind, decent people.

As Traf left, she asked the big butch to walk her out. Then, once at the van, she discreetly handed her friend the two paper-wrapped bundles.

"I never thought you'd remember." Odete looked surprised. "I figured you'd forget since I didn't have the money then."

"Never, my friend," Traf answered. "I have only one word, and I keep it."

"I've got the money for you now." Odete raced back inside. When she came out, she gave Traf a crisp new ten dollar bill and the biggest smile that ever crossed her lips. "Thank you," she said earnestly. She hesitated for a heartbeat and added, "…my friend."

On the drive back to base to return the van, Traf reflected. *This errand was worth more than the time I spent. Odete called me her friend. A person can always find more time… it's much harder to find a friend.*

Later, while telling Ana about her visit, they heard the distinctive sound of Michaela's VW bug. Looking out the window, they saw Gabriela bouncing in her seat and waving happily. Michaela honked the horn once, looking just as eager.

Traf immediately yanked open the front door, joining her friend at the car's trunk. There, Traf handed Michaela a few bundles, including one wrapped in white paper she'd brought with her from Spain. The two butches shared a wink, and then Traf and Ana piled into the back seat of the VW. The femmes, excitement shining from their eyes, hugged awkwardly in the small car. The seamstresses almost never had adventures and both had looked forward to this day for months.

"Everyone ready?" asked Michaela.

"Ready!" the rest answered. The VW pulled out onto the cobblestone street and they all settled in for the drive. They headed to a sheltered area Michaela and Traf found while scouting around in Caldeira, a cove created at the ocean's edge by the island's banked but still simmering volcano. The four friends planned to camp overnight, a first for the two excited femmes.

Because their girls were along, the butches teased and grumbled.

"Why do we have to bring cooking utensils, food to cook, and all these other things?" Michaela demanded. "Traf and I usually make do with whatever's at hand. We find our own food." She grabbed Gabriela's pack, adding it to her own, and started down the steep path that led to the beach.

"Most of this stuff the two of us would gladly do without, such as a change of underwear or blankets to sleep on," Traf added helpfully.

"Eww," chorused Ana and her best friend.

"But," Gabriela teased Michaela as she started down the trail after her, "doesn't the pleasure of our company make up for the inconvenience of carrying a little extra weight down the cliffs?"

Michaela laughed and reached up to take her hand and steady her. "I agree wholeheartedly! You two are worth every kilo!"

"Agreed!" Traf said, slipping Ana's bundle over her shoulder. She gestured for Ana to follow Gabriela as everyone laughed. With high spirits, they all looked forward to their weekend.

"Do you think you'll find enough limpets to make a dinner?" Gabriela asked as she jumped the last bit down to the ground, turning around to look at the two still descending.

"Of course they will," answered Ana. She patted Traf's arm. "These two will find enough limpets for all four of us, and we'll have some left over!"

"No." Michaela shook her head, reaching up to help Ana down, glancing over her shoulder just long enough to throw a wink at Traf.

"We're going to find only enough for the two of us, and you two little ladies can eat whatever you're making us carry down these rocks!"

"Sure," Traf agreed. "You girls brought enough to feed us even if we don't find a single limpet. So what are you worried about?" She waggled one eyebrow saucily at Ana, who giggled and ducked her head, making the casual braids hanging over her shoulders dance. She looked very pretty in her pleated skirt and white blouse.

"This is going to be so much fun!" Gabriela said, shivering deliciously. "I've never done anything as daring as this before! I feel so brave!" She didn't usually travel far from home, the very idea brand new and exciting.

By early afternoon, they had two tents set up on a small grassy meadow, protected from the worst of the weather by tall cliffs on three sides. Michaela and Traf were eager to get down to the shore to search for the shellfish delicacy they all enjoyed so much. They tore off through riotous bamboo shoots between the meadow and the beach and soon clambered over the igneous rocks that sheltered thousands of tide pools, each hiding its own treasures.

Watching them go Ana said, "I'm a little nervous about being left here alone. Do you think it's safe?"

"It must be," Gabriela said quietly. "Michaela wouldn't have left me here if it wasn't safe." But they took a few moments to reassure themselves that the tall walls of rock surrounding the camp truly isolated the meadow. Reassured, they wandered around, exploring for at least an hour before they set about creating a cooking area, by then thoroughly enjoying the freedom of the outdoors.

Together they gathered some loose rocks and built a fire ring. Then they went looking for firewood, carrying several armfuls back and stacking sticks and branches to one side of the campsite. Gabriela found four larger stones, all roughly the same size, and placed them in a square just inside the ring of smaller stones.

Ana reached into one of the bundles the butches had carried down on their backs, and unpacked a large piece of metal, the sides of a discarded ten-gallon aluminum can from the base that had been cut open and hammered flat. Later, to cook the limpets, she would lay the metal over the fire across the four larger stones. As it heated, it would warm a pan filled with fresh water from the jugs they brought, and fresh herbs she packed along. At the last minute, Ana would pop in the fresh shellfish. What a delicious dinner it would be.

Having finished the preparations, the two femmes finished unpacking. They made beds out of blankets and created a homey environment in each of the tents. They picked some wild flowers and spread them around the laid fire; later their scent would warm the air. By the time they finished, it was late afternoon, and they expected their butches back at any moment. Gabriela filled the pan with water while Ana lit the fire. The fresh air fueled their appetites.

Nimble as crabs, Michaela and Traf scrambled among tumbled boulders in search of their dinner while the shadows on the cliffs grew taller. As the sun began its long descent toward the hills behind them, Michaela looked up long enough to realize they had rounded a curve of the island and entered Caldereinha, a small inlet.

"Traf!" she called. "We've wandered all the way over to the next cove. I think we ought to go back soon."

"Sure. But look over here, Michaela! I've found a whole cluster right here!"

Michaela hurried over to look and sure enough, determined limpets clung to the rocks lining the entire tide pool. Greedily, they pried the delicacy loose and plopped them down into tin buckets. Every few minutes one of them would wander a little farther, finding yet another bounty.

Finally, their full buckets could hold no more. They stood up and stretched their backs, balancing on uneven boulders. As they looked around, Traf gasped.

Gabriela started pacing back and forth across the campsite. Ana sat on the ground, stoking the campfire. The water in the pan boiled away an hour earlier. Both grew more nervous as time passed, the sun lowering as inevitably as a guillotine. They passed the time in idle chitchat, neither one ready to voice her concern. Each one thought about her butch, but they talked about sewing, and cooking, and things they did well. The bravery they felt earlier speedily turned to bravado.

"Oh no," Traf cried, grabbing her friend's arm and frantically pointing. "Michaela, look at that!"

Behind them, tall waves rushing in blocked their access to Caldeira. While they weren't looking, intent on finding dinner, the tide rose. The narrow pathway back to their campsite now lay under water, impossible to cross.

"Those waves will smash us on the rocks!" Traf cried. "They'll knock us off our feet and then drag us into the ocean!"

A lot of people on the island couldn't swim, Michaela and Traf included. A little rough, the waves crashed into the jut of rock between the two coves, exploding into foam-white spray taller than either of them. They stared at each other bleakly.

"We're safe enough where we are. The water will continue to rise for a while, but we can move farther in onto the land and wait it out."

"Or," suggested Michaela, "we can climb up the cliff side here in Caldereinha and then walk over and around until we get back to Caldeira, then climb back down again."

"That's too dangerous and will take just as long," Traf complained. "We'd have to climb up a cliff, then down another in the dark, without any rope. Let's just wait for the tide to go down, and then we'll cross back the way we came."

"What about the girls?" asked Michaela. "Don't you think they'll worry about us?"

"They'll have to worry one way or the other," Traf muttered morosely. "We won't be able to get back to them for hours, no matter if we go up and over, or wait here until we can just go around." In the end, their heavy buckets of shellfish won, and they decided to sit on the rocks and wait out the tide. They certainly weren't the first to do so and surely wouldn't be the last.

"Ana," broached Gabriela finally. "Where do you think they are?"

"I don't know," complained Ana eagerly, glad one of them had finally broken through the mundane to the immediate. "Do you think they're hurt or something?"

Gabriela looked off toward the bamboo shoots where they last saw their two butches disappearing. "I just don't know," she whispered. She turned around and looked behind them at the sun starting to set. "It's going to be dark soon. What should we do?"

Ana stood up and brushed the dirt from her skirt. "I think we better go look for them." She disappeared into her tent and came out with a tiny flashlight she brought along. She shook it a few times, then found the switch on its side and flipped it up. A beam of light shot out of its end, creating a pale circle on the grass.

The long twilight hours of summer darkened to dusk. Shadows grew tall and would soon knit the night around them. The two friends walked shoulder to shoulder toward the stand of bamboo. Their steps were sure-footed and light until they reached and began to move through the tall, dry reeds. The late afternoon sun dissipated above their heads and the tiny flashlight couldn't push far against the bamboo pushing back.

"I can't see where we're going in here," said Ana, completely unaware her voice shrank with fear.

"Me either," whimpered Gabriela. "I don't think we can find them this way. Maybe we should go back and wait. They're probably just playing a trick on us, trying to scare us!"

"It's working," Ana muttered as they turned and retraced their steps. They sat down near the fire once more, relieved by its light. Ana turned off the flashlight but left it nearby on the ground. A blanket of darkness soon surrounded the fire, trying to smother them.

"This is boring," Traf complained as the tide continued to rise. The water had completely swallowed their pass by now; they traveled inland to wait. The sun set, darkness descended, and climbing the cliff walls became impossible. They had no choice, now, but to wait for the tide to recede.

"It may be boring," answered Michaela, "but it's safe. Unless you want to learn how to swim in the dark?"

"Um, no."

"Are you hungry?" asked Gabriela. She had put more water to boil and they nervously sipped coffee. In the warm evening they shivered, chilled to the bone.

"No," answered Ana. "I couldn't keep it down." She looked small and frightened sitting beside the fire. Gabriela heard a noise in the bushes, and before she could say so, Ana grabbed the flashlight and shone it at the bamboo looming in front of them in the dark. The noise came again, and through the gleam of electric light, they saw the confused fluttering of a bird taking refuge in the relative safety of the sheltering reeds.

Gabriela grinned at Ana, who smiled back sheepishly.

Edgy with nerves, horrible ideas began to creep into the conversation. "What if one of them is hurt, and they need to be rescued?" asked Ana of the night, unwilling to see her fear reflected on Gabriela's face. "What if they're both hurt?" Their smiles vanished.

"What if they fell into the sea and drowned?" was her best friend's response. A bleak silence settled around them. There was nothing left to say, the worst already voiced.

"Is the tide going down yet?" Michaela asked for the thirtieth time, cursing her poor night vision. Traf peered out over the dark water. The sea finally started to slink back into the belly of the ocean, reluctant to leave the area it claimed for its own each night.

"It's going down," she assured Michaela as her fishing night-eyes played over the path they needed to cross. "But it's still too high."

Ana began wringing her hands, although she seemed oblivious to the action. Time after time, she fingered the gold ring her lover gave her last Christmas. Gabriela noticed in her friend a tendency to jump every time she heard a noise. They were both so nervous it was a wonder neither had started to cry yet.

The moon had not yet risen, and darkness surrounded them. Old nightmares from childhood joined forces with the legitimate fear they felt for their missing lovers. They huddled together, weak, vulnerable, and very frightened.

"Okay," Traf finally announced to Michaela. "I think I've noticed a pattern. If I'm right, I think we can get out of here pretty soon."

"What pattern?"

She gestured toward the area they needed to cross. "I've been keeping track, and I think there are three large waves, and then a really weak one." She squinted into the darkness, counting, keeping track for several minutes.

"You're right," agreed Michaela excitedly. "That was three large waves, and then a small one. Now what?"

"The tide's going out pretty fast now, and if we keep count, I think we can make it across during the short wave."

"What if you're wrong, and the short wave doesn't come for some reason?" asked Michaela.

"Then you better hope you're stronger than that wave," Traf answered, flippant but determined.

She began picking her way over the rocks and boulders toward the pass they had to cross, Michaela close behind her. Waves splashed them with spray, drenching their pants and folding them against cold legs. Traf felt invigorated, challenged.

"I don't know," hedged Michaela when they neared the pass. "The waves are still pretty high, Traf. Maybe we should wait a while longer?"

"I'm tired of waiting. We both run pretty fast. If we're careful where we put our feet, I think we'll make it just fine. We'll run together," she said, counting waves. "Now get ready, this is the last big wave coming in."

Michaela crouched, ready to spring forward and run as fast as she could.

"I think we better go get some help!" announced Gabriela. "They're in trouble out there somewhere and we're just sitting here!"

"You're right!" agreed Ana. The two jumped up, then looked around the campsite. With both tents up, and their belongings spread out all around the camp, they looked at each other in exasperation and started hurriedly packing everything up. They knew better than to leave things lying around out where anyone could find them. It was too hard to replace anything. Tears of frustration and fear leaked from the corners of their eyes as they labored on the last bit of packing.

Abruptly, Michaela and Traf burst through the bamboo reeds and nearly startled them to death.

"Aaaieeeee!" shrieked Ana, throwing herself around Traf's neck. Gabriela stood still as if rooted to the spot until Michaela raced over and hugged her. The two femmes burst into the tears they had so valiantly held back. For the next few moments, questions flew like daggers.

"Where have you been?"

"Stuck waiting for the tide to go down."

"Didn't you know we'd be worried about you?"

"Yes, but we stayed too long on the rocks, and there wasn't any way back."

Then the recriminations started. "You should have come back earlier!" This said with a distinct tinge of anger.

"You frightened us!" Accompanied by a shove.

"But we brought back buckets of limpets! Look!"

"I don't care about limpets!"

"We thought you were hurt, or maybe even…"

"Dead!"

Traf tried soothing words. "Oh, honey, don't cry! I'm fine…"

"But…" shouted Ana as Gabriela swung and connected a good slap across Michaela's face. "…two minutes ago you were lost, mangled, drowned."

Michaela grabbed Gabriela's hand as she swung again, pulling her femme close. "I'm safe, sound, and breathing, sweetheart."

"Thank God!"

"What about you two? Are you okay?"

"Now we know you're not dead!"

"Thank God!"

"We were so worried about you being worried about us."

"I wasn't scared but she was."

It's amazing how swiftly the range of human emotions can be expressed once unleashed. Tears flew, anger raged, relief burbled, but finally love won out. The femmes threw their arms around their butches' necks. After a few consolatory hugs and snuggles, they all settled down to a late supper. While Ana and Gabriela fixed the food, they ordered Traf and Michaela to unpack everything they had packed back up while "…getting ready to climb cliffs in the dark to seek help for whatever rescue was required to save our sorry-ass butches."

Sheepish, tremendously sorry they had made their lovers worry, Traf and Michaela did so without complaint. The two resurrected the tents, remade beds, and spread soft blankets near the fire. The femmes, relishing their lovers' penitence, took special care and created a delicious feast.

They sat around the rekindled fire for several hours, sharing stories, leisurely enjoying the shellfish, telling each other how brave they had been, and enjoying the scent of fresh ocean air. Much praise fell to the talented cooks and even more on the intrepid fisherwomen who'd supplied the feast. Traf tucked dried flower petals into small pinecones and tossed them on the fire, sending bursts of scent into the air. Michaela told a ghost story, followed up by another from Gabriela. Everyone enjoyed shivering at the 'what if's' by moonlight.

Finally the four friends banked the fire and wished each other sweet dreams. Then each couple spent the night making up the same way lovers have forever, even if this time it was between a butch, a femme, and their chuckie.

Ch. 14 – An Uncivil War

Winter, 1966/67

Over the next several months, Major Brandon sent her overseas to Europe multiple times, usually only for a few weeks, but occasionally longer. Since she wasn't married and had no dependents, she was easy to assign and never balked at traveling. "I want you to apply for Top Secret clearance," he told her. "You're just the kind of officer we're going to need for future assignments."

"Yes, Sir," Trafulha agreed readily. "I enjoy seeing new places." She completed the paperwork and returned it to him promptly, but had learned by then that the gears of the Armed Services move slowly and it might be a long time before, or if, anything came of it.

When finally assigned for the first time in the United States, it was like a prayer answered. *America!* She'd always known that she would go one day, but here it was, her dream come true. People laughed at her, called her a dizzy fly, and flat out told her she'd never make it. *All but one.* She felt Grandfather's proud arm squeeze her shoulders as she climbed down the ladder of the plane and placed her foot on the soil of her intended homeland for the first time.

But nothing, not even the streets of Rome, prepared her for the speed at which everything traveled in America. As she studied the maps of the routes she would drive the sheer size of it strained her credulity. The numbers astounded her, not to mention mentally converting metrics to whatever they called the American way of measuring. The dimensions must be wrong. Growing up on a small island, and her later experiences in the relatively small countries of Europe, left her unprepared for the endless spaces. Even crossing the border from one state to another confused her. *No checkpoint or any other way to tell except small signs posted on the road as I whizz by.*

"You've got to see it for yourself," Traf told Ana when she returned to Lajes. "What silly children we were to believe the streets of America are paved with gold cobblestones, green dollars grow on the branches of trees, and everyone lives a life of ease and prosperity. But we would never have dreamed of the things I've seen, either. You've got to see for yourself."

"It sounds wonderful," Ana agreed. "I'd love to see it, especially those shopping malls. Are there really that many stores all in one place? Tell me about that again."

To the US Air Force, Ana was officially Traf's next of kin, a cousin. This wasn't true, of course; however, the Americans were very clear - a cousin they would accept but never a lover. If she wanted to travel with Traf, it would be easy to arrange. Ana could be her assistant, someone to make sure her uniforms were clean, pressed, and ready, and even earn a small stipend for doing what she already did.

However the first time the opportunity arose, Ana discovered she had no interest whatsoever in leaving their little island of Terceira, especially since it meant flying through the air. The mere idea of being as high in the sky as a bird terrified her. "I'll be much happier staying home and working at my sewing business," she explained. "I'm busy all the time."

"Are you sure?" Traf raised her eyebrows and waggled them. "It can get mighty lonely when I'm a stranger in a strange place. Do you want me to be all alone? What if I need you?"

"Nonsense," answered Ana. "You're the bravest woman I know." Turning back to the dress she was hemming, she added, "You'll be fine."

So Traf learned how to make friends easily and just as easily let them go. Always billeted in Officer's Transit Quarters, with any number of other women officers, she got used to the idea that she would know them for a few days and never see them again. Others stayed longer, usually eighteen months, and stayed in Bachelor Living Quarters if they were officers or barracks if they were enlisted. Those friends Traf could look forward to seeing again during her various hops.

In late September, she was sent to Germany. The three-month tour became routine, driving VIPs around to various important meetings. As winter settled in, Traf spent most of her off time on base. Glad to have learned to drive in snow and on ice, she didn't mind escaping those elements whenever possible. She'd never experienced such weather, totally different from what she knew on Terceira. She missed home, but she comforted herself with the thought that the dreary tour ended the week before Christmas and she'd be back in time to celebrate with Ana, family, and everyone at Troublemakers. Until then, temporary friends would have to do.

She and Janet Hammond, another VIP driver whose tour in Frankfurt wouldn't end until summer of next year, shopped together for presents at the PX and in town. They whiled away the cold dark days talking, sharing personal stories. Traf heard about growing up in a military family, and Janet learned about life on an island. They described lives completely new to each other, and a mutual respect grew between them.

On December twenty-second, the day her tour ended, a sudden snowstorm grounded all planes. As the snow continued to fall, she waited impatiently for flights to be cleared for take-off. As military transit, she could only take available flights no matter how much they zigzagged around the world. Once, she'd been bounced from Europe to America, to the Mediterranean, and back again before finally landing at Lajes Field, Azores. It could take several exhausting, travel filled days to get home.

Over six feet of snow fell in the next few days, a blizzard of epic proportions. Icy surfaces and strong winds made runways unsafe for landings and takeoffs. Traf still believed she'd make it right up until Christmas Eve when the base announced all flight were grounded for the next three days. She realized with a shock that she'd miss the holiday for the first time in her life.

No way home! She'd never considered this possibility before. *Unthinkable.*

Traf hurriedly sent off a telegram to Ana, letting her know the situation. Dispirited tears almost leaked at the thought of their not being together but she blinked them back fiercely. She was a soldier, an American soldier, and God damn it, she wasn't going to get upset over a stupid disappointment. But she spent the rest of Christmas Eve lying in her dark room, an occasional groan escaping into pathos.

Christmas morning dawned gray-skied and gloomy. By noon heavy drifts of snow still blocked the sidewalks to the Chapel and mess hall. The holiday Mass and meals were postponed until paths could be cleared. Traf look at her packed garment bag, stuffed full of presents and boxes of candies and delicacies she should be sharing with family and friends. Another bleak sigh escaped her.

A restlessness nibbled at her until she rather despondently began walking around the BOQ. She headed for the section of rooms reserved for women officers stationed during longer tours. From Janet's open door the joyous sound of the Vienna Boys Choir singing German Christmas carols floated through the air into the sterile hallway.

Standing in the doorway to listen, she saw her friend sitting on her bed and talking to another woman officer, a radio playing in the background. "Hey Traf," Janet called out as she waved her in. "You know Tracey, don't you?"

Traf grinned, hailing them with a wave. "Sure I do," she said, walking into the room and extending her hand for the other woman to shake. "Nice to see you again, Lieutenant."

"We're just sitting around feeling sorry for ourselves." Tracey waved a Christmas cookie decorated with red sprinkles in the air. "Pull up a chair and join us, why don't you?" She indicated an open tin box. "I was hungry so I raided the presents I bought for my family. I'll have to replace it before I go, now." She laughed. "Help yourself," she offered expansively.

"And I've got a pot of coffee on, so sit down and join us," finished Janet, gesturing to a hot plate set up on her desk. A bowl of sugar, its hill of white glittering like the snow outside, sat beside it.

Traf couldn't stop grinning. This sure beat sitting alone in her room watching a snowstorm out the window. "Wait a minute," she blurted. "I'll be right back."

She raced off down the halls back to her own quarters. Unzipping her travel bag, she reached deep inside to pull forth a five-pound box of Christmas candy. Tucking it under her arm, she happily retraced her steps, enjoying the sound of the carols growing louder as she approached.

Two other women had joined the party by the time she returned, and each brought along some goodies they'd planned to share with their own families. Over the next several hours, other lonely souls found their way into the light and laughter until a dozen or so had gathered. Everyone contributed to the party and when the path to the mess hall finally cleared, they trooped off together to a turkey dinner complete with all the fixings.

After the feast, the base chaplain celebrated Mass in one corner of the mess hall; Traf and several others attended. It ended just in time to take several thoughtfully packed baskets of leftovers and pies back to the BOQ where the party continued into the wee hours of the morning. Someone brought out two bottles of cognac, others shared good German wine and beer, and everyone got merry.

During one part of the evening, the conversation drifted to how each celebrated the holiday and Traf enjoyed hearing the other women describe their family traditions. She heard for the first time about mistletoe, plum puddings, and Hanukkah, and tried to imagine their homes the way they described them; perfect American families where no one knew trouble or experienced poverty.

When it was Traf's turn, she sighed. "When I was a kid, I'd leave my shoe by the cooking fire. On Christmas morning, the baby Jesus had pee'd in it, filling it with candy and fruit." Some of the other women laughed. "Not that much different than a sock filled by a fat saint," she said, a trifle defensively.

"True," Janet acceded with a warm smile. "I love hearing about different heritages. That's the best part of traveling in the Air Force."

Mollified, Traf went on, "Every year, I created something new for the wooden nativity scene. With my pocketknife I carved the holy family first, and then the shepherds, followed by the kings. Then I did the animals, the cows and sheep. I'd beg my mother for left-over paint to finish them." Remembering those early years, she added, "My parents were too old for Christmas decorating, so I'd drag in a tree, set it up, and hang small oranges and wrapped pieces of candy on it." She laughed. "I'd pick one off each night to take to bed with me. They were almost always gone before Christmas Eve."

After consulting her watch and doing some fast math, she described the special meal that was, at that moment, being served at her sister's house. "Alice is pulling the alcatra out of the brick oven."

"What's alcatra?"

"For Christmas it's usually beef but you can use fish, or pork, or beans for that matter," Traf explained. "A large clay pot is stuffed with meat, covered with good red wine…" Janet raised an open bottle of pinot noir and the group cheered. "…and a bag of spices is thrown in, too. Then it's cooked slowly in a brick oven, allowed to cool, then reheated over and over again for the better part of a week. By the time Christmas comes, it's…" her voice trailed off as she remembered the familiar flavor, "…delicious."

Traf cleared her throat. "We spend the rest of the day out, visiting friends, family, and neighbors, chatting and hearing good news. Then we go home and wait for our own visitors. Everyone shares the delicious puddings, candies, and other delicacies we've prepared especially for this day." Finishing her description of what was going on at home, her eyes stung with hot tears held at bay by sheer will. *I don't cry*, she reminded herself sharply the same way she had as a child when Father would start on her with his belt.

Perhaps to divert attention from the struggling young lieutenant, Janet raised her glass. "Sharing is the best part of Christmas, no matter where you happen to be." She looked around the jolly group. "To us and ours, and a future filled with other Christmases we're blessed to share with family, strangers, or strangers who become family."

"To us and ours!"

While saying her prayers that night, Traf realized that this had not been the worst Christmas of her life, but one of the best. She had expected to spend the day depressed, melancholy, and missing home. Instead, she found something completely unexpected.

Another new family, not one to replace the Troublemakers, nothing could. But they're a new kind of family of friends, my sisters in the Service. Most of these women she'd never see again and yet for the rest of her life they would live vibrantly in her memory just as they were now, caught in this moment of time and remembered with great affection.

When she finally returned to Lajes, she didn't get to stay long before receiving an emergency posting. Another VIP driver with the rank necessary to drive high-level officers had a sudden appendectomy and was now recovering in the hospital. Traf went to Turkey, assigned as her substitute until she could return to duty or her two-week tour ended, whichever came first.

Traf's first visit to the Middle East captivated her imagination. Ankara was a very different city than she'd ever seen before. Beautiful women wore colorful long tunics covering pants gathered at the ankle. Bright smiles lit their faces and their dark eyes sparkled. Gold jewelry hung from ears and necks, decorating round brown arms and wrists.

Some WAFs who'd been stationed there for a while took Traf to a street market with mountains of food. Her eyes widened in wonder. Piles of tangerines rose taller than herself. Watermelons stacked in the open air looked like a green-striped stairway to heaven. Whole lambs roasted on open fire spits. Live chickens squawked from cages. People milled here and there, eating or browsing through fascinating edibles. Traf had never seen such joyful abundance!

She wandered around, absorbing the exotic scents unique to that place. The strange language sounded unlike any she recognized; there were no Latin roots for her to cling to. Entering an area full of tented vendors, she had to negotiate with hand gestures to buy trinkets since nobody there spoke English, much less Portuguese. Luckily, the business of buying and selling is nearly as old as time and has conquered many a national boundary so eventually she carried off her purchases, happy with the exchange. She left the vendors pleased enough also, although the vendor grapevine warned an American with a strange accent drove a harder bargain than usually struck with someone in uniform.

When a WAF told her that she laughed. "They're not wrong. We Portuguese always bargain hard but we respect fine work and craftsmanship." They were strolling through a far section of the marketplace when she caught sight of the local government's public mutilations and executions, rooting her to the spot.

Even on Terceira where the police often operated independently of the law, such cruelty could never pass as justice. In numb shock she watched a man lose his hand at the wrist for theft, but her feet found wings when another was brought to the block to lose his head. Even as her footsteps carried her swiftly to the bus that would take her back to the base, she heard the heavy 'thwack' of the ax cutting through human flesh and embedding in the chopping block, accompanied by the anguished, horrified shriek of the new widow. The same air whose scents she'd enjoyed mere moments earlier seemed suddenly tainted with the stench of blood. It took two showers to drive the smell from her nose and she never returned to the market.

Driving a brigadier general from the base to the American embassy and back several times a day seemed like easy duty. It fed her pride to have the flag with its bright star waving from the antenna of her vehicle, indicating she drove a general. Seeing the two guards at the embassy gate snap crisply to attention became a daily pleasure. A few years back, the island of Cypress had accepted the U.N. resolution calling for a cease-fire, but bitter fighting had broken out between Greek Cypriots and the Turkish Cypriots who shared their island. The General she drove went to and from the embassy hoping to negotiate a more lasting peace.

Still cold in this part of the world, Traf loved wearing her winter blues. The thick warm material made it much easier to keep her uniform looking sharp and pressed throughout the day, an important aspect of her job. Always very exacting in her dress, her evaluations reflected her efforts.

That quality often led her superiors to select Traf to drive the highest-ranking VIPs.

Already after ten, she drove the General to the embassy for the second time that morning and parked her van on the long driveway to await his return. Lost in thought, just gazing about, she was surprised when three young Turks approached out of nowhere.

"Get out of the vehicle!" one of them ordered.

Startled, she considered the young men. They dressed like locals. One's beard still grew in patchy tufts, and the others seemed not much older. Each held a glass bottle filled with a yellowish liquid, cotton stuffed in the necks. As blood pounded on her eardrum, she scanned the area for any kind of help. The two uniformed guards a significant distance down the driveway looked out of the compound for trouble, not in.

Panic fought with reason and her shoulders squared. "What are you going to do?" She addressed the one who spoke.

"We're going to blow up the general's car." He smirked at her.

A second one held up his hand, quieting the speaker. He stepped a little closer to her door and asked, "American?"

She nodded sharply at him holding her head high. "United States Air Force."

He cocked his head listening to her, then said, "You speak American with an accent. Where are you from?"

"I'm Portuguese, I work for the Americans," she answered proudly.

The men turned aside and ducked their heads together, speaking hurriedly to each other while she glanced down the driveway to see if anyone noticed anything. No one did. She was on her own in this.

The first one spoke to her again. "Step out of the car, Miss. We're going to blow it up, but we have nothing against you Portuguese. Move away, now!" His arm rose, the bottle glittering dangerously in the clear morning air.

"Wait!" She gave him a slightly desperate look. "Let me at least get my coat and hat. They're expensive and it's cold here!" She started leaning over, reaching for her jacket draped over the passenger seat.

"All right, but hurry up." The young Turk smirked at his friends.

She kept her eyes focused on him as she deftly opened the glove box and pulled out her service revolver. She leveled it directly between his eyes.

"This is American property," she explained to them reasonably as their eyes bulged with dawning awareness. A look of worry entered their dark flashing eyes at their sudden change in circumstances. "I have sworn to protect and defend everything American. I don't want to shoot you but if you attempt to harm me or my vehicle, I will."

The young men looked at each other, dropped the bottles, and took off running in three different directions. The odor of gasoline wafted on the breeze. The threat dealt with, she settled back into the driver's seat but kept the revolver in her lap. She started mentally preparing the report she would make when she returned to the base.

The wail of sirens shattered the serene quiet of the morning a few minutes later; an Ankara police car drove right through the embassy gate without stopping, and before she knew what happened, Turkish officers surrounded her, guns drawn and aimed at her head.

"Step away from the vehicle," barked a man whose uniform had more decorations than the others.

She climbed out of the car and one of the officers snatched her revolver from her hand. "What's happening?" she asked.

"You're being arrested for threatening to kill Turkish nationals," barked the one clearly in charge. And without another word or a chance to notify anyone inside the Embassy, she was shoved into one of the police vehicles and driven off the grounds. After a quick drive through narrow streets, they arrived at police headquarters where she stood for several very long minutes in the interrogation room as they questioned her. By the time she figured out that the three Turks who threatened to blow up the car had run to the police and now claimed she pulled her revolver and threatened to kill them, a lieutenant colonel from the base and a delegate from the Portuguese embassy were being shown in.

"What are you doing here?" barked the chief of police at the politician.

"The woman is a Portuguese citizen," he answered just as heatedly. "We will be involved in whatever happens to her."

"And as an officer of the United States Air Force, Mendes is entitled to the best defense we can offer," announced the lieutenant colonel barely sparing her a glance.

Abruptly forgotten, she stood waiting while the men in power adjourned to the police chief's office to debate her fate. It was an hour or more before they filed back into the interrogation room to speak with her again.

"First Lieutenant Mendes," began the lieutenant colonel, "this is for the official record. Exactly what happened at the embassy this morning?"

Thoroughly prepared, she said briefly and to the point, "Three local men approached me while I sat in the vehicle, sir, waiting for the brigadier general. Each of them held a glass bottle filled with a yellow liquid, the openings stuffed with cotton. They ordered me from the car and told me they were going to blow it up. I asked them to let me get my jacket, and while reaching for it I retrieved my revolver. When I showed them my weapon they fled, abandoning the bottles on the ground. A few minutes later I was arrested and brought here."

The delegate from the Portuguese embassy spoke to her in Portuguese, assuring them some privacy. "You are in big trouble here, little lady," he lectured sternly. "They say you began the problem by leaving the American car and pointing your weapon at them. It's a case of your word," he looked ruefully at her, a small Açorean woman not quite nineteen years old standing before him, "or theirs. It looks to me like you're liable to spend some time in a Turkish prison." Clearly, he thought her case lost. His eyes glazed over to hide his fear for her.

She turned to the lieutenant colonel and said, "Sir. The three locals dropped the bottles on the ground when they ran. They should still be there unless someone has collected them."

The lieutenant colonel immediately dispatched his VIP driver to return to the US embassy grounds to search. The delegate from the Portuguese embassy accompanied him. The lieutenant colonel, the chief of police, and Traf waited in tense silence for their return.

Less than a fifteen minutes later they came back carrying three bottles between them. One was broken, its contents lost. The smell of gasoline filled the small room. Traf was instructed to wait there again while the men adjourned to discuss the situation. Involuntarily inhaling gasoline fumes, she spent the time imagining what it would be like to be locked up in a foreign jail. *Or will I be taken to the market square and get my head chopped off?*

It took several hours, but the chief of police finally released her. Upon reaching the base, she reported immediately to her commanding officer. In his office sat the brigadier general who'd been surprised when his young driver disappeared. He demanded she tell them the story from start to finish and did not interrupt her once. When finished she stood there at attention, wondering what would happen to her now.

The two men gazed at her with hooded eyes. “I see,” her CO said after a brief silence. “Tell me, why didn’t you just get out of the vehicle and let them blow it up, Mendes?”

“Because, sir,” she answered him straightforwardly, “that car is United States property, it flies the brigadier general’s star. I swore an oath to defend and protect America and her people, and that means everything that belongs to her. The vehicle was checked out in my name and I couldn’t let them destroy it, so I protected it. That’s why, sir.”

The brigadier general rose from his seat at the CO’s desk, pinning her in place with his stare. Not once did he blink as he came around and stood before her. Although she’d opened the car door for him many times, somehow she’d never realized how tall he really was. It seemed to take forever for her eyes to rise to his.

“First Lieutenant Mendes.” He shook her hand. “I wish every American soldier was like you. Well done.” He smiled for the first time since she’d entered the office. “Foolish as hell, but well done.” He dismissed her brusquely after telling her to remain in her room at the BOQ to await new orders.

Two hours later, just a little after six in the evening, the US Air Force abruptly flew Traf out of the country before the Turkish government could change its mind.

She arrived in Greece that evening, surprised by the warm weather. Suddenly, her heavy blues were cumbersome and she shed them as easily as her fear of the executioner’s block now that she was safely away.

She spent her nineteenth birthday in Greece, waiting to receive new orders, hoping to go home. However, a few days later she received a transfer for another three-month rotation in Germany. It was nearly April and she’d been gone well over six months by the time she returned to Lajes. She hoped Major Brandon would had forgotten the ‘incident’, as she thought of it, by now. No such luck; when she reported to him, he had some choice words he’d saved for just this occasion.

“What were you thinking?” His voice thundered down the hall where the secretarial pool eavesdropped. “Do you know how close you came to being killed? Or worse, locked up so deep in a Turkish prison you’d never get out?” Everyone on base knew what she’d done and while most agreed she’d been naïve, even stupid, she’d impressed people. “I ought to kick your sorry butt for taking such a stupid risk.” Major Brandon’s voice rose so loud even those passing by outside could hear him. “You’re just a kid, for Christ’s sake!”

Up until then, he'd viewed the Portuguese who joined the service as children playing soldier, youngsters to be tolerated in deference to the host country. He didn't expect any of them to last the ten years required to transfer fully into the American military, especially the women. In his casual American bigotry, he'd considered them native servants, chauffeurs, mechanics, secretaries, and telephone operators easily left behind if the base closed. Traf changed all that when she responded to an emergency situation as the professional soldier the Air Force trained her to be. A grudging admiration advised Major Brandon never to underestimate her, or any of his Portuguese officers, again.

That hadn't prevented him, however, from bolting awake with nightmares ever since it happened. How could he have explained it to the Portuguese government if she'd disappeared inside a Turkish prison, never to be heard from again? To her parents if she'd been shot defending…what? A car? He had children stateside her age; his conscience refused to give him rest. It was imperative she understand.

"Mendes," Major Brandon bellowed, "you are a much more valuable asset than any vehicle." He glared at her, determined to get his point across. "I don't suppose it ever occurred to you that the United States would far rather lose a car, than a skilled officer?"

"No, sir," she said, surprised. "But isn't it lucky they didn't have to lose either?"

He held his body rigid even though it shook with suppressed laughter. "Get out of here." Brandon saluted her first, causing her eyebrows to rise. As she returned the salute, he added, "You've got two weeks leave. Try to stay out of trouble."

She'd sent a telegram to Ana announcing her return to the island but for once she'd gotten a direct flight and beat it home. No one outside the base expected her, which gave her a chance to surprise Ana.

She reached her front door by early afternoon. Surprised to find it locked at this time of day, she grabbed the key they kept under a rock and let herself in. She heard the sound of the sewing machine down the hall and through the open door she could see Ana bent over her work.

Sneaking up behind her, Traf snaked both hands over her girlfriend's eyes. "Guess who?" she was saying as a scream rent the air. Startled, she dropped her hands and swung a shaking Ana around by her shoulders.

"What? It's only me." Traf cupped her cheek and made eye contact.

"Oh, thank God," Ana cried, launching herself into Traf's arms. "I've missed you!" Being mindful of the open window, she pulled her lover to the side and covered her with kisses. "Thank goodness you're home." Breaking free of their embrace, Ana rushed to close the window and shutter it. "Did you lock the door?"

"No, but I will," answered Traf, happily excited by the enthusiasm of her reception. *I'll have to surprise Ana more often.* She locked the door and made sure the windows were shuttered as if no one were home. Gleefully, she started removing her uniform, dropping each piece to the floor as she made her way to the bathroom.

"I need to wash the travel off me," she called. "Come join me, my love."

Ana needed a little coaxing, but after a while she pulled back the curtain and stepped naked into the shower. They took turns soaping each other up and washing each other down. Firm young bodies slid sensuously together while hands roamed and lips kissed. Not bothering to towel dry, Traf whisked Ana off to the bedroom where they made love until night fell.

Afterward, Traf lay easily in bed, still naked. Her skin glistened in the rich glow of the kerosene lamp she'd chosen over the glare of the electric light. Ana, always shy, had already dressed in a long, modest nightgown. "Come here," Traf whispered, pulling her girlfriend down to lie beside her, stroking Ana's head on her shoulder, "and catch me up on everything."

To her total surprise, within the safe circle of her arms Ana burst into a torrent of tears. It took a long time for her to quiet enough to explain through shuddering sobs.

The past winter had been brutal. Things on the island grew worse while she was away. People cooped up too long by harsh weather gave vent to pent-up feelings they nurtured in dark corners of homes and hearts. During the past six months Terceira suffered tidal waves of violence built on frustrations, imagined injuries, and recriminations. Self-righteousness simmered into a cesspool of indignation. Anger and resentment sprouted a cold winter's flower full of spiteful thorns.

"The attacks started just after New Year's," Ana explained. "Poor Lucy and Odete were the first to suffer. They were attacked again just after the new year, this time in their own home." Traf's eyebrow rose questioningly.

"No, it wasn't Lucy's cousin Mike, but maybe some of his cronies." Ana shook her head, rolling it back and forth on Traf's shoulder. "Three of them beat Odete unconscious while a fourth raped Lucy. This time they warned her she'd better learn her lesson and give up her sinful way of living.

"I haven't seen either of them since, although every so often fresh bread or salted meat shows up in the kitchen." Odete, generous by nature, never forgot what Traf had done for her and took to leaving presents for them to find. Aware that Ana lived alone during Traf's assignments overseas, Odete visited often. "She checks on me to make sure I'm all right whenever you're gone."

"She's trying to prevent what happened to Lucy from happening to you." It twisted something in Traf's heart to know she'd left Ana so vulnerable. She'd defended a stupid car with her life; what if she hadn't been here to protect the woman she loved? Thank God Ana kept the front door locked. Traf realized the big, shy butch from Serreta understood the danger far better than she, which made the second attack on Odete and Lucy during her absence even more horrible.

But theirs wasn't the only terrible news. Friday night, Traf's first back at Troublemakers, people surrounded her telling of a series of attacks waged against the butches. In February a passenger pulled Teresa from her taxi and beat her unconscious, breaking three ribs. Two butches reported being attacked in their own fields during broad daylight.

Just a week earlier, Berta got caught walking down a lonely road. No longer able to breathe freely, her swollen, broken nose whistled as she shared her story. "I never stood a chance. Two guys got me from behind and beat me up." Her two blackened eyes glared. "I never even got a punch in."

More than a few femmes spoke of men, brave in their bigotry, who used foul language to harass them in public. Followed on the streets and spoken to as if they were whores, they were outraged but otherwise unhurt.

With the sole exception of poor Lucy, only the butches who wore men's clothing seemed to be selected for physical abuse. In the brutal fashion of inadequate men, their attackers beat and defiled women to subjugate them and destroy their independent personalities. During Traf's absence, the Night Avengers had revenged six butches.

Even on this particularly warm and inviting April night the story of an attack earlier that day was spreading from one group to another in hushed tones. The swine wore a cloth over his face and Michaela could not identify her rapist.

Traf sat shocked to stillness, horrified. Sick terror filled her belly. Her thoughts filled with Michaela, her best friend, a strong woman, almost a mirror image of herself. They'd known each other for years since they'd both joined the Service. *If it can happen to her it can happen to me*. Traf saw her own foreboding reflected plainly in many butch eyes.

She and Ana left the club to go to their friends. When a pale Gabriella unlocked the door to let them in, Traf's eyes immediately sought Michaela's face and found it closed tight as the two fists clenched by her sides. Black, dried blood covered split white knuckles. A long scrape painted red with mercurochrome crossed her forehead, still seeping blood. Two small Band-Aids crisscrossed a cut on her cheek where purple bruises swelled. Although Michaela's eyes registered Traf's face, overwhelming emotion and indescribable pain kept her from speaking. Though she recognized her friend's voice, or perhaps because of that, Michaela turned inward to a fortress of silence no sound could penetrate.

Gabriella went into the bedroom with Ana and cried scourging tears of fury and anguish. Clutching an untouched bottle of beer at their kitchen table, Traf sat silently beside Michaela, restrained from offering worthless words. The attack and its consequences couldn't be undone. Nothing she said would make it more bearable. No discussion could soothe Michaela's pain, or touch be tolerated no matter how kindly meant. She couldn't do anything for her best friend, the sister of her soul, except give her time to heal in private and in her own way.

Traf felt crippled with fear, which served to fuel her anger. Only direct action would put an end to future attacks. She left Ana and Gabriela to convince Michaela to go to the American hospital and returned to the club to form a battle plan with the other butches.

For the next few weeks an uncivil war raged across Terceira. Since the men now used disguises, the Night Avengers took to wearing their own dark masks. Every night each group hunted the other. Bones broke, teeth disappeared forever, bodies and minds savaged one another. No one ever traveled alone, many carried weapons, and doors remained locked both day and night.

Since no one made a report the authorities did not investigate any incidents on either side, leaving the community to sort things out in their own way. The little island, pounded by waves of hate, suffered a storm that soaked the ground with blood. At last both sides, too battered to fight anymore, fell exhausted into an undeclared ceasefire. The tempest of violence ended as a hot, humid summer began. An enervated peace fell over the island, but the pestilence of hostility churned like magma simmering in a slumbering volcano.

Ch. 15 - Do you like girls?

Summer, 1967

VIPs often request specific support personnel. They do this for several reasons. First, it's always easier to achieve goals with experienced help. And second, if things are comfortable for the specific VIP, his or her mission runs more smoothly. So, like powerful people everywhere and everywhen, high ranking officers visiting Lajes Field exercised their privileges.

Colonel Davis, a consummate officer and model of military service, was known for his integrity, courage, and skill at negotiation. He stood an easy six feet tall with dark wavy hair graying in two streaks from his temples and honest blue eyes that could pierce the most hardened shell. For some reason he took a liking to Traf.

He requested her with increasing frequency whenever he needed a VIP driver. She clearly fascinated him, a little spitfire with officer's bars. Her perfectionism rivaled his own. He sensed in her a deep respect for America, increasingly lacking in young people during 1967.

She, for her part, enjoyed driving for Col. Davis. In her estimation a perfect officer, he conducted his business with grace and style, always returned her salutes promptly, and carried himself with head held high. Generous with compliments, he often told her how nice she looked in her uniform. Since no man she knew ever thought her attractive in uniform, he earned her undying devotion each time he said so.

Although perfectly proper in word, look, and deed, Traf did notice he seemed to treat her differently. Other drivers usually parked outside a restaurant, making do with boxed meals in a military van while waiting through dinner meetings. Traf ate inside the restaurant at a table across the room. The first time he arranged it, Colonel Davis explained it was so she could see when he rose to say his good-byes and have the car ready the minute he wanted to leave. *That's reasonable*, she told herself, *but he never seems to go anywhere in a big hurry*. She got the impression he simply wanted to know where she was.

The colonel became the only officer she ever introduced to her parents. Traf had requested time off to help slaughter a pig, just as she did every year. While explaining to Col. Davis why he would need another driver, he asked to be allowed to watch her family and friends at work, and to her surprise her parents agreed.

Treated with full guest honors, the colonel enjoyed himself thoroughly. He took photographs as they slaughtered the pig, prepared it, sorted the meat, and packed it away. He helped with the most menial tasks, fetching firewood and cleaning intestines for sausage casings. He smiled often and seemed to shrug off his mantle of authority for the occasion, relaxing among hard working people.

He shared his American cigarettes with Gaspar. At lunch, he complimented Amalia on her cooking and admired Alice's growing children. He teased Hermione and Traf about their perfect synchronization when stuffing sausages, well-practiced over the years. And when the work was finally done he shared a bottle of good port wine with Jack and Johnny while the three of them swapped military stories. He impressed them, and they accepted him.

Because of Colonel Davis, Traf went to the French Riviera that July. At the last minute, he requested her and she flew over to drive him around while he conducted important affairs of state.

To her surprise, she was housed in the same hotel as the colonel. For the first time in her life, she experienced five star treatment. Traf's room, luxuriously filled with every amenity, looked out over the Mediterranean Sea. She promptly suggested she stay in more modest accommodations, but Colonel Davis insisted she have her own room in his hotel. After spending the first night diligently studying local maps, she spent the next few weeks driving him to and from various locations during the day to conduct his business. However, in the evenings they experienced fine dining and the entertainments of the area together, often with other high-ranking American officers. In the company of these mature, perfectly polite, and well-traveled men, she learned to comport herself with composure, to mingle socially with her superiors, and to catch glimpses of the world through older, wiser eyes.

It also did not escape her that the ladies of the French Riviera were as varied as women everywhere and very beautiful. What did come as a surprise to Traf, however, was that no matter what their social standing it seemed quite fashionable to wear almost nothing.

One night, she was sitting with several officers watching the floor show in a nightclub. She had to keep tight control over herself not to openly ogle some of the enticing female flesh on display, both onstage and off.

I'm in heaven and hell at the same time.

The higher-ranking male officers certainly felt no need to keep their eyes to themselves. Only the colonel's paternalistic attitude toward his young driver kept civil tongues in their heads. The parade of mostly bare feminine beauty seemed to strip them of all inhibitions.

During a particularly daring dance called a striptease, one of the women dancers threw her freshly discarded panties directly at Traf, quite clear about who she wanted to have them. Traf felt her face flush. Yes, the woman was beautiful and if they were alone she might offer to buy her a drink, but the laughing attention of Colonel Davis and the other officers paralyzed her. She whipped the scrap of red silk out of sight and refused to meet the openly inviting gaze of the dancer.

Later, as they left, Traf surreptitiously tried to leave the panties behind on the seat of her chair. Colonel Davis, however, reached over and plucked them up, handing them to her. Captain Binghamton later reported to a fascinated crowd of listeners that he distinctly heard the colonel tell his driver, "Don't forget your panties."

The following day, Colonel Davis asked Traf to take him for a pleasure drive along the coastline. As that inordinately beautiful seascape rolled along beside them, he leaned back and relaxed. When she glanced at him in her rearview mirror, she saw him close his eyes and let the sunshine warm his face. In a calm and measured voice, he spoke about his daughter for the first time.

"Eleanor is my pride and joy," he began. "Every inch a military brat from the moment she was born. Her two older brothers think she should be dainty and typically feminine, but even they have to admit she can soldier every bit as well as they."

The colonel's eyes opened, and his gaze focused on the passing scenery. Traf glanced at him often, but his eyes never rose to meet hers. "Ellie was a fine officer, perhaps one of the best. She worked hard at it like some people do," he watched the waves rolling offshore but nodded in her direction, "like you do, Lieutenant Mendes. Never a hair out of place, shoes shining like mirrors, every nip, tuck, and fold perfect. She advanced rapidly and made Captain at only thirty." He laughed at this, and finally glanced into the mirror to find her eyes. "You got an earlier start and will make it before you're twenty-two, or I miss my guess." Traf smiled back at him, nodding her agreement.

"Ellie was meant to be a lifer, and no doubt could have been the first woman General one day." His gaze returned to the window, watching the past roll by. "She fell in love with someone she shouldn't have, another woman officer. They got caught one day and dishonorably discharged the next, both of them."

I have to act surprised. Hell, I am surprised. "Oh?" she managed lamely and felt the hair on the nape of her neck stand on end. She held her breath and kept her eyes on the road. *Why is he telling me this? What does he know about me?* A cold trickle of sweat ran down her side.

"To this day, she regrets losing her commission. The Air Force was her home, and she's never really been able to put down roots since. 1967 America isn't exactly a comfortable place for women gifted at giving orders."

A heavy silence descended between them. Traf's heart finally found a regular rhythm again, but her shoulders crept steadily toward her ears as she drove.

The quiet lasted until they returned to the hotel. Traf parked the vehicle, and only as they crossed the parking garage together did he finally add, "If Eleanor had been more discreet she would have made it."

He looked her in the eye as they reached the door of the hotel. He placed a hand on her shoulder, the only time he ever touched her. "No one knows but me, and that's only because I can see so much of her in you. You're doing an excellent job, Lt. Mendes. Keep up the good work. Go the distance, be a lifer. Do it for yourself, for Ellie, and for the other deserving young women out there like you." Then he opened the ornate glass door and ushered her through it.

She kept her shock to herself. Alone in her room she thought about Ellie, trying to picture her. *Was she butch, like me?* She thought about Margarida, and Michaela, and herself. *I wonder, how many butches are in the American military*? Surprised, she realized there were lesbians in every part of the world. Not just dancing strippers, like the one that threw her panties in Traf's face, or whores who'd go with anyone with enough money to pay, like Bella. Most lesbians were probably women like herself, living their lives day by day exactly like everyone else. *We must be everywhere*.

Hero worship is a hard horse to ride. A prince in her eyes, Col. Davis could do no wrong. Outside the world of the Troublemakers, he alone knew the real Vitória and approved. Traf swore, with God as her witness, she would gladly take a bullet for him.

However, she also knew jealousy of her perfect performance ratings made others in the military sometimes difficult to get along with. Traf's outstanding reviews often became the topic of sour discussions by those who didn't perform as well. Many of the Americans, enlisted and officers alike, considered her a kiss ass. So she decided to be discreet in her devotion to the colonel.

Gossip, however, needs no fuel. Mere supposition, innuendo, or a single snide remark can ignite it. Fanning it into full-blown flames is as easy as telling a joke, whispering behind someone's back, or just lazily encouraging idle speculation. After returning from their assignment in the French Riviera it wasn't long before the tale of the red panties had been told and retold until everyone on base heard it.

Water cooler chitchat had the colonel and his driver in a lustful tryst. Afternoon break conversation suggested it had been going on for a while. After-work drinkers insisted the relationship between Col. Davis and Traf was an openly acknowledged extra-marital affair. Acknowledged, that was, by everyone but the two principles. They knew nothing about it.

No one said anything to Traf directly, but the sound of snickering laughter followed her down the halls. Other drivers looked at her with open hostility and contempt. The mechanics, most of them male, casually baited her with sexual innuendos whenever she entered the motor pool.

One afternoon, as she checked the duty roster for upcoming assignments, one of the secretaries make a snide remark concerning her "boyfriend." Traf's head swiveled, pinning the woman to her chair.

"What are you talking about?"

The secretary, a busty young redhead, grinned knowingly back at her. "I said, your boyfriend must be busy. Colonel Sugar Daddy didn't request you even once next week. Maybe the party's over?"

Hiding her shock at being romantically connected with Col. Davis, Traf immediately realized she must nip this in the bud, completely unaware it was already in riotous bloom and she was about to add fertilizer. She frowned at the lower ranking secretary and answered her in a low, threatening voice, "Nothing's over. It never began." Both arms on the secretary's desk, Traf leaned down until they were face to face. "You don't want to get on my wrong side. I'm Portuguese," she made a point of staring at the woman's nametag, "Sgt. Bendix. With us, nothing's ever over until we decide it's over." She turned on her heel and left the room steaming.

That's why I've been hearing laughter for over a week. Well, at least they're not wondering if I'm a lesbian. That's the farthest thing from their minds right now. She immediately felt guilty over the thought, however, because Col. Davis never behaved improperly with her. His reputation was at stake, as well as her own.

Not knowing what to do, she stewed about the situation. She wanted to talk it over with Michaela, but her best friend was still dealing with the pain of being attacked and Traf didn't want to interrupt. Ana might understand, or she might grow jealous herself having wondered aloud more than once about the colonel's interest in her. She thought about going to Major Brandon, but that felt a lot like tattling. Traf worried obsessively for days.

At the end of the week she received new orders to drive Col. Davis and in his calm and approving company her reservations melted away. So much so that when the day's business was over she broached the subject during the drive back to his quarters.

"They think what?" asked Col. Davis incredulously.

Traf blushed a brilliant red but kept her eyes on the road. "They think you and I are having an affair, Sir," she repeated.

"How do you know this?" he demanded.

"I just found out about it myself." She glanced at him in the mirror. "It has to do with those red panties and the French Riviera." Traf shook her head disgustedly. "Someone started talking, and it got blown up into a nice juicy story."

"Well," he said to the back of her head, noting the crimson of her ear tips, "I'll have to do something about this. I hope things don't get too rough for you, Mendes, but if they do let me know."

Right. She looked at him in the mirror. *I have to ride this one out and you and I both know it.* But all she said was, "Yes, sir."

Over the last week of July and the first week of August, Major Brandon called a number of people into his office. Many threw irritated looks Traf's way and let loose the occasional snide comment about snitches. As one gossip was chased down another was exposed until the trail finally led back to one of the officers in the colonel's entourage during their time in the French Riviera.

Captain Binghamton received orders to report to Lajes Field. On the day he arrived, his VIP driver took him directly to Major Brandon's office. There followed a long interview with Col. Davis, who flew in to deal with the situation personally. During the third hour they spent together behind closed doors, Traf received a summons to report to her CO's office. Standing ramrod straight in front of Col. Brown, the Base Commander of Lajes Field, and Maj. Brandon stood a thoroughly miserable Binghamton, newly demoted to First Lieutenant and now her equal. He formally apologized to first Col. Davis and then Traf, his face red as a ripe tomato.

Before being briskly dismissed with a sharp salute, she had time to note a subtle twinkle in Col. Davis' eye indicating his awareness that her name being linked with a heterosexual scandal was not as bad as it might normally have been for a young woman officer.

After the formal apology everyone behaved in an exactingly proper way with Traf. Laughter no longer followed her down the hallway and the male mechanics kept their thoughts to themselves. No one seemed particularly friendly to her either, and while this might have been a painful shunning for someone temporarily stationed on Terceira, for her, with plenty of family and friends available every day, it came as a great relief. Traf continued to do her job as professionally as possible. Colonel Davis still requested her as a driver, but perhaps not quite as often as before.

In the middle of the month she received an assignment in Spain for two weeks. Traf, familiar with Spaniards by then, found it an easy, if uneventful posting. Her top-secret clearance came through and she ferried papers in briefcases more often than not. Every now and then she carried passengers, but most of the time she drove simple deliveries from the base to the embassy and back again. She had plenty of off-duty time and spent it with casual friends.

Traf sat in a bar one night, drinking with several WAFs, when her world turned upside down. She didn't know it at first of course, no one ever does. But, as Second Lieutenant Chris Atwater arrived, Traf glanced up to greet her and became instantly captivated by her beautiful gypsy companion.

Since their meeting a few days ago, Traf wondered more than once if Atwater might be an American lesbian. There was nothing obvious about her; she looked like any other VIP driver, but something told Traf that Chris would feel right at home among her butch friends back at

Troublemakers. Approaching the table, the second lieutenant said, "Hi, everyone. Sorry I'm late. On the way here I ran into an old friend." She took a seat on the opposite side of the table as her friend pulled an extra chair up next to Traf. "This is Carmen, like the famous Opera, and she only speaks Spanish."

As if dying of thirst, Traf drank in the sight of the alluring woman in her billowing white peasant blouse threaded with colorful ribbons. *I wonder if they're together.* She paid attention to their body language. Oddly reassuring, it appeared they shared only a friendship. She chatted casually with the charming woman in a mixture of Portuguese, Spanish, and hand signs.

Several years older than Traf, Carmen was in the full bloom of her beauty. Long black curls caressed smooth olive-skinned shoulders, sharp green eyes danced, and full lips pouted playfully as the gypsy explained in Spanish that she was waiting for a cousin. They would travel back to their caravan together.

"Your what?"

"We live in our family's caravan. Each of us has our own caravana." Seeing Traf's confusion, she asked in Spanish if Chris Atwater would explain.

The second lieutenant nodded and said in English, "Kind of like little houses on wheels. The Romani hook them up to horses when they want to move."

They must want to move often. "Romani?"

"That's what our people call ourselves," Carmen said, offering a warm smile. "How can I reach you?"

"You can leave a message for me here." Traf wrote the phone number for the BOQ on a paper napkin. Shortly after that, Carmen's cousin arrived and she left, the sway of her hips hypnotic as she walked out the door.

Please call, please call, please call. She shook her head to free it of the repeated wish.

Carmen phoned a week later and offered to show Traf the local sights. They met several times casually for coffee and drinks and found each other easy to talk to regardless of language differences. Carmen was good company, as well as being deliciously easy on the eyes. One Thursday night she suggested Traf get a weekend pass and spend it with her in the caravan. She had already asked permission of her father, the leader of her family tribe, and he agreed Traf could go with them while they traveled to Seville to watch some friends perform.

I'm interested in seeing the gypsy camp... exposing myself to a foreign culture. But in those rare moments when she escaped her denial, she acknowledged the truth. *I crave more time with Carmen.*

She met the delightful beauty Saturday morning and they took a cab to the caravan. Carmen introduced Traf to her father, an average-sized, dark-skinned man with a rather intimidating mustache. He welcomed her formally and left her in his daughter's care. A quick tour of the caravan followed. She saw the cooking and eating areas, a performance square that doubled as rehearsal space, and the brightly colored wooden wagons scattered around, ready to be hitched to teams of horses but settled for the time being.

When it was time, Carmen's father called, "All going!" A dozen or so people crowded together, piling into an open wagon. Everyone laughed and sang popular songs as the six-horse-team, expertly driven by the gypsy leader, carried them down the road. The journey took several hours but it passed pleasantly in the company of such entertaining people. The Romani accepted her presence easily, soon calling her by name. Even though they spoke one language and she another, they found enough common ground to communicate.

Carmen's father drove through Seville to the performance area of a market square, and there Traf saw her first flamenco dancer. She climbed down from the wagon and stood mesmerized by a gorgeous woman dancing rapidly, heels tapping a quick tattoo. So enraptured was she that Carmen thumped her on the arm and announced, "I dance flamenco, too."

Traf tilted her head, considering. "Will I see you dance like that?"

"Not tonight, no. These are cousins who have their own show. We're here to help them open in Seville."

They spent the day wandering through the market area, examining items for sale and listening to musicians play for talented singers. Traf impressed Carmen when she produced Spanish coins, pesetas, and bought cold drinks for both of them. They shared a packed meal of figs and olives, rustic bread and cold fish while sitting in the shade of a tree, entertained by skits and comedies.

A few hours after sunset, they returned to the family's camp. Carmen flashed Traf a bright smile as she led the way to her personal caravana, a compact little wagon holding a bed, a chamber pot, and Carmen's few belongings. They took turns changing into nightclothes, then slept back to back. Traf, although very aware of Carmen's proximity, nevertheless maintained the same decorum she used when sharing a bed with her cousins.

Sunday they rose and spent the day talking. While strolling under the trees in the heat of a bright late summer sun, Carmen's every movement entranced. The vibrant colors of her skirt, the ribbons and laces she'd sewn to it here and there, dazzled Traf's senses. Gold bangles encircled slender wrists. Beautifully wrought chains graced her long neck, drawing Traf's eye to a captivating cleavage revealed by a blouse that fell gracefully off one shoulder.

"Do you like girls?" Carmen surprised her by asking. Traf understood her perfectly, but pretended not to, defenses up as always.

"Of course I like girls," she answered as they walked along. "I like most people."

"But," Carmen insisted, slowing down to look Traf in the eye. "Do you like girls?"

Luckily, they were called to lunch then, served communally to everyone in the tribe at the same time. They joined the meal and conversation, and once again Traf saw for herself how easily the Romani included her, obviously used to visitors.

Traf had to catch a bus back to the base by four o'clock. They spent their last hour together in Carmen's little caravana, supposedly catching an afternoon nap. But the clever girl wanted information, and she set about getting it.

As they lay side by side on her bed, facing each other, Carmen asked. "Do you sleep with girls?"

Traf didn't want to be evasive, but she also didn't want to invite any trouble. She couldn't imagine Carmen being a spy for the US Air Force, but stranger things had happened. So, once again she dodged, deliberately vague.

"Yes, I sleep with girls," she answered cleverly. "I slept with you last night, didn't I?"

Not knowing the exact terms that she wanted in Portuguese, Carmen seemed frustrated by her inability to convey her meaning. "I mean like Chris Atwater and my cousin," she insisted.

Traf's eyebrows rose. *So, I was right. The second lieutenant is an American lesbian and apparently involved with a local woman.*

Interesting. Still, she couldn't afford to admit anything. Traf shrugged her shoulders, indicating she didn't understand.

"Like this," Carmen finally insisted, leaning over and kissing Traf.

As lip touched lip, unspoken promises were offered. Desires boiled over and delirium ensued.

That wild kiss taught Traf more in an instant about herself than all her cautious and correct years of living with Ana. As Carmen's delicious tongue teased hers, she felt a sudden hunger in her belly, fiercer and more insistent than anything she ever experienced before. Traf desperately wanted to gather Carmen to her and explore her thoroughly. Her head swam with yearning. *If I didn't need to catch that damned bus I'd show you just how much I like girls.*

The whole ride back to base she berated herself for not requesting a pass until Monday morning.

Traf spent an uneasy week hungering for forbidden fruits. Frequent thoughts of sweet Ana keeping their home together during her absence, tormented her conscience. Traf pictured her scrubbing the house, working in her sewing shop, cooking delicious meals, and lying beneath her as they made love. Traf's culpability knew no bounds and so far she was only guilty of a single kiss. Her mind taunted her, labeling her with vicious, foul names for her wishful infidelity.

Her body tortured her too, imagining Carmen's curves sliding against hers and the touch of those luscious breasts in her hands. The sexy Romani's voice planted itself in Traf's ear, and in her absence blossomed into memory. The softness of Carmen's skin beckoned her fingers, even while clutching a steering wheel on duty. She needed to taste the feisty woman's lips again.

Ah, who am I fooling? If I'm honest, I won't stop with just a kiss.

To avoid temptation Traf dodged Carmen, not returning messages and staying away from the bar where they met. Relieved when her duty ended a few days later, she returned to Lajes chastened.

Ch. 16 - Enough for a Lifetime

Late Summer to Autumn, 1967

As summer advanced and the crops began to ripen, Traf helped in her family's fields just as she always had. Her brother Johnny, as many local soldiers did this time of year, requested leave from the Portuguese army to come and help. Almost like old times again, they tried to outdo each other with stories of their adventures in the different militaries.

Johnny took a lot of pleasure in telling her all about his love life, spending a lot of time talking about girls he'd dated. Slowly but surely, Traf began to joke with him about women, letting him know that she, too, felt the same way about them. He never blinked, didn't once hesitate in the conversation. It wasn't long before he teased her about getting all the best girls, leaving him with her leftovers. Neither of them mentioned the word lesbian. They behaved the same way with each other they always had. Nothing changed.

Johnny, always a very decent human being, had become the only man she knew who understood a woman could be his equal in every way. Of course, he grew up watching Traf develop into the young woman she was today. Being a big brother, he'd goaded her to accomplish impossible things, and became her loudest cheerleader when she succeeded. Long ago, he got used to the idea that he competed with, and often lost to, his baby sister and wouldn't have it any other way.

One late afternoon in the last week of August, as they harvested long rows of sweet corn, the conversation turned to the adventures of their childhood. Johnny reminded her of the night so long ago when they hid on the roof of the whorehouse, baptizing the patrons with her urine.

"I forgot all about that." Traf snorted. She tucked three ears of corn into the bag slung on her back. She stepped forward and began stripping the next stalk. "We really did that, didn't we?" They laughed together in the good hot sunshine, content with the knowledge that after their work was done there would still be hours of daylight. Plenty of time in a day during summer.

"Hey," said Johnny, suddenly standing erect and looking over rows of corn plants at her. "Do you remember earlier that same day?"

She clasped both hands over her head and stretched, trying to remember so far back. It had been eight years, and so much had happened since then it wasn't easy to isolate specific incidents. Her silence prodded Johnny into supplying a clue.

"We were playing war," he prompted.

Suddenly, a connection clicked in her memory. "Oh yes! The man in the tree! We thought he was the target." She threw her head back and laughed loudly, remembering. "We scattered like the wicked children we were as soon as we heard him shouting!"

Johnny looked at her with a grin and said, "Do you remember Mary Katherine, the girl I was dating?"

She arched one eyebrow and questioned, "Was dating? As in, last weekend?"

"Long story, I'll tell it to you sometime. Anyway, her recently widowed uncle attended a party the family hosted one night and told us a very strange story." Johnny started harvesting faster, tossing words over his shoulder as he continued down his row.

"He talked about the only time he cheated on his wife. He met a woman from Pico and she invited him back to her rented room. They spent a wild night of intense passion together, but the next day he began to feel guilty. He spent the afternoon working in his orange grove to daydream about his new lover, and get away from his wife and the sense of shame he felt in her presence.

"Up in the branches, trimming away dead growth, he asked God whether it was wrong to have a mistress. God answered him by sending stones down from heaven onto his unprotected head. He remembers calling out, "Oh. Oh! Lord forgive me!" and just as suddenly the rain of rocks stopped." Johnny turned to look at her, grinning wickedly as he saw understanding light up her face.

"He claimed he'd been blessed with a direct intervention by God and he never cheated on his wife again. Telling his story he insisted, even though several guests teased him, that God sent him a sign that day and saved him from eternal damnation."

Traf's loud guffaws sounded like a donkey braying, and then when she tried to get them under control, she suddenly snorted like a pig. They both laughed hysterically. After calming down, they took delight in their accidental participation in God's great plan. It brought back the good old days, and pleased with themselves, they knocked off early to go home.

Being an instrument of the Lord was the first thing Traf was going to tell Ana as she opened the door to their home later that evening, but the words died on her lips. Not for the first time in recent months, she found Ana sitting alone in their darkened bedroom, shutters closed, eyes red and swollen from crying.

"Ana!" She was worried, just as she was every time she found her lover like this. "What's wrong, sweetheart?" Traf sat beside her on the bed and put her arms around her protectively, hoping that this time she would find out the reason for the tears.

"N-n-n-nothing…" stammered Ana, hurriedly wiping her eyes and jumping up from the bed. Traf rose and followed her as she left the room. This scene seemed all too familiar.

"Then why are you crying?" she insisted. "Why have you been crying so often lately?"

"It's nothing, I tell you," Ana evaded as she busied herself with preparations for dinner.

A sudden horrible thought shot through Traf's head. "Did someone hurt you?" Her heart broke and her soul turned to stone. "Tell me who it was and I'll break his neck!"

"No one hurt me, I'm just miserable," answered Ana, crumbling into a chair.

Puzzled and completely disarmed, Traf sat down next to Ana and took both hands in her own. She bent close and said urgently, "Whatever it is, tell me, Ana. We'll solve the problem together."

"It's you, okay?" Ana shook angry tears from her eyes.

"Me?" Traf blurted. "What have I done to you?"

"That's it, exactly!" Ana exploded. "You don't *do* anything to me. You don't love me!"

"What are you talking about?" Still confused, all Traf got in answer was another storm of tears raining down her lover's cheeks. Nothing she did stemmed the flow of those tears, and more followed over the course of that evening, the next day and pretty much the whole week.

She talked to Michaela about it. They puzzled over Ana's reasons, and as much as they talked it over, they could not find an answer that satisfied. Finally, Michaela suggested she take Ana to the therapist she'd seen as a young woman. She confided in her best friend that she'd been seeing Dr. Duarte again to help her deal with the rape.

Traf remembered Michaela bringing to the fire the definitions of butch and femme, and having gotten them from a doctor. "That might be a good idea. Write down her name and address, will you?"

A week later, Ana and Traf sat in Dr. Duarte's office in Angra. Tall for a Portuguese woman and very slender, she kept her hair, streaked with fine silver threads, swept back from her open face. Piercing light brown eyes calmly examined the two young women sitting before her, Traf with her arms crossed over her chest and Ana, shoulders hunched and bent inward. Both of them, the doctor noted, felt a need to protect their hearts.

"Tell me why you wanted to see me," she said.

Traf leaned forward and placed her elbows on her knees, fingers folded together. "It's Ana," she said, indicating her lover sitting beside her. "She cries all the time. She says I make her miserable, but she won't tell me how." Satisfied that she'd done her part, Traf sat back and refolded her arms, waiting for the doctor to set Ana straight.

Dr. Duarte looked expectantly at Ana, still hunched over. "Is that how you feel?" she asked gently.

Ana's shoulders sagged even further, if that was possible. She looked up bleakly at the therapist. "It doesn't make any sense. It's just stupid. We shouldn't even be here." A single tear leaked slowly down her cheek.

"Ana?" asked Dr. Duarte. When the girl looked up again, the therapist leaned forward, lessening the distance between them. "It's clear you're not happy. Why don't we start there?"

It took a while, but Ana finally got around to the real reason for her unhappiness. Her white, embroidered handkerchief was sodden with tears by that time. "Lots of my friends get h-hit by their butches," she stammered. "It's h-how they know they're loved." More tears streaked down her face. "Traf never hits me."

Dr. Duarte noted the surprise on Traf's face. "And you think that means she doesn't love you?"

"A butch who corrects her woman really loves her," insisted the miserable Ana. "Traf doesn't correct me; she just redoes my work for me! I'm so ashamed!" Her sobs became truly heartrending and it took over five minutes to calm her down.

The doctor waited for the distraught young woman to meet her eyes before asking, "Is this your first relationship, Ana?"

Traf again answered for her. “No, Doctor. She had a butch before me. A woman named Antonia.” Contempt dripped from her voice. “She’s a brute. Ana was very young when she was with her and Antonia treated her like a slave.”

Ana looked up defiantly. “At least she loved me and wasn’t afraid to show it,” she threw out like a dare.

The doctor sat patiently, watching the exchange.

“I don’t beat women,” Traf shot back hotly. She searched for other words, but those four said all she had to say. She sat fuming.

“You don’t love me,” accused Ana. “You clean up the house before I have a chance. Why don’t you just hit me and tell me to clean better, the way you like it?” Ana shook her head, releasing tears that streamed down both cheeks.

Before Traf could answer, Dr. Duarte raised her hand for silence. “Wait, Vitória. Let her tell us all of it.”

With that encouragement, Ana tumbled forth one accusation after another. “I don’t cook the way you like. Sometimes you do the cooking yourself! And… and… you wash the dishes with me as if you don’t trust me to do them right by myself! If you sleep in late, you make the bed yourself instead of waiting for me to do it.” She sniffled a little, and then added, blushing, “You never force me in bed. You don’t even love me enough to take what you want when you want it!”

Traf paled at the accusations, recognizing some truth in them. Her confusion ran rampant, however, because it still wasn’t clear what she had really done wrong. The doctor waited silently to see what she would say.

“I’m sorry if you think I don’t love you, Ana.” She took a deep breath and let it out slowly. “I do love you. I love you so much I hate to see you doing all the work yourself. I mean, I’m a woman, too. I know how to help with stuff around the house.”

“No.” insisted Ana. “You’re supposed to come home from work, put your feet up, and smoke your pipe.”

“Is that why you bought me a pipe?” Traf asked. She enjoyed the gift but had no idea where Ana got the idea to give it to her.

“Yes!” insisted Ana. “But all you do is follow around behind me, dusting this, cleaning that!”

“I just want us to have more time to spend together!” Traf sat up straight and ran her fingers through her curly hair distractedly. “Is that so wrong?”

Once again, Dr. Duarte raised her hand, effectively reminding the two of them that they had come to her for help. “Ana,” she said, “Vitória says that Antonia used to beat you. You say she ‘corrected’ you. You say that Antonia demanded sex whenever she wanted it, and would sometimes force you. Is that right?”

“Yes,” cried the miserable femme. “Afterward, she always told me she did it because she loved me. I believed it.” She sobbed openly. “I still do, I guess.”

“But,” insisted Dr. Duarte, “did you feel loved when Antonia hit or forced you to have sex?”

Ana sat stunned for a moment. Thoughtfully, she answered, “Not right at that moment I didn’t. But afterward, when she spoke gently to me and told me it was only because she loved me that she did it, I believed her then.”

“But at the moment she was hitting you, hurting you, how did you feel?” pressed the therapist.

“Scared, ashamed, afraid, in pain,” said Ana softly, remembering, listening to her own words. Traf watched the interchange between the doctor and her lover in silence.

“Is that what you want Vitória to feel when you say you love her?” asked Dr. Duarte. “Scared? Ashamed? Afraid?” She took Ana’s hands in her own. “In pain?” Older, wiser eyes forced much younger ones to see their own reflection. “Is that really what you think love is?”

Confused, Ana blinked away tears that were swiftly drying in the aftermath of reason. “Of course not.”

“Of course not,” agreed the therapist reassuringly. “That’s because you know how to love, but not how to be loved. Antonia taught you lies when it comes to love and being so young, you believed her.”

Ana nodded. “Like being told that babies are brought by airplanes, and never learning differently.” Traf flinched but nodded.

“If you want to put it that way, yes,” said Dr. Duarte.

In almost a whisper, Traf added, “It can be very hard to love you, Ana. Sometimes you won’t let me love you at all.” She thought of nice things she’d tried to do on occasion only to be met with ambivalence, resistance, or outright resentment.

Ana sat in silence for a long moment, her eyes turned inward toward her own memories. They waited for her. Finally, she said softly, “I love Traf, uh, Vitória. I want her to feel happy not sad, pleasure not pain.”

"Exactly," encouraged Dr. Duarte, sitting back in her chair and relaxing, letting her hands rest peacefully in her lap.

"I want to do nice things for her," Ana continued, not looking at Traf. She concentrated on the therapist. "I want to make her feel good about herself. I want to know she's proud of herself, and of me."

They both watched Ana's face as Traf calmly stated, "I want to do nice things for you." She paused, letting the silence draw out until Ana's eyes finally turned to meet hers. She continued, repeating Ana's own words. "I want you to feel good about yourself. I want to know you're proud of me, and yourself."

Ana looked at her with newly awakened eyes. They spent the rest of the hour discussing ways they could counter the behavior and responses she had learned from Antonia. Dr. Duarte gave them some sound advice and sent them off with words of encouragement.

As the summer began giving way to autumn, things at home settled into a nice, easy rhythm. Ana was a bright young woman and once she saw the truth of her behavior, worked hard to make changes in herself. Eventually Traf could help with the dishes while Ana teased and laughed about it, gradually relaxing enough to enjoy the experience. She began accepting help in making the bed, dusting the house, and sweeping the floors. Traf pointed out, at the end of various chores, how much time they saved by doing the task together and let Ana decide how they should spend it.

Days shortened as September grew cooler, a welcome change from the steamy summer. Ana and Traf now found enough time to sit out on their veranda like an old married couple, simply enjoying the evening. They drank cold coffee, sharing idle chatter with neighbors and friends as they came and went. Life settled into a pleasant, comfortable routine.

Troublemakers' membership had grown steadily, now open to supportive friends and families of club members, and catered for special events. On Friday, the twenty-ninth of September, they held a large dinner party in honor of Teresa paying off her taxicab.

Artie, Teresa's older brother, hosted the event with the interest she'd tried to pay him. He'd financed the loan on her taxi since the bank wouldn't take a chance on her, and she'd finally managed, after six long years, to pay him back in full. The close siblings invited all of the original founding members, and their guests, to join them for a private celebration. Beatrice, Teresa's femme, and her girlfriends decorated the clubhouse with festive paper streamers, candles, and fresh flowers. Artie stocked the bar with beer and wine for twice as many as expected, and the kitchen with steaks, onions, tomatoes, and potatoes for frying. Mary Jo, a talented femme with a flair for traditional cuisine, volunteered to command the stove as she loved to do.

The group settled in around cloth covered tables enjoying appetizers and drinks. They teased Teresa, asking for free rides in honor of the occasion. Everyone felt festive, happy to be together, glad to share in their friend's good fortune. Then the front door opened.

Two figures, completely dressed in black, straggled in – Mr. Silva, a familiar farmer around the marketplace, and a skinny, bent woman. Both seemed old and rather fragile, although Traf knew him as a man of robust middle age.

A hush fell over the room as he introduced them both. "I am Richard Silva, and this is my wife, Mercy." He nodded at the pale woman standing beside him whose skin appeared stretched paper thin, barely holding her together. As he looked at them his haunted eyes silenced every murmur. "Odete Silva is our daughter."

A cold shiver ran down Traf's back, but she stood up and warmly welcomed them to the club. "Come in, join us for some dinner. Where is Odete this evening? She and Lucy were supposed to join us."

She noticed his hand shaking as he pulled several envelopes from his pocket. "We have a few letters to deliver. One is for you, Vitória," he said, "and there are four more." He took a deep breath, then released it tentatively. His eyes fell closed as he said, "Odete and Lucy are dead."

Gasps sounded all around her as Traf's mind swirled, unwilling to understand his words. She struggled for breath. Mr. Silva reached out a concerned hand and grasped her arm to steady her.

The world inside her head grew dark. She stared into the eyes of friends she'd known all her life as if they were strangers. *It can't be true. I'm hallucinating.*

The group sorted itself in two, the femmes gathered on one side of the room to give vent to tears and wailing while the butches met on the other. They stood in a loose circle facing inward toward each other in unconscious imitation of their first group fires. No one spoke but jaws clenched, muscles bunched, and teeth ground in their battle with their emotions. They couldn't cry but what words could express how they felt? Refusing to look too closely at each other in case they lost what control they still held on their emotions, they started chain smoking.

When she could speak again Traf managed to ask, "What happened?"

Mr. Silva stood behind the chair where his wife sat with her thin ankles crossed and fingers working worn rosary beads. "I found them," he said. "Odete didn't meet me in the fields this morning. She's never late, you know. I waited for an hour, then went over to her house to see if she was sick or needed something." He covered his eyes and moaned. "Can it only be this morning?"

Several femmes sobbed unashamedly. Traf's throat sealed shut, never to swallow again.

After a moment, Mr. Silva regained his composure. Unsure whether she wanted the answer but knowing they had to have it, Traf leaned toward him and croaked, "How did they die?"

He looked at her bleakly. "They drank poison. I found them in their bed together."

Gabriela managed to ask, "Why?" before dissolving once more into tears.

Mr. Silva answered only, "I…we don't know. I was hoping one of these letters might give us the answer." He handed Traf a sealed envelope with her name lettered across it in Odete's clear, strong hand. Her heart clenched as she forced herself to take it from him.

"Read it aloud, please?" he begged her.

She didn't know if she could, but Traf tore the envelope open and removed the sheets of paper inside. From the same familiar penmanship, she slowly read aloud.

Traf,

I am dead. Lucy is with me and we are either in the arms of our Lord or facing the tortures of Hell. Whatever our true destiny, we face it together. Try not to be sad. We had to do this.

They came for us again.

Lucy's family will never accept us or leave us in peace. We know that now. The men they sent this time raped her while holding me down, then made Lucy watch while they took turns beating and, well you know what else they did. By the time I came to, they were gone and my poor Lucy was wild with grief and pain.

Why do they torture us?

We tried to comfort each other again but our wounds are still fresh from the times before. We know it will never end.

There is no hope.

Traf, you are my best friend and you need to know there was nothing you could do about this. You know as well as I do that they will never stop. Ever. Never.

When I met Lucy, my life suddenly made sense. I dreamed of a future together full of fun, happiness, and love. Instead it all turned to darkness and there is no way back to the light. We belong together and if that can't happen in this world we will take our chances in the next. Surely God will show more mercy than men.

Take good care of yourself and sweet Ana. We will be here to welcome you when it's your turn to come.

Missing you already my friend,

Odete

Traf's voice broke as it faded away. No longer giving a damn who thought what, her head dropped to her arms and she wept hot, bitter, scalding tears, sobbing inconsolably. Like a line of dominos falling, the other butches also let go and shed tears they'd dammed up for years.

One at a time Mr. Silva handed out three more letters. They all listened as first Ana and then Gabriela read their letters from Lucy aloud. When it was Michaela's turn, she couldn't finish when she learned that the final attack happened mere moments after she'd dropped the two at Odete's doorstep.

"They were nervous, talking about getting a taxi to drive them home." She sobbed raggedly. "I took them so they wouldn't have to w-w-worry…" Her body shook as she struggled for breath, "…about traveling alone in the dark." Haunted eyes sought Traf's, begging for understanding. "I should have gone in with them…"

Is she wondering what would have happened if she had? Traf wondered. *Her own rape changed her, made her afraid. Is she wondering, as I am,* she realized, *if she would have gone in knowing what was to happen?* Traf looked around, seeing fear and self-doubt on every face.

Artie and Teresa held a brief discussion, then passed out the food and set around bottles of wine. The group ate a somber meal while struggling to come to grips with the news. They shared what they knew with each other, trying to make sense of things.

Mrs. Silva sat across the table from them, the food on her plate untouched. "I don't understand what she meant by Lucy's family coming for them again, do you?" Seeing her hand tremble, she set her empty wine glass down. Teresa refilled it.

And so Traf explained that the first attack, which they knew about, was by Lucy's cousin, Mike. Ana somberly told of the second time last winter, which Odete somehow managed to keep from them. It was now clear that Lucy's vicious family had violated them yet a third time.

"How do you know they used poison?" someone asked. There was a general need for every detail.

"They were holding each other in bed when I found them," answered Odete's overwrought father. He'd already devoured one steak and Artie brought him a second, which he acknowledged with a grateful nod. "An empty bottle of rat poison from the barn was sitting on the kitchen table with the glasses they used." He wiped his eyes dry and took a deep breath. "At first I thought I'd walked in on them sleeping." Mechanically he picked up knife and fork and began eating again as the only tear they saw him shed slid slowly down his cheek.

An image of Odete lying with Lucy's head on her shoulder, exactly as she and Ana slept, wouldn't leave Traf's mind. She almost didn't hear Mrs. Silva say, "There is a final letter addressed only to 'The Group at the Club'."

"This one I will read to you myself." Mr. Silva wiped his mouth and rose from his seat. "And then we have something important to say to you all." He unsealed the final envelope.

"Our sisters," he began, then startled, he paused. With great deliberation, he looked at every face in turn, memorizing each.

Our sisters,

We love each other, in this life and beyond, and are grateful our mortal pain is ending. Please pray for us, knowing what we have been through, and ask God to be forgiving. Remember us in happier times.

Thank you. Lucy and I are so grateful to each and every one of you for being our friends. Troublemakers is important. It gave us a place to go where there are others like us, people who understand and don't judge. We found that here, keep the club open for as long as you can.

We leave each of you a piece of our hearts. Know we left this world wrapped in the love you gave us.

I am Odete Silva, a lesbian, a butch, an outca…

Her poor father's voice broke. He cleared his throat, wiped his eyes, and started again.

I am Odete Silva, a lesbian, a butch, an outcast. Lucy is my beautiful, kind, lesbian wife, my life. With you as our friends we knew kindness, acceptance, even respect. We wish each of you the same, forever.

Pray for our souls.

Your sisters,

O and L

Mr. Silva looked up. A wan smile creased already seamed cheeks.

Around the room all pretense of stoicism evaporated as people turned to their neighbors for support. They comforted each other as best they could. Amongst the rising hubbub, Mrs. Silva stood, a bereaved mother forlorn in black, a bony specter silencing them all.

"Girls, I have something to say." She cleared her throat as they quieted. "We didn't know about you before. A club just for women right here in Praia, imagine." Her words sank to a near whisper. "I had no idea that a place such as yours existed."

Her voice strengthened. "If I had, I don't know what I would have thought about it." She seemed determined to be honest, no matter the cost. "I might have disapproved, I don't know." She shook her head. "I didn't try to understand my daughter, and now I wish I had." Fiercely, she swiped a tear from her cheek. "In my pride I thought it far more important she understand me." She swiped another.

"You're her friends. When my Odete was troubled she turned to *you*, instead of me." She clutched at her heart. "Was it because she was afraid of what I would say? My husband," she paused and gripped his hand hard, "understood her far better than I did, and even he didn't know the half of it. You are the family we should have been for our Odete and her Lucy."

Mrs. Silva's ravaged face lighted with an ephemeral beauty born of loss. "My husband and I have taken a solemn vow." Her soft voice took command of the room. "It's what I would have promised my daughter but now I can't so listen well: If any of you, at any time, feel as Odete and Lucy did that you have no choices, you *must* come to us! We will help you no matter what trouble you face or how dark your life may seem at the time." She looked around the circle, searching each and every face until she found acknowledgment. "We promise to help you as we should have helped them." Her voice faltered, failing on her last word.

Mr. Silva spoke up. "You are our adopted daughters now, one and all. We do this to honor the memory of the daughter we lost through our own ignorance. We will be your Godparents, knowing exactly who and what you are. We love you because you loved Odete. When you are in pain, we will help ease it. When you have victories, we'll celebrate with you. When you need voices to join with yours, ours will be the loudest. Never again will any of you have to face trouble alone."

"Never again," agreed Mrs. Silva. "We'll give you all the love we have for our daughter," she said, a hand at her throat, "and that is enough for a lifetime."

The Troublemakers took turns hugging Odete's poor parents as they left to sit with their only child's body through the night before burying her in the morning. Out the door with them went all incentive to talk and slowly the group, grieving their lost two members, left their beloved clubhouse to go home. For the first time Traf was glad to see the place closed, silent, and dark.

Later, lying in their bed, Traf stared at the ceiling. Her head knew they were gone, but her heart expected to see Lucy and Odete again. Thoughts chased themselves in, out, around, up and down her brain and none of them made sense, but one returned again and again.

I didn't know I was her best friend.

Ch. 17 - A Hell of a Sendoff

Autumn - Winter, 1967

During the month of October conversations at Troublemakers fell flat before they were well begun, and a general sense of unease settled over them all. Questions haunted everyone: *Who else among us might choose suicide instead of life? Which of us could be next?*

Everyone went out of their way to be kind to each other. Femmes gathered in groups to discuss their feelings and check in with each other, their opinion being that problems shared are halved. The butches, on the other hand, offered each other favors as quickly as prayers and slapped each other on the back to buck themselves up. Their support came in buying rounds of drinks, telling bad jokes, playing cards, and lighting each other's cigarettes. No one mentioned their loss of control, the hot outburst of tears they'd held in check for years; it was too embarrassing. Although they approached grief from different perspectives, both butches and femmes kept close watch over everyone, fearing for themselves as much as anyone.

An island is a small world and news of a double suicide, even one that takes place in a remote village, eventually reaches everyone. While many didn't approve of the lesbian lovers and thought the miserable sinners were right to kill themselves, they understood too well the anguish of parents who lose beloved children. Righteousness warred with compassion, and the families of lesbians and gay men became concerned.

One afternoon in late October, Amalia stopped in at Ana's shop to invite them both to dinner that night. Gaspar would be away helping his brother make wine and they'd have the house to themselves. It was that time of year between the last festival's end and the beginning of their Christmas rush so Ana had plenty of time in the evenings, especially now that she allowed Traf to help with household chores.

"Certainly," she answered.

"You can be so sure without even checking with my daughter?" she asked. "My, how you've changed her."

"Is that a bad thing?" asked Ana with a twinkle in her eye.

"No. She's at her best with you." Amalia turned and started walking home. "I'll see you at seven," she called over her shoulder.

Traf was pleased. "Of course you were right to accept for us both," she said. "I'm looking forward to it. I've missed Mom's cooking." Seeing the glint in Ana's eye, she hurriedly added, "Not that I don't love yours, sweetheart."

They arrived just before seven, Traf holding a bottle of good red wine and Ana with a covered basket of richly spiced sweet bread. Amalia was ready for them, the table laden with steaks and fried potatoes, sliced tomatoes and fresh made pickles.

"Will you do me a favor?" she said, motioning for them to sit down at the table, looking at Ana and her daughter.

Traf's mouth watered as she helped herself to some of everything. "Sure, Mom," she answered around a mouthful of pickles. "What do you need?"

"You remember my friends, Anita and Esmerelda?" she asked.

Traf chewed thoughtfully. "Yes, the two old lady sisters, right? They live over in the village of Biscoitos?"

"Yes, you've been with me at their house in Biscoitos." Amalia cut up her steak into many small pieces. She'd lost some teeth over the last few years and found small bites easier on her gums. "They're having a fifty-year anniversary party and I've been invited. I've got something else to do and can't go, so I want you to go as my representatives."

Ana looked up, pleased at the idea of going to a party. Traf shook her head. "Don't get too excited," she advised. "These ladies are elderly. Their friends are probably ancient," her eyes twinkled, "like Mom. It won't be a very lively party."

Her mother slapped her hand. "Now you behave. Their actual anniversary is sometime around Christmas, but Anita has cancer. The doctors say she probably won't live to see out the year, so my friends decided to have their party early. I want you to represent our family and give them my gift and best wishes. Do you think you can do that for me, or is it asking too much?"

Chastised, Traf answered, "Of course we'll go for you. When is it?"

"Tomorrow," Amalia answered.

"Well, thanks for the warning." Traf raised a glass of wine.

"You're welcome," her mother answered graciously, heaping another spoonful of fried potatoes on her plate. "I have the gift wrapped and ready to go. Tell them I'm sorry to miss their big party, but it's unavoidable. Give them my best wishes, and tell them I'll visit next week."

After work, Traf signed out a van. She and Ana drove to the village of Biscoitos and the home of Esmerelda and Anita. They entered the open front door of a small, spotlessly clean, and wonderfully decorated house. Tastefully framed copies of art masterpieces hung on walls in every room. Fine furniture, not a set but perfectly arranged, might have been preserved in a museum, evidence of a finer era. Strategically placed mirrors appeared to double the size of rooms.

At least fifty guests were in attendance and wine flowed freely. Traf, led by Ana, made her way through the crowd to the main sitting room to congratulate the two women and pass along her mother's greeting. Small, frail looking Anita held court on a long sofa, her fine white hair escaping a thin bun on the top of her head, landing in wisps around her face. She dressed in a finely tailored lavender suit and a frilly white blouse buttoned up to her wrinkled neck. She wore a corsage of red rosebuds pinned on her lapel, and ruby earrings dangled from drooping lobes. Clever eyes, bright with pain, smiled up at Traf as painfully thin hands tugged a colorful crocheted blanket up to her chest.

Esmerelda, a woman not much larger, sat on a folding chair beside the couch. In fact, her feet didn't quite reach the floor but healthier, stronger, and quicker, she efficiently tucked the blanket in around Anita. Her still thick hair, silver with white streaks, crowned her head in a coiled braid. A large beak of a nose met her single eyebrow, separating small dark eyes that could pierce a soul. Esmerelda wore a simple blue wool dress that reached her ankles. Her feet were dressed in church going flats, sensible yet stylish.

As Traf looked at the two, she noticed their faces seemed very unlike each other. A thought suddenly struck her. *What if, maybe Esmerelda and Anita aren't sisters, but lovers?* Just as quickly, she dismissed the idea as absurd. *No, love exists for the young. These women are old, long past the time of physical love. They have to be sisters.*

"My mother, Amalia Mendes, sends you this gift and her very best wishes," Traf said, handing the present to Esmerelda. "She deeply regrets not being here, but sent us to represent her."

Anita, ravaged by her disease, looked so frail Traf was afraid to touch her but Ana reached forward and gently shook her hand. "Congratulations on your Fiftieth Anniversary," she said. Distracted by a particularly loud voice in the chattering around them, Ana briefly turned away.

For a split moment, time stopped. Traf watched, unnoticed, as Esmerelda tenderly turned to Anita, leaned in very close to her ear and whispered, tucking a tendril of white hair back into the thin bun and then trailing a fingertip along the withered cheek. Anita nodded her head tremulously in acknowledgment. They both fixed their eyes on first Traf and then Ana, and smiled knowingly at each other.

Witnessing that completely intimate exchange, Traf knew without a doubt that these two spent their lives loving each other as much as human beings can. In that instant, she discovered that true love could never be based solely on physical pleasure, for that fades away in time. These two women loved each other's souls and, more importantly, recognized the same potential in Ana and Traf.

"Thank you *both* for coming," said Esmerelda in such a manner that only Traf heard the intended inflection. "Give Amalia our thanks. Tell her we think of her often, and remember."

"She said she'll visit next week," Traf said. She chanced a saucy wink that caused Anita to dimple with delight. Esmerelda laughed and then turned to greet the next guest waiting to present her gift.

Traf pulled Ana away and told her what she'd seen.

"Do you really think they're like us?" asked Ana, peeking curiously through the crowd at Esmerelda, still plump with health, sitting comfortably beside razor thin Anita. "I thought they were sisters?"

"I thought so too, but now I don't," Traf answered. "Think about it, Ana," she insisted. "They're both in their seventies at least. Why would two sisters have a fifty year anniversary together?" She let the question hang in the air.

Musicians hired for the event began to play and soon people sang along in the main room. Golden oldies, the young women heard the songs occasionally on the radio. People sang along not caring if they were in tune or had the lyrics right, just enjoying the feeling good music gives when shared with others.

Out on the veranda several folks chatted. Traf listened in.

"Did you hear a Russian actually walked in space?"

"Imagine that! Before you know it, they'll put someone on the moon."

"I bought a new album of the Miles Davis Quintet when I was shopping in Angra, yesterday. I really enjoy his music. It's called jazz."

"Jazz? No, give me fado any day."

"What's going on with the Americans in Vietnam?"

"They better watch out. It'll be another Korean War for them, mark my words."

The conversations were sharp, witty, and very interesting. The young butch and her femme hopped from one group to another, always welcomed and included.

After a while it occurred to Traf that the only men present were entertainers or servers. Every one of the guests was a woman and significantly older than she. They looked like her mother and aunts. Not one looked like a lesbian.

Waiters passed among them with trays of hors-d'oeuvres. Esmerelda carved a huge cake, decorated with the number fifty in silver icing, into small pieces which Anita handed out to everyone from the chair beside her. Traf kept watching the two old ladies for any further signs of intimacy, but even when sharing an occasional hug they acted exactly like two devoted sisters.

It was an enjoyable, stress-free night. Anita's friends came to say goodbye, but more importantly, they'd come together to celebrate two lives that added immeasurably to their own.

Funny stories of times gone by brought shared raspy laughter from the old ladies. "Remember when Anita chased away the chicken thief?"

"Yes, but it turned out to be Esmerelda!"

Their friends heaped glowing admiration on the old girls for daring deeds done long ago.

"I'll never forget when you slapped him right in the face, Anita, and you're so little! I'd never have been that brave."

Many favors and acts of altruism received tributes and thanks. "Esmerelda rode bareback through that storm, from one end of the island to the other and back again, to bring my mother the medicine. You saved her life, my friend."

"Anita, I never told you, but those talks we had when I lost the baby made all the difference to me. You gave me the strength to go on. Thank you."

The women who loved them paved Anita's path to heaven that day with their memories. Through their stories they reassured her that after she went on leaving Esmerelda behind, they would care for the love of her life. While no one said the actual words, they thanked her for a life well lived and wished her their best on her next grand adventure. It was a hell of a sendoff.

Traf stopped by her mother's house the next day after work to ask about the pair. "Anita and Esmerelda are sisters?"

"I don't think so. Did you have a nice time?"

"Yes, I did," Traf answered honestly.

"I thought you might," answered her mother. She looked at her last born, the one out of step, marching to a music only she could hear. "There is a future for you and Ana," she said. "Most problems are temporary; they don't demand permanent solutions. Remember that, my headstrong daughter."

"I think she sent us to Esmerelda and Anita's anniversary party to see for ourselves a successful lesbian couple," Traf explained later to Ana. "And it is nice to know love like ours has existed long before us, and will continue long after we're gone."

"Fifty years," mused Ana, "and we've only had two. Imagine all they've been through together."

"I wonder how Mom knows them."

A few weeks later they heard Anita had conceded the fight to her disease, dying peacefully at home. Traf's first thought was to wonder how long Esmerelda would live without her. "How do you go on living when half of you is missing?" she asked her lover.

"Maybe that's why Odete and Lucy died together, because neither could live without the other," answered Ana. The two sent flowers to Esmerelda's house instead of to the church, hoping to soothe a widow's aching heart, a thoughtful gesture gratefully appreciated.

Thanksgiving was an American holiday that Traf embraced with great enthusiasm. It was four weeks after All Saints Day, and still weeks away from Christmas. Best of all, since it was totally new to her family, she got to host every year. Thanksgiving combined food, family, and fun, three things all good Portuguese celebrate.

She and Ana learned how to roast a turkey, prepare stuffing, mash potatoes, and slice cranberry sauce into pretty red discs of jelly. They borrowed tables, chairs, and china from neighbors, pulling out Ana's stash of tablecloths trimmed with rich embroidery. It was a pleasure to provide a uniquely American meal, delicious and exotic, for friends and family.

Invitations were extended to both sets of families, on into the aunts and uncles. Traf walked over from her mother's house to invite Hermione personally, even though some of her extended family disapproved of her friendship with a bastard. Her best friend had inherited Tia Betty's house a few months earlier, following her mother's sudden death from pneumonia. Hermione and her husband Louis expected their first child sometime after New Year's Day, and she was getting bigger every day.

Their Thanksgiving dinner that year was once again a triumph. Everyone ate too much, talked too loud, and enjoyed themselves thoroughly. Following the festivities, as they stood next to each other at the sink washing up the dishes, Hermione waited until the kitchen was otherwise empty, then leaned over and whispered, "A letter for you arrived yesterday at my house. The stamp is from Spain, and the handwriting is a woman's." She raised an eyebrow enquiringly at her young friend and said pointedly, "The envelope is perfumed."

Traf's hands stilled in the water. Her heart leaped into her throat as her eyes gleamed hopefully. She turned to look at her friend, wondering if it was a joke. Hermione shook her head, looking disgruntled and unamused. "Carmen," Traf whispered.

Hermione waited, but when Traf said nothing else, she prodded. "Who is Carmen?"

"I'll tell you later when I come over to pick up the letter. Please don't mention it to Ana or anyone else for that matter. Does Louis know?" Traf finished washing a plate and held it out for her friend to dry.

"No. I hid it in the kitchen where he'll never look." Hermione plucked the plate from Traf's fingers. "Why? What are you hiding?"

Traf shushed her as Ana swept into the kitchen, carrying leftovers and discussing with Tia Isobel the process of melting marshmallows on top of sweet potatoes. The two swiftly finished washing the dishes, then Traf excused herself long enough to help carry Hermione's borrowed china back across Lajes for her.

"Here." Traf's oldest friend reached into her spice drawer and thrust an airmail envelope at her. "Now, who is Carmen?" she demanded.

"Just a friend," said Traf, her fingers itching to open the letter.

"How did she get my address, and why does she think you live here?"

Traf explained about meeting Carmen and visiting the gypsy camp. She saw no reason to tell Hermione about the kiss, instead saying, "She's a nice girl and she wants to be my friend. There's no need for Ana to get jealous over nothing, so I told Carmen she could," Traf looked up from the letter flap she was sniffing, "write to me here. I hope that's okay?"

After all of their years growing up together, Hermione knew her young friend well enough to know she was not getting the whole story, but enough of the truth for now. "Okay, I won't mention it to Ana."

"Thanks, Hermione," Traf said with relief. "It's really nothing, maybe a small infatuation on her part but I can handle it. Nothing to worry Ana about."

"Good, because I like Ana," Hermione said with a defensive attitude.

"Good," Traf grinned back, "because I love Ana." She folded the envelope in fourths and stuck it deep into the pocket of her jacket. "I'll see you later," she called as she walked out Hermione's door into the autumn wind. "Thanks for lending us your china."

"Thanks for the dinner," called back Hermione. "Tell Ana I give thanks for her friendship." The last was said with a bit of a bite.

Traf waited until she turned a corner before plucking the letter from her pocket. The wind tore at the three pages of small handwriting, cramped words covering front and back of each paper. She read them quickly, then again more slowly.

Carmen wrote in her native tongue, but with broad interpretations Traf understood her to say she was sorry she hadn't gotten to say goodbye and hoped Traf would be returning to her part of Spain soon. She chatted about some of the people in her tribe, specifically mentioning her cousin, Alfonso, and his boyfriend, Cayo. On the last half of the last page, she mentioned their kiss. 'Your lips were soft and offered so many promises. I would like to kiss you again when we meet and ask once more if you like girls.' She signed the letter, 'Yours, Carmen'.

Still a few blocks from home, Traf's feet took a sudden detour. She entered the base, largely empty due to the holiday, and walked out to the airfield to look at the planes. She felt guilty and pissed off because she hadn't done anything to feel guilty about.

That's not true. I kissed that girl, and now I'm thinking about kissing her again.

Thoughts aren't deeds. I've only kissed her once.

But I'd like to kiss her twice, or even three times.

Ana. Think of Ana. It would kill her.

Yes, but it felt so good, much better than kissing Ana.

Disloyal! We've been together for two whole years. Ana is the woman I love; we're making a home and family together.

Carmen will give me the thing that's been missing, I know it; I feel it. She can get me there because she's not like Portuguese girls. She'll touch me with pleasure, as much as I'll touch her. Think of it.

No. Don't think of it. I'll think of Ana, instead. Pretty Ana...

THINK OF IT, finally reaching that place, riding the highest wave and jumping off. Imagine the pleasure...and relief.

Ana, pretty Ana... Her thoughts stilled as Ana's face solidified in her mind's eye. She felt instantly comforted, happy, and content. Ana was her everything, the meaning of her existence, the very beat of her heart. *Ana...*

...is waiting for me at home! Her feet turned her around and marched her off the base and down the street, pausing only long enough for her to deposit Carmen's letter in a trashcan.

It was a solemn Christmas that year, not sad, so much as weary. The Troublemakers were tired of pain and sorrow. Their youth cried out against their general despondency, but they couldn't quite generate the spirit to be merry. They held their annual party the Friday before the holiday and although quite nice, no one stayed late or partied too hard. Everyone missed Lucy and Odete and while no one felt exactly guilty, a pervasive air of wishing more had been done filled the clubhouse.

Everyone knew the Silvas wanted them buried side by side, even offered to pay for a double plot, but Lucy's family wouldn't allow it. Their poor friend lay in an unmarked grave in the unsanctified section of her parents' local churchyard while Odete slept eternally on a peaceful hilltop overlooking the sea. This final separation, the Troublemakers agreed, seemed excessively cruel.

In the darkened clubhouse late Christmas Eve, the surviving charter members hatched a daring plan. Against the laws of both God and man, it would be extremely risky and the consequential punishment, should they be caught, severe.

Traf asked, "Are we in agreement?" A number of heads bobbed and several women murmured, but it wasn't enough. "No, stand up. I want to see who is with me. The rest of you get out of here so you can honestly say you had nothing to do with it." As people began to leave, she called after them, "We won't do it, anyway. Remember, that's the last you heard. We won't do it, just talk about it." In the end, seven butches and five femmes stayed. They would act tomorrow night, the least suspicious night of the entire year.

An hour before midnight on Monday, December twenty-fifth, they separated into two groups. Traf, Michaela, Berta, Ana, and Gabriela went to the cemetery where Lucy lay, as ignored and disgraced in death as she had been in life, to free their friend from discriminatory hate. Shovels, tools, and other supplies Berta placed in a small cart chained to the back bumper of the blue VW. As they dragged it up dark roads, the conversation waxed philosophic.

"We all live, we all die," Michaela mused, her left arm air surfing out the driver's window. "And in between there's supposed to be a purpose, a way to leave the world a better place than you found it, right? Well, what's my purpose, I wonder?"

"To be a good Christian, and to worship in His Name," answered Gabriela promptly.

"That's not enough," disagreed Ana. "You have to make a difference to people, too, and the more the better."

"Then, I guess Odete and Lucy fulfilled their purpose," said Traf. Her eyes were focused out the window on the barest crescent of a moon as if God himself winked at them.

"What do you mean?" questioned Gabriela a little sharply. "They violated one of the most important rules. They killed themselves." She crossed herself and kissed the rosary she wore around her neck.

"Which affected people, a lot of people. Every member of the club knew them, and these days, that's a lot of people." Silence followed Traf's words.

"Yeah, but I don't understand the way they made a difference to people." Berta fidgeted in her seat. "For the good, I mean." She ducked her head and glanced around, "Not to speak ill of the dead, you understand."

They did. Several kilometers passed.

Traf still stared out the window. "Well, I guess losing Odete and Lucy taught me how important it is to hold on, no matter how bad it gets."

"Huh…" said Ana, "to me, it meant I should ask for help when I need it. And that not everyone is against us."

"Yeah, I agree with both of you," said Michaela, pulling her arm in and rolling up the window. "We're here." She pulled the VW up close to the churchyard gate.

At the same time in Serreta, the other seven volunteers vaulted an easily crossed wall and began excavation of Odete's ornately fashioned chestnut wood coffin. The dirt hadn't settled much, and it wasn't hard to shovel. Taking turns, they had it uncovered a full hour before the other group arrived with Lucy's slight corpse wound in a long sheet of white satin left over from a redesigned wedding dress. Although white was for babies untouched by sin, the grieving women found it sadly profound.

Traf climbed to the top of the cemetery wall, accepted the light bundle from Michaela, and handed Lucy over to Daniela, a tall woman in her mid-thirties with fully fleshed laugh lines and a thickening middle. She didn't fit as either strictly butch or femme, but some of both, and neither.

"Are we disturbing their final rest?" Unwilling to lay the white silk on disturbed dirt, Daniela held their friend's body as she would a child, cradled against her chest.

"No, we're making sure it's a good one," answered Teresa, climbing out of the open grave, two dozen nails and a hammer in her jeans pockets. She leaned on a shovel.

"The right one," agreed Beatrice. "Their rest has been disturbed up until now, but we're setting it right. Now their souls will be at peace because they'll spend eternity together."

A number of people murmured their agreement, identities largely disguised by night shadows. Everyone kept their voices low. No one could afford to get caught.

"Do you think they'll be allowed in heaven?" asked Mary Jo in a whisper.

"You mean because they're lesbian?" asked Daniela. "No, but maybe Limbo."

"What? You're crazy." Teresa glared around in the dark. "They didn't do anything wrong, the bastards who kept torturing them did. These two took as much as the Good Lord could help them carry, and then they died. End of story." The fierce butch was intimidating as she threw the shovel aside and faced Daniela. Teresa gently took Lucy from her, then turned her back to the rest of the group as she murmured a private good-bye. Traf noticed a tear stain on the white silk when the rough butch gently deposited the small bundle in her arms. One of her own soon joined it.

A butch never cries, she reminded herself, desperate to be strong and do the right thing. Hugging Lucy's body gently, she stared down in the opened grave at Odete's closed eyes. *They will never see me again. I'll never see them again. They're gone, and I can do nothing to bring them back, make things better, save them.*

One tear, followed by another, fell down her face. Trying to slam shut the floodgate of her emotions she blinked fiercely, but it was hopeless. She rapidly, but carefully, placed Lucy's body in Ana's waiting arms and turned away.

She looked to Michaela, hoping for bracing support, but her best friend's eyes brimmed full as she watched, and spilled over. Berta was facing away, her shoulders shaking with sobs. Looking from one to another of the dozen friends gathered, Traf realized all the Troublemakers were weeping. *Anyone will cry*, she realized, *if they hurt enough.*

Teresa jumped back into the open grave, one foot straddling each side of the coffin, uncaring that tears covered her cheeks. "Odete and Lucy are going to heaven," she said vehemently. No one contradicted her.

They passed Lucy's body gently from one to another until Traf finally carried her to Teresa, who lowered her into Odete's opened grave. The tough taxi driver tenderly unwound the covering and took care to arrange the two lovers facing each other, cradling them in each other's arms, before covering both with the sheet of white silk and once again nailing the lid shut. They came prepared to enlarge the casket if need be, but Lucy was so small she fit easily beside the much larger Odete in her generous coffin. They all helped fill in the grave, patting the dirt down as it had been before their visit.

"Did you cover your tracks over there?" Teresa asked Traf as they packed up the last of the shovels.

"We stamped the dirt flat again," Traf assured her. "No one will notice except maybe a groundskeeper wondering who would tend the grave of the damned. They had her tucked way back behind a wall. No one ever visits that spot."

"Shouldn't we say something?" asked Ana, looking expectantly at Traf.

Everyone looked at her, Teresa, Berta, Gabriela, Daniela. Everyone expected her to know what to do, so she opened her mouth to see what she'd say.

"Thank you, everyone, for helping do this tonight. You've done a good thing, a noble thing, bringing Odete and Lucy together again." Instead of bowing her head she looked up into the darkest part of the early morning sky, eyes reflecting a million stars. The others followed her example.

"Dear God, hear our prayer. We commend to You Your loving children, Odete and Lucy, with hope You will forgive them their earthly sins and accept them into Your kingdom." Her voice grew argumentative. "They love each other, You know, the same as men and women do. Their love is true and honest, good and kind." Traf nodded at God, as did the others, a group testament for their friends.

Her voice turned supplicating. "You made them lesbian, You know You did." She paused and swallowed. "Now do the right thing…" Everyone gasped but Traf plowed on with firm conviction, colored with a hint of a scold, in her voice, "…and reward them for being Your good servants, because that's what they are. Hey, You've made martyrs into saints for suffering less than these two endured."

Traf gestured at the gravesite. "Oh, and please forgive us for all this." She paused. "Or, You're welcome." She winked at the sky. "After all, I know You honor love above all."

She crossed herself and kissed her rosary. "Amen." Everyone did the same. They'd all brought rosaries, a necessity for clambering around graveyards after midnight. Helping each other scale the cemetery wall, they piled into the two vehicles. The grave robbing Christmas Night Avengers fled into the darkness.

Content with their night's work, Traf and Ana washed and landed in bed no more than an hour later, but neither could sleep. Life and death forced them to ask questions and they weren't sure they wanted the answers.

"Do you really think our love, lesbian love, is the same as the love between men and women?" asked Ana.

"In God's eyes?" Traf asked. "Maybe, but I won't know for sure until I die and meet Him face to face. Some people think He hates us, others say it's love He offers. I'm not in any hurry to find out, one way or the other."

"Yes, I know what you mean. But I'm talking about the way they feel things with their hearts."

"Well, I'm fairly sure they feel things, like lips and breasts, the same way we do," Traf teased. "Why not their hearts as well?"

"So you think our love is as good as theirs?"

"Oh sure. No one can enjoy touching anyone more than I do you." Traf's fingers traced shivers down Ana's arm.

"No, I mean do you think they feel different inside than we do?"

"Oh, Ana. Who knows how other people feel inside? We're probably, each and every one of us, different inside. Isn't that the miracle? That we're all uniquely different?"

"And uniquely the same," agreed Ana thoughtfully, tracing Traf's jawline by the pale moonlight peeking through their window shades.

Drawing Ana's fingers to her lips and kissing them, Traf sighed. "It doesn't matter what other people feel; I don't care. What matters is how we feel. I love you with all I have to give. That has to be enough."

Ana twisted onto her side and raised herself up to kiss Traf's lips. "It is. I feel the same." Arms wrapped around each other, they kissed again.

Unhurriedly, with slow and deliberate touches, Traf explored Ana's body. The heat between them grew gradually, melting the cold of death away from their hearts. Tongues kissed lips, eyelids, cheeks, and throats while Traf's hands cupped and squeezed, fondled and teased. Ana pulled her nightgown up to her neck, then raised her hands over her head and surrendered. Pulling sighs and moans from her lover, Traf reached for that ever elusive something to quench her own desire. Riding atop her lover's thigh, it escaped her yet again, even as Ana crested beneath her, throwing both arms around Traf's neck and covering her face with kisses. She willed the hungry fires within her to cool, but just as she was succeeding, Carmen's face flashed before her eyes. Desire surged through her again, and she rubbed herself against Ana's leg in desperation, but it was no good. Her lover's questioning stillness quenched the fire instead.

"I do love you, you know," Traf whispered into her lover's ear, more to reassure herself than Ana.

"I know you do. I love you, too."

The trust in those words was enough. Traf let her heart take command of her thoughts and loins. "When we've been together for fifty years," she said, rolling off Ana, "let's have a huge party." She watched her lover demurely pull her nightgown down.

"That sounds like a great idea. We'll invite all our friends and celebrate a long and happy life together," Ana called, surreptitiously enjoying her lover's naked bottom as Traf streaked to the kitchen for two glasses and a bottle of wine. "I wonder how many of the Troublemakers we know will be there?"

Traf filled the glasses and handed one over. They drank in silence for a moment. "All of them," she answered, silently toasting Odete and Lucy, "in one way or another." Taking Ana's glass, she settled both on the floor.

"Merry Christmas, my love." She resolutely pushed away the next thought that came, *And Happy New Year to you, sweet Carmen.*

They kissed and settled down into the position they used every night to drift off to sleep, with Ana's head pillowed on Traf's shoulder. Although neither shifted position, both women felt a chilly premonition. The position they lay in was the same as two dead lovers locked in each other's arms for eternity on an island hilltop overlooking a vast, uncaring ocean. To chase away any foreboding each listened to the other's heart until they beat in rhythm, stronger together than they'd ever be apart. Ana, smiling contentedly, drifted off to sleep.

Traf lay awake listening to her lover's gentle breathing and wondered why she hadn't yet told Ana she'd been stationed in Spain for the next three months.

About the Author

Genta Sebastian runs with scissors, laughs without shame, sometimes writes naked, and can't help dreaming big. A multiple award-winning author, she writes Sapphic romances, like The Troublemaker series:

1. A Troublemaker Never Cries (2nd edition of When Butches Cry)
2. A Troublemaker May Surprise
3. A Troublemaker Sometimes Lies (expected release date February 2024)

She's also written two novels for children living in Rainbow Families:

Riding the Rainbow (GCLS award winner 2015) for middle-school readers, and A Man's Man for Young Adults.

She stepped into the horror genre with We Don't Say Gay in Tranquility Bay! a trigger-warning horror story with a twist.

"Lost" is a novelette worthy of the "Twilight Zone". A grieving widow finds a strange child lost in a snowstorm, made of snow and ice.

But she started out writing wlw (women loving women, i.e. lesbian) erotica short stories that range from super-hot sexy sci-fi

Martian/human first contact, to culinary cunnilinguists, to drag kings, to college and tropical vacations, exotic settings, unforgettable characters, and quirky situations. These stories are fully adult and not intended for young audiences.

Other Books by This Author

A Troublemaker May Surprise

It's 1968 and the Troublemakers, a band of merry lesbians living on a tiny island in the mid-Atlantic, are braving the shockingly decadent waves of a European sexual revolution, except for Traf who still flounders.

Capt. Traf Mendes, a VIP driver for the USAF, craves sexual fulfillment almost as much as she wants to present her girl with everything her heart desires. Unhappily her sweet Ana, faithful to a fault but a lukewarm lover at best, wants something Traf can't provide – a child to raise together like a respectable married couple.

A prostitute's unwanted newborn might be the answer. If Traf adopts the child in secret to present to Ana as a surprise, perhaps this ultimate act of love will solve all their problems.

But will it cure Traf's fascination with alluring Carmen, an exotic Spanish gypsy whose bedroom eyes promise so much…and her hips even more?

Don't Say Gay in Tranquility Bay!

If you've ever been bullied or stood by helplessly watching it happen, this novel is your next must read. If you were once a bully, or helped someone else to bully, this book offers redemption. If you stood by then but wonder now if you can make a difference, Don't Say Gay in Tranquility Bay! will bring you inspiration.

High school juniors Nick and best friend Penny are attacked by bullies on campus who start internet rumors they're both gay. Things seem bleak when a video of Nick being stripped followed by his boxer shorts flying from the school flagpole hits the internet, goes viral, and threatens to become a full-blown scandal.

But the situation really deteriorates when one of the bullies turns into a psychotic killer.

Don't Say Gay in Tranquility Bay! is a suspenseful thriller, a modern coming-of-age tale about the dangers surrounding today's teens. Taut and compelling, it tackles the grim issue of bullying with biting, sometimes savage humor.

Intended for mature readers, *Don't Say Gay in Tranquility Bay!* is not recommended for children or the very sensitive. **CAUTION**: People bullied in their teens report being triggered by the frank language, and the brutal, horrific behavior of the bullies.

Seriously, you've been warned.

Riding the Rainbow

Lily loves her two out-loud-and-proud moms almost as much as she loves horses, but bullies makes life tough during bus rides, in class, and on the playground. Clara sits across the schoolroom, still as a statue, never volunteering or raising her hand, keeping her family's big secret; she has two in-the-closet dads.

If they become best friends, what's the worst that can happen?

Blackmail? Kidnapping?

Maybe even...murder?

"Riding the Rainbow is a heart-warming read, filled with all the trials and tribulations of pre-adolescence. Lily struggles to understand the prejudices of adults around her, faces down school bullies, grapples with her body image, and struggles to accept her family is different, all the while stumbling her way towards the secrets of real happiness: being true to yourself.

Happy and sad surprises hide behind every page. Throughout the story I felt like Lily's third mom, rooting for this strong little girl to claim her place in the imperfect world. Sebastian doesn't shy away from showing the brutal reality of prejudice, but she also doesn't shy away from highlighting the goodness in people's hearts. She has a way of writing that adds depth to every character that enters the story, no matter how brief a time they are present. Riding the Rainbow is a great book, and I highly recommend it!"

- Lindsey Taveren, F-BoM (named Feminist Book of the Month, July 2014)

A Man's Man

Thirteen year old Bobby is terrified he'll grow up to be gay because his father lives with his boyfriend, Stephen:

It's like this, see. My dad's a fag, his boyfriend's a queer, and I think I might be gay. I mean, I think it's catching or something.

I never used to think about it, back when I lived with Mom. But now she's dead and I have no one to live with except Dad and Stephen. Everyone knows that kids raised in faggot families turn out all messed up. I figure it's just a matter of time before I start prancing around, or my wrist goes limp, or I start speaking with a lisp.

I tried to talk to my Dad about it once, but all he said was, "R.J.! Those things don't really happen!" and then he changed the subject. I guess he doesn't see it as a problem if I grow up to be a homo, but to me it's a death sentence. I think I'll have to kill myself if I start liking guys.

Back when Mom was alive, things were easier. She could talk to me about anything and I'd understand. If I didn't understand at first, she'd take her time and talk it out with me until I did. Now I don't understand anything.

Genta Sebastian's Author Page on Amazon

Visit GentaSebastian.Net for contact information.

www.ingramcontent.com/pod-product-compliance
Lightning Source LLC
LaVergne TN
LVHW020042110826
845155LV00029B/597

* 9 7 8 1 9 4 2 5 9 4 0 9 3 *